STRANGER WITHIN THE GATES

STRANGER WITHIN THE GATES

SHORT STORIES BY
BERTHA THOMAS

Edited by
KIRSTI BOHATA

HONNO CLASSICS

Published by Honno
'Ailsa Craig', Heol y Cawl, Dinas Powys
South Glamorgan, Wales CF6 4AH

This collection 2008

British Library Cataloguing in Publication Data
A catalogue record for this book is available from
the British Library

ISBN 13: 978 1870206 945
ISBN 10: 1870206 940

Published with the financial support of the Welsh Books Council

Cover image: Herbert Gustave Schmalz/Getty Images
Printed in Wales by Gomer

ACKNOWLEDGEMENTS

My interest in Bertha Thomas wouldn't exist were it not for Jane Aaron's pioneering work in the field of Welsh women's writing and in particular her book, *A View Across the Valley: Short Stories by Women from Wales c.* 1850-1950, which included a story by Thomas. *A View Across the Valley* remains a powerful marker both of the progress which has been made in recuperative feminist studies in Wales and a provoking reminder of how much more there is to be done to map and fully assess the contribution of women writers to Anglophone Welsh literature. The role of the Honno Classics series is central to this endeavour and it is a privilege to publish under this imprint.

In my research, I have been helped by a number of generous archivists and librarians and others. I would particularly like to acknowledge the invaluable help of: Keith Tompsett, of Cefncethin Farm; Cliff Davies, Keeper of the Archives, Wadham College, Oxford; Anna Greening, Parish Archivist, All Hallows by the Tower; Anne Williams, St Teilo's Church, Llandeilo; Alice Blackford, Assistant Keeper of the Archives, Oxford University Archives; Brian Elvins, Shelsley Beachamp. My thanks also to Virginia Blain for information about research on Bertha Thomas conducted for the entry in *The Feminist Companion to Literature in English: Women writers from the Middle Ages to the Present* (London, Batsford, 1990).

I am extremely grateful to the Honno Classics series editors (Jane Aaron and Katie Gramich), for their help and support in bringing this book to press and to Katie Gramich in particular for her helpful comments and suggested revisions to the introduction. My thanks too to Lindsay, Helena and all at Honno.

CONTENTS

Introduction by Kirsti Bohata   *i*

The Madness of Winifred Owen   1

The Only Girl   21

The Way He Went   35

An Undesirable Alien   109

Comic Objects of the Country; Being the
    Impressions of an Industrial School Boy   121

A House that Was   131

The Courtship of "Ragged Robin"   145

The Castle of Sleep   155

Zebedee; or, A Latter-day Prophet   175

Hand in Hand; A Comedy of Yesterday   195

My Friend Kitty   247

Latest Intelligence from the Planet Venus   263

INTRODUCTION
BY KIRSTI BOHATA

Bertha Thomas is probably best remembered for her satirical article, 'Latest Intelligence from the Planet Venus': a witty, pro-female-suffrage parody of the arguments against giving women the vote. The article appeared in the major Victorian periodical, *Fraser's Magazine,* in 1874 and was also issued as a booklet in 1875[1]. In 'Latest Intelligence', Bertha Thomas imagines a country very similar to Britain in all but one inverted detail: 'Women only have the right to vote or sit in the House of Commons, and the Upper House is formed of the eldest daughters of deceased Peers'. Men are excluded on the basis of their being constitutionally unfit for such tasks and being more concerned with pursuing physical adventure than capable of quiet application to sedentary learning, diplomacy and legislation. Charlotte Carmichael Stopes, in her 1894 book, *British Freewomen: Their Historical Privilege*, refers to Bertha Thomas alongside John Stuart Mill as having made a significant contribution to the education of the nation in the matter of women's political rights through this humorous, satirical piece.

> The publication of John Stuart Mill's "Subjection of Women" [*sic*], in 1869, educated many minds. The humorous treatment of the question in *Fraser's Magazine* in the article entitled, "Latest News [*sic*] from the Planet Venus", where logical objections against Male Enfranchisement are supposed to be urged by women, taught others that there were two sides to the principles of exclusion, and that those against the Enfranchisement of men, were, to say the least of it, quite as valid, as any that have ever been brought against the Liberty of Women.[2]

But in addition to this intervention in the suffrage debate, Bertha Thomas was a relatively prolific and popular writer in her time whose often humorous and observant writing includes careful treatment of gender and the role of women. She is also fascinated by social outcasts or misfits in terms of class, gender and national or cultural heritage, an interest which culminates in her last book, *Picture Tales from Welsh Hills* (1912), in which she turned her attention exclusively to her father's native Wales.

Like many writers of her day, Thomas depended on romantic plots for her longer works, although she also experimented with and often adapted other forms, such as sensation and gothic fictions and she was adept at shorter, satirical sketches. A contemporary reviewer remarked on Thomas's ability to make even minor characters 'stand out in a distinct shape by a skilful stroke or two of the pen'[3]. And while these stories are entertaining and engaging on first reading, they reward a second or third reading, with time enough to appreciate the often subtle and dry humour or the telling but unobtrusive details she lavishes on even the most peripheral figures such as the schoolmaster, Macpherson, in 'The Way He Went', 'whose career had been checked by a moral scrape of his youth', and whose ambition, 'under the slur of it, had finally settled down to the lifelong position of an assistant master, manufacturing brilliant products rather than shining as one himself'.[4]

The stories selected for republication here have been chosen largely for their Welsh content and the first nine stories are taken from Thomas's last book, *Picture Tales from Welsh Hills* which appeared in 1912 (an American edition followed in 1913). Another (long) short story with a Welsh setting, 'Hand in Hand', comes from an earlier collection *Camera Lucida: or, Strange Passages in Common Life* (1897) while two other short pieces that are overtly concerned with the Woman Question have been included: the satire mentioned earlier, 'Latest Intelligence from the Planet Venus' and a short story from *Camera Lucida*, 'My Friend Kitty'. These early 'feminist' pieces give some context to the way Bertha Thomas approaches Welsh women and offer some background against which Thomas's ambivalence about urban New Women versus rural female domesticity may be read.

BERTHA THOMAS AND WALES

Like many of the lesser-known Victorian women writers, the details of Bertha Thomas's life are scant and indeed the few biographical details available (in *The Feminist Companion to Literature in English* and Jane Aaron's *A View Across the Valley*) are only partly accurate. Thomas is described, in the *Feminist Companion* as the daughter of Maria Sumner and Rev. John Thomas 'of Glamorganshire, Canon of Canterbury from 1862'[5], but while Thomas's father was indeed Canon of Canterbury from 1862 (and also vicar of All Hallows, Barking from 1852 until his death in 1883), he was not from Glamorganshire at all.

John Thomas (1810-1883) was in fact from Carmarthenshire and he was born at his parents' farm, Glanyrafon, in the parish of Llandyfeisant on the banks of the river Towy, near Llandeilo. The confusion over John Thomas's birthplace, and therefore Bertha Thomas's own connections to Wales, appears to arise from a series of conflicting or misleading entries in various records produced during his time at Oxford University (Trinity College and Wadham College)[6], and a *Times* obituary in 1883 which incorrectly gives his place of birth as Glamorgan. The confusion in the Oxford records seems to arise largely from the unfamiliarity of Welsh place names, and perhaps the lack of standardisation in spelling. Rather than being the daughter of a Glamorganshire vicar who later moved to Canterbury, then, Bertha Thomas was related on her father's side to relatively minor gentry from the heart of Welsh-speaking Carmarthenshire. Bertha Thomas herself, however, seems never to have lived in Wales for her father's career and marriage took him to England.

Bertha Thomas was born on 19 March 1845 at the Rectory, Shelsley Beauchamp in Worcestershire. She had one older sister, Florence, who was born in Rome two years earlier; Florence became a noted musician and amateur conductor and wrote the authorised biography of Mary Shelley[7]; she was the only sister to marry, becoming Mrs Julian Marshall. A younger brother, born in Durham, died a relatively young man, and Bertha Thomas and her youngest sister, Frances, lived as adults with their widowed father in Gordon Square, London. After his death in July 1883, they lived together at various addresses in London. Like her oldest sister, Frances describes herself as a musician in census returns and perhaps following this family interest, Thomas's fiction regularly features musicians and she wrote articles about music. For her own part, Bertha Thomas variously describes herself in census returns as an author, a lady of independent means and, once, when she was a young woman, as an artist. Bertha Thomas's writing career spans about forty years: she published her first novel in 1877[8] but contributed to the periodical press from at least the early 1870s, and her last book appeared in 1912-13.

Bertha Thomas's Welsh family was of considerable local standing: her grandfather was Magistrate and Deputy Lieutenant and the obituary in the *Carmarthen Journal* on the occasion of his premature death suggests he was held in high local esteem. The family were also comparatively wealthy in local terms.[9] On her mother's side Bertha Thomas was related to the illustrious ecclesiastical family, the Sumners. Her grandfather was John Bird Sumner (1780–1862), Archbishop of Canterbury and Bertha Thomas and her family lived with her grandfather at Lambeth Palace for some years during her early childhood. She was also related to other senior figures in the Church as well as to Mary Sumner, founder of the Mothers' Union. John Thomas's career as a vicar was shaped by his father-in-law, who gave him his various livings before and after his marriage. Although this kind of patronage was common practice, testimony to John Thomas's personal and professional qualities suggest he was a worthy and dedicated man in his own right: his long and diligent service as vicar in the poor riverside parish of All Hallows, Barking, is commemorated by a sizeable memorial on the wall of the church. The inscription below a full length 'portrait' reads:

Sacred in the memory of the Reverend John Thomas DCL
Canon Residentiary of Canterbury and for thirty one years the
much loved vicar of this Church, who died the 18th July 1883.
"Thou shalt be remembered at the resurrection of the just."

Most of Thomas's fiction is set outside Wales, but the family home on the western tip of the Black Mountains, just outside Llandeilo (which appears as Llanfelix or St Teilo in her stories) seems to have offered a base from which Thomas could explore her father's native region. This part of Carmarthenshire that is the setting for all her Welsh short stories. When Thomas's father was just an infant, the family moved from the river-side farmstead of Glanyrafon (which may have suggested the model for the similarly named Trearavon in the story, 'The Way He Went'), to the estate of Cefncethin in the neighbouring parish of Llandeilo Fawr. This property was purchased for the family by John Thomas's maternal grandfather, Rev. Thomas Thomas Stanley, from Gloucestershire.[10] If we are looking for biographical sources in Thomas's fiction, then this English, Anglican vicar might be seen as the model for the revered uncle in 'The Way He Went', and the fact that John Thomas's own mother, Mary, would have been an English-speaking woman perhaps finds a parallel in the protagonist's mother who only speaks Welsh as a second language (significantly however, the fictional mother is from an English-speaking Welsh shire, Radnorshire, rather than an English county on the border of Wales).

Other biographical sources for Thomas's stories may be discerned in the history of the Cefncethin estate. For much of the time, it was a home and estate headed by women, with Bertha Thomas's widowed grandmother and five maiden aunts listed as head and occupants in the 1841 census while by 1871, four maiden aunts in their fifties remained, all listed as 'landowners'. Thomas's earliest known Welsh story, 'Hand in Hand', depicts an all-woman household on a similar estate in Wales and the name of this fictional family, the Rodericks, is that of Thomas's Welsh great-grandmother. After a series of deaths in the years up to 1881, the house ceased to be a family home (although it remained in family ownership until 1926) and by 1891 was being rented to agents of Industrial Schools (institutes for correcting delinquents as well as providing education for destitute children) and their wards.[11] It is surely no coincidence that Bertha Thomas wrote a comic short story featuring a cockney boy from an Industrial School who has been sent to rural Wales to curb his criminal activities.

What is remarkable about Thomas's Welsh stories, given that she was probably no more than a visitor to Wales, is the sensitivity and respect with which she portrays lives from all classes: the Wales she describes is no mere romantic or gothic backdrop. This is not to say that Thomas does not indulge in some light-hearted gothic fantasy. She plays with supernatural themes in her Welsh stories, drawing in a fanciful way perhaps on the work of Wirt Sikes who published *British Goblins: Welsh Folk-Lore, Fairy Mythology, Legends and Traditions* in 1880[12], or maybe on more locally and personally obtained versions of such folklore. Nevertheless, her treatment of Wales and the Welsh is never wholly or even predominantly whimsical. Her depiction, in 'The Way He Went', of a man torn between his Welsh roots and his English wife and future is carefully, sympathetically and insightfully told. While her narrators are usually outsiders bringing back to a London (or even an American) audience tales of the exotic 'stranger within England's gates' (as Wales is described in one story), these narrators are either well-informed or sensitive and sympathetic to the characters and ways of life of the Welsh-speaking characters who are featured.

A contemporary, anonymous, reviewer for *The Academy* described *Picture Tales from Welsh Hills* as offering 'students' wishing to acquaint themselves with unfamiliar Wales 'many illustrations of habits of thought and life as foreign to their ken as those of a far country'.[13] Thomas's stories are seen, by this reviewer at least, as offering an authentic, insider's picture of a very different nation. Difference is figured in the review in fairly typical colonial terms and Wales is portrayed as a place peopled by wilful and unco-operative natives, and inaccessible to strangers and the uninitiated: 'Speaking from personal knowledge we can say that there is no corner of the world in which an Englishman feels so strange and out of touch as in some Welsh valley where the people cannot or will not speak English'.[14] But this is not Thomas's own position: Thomas is not a stranger, indeed she includes an epigraph in *Picture Tales* which is an inversion of the old rhyme which alludes to a history of raids and violence between the English and Welsh to suggest her sense of belonging in Wales and this verse is quoted in full in the review in *The Academy*:

> Taffy was a Welshman, and a thief was he;
> Taffy came to my house, and stole my heart from me.
> I went to Taffy's house, as one goes from home…
> There I set my own house, and seek no more to roam.

Moreover, Thomas does not share her reviewer's sense of linguistic exclusion and is certainly not hostile to the Welsh language which is the native tongue of many of her fictional creations. Interestingly, another reviewer in an otherwise favourable notice, criticised some 'aberrations' in Thomas's English which, it is suggested, 'perhaps attributable to the contagious influence of the Welsh idiom'.[15]

Bertha Thomas died on 24 August, 1918. The war left little space, perhaps, for obituaries of elderly spinsters and although a popular writer in her day, who was published in multiple editions on both sides of the Atlantic, it seems Bertha Thomas was quickly forgotten. Today, apart from one story in *A View Across the Valley,* all her work is out of print and most of it impossible to find outside the rare books room of the British Library.

WOMEN

Bertha Thomas sustained a complex and at times, an ambivalent treatment of 'the Woman Question' throughout her fiction and other writing. She is closer to Allen Raine's generation, rather the generation of New Women writers who burst on to the literary scene in the 1880s and 1890s, but her pro-female stance, her interest in androgynous or 'masculine' women and playing with traditional gender roles as well as her depiction of strong female characters, justifies her inclusion among the more self-consicously feminist writers of the late nineteenth century. Her treatment of the iconic New Woman, however, is not always positive: although the New Woman narrator of 'The Madness of Winifred Owen' is an admirable characterisation of independent young womanhood, complete with iconic bicycle, Thomas also caricatures some of the more absurd traits of the stereotypical, fast New Woman of the turn of the century. But if her work is not as radical or as explicit as that of the generation of women who shocked contemporary audiences with their forthright handling of issues of sexuality, marriage and female independence, Thomas nevertheless firmly states, restates and reinforces the competencies, strengths and intellectual equality (or, indeed, superiority) of her female characters in whatever social and cultural circumstances they are to be found, and these are various.

As well as asserting women's intellectual and practical

capabilities, Thomas is interested in testing ideas of gender, through cross-dressing and inverting gendered tropes of insanity and imprisonment. In *Elizabeth's Fortune* (1887) the narrator is a girl who begins the novel working on the streets as an orange-seller. She manages to find a position as a maid in the house of a vicar and thence becomes an actress in a company led by a cross-dressing, ambiguously gendered lead actress and director; cross-dressing features again in other novels, including *The House on the Scar* (1890). In her last novel, *The Son of the House* (1900), Thomas pursues her fascination with destabilizing gender roles in a plot which turns a typical scenario of the sensation novel (a form she adopted or adapted more than once) on its head. A mother struggling to overrule her son's control of the family inheritance imprisons him in his own house, confining him to his bedroom on the pretence of illness. She later has him incarcerated in an asylum, from where he is finally rescued by the female romantic lead. The mother, odious character though she is, is forced into this action because she has no property of her own since her deceased husband entailed the estate to the son.

As well as putting a man in a typically female role, Thomas tests ideas of insanity as a 'female malady' in other ways. 'The Madness of Winifred Owen', included in the present volume, offers a fascinating and complicated instance of a woman using an induced bout of temporary madness to enable her to enforce her will over that of her father: in this story madness is not a metaphorical 'escape' as in other turn of the century writing, but genuinely leaves Winifred free to organise her life as she wishes. In this story, the narrator is a positive representation of a New Woman, who has travelled from London to Wales on her bicycle to look up old Welsh ancestors. She is clearly Winifred's social superior in terms of class, something acknowledged by both the narrator and Winifred in their social exchanges, yet she describes Winifred as 'intellectually towering' over her. Winifred is completely in control of her busy inn, firmly dismissive of the narrator's 'commonplace, middle-class [and misguided] suggestion' of how she might 'develop' her thriving business. Winifred tells the narrator about her experiences as a young woman describing how she chose her own husband, a foreign (English) sailor, in the face of intense pressure from her father who uses the power of 'the old Welsh tongue of his forefathers' to reproach her for being 'false to ties of home, country, kindred and religion – every holy thing'.

The method of Winifred's 'triumph' over her father's will is disturbing and fascinating in terms of Bertha Thomas's manipulation of the literary tropes of gothic and sensation fiction – Winifred doesn't 'escape' *into* insanity, but *through* a temporary bout of insanity as mentioned above. To complicate matters further, however, this insanity is induced by a potion given to her by an English gentleman scientist, or 'witch doctor' as the locals call him. The struggles of other women haunt this short story both in terms of its gothic elements and in the references and associations drawn by the central character herself who refers to having 'read once of a girl who disfigured herself – spoilt her good looks – to get rid of a suitor. I thought it something too terrible to be true, but feel now that I could do it myself!'. This disturbing image of powerlessness where a woman may resist an unwanted marriage only by recourse to self destruction is reinforced by the doctor's confidence that her unwanted suitor will reject her as damaged goods once he hears of her insanity (although he is equally confident that a quiet and authoritative word from himself will reassure the man she wishes to marry). Though a risky and desperate measure, Winifred's courage in taking the potion and putting herself at the mercy of another patriarchal figure, motivated by scientific discovery and (implicitly) sexual conquest, is ultimately rewarded with a happy marriage and travelling the world. Indeed, Winifred's exceptional personal qualities, we are told, are part native and part due to her experiences beyond

Wales (one of many positive examples in Thomas's writing of the personal strengths to be found from cultural hybridity and mixture).

The present volume includes two of Bertha Thomas's most overtly 'feminist' pieces, the satire, 'Latest Intelligence from the Planet Venus' mentioned above, and a short story in a similarly satirical mode, 'My Friend Kitty' from the 1897 collection of short stories *Camera Lucida*. Both of these are indebted to the school of thought which argued that women's work in the home and 'natural' feminine characteristics were proof both of the capabilities women and the value their feminine qualities could bring to public life:

> Kitty at home found no difficulty in killing time, nor had she been a Napoleon in petticoats would scope for her universal genius have been wanting, if she proposed to be perfect in all her parts: social treasure, medical companion, mentor to six servants older than herself, special providence to a curly-headed imp, and mistress of all the knowledge— chemical, mechanical, sanitary, aesthetic, ethical and economic—whose practice we disrespectfully lump together as 'good housekeeping'.

The Welsh stories which make up the rest of the volume tend to expand on this position by showing how intelligent, autonomous women (as well as weaker or damaged characters) fill key roles in family and wider society. But in attempting to confer value on the domestic roles of women Thomas did not imply that women ought to be confined to or entirely satisfied by domestic duties alone.

In 'The Only Girl', Thomas holds up the domestic sphere as one in which women may not only excel but prove invaluable to the family and economic unit of the farm. Although a potentially conservative stance and one which often appears to be linked with the rural Welsh life she is depicting, the story is clearly conferring value on an otherwise underrated female role and this theme is picked up again in 'The Way He Went' (both included in the present volume). 'The Only Girl' is a humorous and fanciful account of life on a remote farm in the Black Mountains where the daughter, Catrin, described as 'Caliban's daughter', is a superstitious, other-worldly teenager who has suffered some form of mental impairment as a result of childhood epilepsy. Nevertheless, she is not remotely an invalid, doing the work of several with a joyful dedication. It is hinted that she has a close connection with nature and, through her odd superstitious habits and rituals, with the fairies who are presented both as the original inhabitants of Wales, and conflated with the modern Welsh. Catrin is deliberately contrasted with the modern Londoner, Edith, who is little more than a parody of the new breed of urban young woman: 'a specialist in Social and Educational Reform when in town, an indefatigable amateur landscape painter when in the country'.

On one of several visits to Glascarreg farm, Edith is laughingly portrayed by the better informed and more culturally astute narrator, as 'a vegetarian on principle, trying hard to look as if she knew a growing carrot from a parsnip', and satisfying her 'hobby, when in South Wales, of buying up all the new-laid eggs to send to girls in London flats'. Another of Edith's principles, again drawn directly from the textbook of New Woman features which make up this caricature, is rather more sinister. A firm believer in eugenics, Edith declares, sombrely, that Catrin would be 'better dead' (the wider implications of which are complicated by Catrin's association with the 'pixies', who are in turn equated with the exotic elements of the Welsh). Yet, as the whole story goes to lengths to show, a more worthwhile life would be hard to find and, indeed, in the event of Catrin's untimely death the entire household collapses and the farm is abandoned. On the surface this story is a relatively simple sketch of two very different types of women with very different roles in life, and for all that Edith is made fun of, it is she rather than that 'Caliban's daughter', Catrin Jones, with whom readers are most likely to identify. But as well as these two extremes of womanhood, the story draws attention to a tension between urban and rural with the causes of ultra-modern urban 'feminism' presented as hopelessly inadequate to address the issues facing women like Catrin or her mother, women who are dependent for their living on farming. Perhaps this story could be seen to support a rather conservative position on the Woman Question: the modern, urban English woman, Edith – who would have the traditional, rural, domestic Welsh woman, Catrin, dead and her family therefore disbanded and farm abandoned – is surely wrong. Yet this would be a narrow and overly simplistic reading which goes against the grain of the narrative: it is the narrator herself who offers a positive image of an independent, educated woman who possesses insight into (and perhaps identifies with) both the rural Welsh family and the world of women working for social, political and economic change. Thus one might read this story as an attempt to widen the discussion of the Woman Question from a rather narrow focus on the issues which concern middle and upper middle class intellectuals pursuing a life and career in predominantly urban surroundings.

There are many female characters, both visitors to and natives of Wales, who display strength, independence and intelligence in a variety of situations in the stories collected here, and Thomas is interested in exploring gender roles in domestic rural settings, as well as in different social contexts. In teasing out the hypocrisies and contradictions of socially-constructed gender roles and the rigid proscription and prescription of behaviour aligned to gender, Bertha Thomas is never dogmatic and is not writing to espouse a rigidly ideological view; rather her characters and stories are successful precisely because Thomas's vividly depicted individuals are never merely 'types' sketched to serve a cause.

STRANGERS AND MISFITS

Bertha Thomas's treatment of those who don't quite fit in, who transgress norms of class or gender, or those who come from different or mixed national or cultural backgrounds, is an intriguing aspect of her work. The figure of the outsider or stranger is an important presence in all the stories originally published in *Picture Tales*, sometimes as a more or less informed and sympathetic narrator reporting back to a metropolitan audience on the strange habits and spectacles of Wales, but also as a more ambiguous, even sinister, intruder into otherwise harmonious Welsh settings. But a mixed cultural heritage is often represented as an asset for all that it sometimes leaves the individual concerned in painful or uncomfortable positions in relation to the rest of society.

The confusions of multiple national affiliations are highlighted in 'A Compelling Occasion', in *Camera Lucida*, which tells the story of a young man of obscure and lowly origins who has been picked out by a wealthy benefactor because of his gift for singing. He is being trained in Europe and consequently mixing with his social betters. His first name, Evan, is the only hint that he may have Welsh connections, while his surname, Briant, comes from a French grandfather. In an exchange between Evan and another of Bertha Thomas's 'fast' New Woman characters, the latter's attempt to undermine her social inferior is deflected:

> '... pray tell me, for I hear such different accounts. *What are you?* Are you English or French or Dutch or Italian or Japanese or what?'
>
> 'Well, Mademoiselle Mila,' he looked at her crisply, 'I'm a mixture — *like you*.'
>
> Born on Swiss territory, of an Italian father and a Russian-French mother, Mila Oligati's nationality was indeed difficult to decide.[16]

The difficulty in simply and correctly labelling individuals (and thus being able to predict their behaviour) is a recurring theme and Thomas delights in depicting characters and scenarios in which people's first assumptions are undermined.

The 'shape-shifting' abilities of those who cross national or cultural boundaries, so that they can 'pass' as a native or infiltrate supposedly foreign situations is given an interesting twist and an explicitly Welsh and linguistic dimension in 'An Undesirable Alien', one of the stories reprinted in the present volume. Here, a man begs board and lodging of an old couple lifting potatoes outside their humble cottage in return for his labour. He makes a point of claiming to be English, although his surname, Brady, suggests Irish origin and his hostess thinks of him as 'this "Englishman from the Emerald Isle"'. Indeed, most foreigners in Bertha Thomas's Welsh stories are clearly described as English (with the exception of one American), which serves to emphasise the national and cultural differences between the Welsh and the English. During an afternoon rest, the couple, apparently safe in the use of their native Welsh, make reference to where their savings are hidden; that night their guest tries to make off with the cash. He is outwitted by the old woman who has suspected his duplicity and thus it is revealed that far from being simply the 'alien' of the title, he is in fact a Welsh-speaker and either a liar or, potentially more dangerous, an outsider who speaks Welsh and therefore breaches the safety afforded by the Welsh language. This is a story entirely concerned with making the reader rethink stereotypes and assumptions and the identities of the two Welsh characters themselves are far from straightforward or self-evident. The opening of the story goes to great lengths to set up an overly-romantic image of the cottage and its inhabitants only to undermine this superficial image as the folly of an outsider-perspective. The narrator describes how the pair were once sketched as 'Philemon and Baucis'[17], only for the visiting artist to be astounded to discover of his idyllic rustic Welsh couple, that the husband was once a collier in Glamorgan and the wife, herself originally from 'a distant border county', was formerly married to, and raised a family with, an Englishman.

Thomas was finely attuned to the subtle difficulties of various 'in-between' or outsider positions and this interest culminates in the longest and most sophisticated of her Welsh short stories, 'The Way He Went'. Here, she paints a portrait of a Welsh boy who becomes estranged from his Welsh home and culture through a classical English education, culminating in an Oxford scholarship. He goes on to marry an Englishwoman, Aline 'whose very name is strange to us', as Elwyn's mother puts it. Her name is indeed a thinly disguised anagram of Alien, and if this were insufficient, she is introduced to the reader in a section entitled 'Daughters of Heth', a biblical reference which alludes both to a mother's grief at her son's choice of wife and to 'interracial' marriage. Aline is not only an alien in terms of nationality, she is also his superior in terms of class (although the match is obviously very worthy and balanced). His distraught mother plays the part of a staunch nationalist who cannot condone what is considered his betrayal of home and nation, and yet she is herself a complex character with a mixed heritage. Her household is mainly English-speaking as she is from Radnor and she goes to Church rather than the socially more inviting chapel out of loyalty to her husband's uncle, who was an Anglican vicar.

As for Elwyn Rosser, he finds it difficult to sustain his position as cultural and social hybrid. Unable fully to assimilate into the English middle classes (in part due to material as well as social limitations), he yet finds it impossible to return home. He feels himself to have been 'the dupe of a huge educational mistake', having been educated as an English gentleman although intended to become a Welsh clergyman. Elwyn is left in a dangerous cultural no-man's land, pulled in different directions by his various allegiances and able to settle nowhere.

In this story, cultural hybridity is not a viable option and for Elwyn it proves to be fatal. The location and the manner of Elwyn's death are both highly significant: an accident occurs whilst Elwyn is staying in what is depicted as a colonial outpost in South Pembrokeshire, described in the story as the 'Little England beyond Wales'. Elwyn sickens suddenly, having suffered a severe drenching at sea after the boat in which he is a passenger is caught between cross-currents during a storm. These same, heavily symbolic, cross-currents are highlighted earlier in the story during a playful but no less significant drenching, while Elwyn's dual, or multiple, identities are described as 'cross-working on Elwyn' and paralysing his mind. The narrator, purporting to offer an insider's perspective on the nature of Welsh identity, acknowledges the charm of 'a vaster nationality and a still vaster world'. Suggesting that a life in Wales would be unfulfilling for Elwyn, the narrative nevertheless explains that:

> a remnant of him was there, and its clutch on the secret places of his heart he could not altogether escape ... that ancient, traditional virtue of a cherished, indestructible nationality, of which none outside the fold, whether scoffer or admirer, can appreciate the peculiar sanctity and importance to insiders, its indirect or cross-working on Elwyn showed itself thus; prohibiting the shaping or thinking out of his own sentiments to himself. How then should he word them to another? His intercourse with kith and kin remained strictly amicable, but limited to trivial passing matters. No communion nor desire for it, on either side, regarding the things filling their minds—the things next their hearts. It was silence. The door was shut.

'The Way He Went', despite its sad ending and rather pessimistic outlook in terms of cultural mixture and mobility,

Stranger within the Gates

is one of the most detailed and interesting treatments of Welsh
cultural assimilation and alienation in the face of Anglo-centric
education. While this story, like many others, presents the
perspective offered by the wider world as irrefutably attractive,
it is also sympathetic to the difficulty of coming from a culture
which is perceived as inferior to its dominant neighbour.
Elwyn is not the only Welsh student at Oxford and the social
awkwardness and injured discomfort of some of these students
is convincingly portrayed: 'Many of his countrymen failed to
make friends outside their clan, fearful of ridicule, always
on the look-out for real or fancied slights'. These Welsh-
speaking students are depicted as socially excluded in terms of
class and 'cultivation', and divided from that after which they
secretly hanker by the language, the 'restrictions of language
[being] worse than the restrictions of sect'. But while this
may appear to be a call for the language to be abandoned as
a bar to social advancement and integration, the overriding
sense is an effective portrayal of the ambivalence of the Welsh
speakers depicted. A genuine and valid emotional and cultural
attachment to the language is emphasised at the very moment
its restrictions or alienations are felt. Interestingly, these are
the men who will return gladly to their own country, unlike
Elwyn who has enjoyed and immersed himself in life at
Oxford, without a similar maternal tie to the Welsh language.
    Indeed, it is not just his experiences at Oxford that come
between Elwyn and Wales: his delight in the place is prefigured
by his childhood education which is shown to involve a steady
undermining of Welsh tradition and history. Greek and Roman
mythology is what matters to Elwyn, while he comes to see
events significant to the collective psyche of Wales, such as the
Treason of the Long Knives, as 'old wives tale[s]'. Thomas
is not one to allow a simple binary to stand for long, however,
and it is not an English but a Scottish master who is intent on
proving that Welsh grievances are fantasy and who appears to
provide ammunition for Elwyn's denigration of other features

of Welsh cultural life. Furthermore, while classical stories seem to be a threat to more traditional Welsh forms in Elwyn's sympathies, Elwyn's obsession with classical mythology is shown to have an authentic local resonance and relevance. The Romans who once mined for gold in the valley remain an influence: the remains of their temples are still evident; their coins are still regularly unearthed; their mines have recently been reopened; their roads still guide the footsteps of David, the farmhand:

> More than once on a moonlit winter evening would David, taking his sheep along an old lost road, made before the days of Christian men, and now a grassy mountain track, see and hear the phantom legion of soldiery ... passing by with mysterious flash of helmets and clash of arms.

How far 'The Way He Went' is inspired or part-derived from Bertha Thomas's father's experiences is impossible to say, but there are some obvious parallels, from the name and location of the riverside homestead to the scholarship to Oxford and the marriage to a socially superior daughter of an English clergyman. The ending, however, is far from the truth, for it was Bertha Thomas's mother, not her father, who died relatively early, while her father appears to have led a successful career until his death in London in his early seventies.

If 'The Way He Went' is a pessimistic, if sympathetic, portrait of cultural assimilation and adaptation, it is significant that cultural identities and intellects produced through mixed heritage are celebrated elsewhere in Thomas's writing. In her biography of George Sand (part of the Eminent Women Writers series), for instance, Thomas suggests that her subject's particular genius is a product of her mixed heritage, expressed in this instance in biological terms:

The origin of much that is distinctive in the story of her
life may be traced to the curious story of her lineage.
George Sand was of mixed national descent, and in her
veins ran the blood of heroes and kings. The noble and
the artist, the *bourgeoisie* and the people, all had their
representatives among her immediate ancestors.[18]

It seems unlikely that it will ever be possible to do more
than speculate as to whether Bertha Thomas may have felt
similarly blessed by her own mixed, Anglo-Welsh heritage,
but her writing is most certainly enriched by her sustained
interest in the stranger, the cultural hybrid, a figure that comes
into the sharpest relief in her explorations of Welsh-English
duality and cultural exchange.

Further Reading

Kirsti Bohata, 'Bertha Thomas: The New Woman and Anglo-
Welsh Hybridity', in *New Woman Hybridities: Femininity,
Feminism and International Consumer Culture, 1880-
1930*, ed. by Ann Heilmann and Margaret Beetham
(London: Routledge, 2004).

----------------, *Postcolonialism Revisited: Writing Wales in
English* (Cardiff: University of Wales Press, 2004)

Katie Gramich, *Twentieth-Century Women's Writing in Wales:
Land, Gender, Belonging* (Cardiff: University of Wales
Press, 2007)

Endnotes

[1] '*Latest Intelligence from the Planet Venus*' Reprinted by permission from
Fraser's Magazine [Signed B.T.], (Manchester: A. Ireland & Co., printers,
[1875])

[2] Charlotte Carmichael Stopes, *British Freewomen: Their Historical
Privilege* (London : S Sonnenschein & co., 1894), p. 147-8.

[3] *The Dial* (Chicago), No. 55, 16 December 1913, p. 365.

[4] Ibid.

[5] Virginia Blain, Patricia Clements, Isobel Grundy (eds.), *The Feminist Companion to Literature in English: Women writers from the Middle Ages to the Present* (London, Batsford, 1990), pp. 1074. Blain is the source of for Jane Aaron's biographical note in *A View Across the Valley: Short Stories by Women from Wales c. 1850-1950*, which includes one of Bertha Thomas's short stories.

[6] R. B. Gardiner's *Registers of Wadham College 1791-1871* (1895) gives John Thomas as son of Thomas Thomas Esq. 'born at Llandyfeisant, Caermarthenshire [*sic*]'. My thanks to Cliff Davies, Wadham College, Oxford, for this transcription. Fraser's *Alumni Oxonienses* gives 'Thomas, John as Thomas of Glamfrafon [*sic*], (? Llanafan) [*sic*], co. Carmarthen'. The original register of Matriculations (OUA ref SW 2/3) gives 'Glangrafon c. Caern'. My thanks to Alice Blackford, Oxford University Archives for this information. John Thomas is also listed in *Notable Welshmen 1700-1900*, by Rev. T. Mardy Rees (Caernarvon: Printed and published at the 'Herald' office, Castle Square, 1908). Here he is given as 'the eldest son of Thomas Thomas of Glamfrafon (?Glanyrafon) [*sic*] Carmarthenshire' although this entry gives his year of birth, incorrectly, as 1811.

[7] Florence A Marshall, *The Life and Letters of Mary Wollstonecraft Shelley* (London: Bentley, 1889).

[8] Virginia Blain et al give the date of her first novel as 1876 and it may perhaps have been serialised before being published a year later (*The Feminist Companion*, pp. 1074-5). The first edition of *Proud Maisie*, held in the British Library, however, is dated 1877. This is also the date given for her first novel in Allibone (*A Supplement to Allibone's Critical Dictionary of English Literature and British and American Authors,* by John Foster Kirk, Vol. II, [Philadelphia & London: J B Lippincott Company, 1891]).

[9] When Bertha Thomas's grandmother died in 1858, her effects were valued by Thomas Jenkins of Llandeilo as £247.0.5. *The Diary of Thomas Jenkins of Llandeilo 1826-1870*, ed. D C Jenkins, (Bala: Dragon Books, 1976), p. 114.

[10] See Francis Jones, *Historic Carmarthenshire Homes and their Families*, (Carmarthen Antiquarian Society, Cultural Services Department, Dyfed County Council, 1987), p. 27. To add to the confusion of John Thomas's birthplace and overuse of the name 'Thomas' in the extended family as a whole, there are three dwellings named Cefncethin (or variations of that name according to the census or map consulted), clustered near each other: a mansion, a sizeable house and farm and a smaller dwelling, the farm manager's house. Although early on the family give their address as Cefncethin Cottage, it seems that it was the mansion which was the home of the Thomases.

[11] In 1891 an agent of the schools of Feltham (Middlesex) and Mayford (Surrey) is listed in the census, along with his family and several 'boarders', boys aged 14 and 15, and again in 1901 another Industrial School agent and several boys are living there. Industrial Schools began to appear in the

mid-nineteenth century and were halfway between ragged schools (schools designed to admit children too poor to afford the clothes and shoes necessary to attend other schools) and Reformatories, which were for delinquents. The schools aimed to teach children to be industrious and to offer some sustenance for the destitute. Nevertheless, homeless children who 'appeared' to be under 14 could be forced into these schools and children under 12 could be sent there for minor offences, including begging. Older children were often 'farmed' or apprenticed out to learn basic trades and rural locations were favoured as offering experience of upstanding community life away from urban poverty and crime. My sincere thanks to Keith Tompsett whose recollection of local stories of 'Barnardo Boys' at Cefncethin led me to follow up this connection.

[12] 'Welsh Goblins' a review of Wirt Sikes's *British Goblins: Welsh Folk-Lore, Fairy Mythology, Legends and Traditions* (London: S. Low, Marston, Searle & Rivington, 1880) appeared in *The Welshman*, Carmarthen, on Friday December 12th 1879, the same weekly edition in which the death notices of two of Bertha Thomas's aunts appeared. Matilda and Mary Thomas died within a day of each other, at Cefncethin, Llandeilo. Whether or not Bertha Thomas read this review is impossible to say but she was clearly aware of contemporary work on folklore and the connections drawn by folklorists and others between Celts and Fairies.

[13] *The Academy,* 26 October, 1912, p. 544.

[14] Ibid.

[15] *The Dial* (Chicago), No. 55, 16 December 1913, p. 365.

[16] Bertha Thomas, *Camera Lucida* (London: Sampson Low, Marston & Co. Ltd, 1897), p. 100. Emphasis in original.

[17] Philemon and Baucis are figures from Greek mythology. A pious and loving couple who extended hospitality to Zeus and Hermes when this was refused by richer neighbours.

[18] Bertha Thomas, *George Sand*, Eminent Women Series, ed. John H Ingram (London: W H Allen and Co, 1883), p. 1. Emphasis in the original.

From *Picture Tales from Welsh Hills* (1912)

The Madness of Winifred Owen

The Old Face

"Not from an old face will you ever get the same fine effect as from an old house."

The old saying was brought to my mind by the sudden sight of an exception to the truth of it in the person of Mrs Trinaman, landlady of the Ivybush, at Pontycler, in the heart of South Wales.

It was in the summer of 1899, when the cycling fever was at its height in all spinsters of spirit. I and my Featherweight had come three hundred miles from our London home, nominally to look up the tombs of forgotten Welsh ancestors in undiscoverable churchyards; more truly for the treat of free roving among strangers in a strange land. So much I knew of the country I was in – that Wales, the stranger within England's gates, remains a stranger still.

At Pontycler, a score or so of cottages dumped down round a cross-roads tavern in a broad green upland valley, I thought to halt for the night, but was met by objections. The accommodations at the Ivybush was not for such as myself. So the striking-looking woman above named plainly intimated.

A woman well on in the fifties, stout and grey, form and features thickened by years and the wear of life; a woman substantially and spotlessly clad in black stuff skirt, white apron and cross-over, and crowned by a frilled cap as awe-instilling as a justice's wig. Yet, to look at her was to feel that there, once, stood a beautiful girl. There was power in the face, there was mind; but it held you fast in girl's fashion by some indefinably agreeable attraction.

'Board and lodging that are good enough for you are good enough for me,' I thought, and said so.

At that she fairly laughed, and agreed to house me, for one night only.

The Old House

While the room was preparing I strolled out on foot. Led by a habit of avoiding the beaten track, I presently left the road for a lesser lane; the lane for an approach to a farm; the farmyard for a rough upward track between pastures screened from view by hedgerows so tall as nearly to meet overhead.

On a sudden break in the left bank I saw, close by, on higher ground, an old house looking down on me as if it were in surprise at the intrusion. A small, grey-stone, slate-roofed house, in a curious stage of dilapidation. The sash windows, carved wooden porch, broad grass-plat in front shaded by a lofty ilex and dense foliaged yew, also some handsome wrought-iron gates beyond, marked it as a dwelling-place of another class to the snug thatched farm just passed, or the jerry-built Pontycler cottages. Some steep stone steps in the hedge-gap led me up to the little green; and through the broken front windows I saw inside – not solid mahogany doors and marble mantels, but ceilings coming down, floors falling in, and no sign whatever of present or recent occupation.

An elderly shepherd, escorting a few sheep up the track I had left, told me that Cilcorwen – so the house was named – belonged to distant folk who, unable to agree as to its use and upkeep, let it go thus to decay.

I remarked that it bore traces of better keeping at some time or other.

'Ah,' he said meditatively, leaning on his pitchfork, 'that was when Dr Dathan had it, twenty, thirty years back, when I was a lad. Twelve years or more he was living there.'

'Rather an awkward, out-of-the-way residence for a medical man,' I let fall.

'Ah, well, but he – Dr Dathan – was not one who went doctoring the sick, unless in some sudden great need,' said my informant. 'He was always at his books – *and other things* – studying – studying – all the time. A man who knew a lot more than others. Too much, they used to say.'

'Oh, a witch doctor, was he?' said I jokingly, but catching at the notion like a trout at the fly. It suited the weird little place so well.

'I do not know. Some would call him a conjuror, and feared him like a ghost,' the Welshman admitted, adding, with a sour smile, 'As a boy I wasn't afraid of no ghosts, nor anything, unless it was a mad dog or a bull, and that one man, Dr Dathan. And I thought he *was* a ghost! He looked like one.'

'What became of him?' I asked.

But my frank curiosity made my friend cautious and suspicious. He shook his head, repeating:

'It is all long ago. I was a lad. There are those here who could tell you more than I.'

'Mrs Trinaman, at the Ivybush perhaps?' I hazarded, explaining that I was stopping there this night.

'Winifred Owen? She at the 'Ivybush'?' His eye – his tone – woke up. 'Yes, indeed,' he said, nodding gravely and mysteriously. 'She should know. She should remember. I believe he did cure her once, when she went clean off her head – crazed, as you say; and was given up by the regular doctors.'

'What?' I exclaimed, startled. Here was a fact stated, more unexpected, more inconceivable than any tale of demonology or witchcraft. For if ever woman stood up looking like Sanity in thick shoes, it was surely my landlady at the Ivybush.

'Aye. It was the talk of the parish! She was keeping house then for her father, Evan John David Owen, at his farm, away down yonder by Pontycler bridge. She went from here after that, rather sudden; and we never saw her no more till two – three years ago she came back to her people, and set up at Pontycler Inn, to be near her old home.'

His sheep were bleating to him to come on; we exchanged courtesies after the custom of the courteous country, and went our opposite ways.

At the Ivybush

The vision of the old house, posed there as if for a picture, stayed in my mind's eye as I retraced my steps to the Ivybush, there to find, to my dismay, that my hostess had vacated her own bedroom to give it up to me. It was too late to remonstrate. Nay, later on I encroached still further, forsaking the cold comfort of the 'parlour' for a snug corner of the oak settle by the kitchen hearth, watching Mrs Trinaman step to and from the bar serving many comers – greybeard village chatterboxes, tired quarrymen, beer carters, pert cyclists, and tramps; customers very various, but all impatient and out of temper, for a wild wet evening had set in, threatening worse. Half the conversation being carried on in the local dialect – elusive as a secret code – was to me unintelligible; but only to listen and watch her was to perceive she found the right word, way, and tone for each.

No need to teach man or boy how to behave in her presence. By-and-by they ceased to come; the storm had burst forth on a heroic scale.

She closed the door, observing, 'Wherever a man is now tonight, there, if he can, he'll stay.'

Ten minutes later she was sitting opposite me with her knitting, and we were having a friendly chat. Her remarks, her questions, showed a knowledge and understanding of men and things acquired in a wider world than Pontycler; and she readily resumed touch with it, opportunity offering. She obviously believed in class distinctions, accepting these as a social fact, without attributing to the fact such sinister importance as to resent its existence. She neither proffered her company and conversation, nor refused them when invited and welcome. But never have I been more conscious of personal and mental inferiority than in the presence of Mrs Trinaman. She simply towered – not by dint of any self-assertion – but by the sheer sense she conveyed of force of character.

Demented? She? Never! Her part in the shepherd's tale I dismissed as a fable. But I spoke of Cilcorwen and the gossip I had picked up by the wayside concerning its sometime occupier.

'Dr Dathan,' she said, quite freely. 'Yes, I knew him.'

'Was he a pretender to magic, pray; or only a quack?'

'Certainly not a quack,' she replied. 'He – he – never put his hand to cure any one if he could help it. For the rest – well, they said he practised black magic. But, I, for one, should be sorry to believe any harm of him, since to him and his 'sorcery' I owe my life.'

'How could that be,' I asked, 'if, as you say, he left the healing of the sick to others?'

'Not "my life" in that sense.' She smiled enigmatically. 'Yet in more senses than one.' Her grave eyes seemed taking a long view – a backward sweep; her strong, expressive face told of deep and lasting emotional experience undergone – yet not of the sort that corrupts or warps the soul. 'It's an odd story,' she resumed. 'One that wouldn't be believed here even now – *as it happened* – which is why I never tell it,'

But as we sat there over the smokeless, glowing hearth, with the storm-wind howling round, she told it me, as follows.

The Tenant of Cilcorwen

'I was a little girl of ten when I first remember him. I think he had not long come to Cilcorwen, but wonderful tales went abroad about him from the first. A doctor who took no patients, yet who was not taking his ease and his leisure but toiled hard all day; some said, all night! Ned the poacher, whose habits took him out and about mostly at bedtime or in the dark hours, vowed the light was always burning at Cilcorwen. Two of the lower rooms were kept locked, and not even the old woman, lodging in the lean-to hovel attached, who cooked and so on for him, was permitted to meddle with them. We children used to take to our heels if we saw his figure coming down the road. I don't know why. It was odd-looking, and seemed not to belong to these parts. He wasn't of a tall make, but spare and flexible; and he wore his black hair longer than is customary. He dressed carelessly, but always like a gentleman, a London gentleman – in black, not squire or sportsman fashion as they all do here. He was sharp-featured, with eyes like two burning fire-devils; his skin wrinkled and white – yellowish white, like a buried thing dug up again, as they say.'

'And they took him for a ghost,' I said.

She laughed. 'More than likely it was the natural effect of a life spent poring over books; and breathing the unwholesome fumes and vapours of the chemicals in his laboratory. Only the pure, keen air of our Welsh hills kept him alive. Perhaps that was why he had settled down here. But the boys said it was because Pontycler being so out of the way and behindhand he could practise his forbidden unholy arts there without risk of being found out.'

'What sort of arts?'

'Nobody knew; but they whispered he spent his time making experiments on living animals – besides dissecting dead ones; studied poisons; could cast spells; knew incantations that would poison your food. Another story said he was an anarchist and made bombs, but I think that was only because he always wore a crimson tie! Oh, there was no end to their tales. Pat Coghlan, an imp of an Irish farm-hand, boasted that, spying round Cilcorwen one winter evening and seeing the blind awry and the light burning, he climbed up on the window-sill, peeped in and saw—'

'Saw what?'

'Dr Dathan in his shirt-sleeves raising the devil. So he assured us; but it's my belief he was too scared to see anything. For the doctor turned his head, and Pat dropped away and ran for his life. "Corpse candles was a-burning in the garden," he told us. "If he had set eyes on me it's a dead boy would be telling you this now!" We believed every word.'

'Did he make no friends, no acquaintance, here?'

'He avoided company, never cared to see the neighbours, rich or poor, unless on business. But he was in correspondence with great doctors and learned professors all the world over; the letters he posted and the stamps on those he received showed that. Sometimes a visitor from town would come down for a few nights – someone in his own style; and now and then he went there himself for a week, always leaving Cilcorwen securely locked up. Yes, though he harmed no one, he was a mystery, and something of a terror; but no one molested him, and he stayed on so long that we got used to him and forgot to wonder or to pry. He never took the faintest interest in anything or anybody here, but was always civil-spoken and always paid his way.'

The Man in Blue

'One evening father sent me on a message to the Ivybush. A handy-man had been repairing the roof there, and I was to urge him to come tomorrow to make good some damage done at our farm by a heavy gale the night before.

Finding no one at the bar, I walked straight into the kitchen, and was taken aback at the sight there of two men – foreigners – Englishmen, that is. One was a little redcoat, and one was babbling in the foolish, rambling way of a man who is the worse for drink. The other wore a plain dark-blue uniform, and I took him for his mate, but he had such a pleasant, open face and quiet, determined look that I was not afraid to stay waiting. I noticed the tact and judgement with which he treated his companion, keeping him from making a worse fool of himself than could now he helped. In a few minutes the innkeeper came back and told me that the handy-man had gone off to another job, a day's journey from Pontycler. I was very much put out, for skilled labour here is scarce. So I stood bemoaning our predicament, and the landlord shaking his head and chiming in 'What a pity!' when the man in blue, who had been lending an ear, spoke – I seem to hear his voice – saying:

'Now, if you'll listen to me, I'll tell you how you can do what you want done yourselves.'

And he described very precisely and clearly how the thing could be managed. But I could not follow him; I had learnt English and thought I knew it, little knowing then how much there was to know. He soon saw I was puzzled outright.

'Well,' said he, with a funny side-glance at the little redcoat slouching sleepily on the bench where you are sitting now, 'I'm stranded here for tonight. You live near, you say. If you like I'll step over first thing tomorrow and do it for you myself.'

I was shy and suspicious of strangers – as we all are here – but somehow I never once thought of refusing his offer, or even asked myself whether I could trust this man, so knowing he seemed, and yet so simple spoken! My head was full of what seemed to be quite a little adventure as I ran home. But I remember my father scolded me sharply for giving the job without bargaining for a price, and I was vexed to death that he, when the man called next day, began by haggling with him about the charge. He laughed outright; said he was no journeyman tinker, and wanted no pay for lending a helping hand to a fellow-Christian. That so hurt father's pride that he walked off in a huff. The other turned to me with a sort of merry appeal in his eye. 'Come, there's no pleasing you Welsh!' he complained.

'Don't say that!' The words slipped from me without thinking; then I felt overcome with confusion – hot and red. Our eyes had met for a moment, and I turned away, my heart beating fast.

Well, he made short work of half a dozen jobs – leaks, broken panes, and what not; refused payment, but stayed to take a cup of tea at our table.

He told us he was a seaman in the Royal Navy, and that he and the soldier-man had first met in the train yesterday afternoon. He had managed to keep his half-tipsy fellow-passenger quiet, till, on nearing Pontycler, the booby tried to pull the communication cord, then wanted to fight the stationmaster, who turned him out of the train as unfit to travel. Just to save him from further scrapes, the sailor threw in his lot with the culprit, piloted him to the safe shelter, for the night, of the Ivybush and had packed him, sad and sober, off to Cardiff that morning.

All the time I was thinking, 'Presently it will be thank you and goodbye – and all over!' sadly. For I liked him. Then, just as he was taking leave, he told us how, last night, Dr Dathan had come to the inn on exactly the same errand as myself, and persuaded him to stay and help patch up the roof at Cilcorwen. And (father had been called off for a moment) though he didn't say so, he let me know he was glad to be detained, because of the chance offered of seeing me again; and my heart gave a thump of rising joy.

So we did meet, once or twice; but along with the gladness of it I was sorely, sorely troubled. He seemed very far off; and if he and his speech and ways gave me a chink view into a new life and world, it was one with which I had and could have nothing to do. For one thing, he was a servant of war. War was wicked, and all fighting men servants of sin; so said every teaching and preaching man I had ever heard. A stranger too, one of an alien race; while I, born and reared at Pontycler, belonged body and soul to the little Welsh world of my fathers. Add to that I was as good as promised to another man – Vaughan Hughes of Bryngolau, who had been courting me for some time – and father had made up his mind he was to have me. He was a farmer in a larger way than ourselves; and all the girls I knew envied me the flattering offer, and said spiteful things about the power of the pretty face. And though I hung back, feeling shy of the man, no one believed my bashfulness would last long. We were not brought up to consider our fancies, for father was a very masterful man. I knew that with his old and confirmed prejudice against the English and his heart set on the marriage with Vaughan Hughes, he would be frantic if he knew how I was feeling now.

Well, a sailor's wooing is short. The fourth time we met – very gravely, very quietly, very tenderly, Walter – that was his name – asked me to be his wife.'

The Struggle

'The the whole trouble of it plumped like a shower of stones upon me. Walter would not and could never understand why, since he had won my heart, he should not have my hand for the asking. There was no stopping him. He went straight to my father for his consent, startling him out of his wits, poor father! He went into a violent rage; then, as Walter persisted, unmoved, he broke into taunts and abuse, shouting out that all sailor men drank, had a wife in every port; loudly treating the offer as an affront to an honest Welsh girl. Walter, stupefied, turned silently to me. I stood up to my father, for the first and last time, said that I loved and wished to marry the man who had spoken; and that, come what might, I would never marry Vaughan Hughes.

Then father broke out in the old Welsh tongue of his forefathers. Oh, he could use it and make it work, in ways Walter could never conceive of. He reproached me as treacherous and unfeeling – a girl who, for a light passing fancy for a foreign vagabond, could be false to ties of home, country, kindred, religion – every holy thing.'

'What? Can you mean that he considered that for you to marry an Englishman would be a disgrace?' I asked in wonder.

'Well, no,' she half smiled. 'I won't say. Perhaps had there been money or advantage in the match he might, though not liking, have thought it his duty not to forbid it. He knew as little about the English as you – pardon my saying it – do of Welsh people; and he judged them from the worst sort that come here because they have gone wrong in their own country. Walter's quiet assertion that he was in a position to support a wife, he scouted. Here, he had made up his mind, was a tippler, an unbeliever, a spendthrift, whose dupe I should never be if he could help it. Oh, you might just as well have tried to move the Black Mountain yonder as to reason with father on the point. The difference of language rose up suddenly like a wall between them, and father seemed to lose his power of understanding or expressing himself in any but his mother tongue. Even Walter was discouraged; felt it was hopeless to argue or to pray.

He had to join his ship; but made me take heart, hold firm, and in a few weeks he would come back for my final answer. It was with a sinking heart I saw him go. But he wrote, he wrote!

The next fortnight felt like a year of torment. Father was confident I had given in, and tried his best to hurry on the affair with Vaughan Hughes, who had heard about Walter and his suit, but was not jealous – not he! – refusing to take it seriously. 'What, an impudent English sailor rascal from who knows where to steal his little girl?' Father, now that Walter was out of the way, had calmed down; but his pleading was hard, too terribly hard for me to resist. When he stood up and spoke you were moved and awed as by one of the prophets or patriarchs in the Old Testament. How could I want to break his heart and bring shame on the family by giving him the godless English vagabond for a son-in-law – I, the only daughter left? My head had been turned for an instant – he could forgive that. But so heartless, so undutiful, as to mean it – he couldn't believe it of me.

I felt somehow he saw things in a wrong light and would never see them in any other. He was old, too. There was no help anywhere. I was bound to go under. My appointed place in life was here with my people, while Walter, far off in the busy world, would presently forget me. It was bitter, and yet I might have yielded but for the dread of being drawn into the other marriage. After that, no hope in this world for Walter and me – none! My brothers, the neighbours, every one were against me, and full of hard words for him who in passing by had broken, if not destroyed, the peace of our hearth.'

A Critical Interview

'There came the yearly grand fair day at Llanffelix, three miles off. Every one was starting for the town, all the girls in holiday clothes. I was in no humour for sports, and stayed to mind the house. Then, left alone with my trouble, it so possessed me and became so unbearable I half wished I had gone with the rest.

There were butter and eggs to be taken up to Cilcorwen, and later in the day I went over with them myself. And as I went, thinking of father, of Vaughan Hughes, but mostly of Walter, whom I must give up – desperate, and at my wits' end what to do, it crossed my head, not for the first time, to consult Dr Dathan!'

'Did you really look on him as a magician?' I asked.

'Well, I won't say that I did not. And only some superhuman power, I thought, could come to my relief. It seemed a wild notion, yet as I walked on in the loneliness – every human creature was at the fair – the determination grew. I knocked at the house door, and receiving no answer, wondered if he too had gone to Llanffelix. The blinds were drawn, but the door opened to my hand, and the passage door into the sitting-room stood ajar. I peeped in. Dr Dathan sat facing me at a table that seemed lit by magical stars. He was so absorbed in watching something in the glass that he never heard me on the threshold. The room, all misty and queer smelling, was full of strange things whose nature and use were to me beyond conception – mysteriously-shaped bottles, tubes, glasses, and scientific instruments; but the strangest object of all was Dr Dathan, with his peaked, pallid face and lanky hair, under a red smoking-cap. Coming into that sickly-smelling little den straight from the open, the simple fields and feeding cattle, it knocked me stupid. At the moment I believed all the fairy tales I had ever heard of him.'

'Were you frightened?'

'I felt cold; but something seemed pushing me on. Then he looked up at me standing there, and I spoke. 'Dr Dathan, I am in dreadful difficulty. I want to consult you—'

'I never give medical advice,' he said, sharply.

'Nor do I need that,' I answered.

'I had broken up some precious bit of study, and he was impatient and annoyed. But – I was not bad to look at in those days – he hesitated a moment to order me off, and out I came with my story. I made it short. Something warned me not to talk to his pity, but to his power, his wisdom and experience. He knew something of my father and Vaughan Hughes, and had seen Walter and me. Still, having said what I had to say, I felt – oh, so miserably foolish! Unless he were a real wizard, what could he do for me in such a pass?'

'You mean that you cannot hold your own,' he said. 'Well, in this world the weakest must go to the wall.'

'If I am parted from Walter, what my father wills I shall do in the end. He upbraids, he talks of my dead mother, he beseeches, then he cries and sobs. If I defy him, and go off with Walter, it might be his death. With fury and excitement he will work himself into a fit.' My own feelings were getting out of hand, and I broke out helplessly, 'Oh, tell me some way to safeguard myself from from being over-persuaded into this other marriage at least. I read once of a girl who disfigured herself – spoilt her good looks – to get rid of a suitor. I thought it something too terrible to be true, but feel now that I could do it myself!'

'That would be a pity,' he said, and I heard him mutter as if thinking aloud, 'Girl of an uncommon stamp – in more ways than one!' Then he levelled his fire-devils of eyes at me searchingly – suddenly – with an expression so outspoken, I seemed to read it off like writing. It said: "Shall I or shall I not?"

'You can do something for me,' I said hastily. 'I see it in your face!'

He was put out and silent for a moment, glanced down at some papers lying before him, then shot another look at me, as keen as one of his own blades.

'So you think you would face anything that offered you a chance?'

'I would face death,' I said.

'Death ends all chances,' he said grimly. 'Besides, there are worse things than loss of life or lover.'

'What things?' I asked shakily. His manner had changed from one of indifference and become earnest, and he was watching me now as carefully as the chemicals in the glass when I came in.

'I dare say you have heard horrible things told of me,' he began, 'that I make a study of the things of darkness – poisons, and so on,'

I assented in silence.

'It is a necessary part of the physician's art. Disease is a poison they have to deal with, and that we men of science are occupied in tracing to its origin. You or anybody can understand the principle of what we call the "anti-toxin treatment", namely, that by introducing a small dose of some particular poison into the system we bring about a mild attack of the particular complaint, which secures immunity from all danger from it in the future. The extension of this principle is bringing us to the verge of discoveries of tremendous importance. Now I have in this glass a certain liquid,' he laid his hand on a small tube. 'Were I to use it on you it would hurt neither you nor your beauty, yet it might bring about, in the natural course of events, all that you desire. Say that I were to inject a drop of it into your veins—'

'What will happen?' I asked, all of a tremble.

'Ah!' The smile on his face made me shiver! 'Since the experiment is one I cannot make usefully on myself, and no other human subject is forthcoming, I can only tell you what I *believe* will happen. It will affect one organ only – your brain. After a few days you will probably suffer from definite mental derangement. You will think, act, and talk absurdly, just as in a dream.'

'Do you mean that I shall go mad?' I asked, scarcely believing my ears.

'Well, your memory, your reason, will be temporarily disordered. The disorder will pass away. But you will find Farmer Hughes will have cooled in his suit. A man like him thinks twice before wedding a girl who has been out of her mind. Ask yourself! What passes here would of course remain our secret.'

'I shrank, scared at what I thought a demoniacal offer. 'Oh, Dr Dathan, I cannot.'

'Well, well, in that case there is no more to be said,' he replied, his tone changing quickly. 'Go home! I was only joking you little fool!'

Never joker looked and spoke as he had done! I knew better. 'Why, they would put me away, shut me up in an asylum,' I stammered out.

'Even if they did, you would be released soon. But I think I can prevent that. I shall interest myself in the case, and will talk to any other doctor they may summon, and provide an attendant for you at home if necessary. No special treatment will be needed, and in three weeks I say you will be well – and rid of Vaughan Hughes's attentions.'

His urgency and confidence were gaining ground on me. 'But say I consented,' I faltered, 'there is Walter. What of him?'

'Oh – he – the navy man – leave him to me. In any case you will be relieved of what you tell me you dread most. To your lover I will – well, I'll tell him something; not all – but enough. Think now. Will you or will you not?'

'I was agitated, as never in my life before. But the excitement, the eagerness that seemed to devour him, and heaved under his ordinary manner, was a thing I couldn't describe or ever forget.

'Mind,' he said, pulling himself up, as it were, 'the only certain risk is mine. I have gone further into these studies than most; and it may be long before certain processes of protective treatment I would advocate are recognised as safe and proper. I am defying law, public opinion – endangering private and professional standing by proposing this to you. And if you consent, you must speak of this to no one – not even to Walter – until after my death. Observe, I am trusting you, as you will trust me.'

His audacity and zest caught and clutched me like a hawk, and carried me away. 'Yes,' I said, 'I am willing. Will it – will it – hurt much?'

'His whole person lit up with elation and excitement. "Oh, a pin-prick," he said, with the laugh of those who win.

* * *

A pin-prick, and it was done.

Then, from an evil spirit tempting me, he seemed to become

a human being; and talked to me kindly and cheeringly, as to one who has rendered you a service. I went home palsied inwardly with fear, but repeating over to myself his last words: 'Don't think. Don't worry. Wait. Let what will happen; hold on and trust to me. All will be well at the last.'

The Hidden Hand

'The blessed, blind trust we put in doctors helped me to do as he said, at the first. Soon, awful fears came like big waves to swallow me up. He seemed to know – for sure. But suppose he was mistaken – had miscalculated; and the effect were to destroy my mind – make of me a madwoman for life! Had I perhaps committed a sin, though unknowingly, in consenting to let him try the experiment? I perhaps deserved this most terrible punishment. I had seen in his face that it would be nothing to him what became of me. All he cared for was to study the effect on me of the treatment.

In the long after-years I have been in lands where they still offer up human sacrifices to their gods. I thought once or twice then of Dr Dathan.'

'Well, what did happen?' I asked, deeply curious.

'For a few days – I don't know how many – I went about my work as usual. Then one morning I was smitten by an awful headache; could scarcely see or speak. As by chance, Dr Dathan looked in at the farm that very day, spoke cheerfully to me, and advised me to keep very quiet.

It's little or nothing I can tell you from my own knowledge of anything after that. They say I went completely off my head; talked and behaved just as he had foretold, as senselessly as in a dream; persuaded that impossible things were happening; persons there who were not; one thing changing, melting into another. I was incapable of understanding what was said to me, or of making myself understood. My father and brothers were as scared as if I had turned into a goblin or a ghost. They

fetched Dr Dathan in a hurry – he being so near. He managed
to quiet them a little, till the Llanffelix doctor came, who was
perplexed, and not particularly hopeful. Dr Dathan professed
to leave me in his hands, but let him know that he held a
different opinion. He offered to watch the case for the other,
and was as kind as could be, coming every day; and, while
confessing he had never seen an attack like it before, predicted
that in due time I should recover.

And so it happened; gradually – as I was told – but to myself
it seemed as if in one happy hour, I shook off a nightmare – a
heavy cloud; and my wits became clear again, though I was
weak as a little child. 'Patience,' Dr Dathan whispered to me.
'You will soon be as well and strong as before.'

And so it came to pass!

But the whole parish knew I had been off my head, and
some whispered, since Dr Dathan gave no pills or draughts,
that he had cured me by a charm. Vaughan Hughes behaved
just as the doctor had foretold. There must be madness in the
family, he supposed. Certainly I seemed to be Winifred Owen
herself again; but the attack might recur. He had inquired, and
heard how rare it was that patients, though discharged from
asylums as cured, remained permanently sane. I don't see that
he was to be blamed for his caution, but he offended father by
his plain-speaking, and they had some words. Just then Walter
came back; and Dr Dathan took a lot of trouble – got hold of
him and talked to him in private, in the first place.'

'What did he tell him?'

'That he felt certain mine had been a case – a rare case – of
blood poisoning, and that there was not the slightest danger
of a relapse. To father he hinted that a thorough change of
scene and circumstances would be a desirable thing for me
on all accounts. Other admirers might behave like Vaughan
Hughes; while here was Walter, with a bundle of badges and
testimonials from his superior officers, ready and eager to wed
me. Father gave in; Walter Trinaman was married to me three

weeks later, and away with me to England – to Plymouth – and the fleet.'

The Tree of Knowledge

Five-and-thirty years ago she went out with him into a new and complicated world, the world of infinite good and evil, from which Pontycler prudently still keeps its face averted. Yet had she been blessed in her deed. Walter Trinaman proved of the good leaven, one of the best in a line of of life where all must be of the better sort. His officers, his mates, knew it; and his Winifred came to know.

'And when I said I owe my life to Dr, Dathan, I mean Walt's life and mine that we led together!'

Much had she seen, "places and men." Sorrow she had known, "Our little son – we lost!" And that sorrow, I felt, was unhealed, "But we had two dear daughters".

Both married young, she told me; and two years ago Walter Trinaman, then in the coastguard service, was one of the six lives lost in rescuing others from a memorable wreck on the coast of South Devon.

'My own life seemed ended and lived out. Of my girls, one was settled in Canada; the other in Glasgow. My heart turned suddenly – so strangely and unexpectedly – to Pontycler and the old country, and I came over, to find father still living, though going on for ninety years old. My brothers carry on the farm. The people at the Ivybush were leaving, and so it came to pass that I took it.'

'And Dr Dathan,' I asked, 'what became of him?'

'It was about three years after I went away that I read a notice of him in the paper. He was found dead in his bed at Cilcorwen by the caretaker who brought up his breakfast one morning. At the inquest the doctor said his whole frame was wasted and perished, and that it was a miracle he had lived so long, not ailing, apparently; as he might have dropped off at

any moment the last twelvemonth. There are those here like
Caleb Evans, whom you met today, who still half believe that
the devil came for his own and fetched him away. That is not
fair. What became of his researches I never heard; nor do I
think he cared to be famous – only to find out, and to know.'

* * *

On leaving the Ivybush regretfully the next morning, I
suggested enlarging and improving the inn, since so pleasant
a halting-place as Pontycler could not fail to attract numerous
summer visitors of a better class. Surely it would be worth
while.

'If you mean that it would be more remunerative,' said Mrs
Trinaman plainly, 'I, or any one who knows anything about
it, can tell you this kind of thing pays much better!' And that,
I felt, was the proper answer to my commonplace, middle-
class suggestion. But her last words were in another key, as,
standing before her door, a serving hostess to every passing
wayfarer, to the fit and unfit alike, she wished me good speed.
'So long as I stay,' she said wistfully, 'it shall stay as it was
when I first met Trinaman – I've told you where and how!'

The Only Girl

It is my firm belief – corroborated by the most recent prehistoric research – that the original Pixyland was Wales.

The landsmen – the little men, the tricksy men, the unaccountable, elusive, secret people of the hills – mighty for mischief, or for kindness, according as they choose – dark, quaint-headed, quaintly clad – you may call them Welsh, or Picts, or Ibero-Silurian, or the ten tribes, or what you please – I call them Pixies.

Any well-read child will tell you, should you have forgotten, what a Pixie is: an originally sinful fairy, whose pleasurable duty it is to cause accidents in well-regulated families and put to confusion the best-laid schemes of thinking men and women.

They are vanishing, together with their hiding-places, before the spread of County Council schools, steam-rollers, corrugated-iron roofs, and land taxes compelling the felling for sale of timber. Hence seldom seen, but "never," or "nowhere" is a long word. Ask the salmon-poachers in some remote rocky valley of the Towy or Teify River. Ask the head of the family of five generations at a farm by the moorland mountain lake. Nay, in your own field, if you could only bring yourself to wait and watch long years for it, some hint, some eerie manifestation of their presence will reward your super-nature-study.

Everywhere on the Black Mountain, though they dare not show themselves, their spirit is present yet. You wander northward along green roads, and are led south. From some slippery stony slope you step on to firm flatland, and are up to your knees in black ooze. A short cut by a ferny hillside proves to be set with man-traps – holes to baffle the surest feet. You may surprise the little folk themselves by sudden chance, hurrying furtively along, cleverly disguised as miners or quarrymen, dark-faced, with dogs of some unknown breed in their wake, coming you know not whence and bound you wonder whither.

I

It was too fine for Pixies today, a day when their remotest haunts were not safe from prying picnic parties.

There, on a plateau of 2,000 feet – a fair elevation anywhere in the British Isles – I and my guest Edith sat eating our lunch beside a rude cairn, praising our patience that had won for us by waiting such perfect conditions for our mountain walk.

Such a day acts like philtre. Gone was the impression, the very memory, of the last four weeks of perpetual rain and tempest. All that was a dream. This was the reality. We basked, we gloated; we had never been glum, or bored, or run down, or out of spirits in all our maiden lives. The world was a glorious place it was was a treat to live in.

'After lunch we'll go on to the upper cairn. The view from there should be more sketchable,' said my friend.

Edith is a specialist in Social and Educational Reform when in town, an indefatigable amateur landscape painter when in the country.

But between the undoing of a packet of sandwiches and their consumption we were stricken with blindness. We could see the way to our mouths, and no farther.

'Oh, bother!' said Edith.

'Only a mountain mist,' said I. 'They come and go. Still – we'd better get back to the path, quick; for you never can tell.'

Never. No sooner were we down in the track than the fog

vanished, as it had appeared, in a twinkling. But after having descended so far we preferred to pursue our way downward and homeward by a footpath skirting a spur of the Black Mountain under the ridge, a path I knew well and one you could not miss. We had hardly done repenting our hasty bolt in a panic, when that white curtain fell again. A sheet, covering all that was visible. A corner might lift now and then, but beyond a yard or so we were practically sightless. Still, with a pathway under our feet, we could not greatly err. We had just passed Bryn Farm, and had only to go straight on for a mile or so when we should meet the high road. That mile was interminable. When, by our watches, we had marched for an hour, and all to be caught in a thorn thicket where no thorns or briers should be, beside a brook I could not name, and a pond we nearly walked into, I owned that we were lost.

We stood still. There was dead silence on earth – if on earth we were, and if not struck stone deaf as well as blind.

Under such suspension of activity the sense of individual existence droops and fades. We were a helpless part of the universal scheme, with no voice in its least counsels.

> "Rolled round in earth's diurnal course,
> With rocks and stones and trees."

'Where are we?' asked Edith, timorously and low.

'In Pixyland,' I feebly jested likewise.

Then, in that lightless wild a sound arose – whether near or distant you could not tell – a sound indescribable, was it a voice? – meaningless, a whisper, an utterance; low, continuous, and though dimly articulate utterly unintelligible. It wasn't even Welsh! Anything so uncanny never broke upon my ears. It wasn't speaking, or singing, or whistling; it sounded human and yet non-human at once. Spirit-talk – Pixy-talk. Edith is an advanced philosopher, but it went on her nerves. If we moved towards where it seemed to come from, it receded – an audible Will-o'-the wisp, bent on luring us into thorn thickets, stumbling-places, or a swamp.

'Let's get away from this,' I whispered desperately at last, and away we got, somehow, tramping on for another weary hour, when we sighted close at hand a real light coming from a real house. The mist was breaking, rain was falling, and I recognised the farm – Glascarreg, whence a cart-track led straight down to the highway in ten minutes.

There we borrowed an umbrella, and in half an hour were at home, but with that weird, wordless whisper still in our ears, running in our brain as a tune runs.

'Well, Edith,' said I, 'say what you like, I know now how Pixies talk.'

II

The following afternoon we went over to restore the umbrella.

Glascarreg was one of those delightful old Welsh farmhouses of which not a few survive, cheerfully setting at defiance the by-laws of local councils and the dogmas of hygiene. The "living-room" seemed expressly constructed to exclude light and air. Perhaps it was. So is a fox's hole, or a bird's nest. For those who live, move, and have their being in the open the first need, as with foxes and birds, is a close refuge from the fearsome heat of the sun and the furious weather rages. So to the husbandman of old a dusky resting-place, where the hurricanes of wet and wind and the noon-day glare cease from troubling, seemed the ideal thing. Certainly a place never designed for the conning of books and newspapers, or plying the sewing-machine; but time was when needlework meant knitting, play a pipe, and reading was sheer waste of time. A glazed loophole, just to let you know what you were doing, that was enough. Air? Well, the house door was never shut but at night.

Something on these lines had stood where Glascarreg stands and served as a homestead ever since the Pixy men held the land.

'Issachar Jones, the occupier, aged seventy-two, works his hundred acres with the aid of his youngest boy Tom, a lad of sixteen. The wife is a thrifty, industrious body, and they have three stalwart sons in America, running a store. But the only girl—'

I stopped, as a weird figure, bent low over a wash-tub, lifted itself suddenly afar off. A skinny and bony creature, who appeared tall from not having a particle of superfluous flesh on her frame. Her bare arms were long and angular, her lanky reddish hair was blown loosely about her face. She was pallid-skinned, with a high colour in her cheeks, and a countenance plainly observant, plainly uncomprehending. A striking, but scarcely a pleasing, object.

'Caliban's daughter,' suggested Edith wickedly, but to the point.

'No, Issachar Jones's,' I retorted. 'She, Catrin – well the poor girl's what you call feeble-minded; slightly deficient intellectually. She suffers from asthma and epileptic fits besides.'

'Better dead,' sighed Edith somberly. Edith is a eugenist. 'Ah, but we are coming to an age of light and leading when such hapless creatures will not be born – or not permitted to exist. Where is the humanity – the sanity even – of rearing and helping them to live out a life of misery?'

'A painful problem, anyway,' said I. 'Now if Catrin were London-born, she would, no doubt, if rich, be with a trained nurse or medical guardian somewhere out of sight; or, if poor, in an Institution for those similarly afflicted. But the Issachar Joneses have their own point of view. The defenseless and least fortunate member is the last they would wish to banish from the family circle.'

Stranger and wilder still was the scarecrow picture when

we came up to it. Torn cotton gown, tattered apron, piecemeal bodice and crossover, the wearer panting loudly and her arms waving like sails of a windmill as she strove valiantly with the contents of the wash-tub. But the face above was exuberantly kind-hearted and good-tempered, beaming welcome on us with broad and cheerful smiles, though of our English speech she could obviously make but little.

The mother came out and spoke to her in Welsh rather sharply. She took it in good part, and began removing herself and her wash-tub, panting and blowing the while like a grampus. Mrs Issachar Jones, with the dignified courtesy of a duchess, invited us indoors.

Living-room? Tut, tut! The Jones's living-room was the farmyard, the sheep-run, the cow-pasture, the potato-patch. Here within was the cooking-place, the refectory; and overhead the loft (*anglice*: first floor) where you slept. "Life" was lived elsewhere.

But oh the solid comfort, the real beauty, of that farm kitchen! The noble smokeless fire made red-hot with balls of clay and ashes – no fire in the world to compare with it, as the bread coming from that oven bore witness; the old oak dresser, decked with blue china inciting to breaches of the tenth commandment, hung with thirty sacred, quaint-patterned jugs of local ware, glorious with the copper lustre surely invented expressly as a set-off to the dull black oak of old settles, tables, and chairs. Here, in an atmosphere of ease and cosy warmth, we took tea with the old couple. When I asked for Catrin, Mrs Jones answered that she was busy in the garden and would take tea later on. After tea Edith, the new-comer, was taken on a round of inspection – of the dairy and its products, not of the choicest quality but free from suspicion of boracic acid or formalin; the cowhouse, over which she shook her hygienic head a little; the water-wheel which she must come tomorrow to sketch. Lastly, the well-cultivated garden, where with silent veneration we beheld a score of thriving growths of various vegetables; Edith, a vegetarian on principle, trying hard to look as if she knew a growing carrot from a parsnip; celery, spinach, and artichoke by sight.

At the farthest end rose a screen of tall currant bushes, and behind that a hedge. We were just turning back towards the house when from behind the bushes came a sound – at which Edith and I stopped dead, gazing at each other.

A murmur, a song, a whisper, a humming, a whistling – it was none of these, yet partook of them all.

Mrs Jones reddened, annoyed and embarrassed.

'It is my daughter. You will excuse her. She is – well – she has fits … and she is not quite like other people in her head. Ah, she can and do talk so as do others; only when she think to be by herself she go on so you are hearing her now. It shall be her way of thinking loud or of singing to herself.'

I begged to know, if she could tell me, where in the Welsh world her daughter had been wandering to yesterday afternoon about an hour before we came to the door for the umbrella.

'Why, just there in that back piece which she is digging now. The mist was so thick, I was telling her all the time to come in, but she would not.'

We exchanged another glance and … held our peace.

Now Edith's hobby, when in South Wales, is buying up all the new-laid eggs to send to girls in London flats. While the Glascarreg henhouses were being robbed for her gratification, she and I, put to wait in the parlour, saw Catrin enter the porch holding something in her hand. She wore a fixed and purposeful air, and passed without seeing us into the kitchen, whose open door faced that of the parlour.

She walked to the hearth, knelt down, and began sprinkling what appeared to be a handful of the fresh earth she had been digging over the embers. To the little flames that arose Catrin, bending forward, seemed to be speaking in Welsh, confidentially, but too low for me to catch the words.

'And so, Edith,' said I, 'the Pixies of the Black Mountain

were Miss Issachar Jones, of Glascarreg Farm!'

But the strangest thing of all was that we had been nearest home just when we had believed ourselves farthest astray; and that after going forward for another hour by our watches we had found ourselves exactly at the starting-point. Truly you never can tell.

III

During the next three weeks we were often at Glascarreg. Edith was determined to sketch the waterwheel, which, objecting, offered a passive resistance it took time to overcome. There was a growing attraction about the spot. The site, within a sheltering amphitheatre of ferny, rocky uplands on the lower slopes of a mountain ridge, was one a lord might envy. So also was the ever-varying, far-reaching outlook. First the near field, with a reed-fringed mere glistening in the centre – the sun-god's mirror, the day long; then away over intersecting lines of wavy, dreamlike hills to the skyline, and, it was said, on certain days – days that never came to pass – to the sea. Such a prospect is the invaluable birthright of many a cottager in South Wales.

The longer I looked on, the larger the Daughter of the House loomed in the family picture. Low mentality and asthma notwithstanding, Catrin was as remote from an idiot as from an invalid. See her carrying laughingly along a sackful of apples or potatoes, under which many a stout son of Adam would curse and stagger! Or working with digging or weeding fork in field or garden as for dear life, tending the soil she loved; fetching water in gigantic jars from a distant well; or mounted high on a long ladder whitewashing the house walls – her pet employment. 'To shut out the damp,' her mother kept repeating. But her zest and persistence in the uncalled-for task once provoked me to ask in jest if she did it to scare off evil spirits, traditions of a belief to this effect lingering from the olden time.

And Mrs Jones replied, 'The father of me – Catrin was yet a child when I buried him – ah! she was one he did love – he loved her in his heart – and he would have her to run by him in the fields where he was working all day. Now father, he was a great man for poetries and fairy-stories and that sort of thing, and could tell you of all the old customs and believes. But some I do think he make out of his own head. And Catrin was always for hearing them. What she have learn from the school-missis she shall have forgotten; but what father he told her she forget never, though we are telling her, and she know it, it be silly. She half-believe them too. You shall see her, when something vex her, as now, since the new colt be gone lame, take fresh earth in her hand, throw it on the fire and tell her trouble to the flames it make, and she think all shall then come well for sure. Her brother Tom, he do laugh and tease when he see her.'

Catrin gloried in her strength. It might not come up to that of Marged, the famous "Strong Woman of Llanberis", whose strength was as that of the two strongest men; but it served.

Once during a cloud-burst – or shower in her estimate – that sent Edith and me flying to the shelter of the house-porch, we saw Catrin sally forth, and with no more protection than an old sack hung round her shoulders, briskly climb the steep behind the farm, and in a few moments, plying foot and hand together, evolve a rough earthwork that effectively diverted a streaming flood making direct for the homestead. Presently the sun shone again, and Edith and I stood watching an enchanting rainbow effect on the hillside, the prism seeming to spring out of the ground beside a clump of sweet-brier, as it were the first pier of a celestial bridge.

What on earth was Catrin doing now? – toiling uphill again in eager haste, spade in hand? Having reached the thorn clump where the rays met the ground, she started digging vigorously on the spot.

'That is one other of those silly tales,' the mother let fall, 'that in what place you see the bow is springing from there treasure shall lie hid. I do not believe it, nor I don't think she do herself. But when I shall scold her she do say, "Mother, if it should be there now!"'

Which of us has not, like Catrin, sought and found happiness in half-conscious illusions!

Catrin had no wisdom. She would never knit in a field – witches would tangle the yarn. She urged the choosing of cows with a white stripe down the back. Such cannot be "overlooked." She would come in to breakfast joyously smiling, having met a wandering fox, which, in the early morning, means luck; or disquieted because a white swan had alighted by the mere – an omen of ill; while of the semblance of the reading and writing arts so laboriously acquired in her school years she retained not a particle. But in the work of her hands she took pleasure, and showed no small intelligence. Gladys and Muriel Llewellyn Evans, of Bryn Farm yonder, were slim and pretty, and dainty in attire, and studying respectively for the teaching and dress-making professions. But they broke down over the churning, caught cold if they got wet, and were strictly forbidden to lift heavy weights.

There was no more regular attendant at the meetings of the Shiloh Tabernacle than Catrin. What religion meant to her, of what nature were the fervent sensations that agitated her while she listened, entranced, to pulpit oratory or joined in a hymn, is unknowable. The minister, to any scoffing comments passed on Catrin Jones and her piety, would retort that if all the rest of the world were as harmless and of much use in it as she, it would be a better place than we see it today. Low though her intellect, that her moral instincts were good and even high was beyond dispute.

Her kindly feelings towards animals were most marked, and she hated killing any wild creature. Once, on seeing her very much younger brother Tom knock over a rabbit in the garden, her sharp cry of pain and change of countenance startled us. We pointed pleadingly to the devastated cabbage-patch. Catrin only shook her head, and walked away uncomforted.

'She do not think,' let out Tom, grinning, 'that the soul of he may have been in that rabbit there.'

'He? Who?'

'Dan.'

'Who was Dan?'

'Dan Price, Glyncoed, to whom she was engaged.'

When we inquired further of the mother she explained.

'Oh, they were then but boy and girl. Dan was a kind boy, and when he sees others laugh or make sport of Catrin he says he be her lad, and shall marry her when they be grown up. It was all a joke, but Catrin she believe it always. For Dan went out to work in the quarries and two years after was killed there by a fall of the rock.'

That was twenty years ago, and Catrin, proud in her fidelity to his memory, had remained content with her spinsterhood.

'But the rabbit?' said Edith inquiringly.

'Well, they do say some think when a man have die his soul she may pass into some creature.'

Mrs Jones repudiated the shadow of so heathenish an idea for her own part, but a word or two I elicited from Catrin, when Tom was at a safe distance, betrayed that she entertained it.

IV

Once only I saw her in tears. Mrs Jones, who was ailing, had gone into the town to consult a doctor, and I found Catrin, alone, face in her apron, crying in the kitchen. We were friends now, she and I, and I coaxed her to tell me her trouble.

'I – I had gone to the well, and was coming back when I saw a dog spitting on the doorstep.'

'Well, was it Spot, or Fan, or Rover, or—'

She shook her head unhappily, and gave me to understand between her sobs that what she had seen was one of the Cwn Annwn, or the spectral hounds that appear on the threshold when an inmate is threatened with death. It was white, with fiery eyes, and melted away at her approach; but later, on her looking out, there it was again! And mother, she had never – never been like this before, not sleeping all through the night, and her head not better this morning. Catrin was past cheering up till Mrs Jones returned with a portentous bottle of physic, bettered by the mere sight of it, and the assurance of a speedy cure.

On the occasion of Edith's farewell visit to Glascarreg we found the liveliest activity there prevailing. The Shiloh "May Meetings" coming on next week were to be on an unexampled scale. At the Tabernacle there would be no cessation of the proceedings day or night, and the assistant principals were to be feasted at Glascarreg. Mother and daughter were up to their elbows in flour and soapsuds. We could only be in the way, we felt, so cut short our parting call.

The meetings were crowded and successful beyond precedent or expectation. They were the last Catrin was ever to attend.

Three days later we met, hurrying to town on an errand from Glascarreg, one Betty Morgan, a widow of eighty, able and willing as any Boy Scout to render first aid in any emergency.

Catrin, laid low yesterday by a fit, she told us, was in a highly critical condition, the attacks recurring rapidly, and the doctor gave no hope at all.

The emotional strain of the revivalistic concourse, perhaps the effort to grasp more of the significance of the preacher's eloquence than the stunted brain could reach – the unwanted nervous excitement, telling on a frame physically exhausted by the colossal hospitable labours of the days before, had proved too much for the imperfect system. The weak link in the chain had snapped, and within not many days of our last visit there was another solemn feast-day at Glascarreg, the funeral day of the Daughter of the House.

Here in this quiet world there is no shirking of the contemplation of the Inevitable, no ignoring of the part death plays in common life, no effort to keep all reminders of it out of sight. Nor yet any repelling sense of formalism or insincerity in the recognised outward signs of mourning. A simpler feeling dictates what shall be done. Individual sentiments are a thing apart; the general attitude is uniform, unquestioned, with no fear of misconception.

Perhaps the very fact of Catrin's mental infirmity impelled parents, friends, and neighbours to convey her to the grave with all the honour and respect their state could muster.

More than seventy rural equipages, numerously occupied, followed the coffin – followed themselves by a train of mourners on foot – to its destination in the Tabernacle cemetery.

Ghosts?

If from her last ecstatic dream of paradise Catrin has awoken to its realisation, there is no call for her to revisit this poor earth. Yet in the wind on the Black Mountain a dreamer might see her, with her banshee-like face and her yellow hair flying. Or when the white mists extinguish the visible world hear that inarticulate murmur – whisper – signifying what? God knows.

> "A sense of the half-corporeal things,
> That lie where only the nightbird sings..."

* * *

Four months later Edith, on her way to an educational congress in a chief city, spent a weekend with me. How were the old folks of Glascarreg? She did not forget to ask.

'Gone from there these three months,' was my reply. 'The farm has passed into other hands.'

'Gone? Why, what ever made them give it up?'

It had not taken them three weeks to discover that Catrin had been the mainstay of the family prosperity, and that without her the whole fabric of their farm life would come tumbling round their ears. Of the labour she had voluntarily taken the brunt. Milking, washing, churning, cheese-making, treading the clay and ashes for fuel, wood-chopping, byre-cleaning, digging and manuring the garden – what hireling, what other, indeed, could be trusted to fill her part? Issachar was ageing and getting rheumatic, and the boy, they knew well, was only waiting for his eighteenth birthday and the age of independence to start as railway porter at a junction station many miles way.

With their substantial savings they removed to a villa on the town skirts, where they have sash-windows of plate glass, and water laid on, and smart slow-combustion grates, yet to them a poor exchange for the old homestead, where their hearts remain.

Ah, that was a happier time at the old hill farm with Catrin! Those were the happy days – before they lost Catrin – Catrin, who loved and revelled in hard work as few can do who read and write; Catrin, who laughed at toil and fatigue, always ready and cheerful, docile and dutiful. Would, indeed, that all women, aye, and all men, of wit and understanding had fulfilled their parts in life as well as she!

The Way He Went

PART I

An Innocent Renegade

I

Elwyn was the only son of Mrs Rosser, a widow.

Trearavon – Welsh for Riverstead – the home of his fathers, was a small tenant-farm of a type that flourishes persistently in Elwyn's country. No gentleman-farmers, the Rossers. They might even have resented the term as opprobrious. Yet Trearavon, stone-built, slate-roofed, creeper-grown, looked what it was – a residence, with a life of its own, apart from the little pile of farm buildings attached to it. These were there for the home, and not the home for them, as with the real old farmstead in Wales and all the world over.

A fancy spot as to outlook, with the Trothi River at a stone's throw flowing past between broad buttercup meadows; and away on the opposite bank a noble wooded headland, crowned by a castle famous in song and story. From that ruined keep an archer might shoot an arrow down on the roofs of peaceful, low-lying Trearavon. Look up the wide river valley, beyond the little hillside town of Llanffelix, to the far horizon for an enchanting vision of mountain peaks, distinct but involved, remote, as it were sky-high and inaccessible.

Left fatherless in his infancy, Elwyn and his future were a source of the gravest anxiety to Mrs Rosser, poor, proud and conscientious.

'Ah, Elwyn, my little son,' she mourned aloud over him once, while he was still in frocks and lying stretched on the hearthrug before her, 'I am thinking how I shall bring you up!'

The little son was on his feet in a moment.

'But, mother, I can perfectly well get up by myself,' he promptly assured her, provoking a laugh and a kiss.

Yet here was a true word. A happily responsive, pliable-seeming disposition won him the goodwill of old and young; yet in him was a determining power that told insensibly on all those he had to do with, those set in authority over him not excepted.

After his first day at school, Hopkin, the master, came round to compliment Mrs Rosser on the proficiency she had already imparted to this youngster in reading, writing, and the English tongue, till she dreamt wistfully of imaginary heights to which she might have arisen in the world had she adopted the scholastic profession.

But too many boys between six and sixteen had passed through Hopkin's hands for him to find in himself, in the years that followed, the sole cause of this pupil's disconcerting advancement.

'It astonishes me,' he kept repeating to Mrs Rosser. Mrs Rosser refused to be astonished.

'His fathers before him were men of learning,' she said, pointing to an imposing old bookcase full of ponderous, leather-bound theological volumes that occupied most of the wall space in the parlour. 'It was the boast of the Rossers that they always sent one son into the ministry.'

Hopkin assented politely, though feeling that only by special miracle could that boy have learnt from controversial tracts, old sermons, homilies, and commentaries all that he seemed to know. But buried here and there in the library, like currants in a loaf, were a few histories, classical and other dictionaries, lesson books that Hopkin, or any self-respecting Council

Schoolmaster, would consign to the dust-heap, yet out of which an eager young mind of peculiar capacity might suck no small store of facts and fancies.

His boyish bent was only half bookish nevertheless. His keenness over any game seemed crazy to his school-fellows; while to see the spell cast over him by the merest shadow of sport was positively dreadful to Mrs Rosser. Put a horse under him, a fishing rod in his hand, give him a glimpse of the foxhounds, of an otter, badger, or even a rat-hunt, and there was Elwyn, as it were, bewitched. Now sport, it is well known in Llanffelix, spells gambling and ruin. Well, well, he was but a boy, and neither a tall nor a strong boy. The open air was medically recommended for him.

In the natural course of things as they were in that shire from the beginning, are now – and long may they so remain! – Elwyn would succeed to the mastership of the farm. Here, though he performed with characteristic amiability such light tasks as his mother and two elder sisters, Gwladys and Gwen, assigned to him, aptitude was wanting. One marked that, one who possessed it – David, the second farmhand, Elwyn's fast friend and ally.

'Now, Elwyn bach,' David would say on Saturdays, taking the stable-broom from him, 'I'll tidy up, and see to the feeding of the calves for you. Then, after tea, into the barn you comes and tells me over and over again that story of the Fleece of Gold and the Ship of Brave Men and —'

'Oh, I'll tell it you now, or any time,' broke in Elwyn readily. 'You needn't do my work for that' (relinquishing the besom as he spoke, nevertheless). 'Now, look here, David, I'll tell you what – I'll just run down to the river for a swim. Then, after tea, in the barn, I've a far finer story than that – we'll have both.'

If Elwyn was a good narrator, David was a rare listener to tales of wonder. He asked no killjoy questions, as for instance: Were these matters of fact? Did Elwyn believe them? Nor

was he, the narrator, required to prove that Perseus, Jason,
Hercules, or Ulysses were somehow, however remotely,
connected with Wales. David's thirsty fancy drank it all in,
and asked only for more. It was as good as the tobacco he
was forbidden to smoke here, and cost not a farthing. That
Master Elwyn's only fitting future place of action was the
schoolmaster's desk or the pulpit was, to David, as obvious
as that his own was the threshing-floor and the stable. Had
not he gone through exactly the same course of instruction at
the same school, yet without bringing away the shadow of an
impression of all these fine things?

Only after listening to Elwyn he seemed distinctly to see
that strange Roman temple whose remains underlie the
ancient parish church of Llanffelix; the gold mines higher up
in the valley, worked by the Latin adventurers, and recently
reopened after a fifteen hundred years' rest; the noble lord and
lady owners of the coins and medals, gold necklaces, and other
buried treasures, brought to light hereabouts now and again
by the lucky. More than once on a moonlight winter evening
would David, taking his sheep along an old lost road, made
before the days of Christian men, and now a grassy mountain
track, see and hear the phantom legion of soldiery that more
than one late wanderer has told of, passing by with mysterious
flash of helmets and clash of arms. A dreamer of dreams was
David in his own way.

II

'Education,' it is shrewdly said, 'is about the only thing lying
loose about the world of which a fellow can have as much
as he is willing to haul away.' And before Elwyn had quite
done with the supplies pressed on him by the local authority,
his past and present schoolmasters came to exhort Mrs Rosser
to let him stand for an open scholarship at an old-established

college, on English public school lines, some fifteen miles up
the valley. The proposal took her by surprise.

'Gentlemen's sons go there,' she objected straight-way,
stoutly. 'I won't have my Elwyn looked down upon – not by
the highest in the land!'

'Well, and I don't think you will,' Hopkin chuckled
knowingly.

'Oh, there are plenty of farmer's sons at Llanwastad
College,' rejoined the other man. 'They do none the worse
afterwards on the land for what they learn there. Of course,
Mrs Rosser, it's for you to decide. But it would be no discredit
to your son if he failed. Whereas, should he succeed – and
we believe he has a chance and a good one – think, what an
honour! Then, should Providence have destined him for the
pulpit, what an advantage such a preparation would be for him
– for you both!'

'And what a feather in our professional caps!' added the two
professionals mentally.

Not long afterwards they were wearing it, and Elwyn and his
little step upward the gossip of the hour in Welsh doorways.

'Mrs Rosser will hold her head higher than ever,' said her
neighbours.

It was because Mrs Rosser went to church – not to chapel –
and English, chiefly, was spoken at Trearavon that the uppish
pose was attributed to her handsome head. Poor, misjudged
Mrs Rosser! Had her detractors but known what a sore
struggle it cost her steadily to resist the seductions of the smart,
popular, up-to-date Tabernacle of the Congregationalists! But
so long as the library of her late husband's late uncle, the
Rev. Thomas Rosser, forty years Vicar of Chipping Hanbury,
Worcestershire, dignified her parlour wall, she felt as if it
would be playing it low on his memory to desert the older
establishment. As to the other matter, it was her misfortune,
not her fault, to have belonged, by birth and bringing up,
recreant Radnor, that English-speaking shire; and though her

present acquaintance with the vernacular sufficed amply for all workaday farm and household purposes, she had so much more to say that she could express better in the simpler, easier, English tongue.

It must give a lift to her children at school, she reflected, in self-excuse, to come from an English-speaking home.

For the rest, there was no more austere patriot, of more unswerving allegiance, in the parish of Llanffelix; and a proud and happy woman on this score, at this time, was Elwyn's mother. Not only had her son demonstrated the superiority of the national intellect by outstripping the English boys, but here were her two daughters, Gwladys and Gwen, of their own freewill, walking in the wise old Welsh ways. Other mothers' girls rush blindly into school teaching and spectacles, or millinery establishments, regardless of the expense to their parents, shirked the care of the house, and had discovered that farm work was not fit for women. The Miss Rossers had a higher opinion of their sex, and could see in Trearavon at least as fair a field as any other for the display of feminine energy and intelligence. They might not aspire to run a model pony-farm, like Lady Eva Jones of Penlimmon, or even what David, ignorant of the Welsh for incubator, called a chicken-factory. But let not David or his fellow-hirelings conceive of these maidens as unaware of whether field-work of any description was being done as it should, or unable to render efficient aid on occasion. Thanks to their studious care of the newborn and the young, tending to the sick, feeding of the sound, the rate of mortality among Trearavon calves, lambs, poultry, and livestock generally had been reduced to the lowest figure on record. They were running the farm for their mother at present; for Elwyn in the future – if he went that way. If not – well – things might happen. Many a promising land-holder in the bud – cousin Joseph Lloyd Jones Harris for one – had cast wistfully admiring glances at Mrs Rosser's bright-haired, Dresden-china-faced daughters. But, though anything but

over-squeamish in words or ways, there was that about these
comely young women that deterred the most enamoured
swains from approaching the Miss Rossers after the frankly
familiar fashion approved by some other Maids of Arcady.

Little was required of Elwyn at home during the three years
given him to spend storing knowledge for his lifetime, as
you store your coal cellar for the winter. They had put him
where he had to compete with the sons of gentry, starting at a
considerable advantage. He was a favorite with these as with
others; while the masters, like trainers in a racing stable, had
from the first singled him out as a likely colt, to be considerately
handled with a view to his being entered for some important
event. Notably one Macpherson, at that time the moving spirit,
though not the nominal head of the institution, of whom college
legends ran that as a classical scholar and instructor no man in
the world could compare with him, but whose career had been
checked by a moral scrape of his youth. His ambition, under
the slur of it, had finally settled down to the lifelong position
of an assistant master, manufacturing brilliant products rather
than shining as one himself.

However satisfactory Elwyn's reports scholastic, it could
yet not be said of him, at sixteen, that 'he had never given his
mother a moment's anxiety.'

That he was a born pickle, with an inventive genius for
boyish pranks, was the least of it. More than once he had cut
her to the heart by poking fun at some immemorial national
usage, reckoned sacred and beyond criticism. For example,
the assuming, by local minor poets and singers, of pompous,
fancy 'bardic' names.

'Why on earth,' he once let out irreverently, 'if their own
names aren't good enough for them, must they go in for all
that highfalutin? 'The Peacock of the Platform,' 'The Eagle
of Snowdon,' 'The Nightingale of the universe,' 'The Lion
of Llangorse.' Just like the Red Indian chiefs in 'The Old
Trail,' the book Dobson junior lent me, 'Big Bear,' 'Bellowing

Bison,' 'Prairie Warbler." He checked at the sight of the maternal frown, then ended mischievously, 'If I ever go in for a competition, what shall I be? "The Llanffelix Luminary," "The Thunderer of Trearavon," "The Trothi Twitterer"?'

'If your English friends at Llanwastad College,' spoke Mrs Rosser severely, 'teach you to jeer at our old customs, I shall repent that I ever sent you there,' silencing him for a moment.

Another time he came home full of a big school fight, stopped – alack! – by the masters before it had gone far, between a Welsh and an English boy, bosom friends up till that hour. Asked what it was about, Elwyn had to bethink himself, then fell to laughing immoderately.

'Almost nothing. Only Ben Evans said things about the English that would have made a Quaker show his fists!'

'What things?' Mrs Rosser and the girls inquired.

'Things that happened – if ever they did happen – a thousand – fourteen hundred years ago. Macpherson, who knows everything, says they never happened at all. The old story about the Saxon kings, Hengist and Horsa, you know.'

They didn't; but they wanted to know.

'The feast the kings gave to the British on Salisbury Plain, when every Saxon jumped up and slew his next neighbour. I don't know that any of the British chieftains came from Wales – and there's a love story mixed up. It's in the chronicle, but the chronicler wasn't born at the time, Macpherson says; and that most likely he was a sort of newspaper man, and set himself to make a good story out of something quite different. But what made Ben so furious was Jimmy Dobson saying that only a Welshman would make a grievance of a fourteen hundred years old old-wives' fable like that. He shouted back that it cast an eternal disgrace on every Englishman, dead, living, or yet to be born. Then the fun – I mean the fight – began. A born fool is Ben, but he can hit out, and I was half afraid for Jimmy.'

'You do not mean to tell me,' said Mrs Rosser, firing up in a moment, 'that my Elwyn sided against his own people?'

'Ah, I wasn't in it,' said Elwyn sorrowfully. 'But say I had been – mother, would you have me go savage about a bit of ancient history, or ancient fiction, as Old Foxy (that's Macpherson – we call him so because of the colour of his beard) says it is, like that?'

'I think,' said Mrs Rosser definitively, 'that Welsh schools should have Welsh professors only. It is through foreigners, like this master you are always quoting, that the spirit of levity and unbelief is being sown and spread among our young people. I never thought to hear my son talk mockingly or make a sport of things that should be holy to him, as to us all – our Land and our Language; our Race and our Religion.'

Elwyn checked the protest on his lips against what he felt an undeserved reproach. Never again did he shock or distress his mother in like fashion. But he broke out to David now and then.

'David, I tell you the world's a tremendous place. We, keeping sheep in this antediluvian old fold, know no more about it than of the moon.'

David was not in a position to deny that, but retorted that much of it, he believed, was not worth knowing, and a great deal more was better not known.

Elwyn was not in a position to deny that. Then spake David conclusively, 'Solomon was the wisest of men. He had seen it all, and said it was vanity.'

'Solomon was heir to a throne,' retorted Elwyn, considering, 'and took a top-of-the-tree view of things. I don't suppose his father, who began as a shepherd-boy, and wrote poetry – as it might be you, David – ever thought or felt like that for a moment.'

III

Only as a little boy was Elwyn a pretty boy. Nearly full-grown at seventeen, he was rather under the middle height; square and light of build, fair-complexioned, with well-outlined, rather thin features. If not a handsome, it was a harmonious face: eyes, brow, nose, mouth and chin no more noticeable separately than so many letters which, joined together, may yet spell a word of no little significance. Here the word was 'force'; but that force which is born of the spirit. His movements were naturally alert, adroit, and rhythmical. Yes, his appearance told in his favour; and in its remarkable combination of manliness and refinement, went straight to the heart of womankind.

Katie Evans and Mary Hughes were fast friends from early childhood – friends of the sort that sticketh closer than a sister. Never apart, in school or playground, each with a fond arm round the other's shoulder, sharing tasks and toys, joys and sorrows, and, as they grew older, girls' dress-talk and dream-talk.

To both – as to many other maidens in Llanffelix – Elwyn Rosser was becoming an object of rising interest and solicitude, as he passed every weekend between Llanwastad College and his ancestral riverside home.

'Poor boy!' they sighed, 'working so hard – and not strong either! They shouldn't let him!'

Perhaps they shouldn't; and then – oh, then – might the thoughts and affections of one so soft-natured have tended spontaneously in certain other directions; as they should.

There came a black day when Mary, looking into Katie's eyes, saw that they were friendly to her no more.

Yet what had Mary done? Merely besought Elwyn Rosser so earnestly to help her with an examination subject, that he thought help was what she really wanted, and exerted himself to render it. Katie knew better. That a lad and a lass should hang over an exercise book, keeping their minds steadily fixed on dead historical personages, was unthinkable. She spoke for the lass.

Then began a silent strife in the dark between the girls which of them should be the one to wake Elwyn to it that he was living in a dream, that kisses were worth more than songs; and a comely, up-to-date damsel than scandalous heathen goddesses, and Grecian ghosts, who, when living men and women, moved and had their being seemingly in an atmosphere of battle, murder, and sudden death. The twelve years' sisterly bond was snapped, the sworn vows of their joined hearts broken, each striving, as the other knew, to work that other's woe.

The climax came on the day of the Llanwastad Sports.

Elwyn's future career had by this time passed out of his hands, as of Mrs Rosser's, to determine. Sent up at Macpherson's earnest instigation to compete for an open scholarship at a certain Oxford College, one where Honours men are sought – he had carried it off. That his appointed place in life lay among the teaching and preaching classes was now an accepted thing. At this moment he was recruiting pleasurably from the strain of overstudy that had preceded his victory. His laurels sat on him lightly. No one had ever taxed him with conceit, nor could jealousy of his little winnings survive long in his company. Keen to excess on the contest while it lasted, once this was decided he would throw himself so heartily into the next thing, whatever it was – task or sport – as to sweep the losing side along with him, and put his invidious honours at a safe distance. Yesterday it was the scholarship. Today the College Games. Yes, though Macpherson, forgetting himself in his professional glee, had said things that might excusably have turned his ex-pupil's head, and though the lord of the Manor had come personally to Trearavon to congratulate Mrs Rosser on the mark made by her son, and though Katie Evans and Mary Hughes were smiling themselves into wrinkles upon him, for him the Llanwastad College foot-races – although he, a frequent prize-winner as the fleetest short-distance runner, was not on this occasion to take part in them – were the vital interest of the day.

He had come over from home with a troop of Llanffelix excursionists. For these, when the sports were ended, followed tea-drinking, speeches, hymn-singing, then a leisurely, loitering walk to the station. Mary – artful minx – had got hold of Mr Rosser and was questioning him funnily about the ancient Olympic games. No sooner were they on the station platform than Katie missed her parasol, left, she thought, on the playground, and Elwyn was snatched to go back and help her to find it. And the minutes went by, and the last train to Llanffelix came in, and the returning party took their seats, and, as they started, joked facetiously about the belated pair; all but Mary, her heart burning within her, a prey to envy, hatred, and malice, as though a wolf had fierce possession of her lamb-like soul.

She and Katie, students in training for school-teaching, were fellow-lodgers at Llanffeilx at the time. Towards eleven o'clock Mary, sitting up and raging inwardly, heard Katie's knock, and went to admit her now mortal enemy.

Alone together in their sleeping-room, something unexpected in Katie's aspect checked the withering taunts and reproaches, the terrific accusations on Mary's lips. Katie spoke not a word, though it was plainly with a struggle that she maintained composure. Mary, now wildly curious, passed a question, a bitter jibe, unheeded as though unheard, by her companion. Then wrath prevailed, and out came Mary with her invective. The parasol trick was a blind. Katie had hidden it; thrown it into the river; schemed to make Elwyn miss the train and walk back with her. It was mean, shameful, cruelly unfair. Never would she – Mary – have stooped to win a lover in such an underhand fashion – no, though her heart was broken now. Poor, hoodwinked boy! But she would tell him

– warn him what sort of creature Katie was, and do her best to spoil her basely won triumph.

Poor Katie, anything but triumphant to behold – as Mary, had she been in her senses, must have perceived – sat down, threw back her head and burst into a flood of tears – the tears of the hopeless.

'Oh, Mary, hush!' She spoke as one crestfallen in the extreme; but there was a light and a look in her eye that were new to her friend. She seemed to be seeing things Mary knew nothing of. 'Sillies that we are, you and me!'

'What! Did he refuse – didn't he say he – didn't he even kiss you?' stammered Mary confusedly.

'Mary, for shame! Mary, Mary, *dear*,' cried Katie, sobbing piteously. 'The boy is not for you, nor for me neither.'

'For whom then?' asked Mary literally, eager and inquisitive.

Katie only shook her head, continuing: 'How could we ever think so, or that he could care? How should he? I don't know where he belongs, but he's far, far above, as far away from us as man on earth can be. Why, the very thing in him that makes us love him so is why we can never, *never* get any nearer. I've been jealous of you, Mary, but the proof that I'm not so any longer is that you may go and court Elwyn Rosser how and when you please. You'll come back saying, "Katie, you knew; you told me truly".'

Katie spoke as never before, with strange emphasis, as one inspired. So impressed, so carried away, was Mary, that she fell then and there into her open arms. Confidences were interchanged, and half the night they two lay awake talking.

Meanwhile Elwyn the mischief-maker, absolutely un-conscious of the heart-troubles of which he was the guiltless cause, was enjoying his supper at Trearavon, and entertaining his sisters with the liveliest account of how he and Miss Evans had got left behind, and what a glorious moonlight tramp they had had to an eight-miles-distant station – done it in two hours by following the railway track – and there caught a market-train home. And how he had kept talking all the way, about everything that came into his head, just to keep her spirits up, as she seemed frightened of the dark and of getting run over, and how cleverly he had dodged the railway man, who would have taken them up for trespassing on the line.

IV

In every European country but Elwyn's the English are well known for a terribly serious-minded nation – puritanical, taking their very pleasures sadly. The impossible strictness of their moral standard is a byword. Theirs is the land of prudish, dowdy women, dismally dull and blank Sundays, compulsory church-going, censored amusements, even late suppers being ruled out for the public by the law. A land of such rigid respectability and conventional piety as to make virtue odious to the light-hearted foreigner.

In Elwyn's native circle a contrary conviction prevailed. Frivolity, thy name is English wight! There, across the border, was the land of play – or worse. A youth, placed by destiny and reared up in a home like Trearavon, if forced to cross Offa's Dyke for educational or other purposes, had best hold apart, spiritually from that gay, giddy people, who would scoff at his beliefs, and entice him out of his harmless, quiet habits of life. That England spells the world, the flesh, and the devil was a time-honoured doctrine none cared to call in question.

Seated of an evening, knitting or darning by the kitchen hearth, or on Sundays in the parlour sacred to the bookish memory of the Reverend Thomas Rosser, Elwyn's mother and sisters would be speculating anxiously on his probable doings or misdoings at the particular moment, Mrs Rosser seeming simply to revel in the darkest, gloomiest apprehensions, founded on lamentable antecedent.

'There was Jones, Brynmawr, whom we all thought so lucky to step straight, at seventeen, into his clerkship in that big London firm. Where is he now?'

Fallen among idlers and evil-doers, he had neglected his work till his employers lost patience, and Jones his place. Was found to have contracted drinking and gambling habits, and had been a millstone round his mother's neck ever since – he who should have been the mainstay, the pride of his family!

'But Rhydychen' (Welsh for Oxford) 'won't be so big a place as London. There can't be so much wickedness there,' ventured Gwladys hopefully. But Mrs Rosser sorrowed on—

'And Price of Pontsimon, poor lad! The greatest musical genius, they said, the world has ever seen – whose parents pinched themselves to help him to a good start out there. He lies in the chapel cemetery!'

He had followed strange gods and goddesses, married a music-hall hussy who left him; and, after picking up a living awhile in uncertain ways, had returned home, ruined in health and in prospects, to die prematurely.

'Mother!' protested the two young things in a breath, 'Why should you think so badly of Elwyn as that?'

'Dear boy! It's the company I fear for him,' and she shook her head. 'Impatient already of the quiet, sober ways of his Welsh fellow-students. What was it he said of Jehoiada James? He called him a dull dog!'

The girls tittered and exchanged a mischievous glance. What they thought is no matter.

'But even those who stay here go wrong now and then,' said Gwladys, naughtily. 'There was Morgan of the Bank…' Mrs Rosser silenced her with an awful look.

That was a bad case! But why drag it in? Moreover it was an undeniable fact that, for the black sheep who stayed at home, their misconduct was mostly less tragic in its ultimate results. Sometimes they reformed; but even if they didn't, thanks to the freedom from temptations, the calming, restraining influences of their social medium, they seldom went under.

'Dr Elsworthy was an Englishman,' persisted Gwladys, naming a recently deceased local resident, 'yet I have heard you say yourself that they buried one of the best when they buried him. Then his college neighbour of Elwyn's, with whom he has made such particular friends – this Mr Brownjohn – he describes as steadier and more hard-working than himself. Why, he might even be half Welsh, from the name, John,' she concluded ingeniously.

Elwyn's letters home were regular, and in a lively vein, but dealt chiefly with little matters of fact – or weight, naturally, to Mrs Rosser – college dues, food, clothes, furniture, and a freshman's expenses generally. But already his intelligence was telling him that Oxford and Oxford University – a mystery to those dear women – were one it would be past his power ever to make intelligible. They plied him with questions that showed it. It was bigger than Llanffelix, they supposed! Was it as big as Swansea or as London? In what respect was it superior to Bala, Lampeter, Bangor, and other founts of learning nearer home? What was the sense of a place of tuition that only admitted you for six months of the year and ruthlessly expelled you for the other half? where nothing seemed compulsory – least of all hard study – and where young men seemed invited to waste their time, and at a great cost? The extraordinary elasticity of the arrangements scandalised Mrs Rosser. And, though the little group of money-prizes won by Elwyn at and soon after his first going up enabled him to pay the best part of his way unassisted, the demands pecuniary, put forward as modest, and for inevitable extras, seemed to her immoderate and for wild luxuries or useless formalities. She complied with them, but under protest, as of necessity. Elwyn, as even she must own, had not been sent to Oxford to reform it or criticise, but to get the best he could out of it.

He was putting the best he could into it, unsolicited. He had gone up at a time when, had its constitution not been founded on a rock of ages, it must have perished from being talked and written about. Critics from within and without were busy doctoring it to death – on paper; some bewailing its downfall and abandonment of the ancient ways; others depreciating it as the home of lost causes, or denouncing it as mediæval, fossilised, obsolete, and finding its only chance of continued existence in the increasing changes, the new pieces of cloth that were in due time to supersede the old garment.

Young Elwyn, arriving without any definite anticipations, unconcerned and irresponsible, had taken it as he found it – so wholly to his liking that its unfamiliarity brought with it no displeasing touch nor any sense of embarrassment. He dropped into his place there as neatly as a billiard ball into the pocket.

The particular place was one belonging, rather to the old, now dethroned order – classical, academic, and social. To him it was new, incalculably newer and more revealing than the most revolutionary modern, democratic additions and devices. And something in him went out to meet the immortal spirit, hugged it, loved it, throve upon it.

Like some choice plant, reared up successfully in a dour climate, then removed to a warmer soil and more genial atmosphere, and responding by unlooked for, undreamed of expansion – so it began to be with him now.

From Trearavon to Llanwastad had been out of a cage into the open; still, with a string tied to his foot, pulling him back incessantly, denying him the use, even the sense, of his wings.

But even then his mind had been full of wants and ideas that had nothing in common with those of his own household, and that he instinctively kept to himself. "They" did not know. "They" could not understand. They were so near, and yet between him and them a gap had sprung, that was now widening daily. Already Llanwastad seemed remote – provincial – Lilliputian in its outlook. Here he was in the thick of things, and invited to walk by himself in the way that he might choose. The gap was fast becoming an impassable gulf.

Some dim inkling of estrangement now and then visited Mrs Rosser, and when one day Macpherson, his ex-preceptor, a bigoted Oxonian, came over to Trearavon, hankering for some report of one whom he regarded, secretly, as the work of his hands, she hailed the opportunity of expressing her feelings on the subject.

That Elwyn would never now be seen working on the parental farm had been a foregone conclusion when first the university marked him for her own. But what of the path of training he was treading now, that was to lead him to the ministry? Already the Oxford system – or want of system – stood condemned in her heart as a dangerous and expensive imposture. What was the principle – the object of it?

'General culture, Mrs Rosser,' returned the tutor, as one smiling from a height, stooping to conquer, 'general culture on a sound classical basis.'

'How can it be sound,' she objected, 'when the languages are dead, and the nations they belonged to vanished from the face of the earth?'

'I don't say that the University is the place for every one,' he conceded temperately, 'but I have always regarded your son, with his imaginative and literary temperament, as one of those for whom Greek and Latin were specially designed by Providence. So apt a pupil I have rarely found.'

'But such studies should come second and not first, absorbing the time and mind of a youth who has his living to earn, and his appointed place to fill in the world of the present day,' asserted the anxious mother.

Macpherson spoke of the Greek temper, of the training of the mind, the high qualities their authors had power to instill into the student, the gain to his general intelligence, mature judgment, foresight, lucidity of thought and expression – the importance of maintaining lofty standards and ideals, a crying need, he averred, so far from being an anomaly, in the present age. It was all as mere sounding brass in her ears. Classical knowledge to her was just a matter of formal scholarship, whose actual uses, unless as an occasional aid to Biblical interpretation, were nil.

'Can you not conceive, Mrs Rosser, of the desire of learning without thought of material reward?' he asked.

Could she not! It was no uncommon thing thereabouts to find a studiously minded man burying himself alive in curious but barren lore – genealogical, botanical, archaeological – and even highly venerated on that account. But to supply a hobby or pastime suitable for old age and leisure was not the business of a teaching institution, said she, and to that she stuck.

Once again he held forth on the larger aspects of education, the broadening of sympathies and interests, wider knowledge of humanity, the real culture thus acquired, leading to a better sense of perspective, of proportion, and the relative importance of things, thus fitting a man for personal independence and diversity of pursuits, and for entering into the life and doings of other nations as well as of his own country; the cosmopolitanism of experience, raising the standard of his duties and possibilities in life, whether public or private – uncomprehending that every word of his powerful pleading was telling in the contrary direction.

(And Gwladys and Gwen, making golden marmalade in peace and concord in their kitchen sanctuary, wondered what on earth the wrangle, of which the echoes reached them, was about!)

'Serves rather to conduce to moral laxity, and a taste for idleness or roving and miscellaneous amusements,' she retorted, 'and to make him impatient of home ties and put him out of conceit with the state of life to which he was called.'

'Even you, Mrs Rosser, must be aware that for the proper exercise of the clerical profession some knowledge of Greek and Latin is requisite.'

'For Elwyn, a knowledge of Welsh is a first necessity. He has been tempted to neglect the study of his own language, with which he is very imperfectly acquainted.' 'Tempted by you' was implied, though unspoken.

'Oh,' said the Scotchman unconcernedly, 'a lad who has shown such aptitude for the classic tongues, will, when he sets to it, soon make himself master of the jargon here.'

'Have *you*?' she returned crushingly. For, after ten years at Llanwastad, Welsh was still to the scholar Macpherson as the language of the birds.

Here the two girls – as if by chance – intervened. It was impossible to go on quarreling in their pretty presences. Instinctively Mrs Rosser shifted her indictment to less debateable ground.

'*And the expense of it all!*'

'Ah, college life there is not conducive to economy,' the ex-Oxonian admitted feelingly. 'Is that the trouble? Bills, eh?'

'Not now – not yet – his first year!' answered the mother, horrified. And did he, Macpherson, defend the length of the vacations?

Evading the issue, he expressed his desire to take Elwyn with a reading-party to a quiet nook he knew, for the Long! The advantage to Master Elwyn, with examinations ahead, was not to be gainsaid. Finally, over the subject of Elwyn's photograph in cap and gown, they made peace in unanimous approval.

'A stubborn old lady. Must have been a handsome one in her time,' mused Macpherson as he went from the door. 'Clever woman, too, in her way, but keeps her eyes fixed on the surface; sightless to the heart of things. Now did she expect that young son of hers to settle down for life as a member of the Llanffelix Mutual Admiration Society, I wonder?' added the profane, the unspeakable Scot.

V

Could the magic mirror of mediæval romance, or the cinema of present reality have enabled Elwyn's family to look on at a day of his college life as a freshman nothing could have appeared more fully reassuring.

An earlier riser than most, more regular in his chapel attendances, zealous in application to his after-breakfast studies, quite as keen on afternoon athletics as his mother cared to see him – left to Elwyn to deplore that his somewhat slender physique, and still slenderer purse, debarred him from over indulgence in what she held to be the most mischievous of modern crazes. Long walks, long talks with his chum and stair-neighbour, one Brownjohn, who, if he had been Welsh, would have been the very companion she would have chosen for him – quiet, studious, fairly well-off, socially better placed than Elwyn, but, like him, cut off awhile from his home people, now stationed in India – himself a 'paying guest,' as he put it, in the house of two maiden aunts at Richmond, where he spent the vacations.

Lectures, of course, and a tutor, of whom he wrote disparagingly as 'not a patch upon Old Foxy' – yet whose ripe age and knowledge had presumably something to impart to the most uppish pupil. Pranks and frolics – the jokesome disposition had not gone out of him – but the authorities were lenient to such; and the worst a fond mother could say or think of them was that they were utterly nonsensical. The picture should have lulled the anxiety rife in those three female hearts. Such was the harmless, happy, ideal life that, none the less, was parting him, past reunion, from the only souls on earth that loved him.

Not the explorer, setting foot in an undiscovered country, not Israel, treading the Land of Promise, entered in with more zest and elation than Elwyn into, so to speak, the heritage of the ages. The larger, freer life absorbed him. Books apart, fields of interests of all kinds were opening to his view – the social, sporting, artistic worlds of which hitherto he had had no glimpse. Great musicians and actors, political leaders, British and foreign, first-class men in all life's departments visited the place. He was invited to widen his mental horizon to the utmost limits of his powers of mental vision, which were keen and comprehensive. The sense of escape – the exultation of it rang through his letters home that second year. He could not keep it out. His mother trembled, warned, exhorted; he bore with it all in silent impatience. It was well meant, it was good advice – only it was utterly irrelevant.

From the first start, when Elwyn, the successful product of that brilliant failure, Macpherson, won admission to his college as its scholar, and Elwyn the pert undergraduate, on entering its ancient porch for the first time, and reading the notice paper on the wall, *A bonfire will be held tonight in the field by the river*, instantly pencilled underneath, *How is this done?* to his companion Jehoiada James's utter dismay and apprehension of instant expulsion for them both, he found himself a *persona grata* with tutors and freshers alike, gathering the best fruits of his position as with simplicity and ease.

Numbers of other Welsh youths, from obscure homes like Trearavon, were undergoing the same experience; but, for the most part, seemed dissimilarly affected. To these proud, shy stranger students there was much in the new social medium that was frankly repellent, antipathetic, or at least dubious, to be viewed with suspicion, and that held them aloof; these same things being accepted by Elwyn without shock or hesitation, nay, as natural wants of his, of which he had been deprived until now, but for whose satisfaction he had been waiting.

Many of his countrymen failed to make friends outside their clan, fearful of ridicule, always on the look-out for real or fancied slights. Not a few such hankered sorely after a wider social expansion, but found themselves not at home in the modes of expression habitual among the more cultivated, hence ill at ease; and preferred to hang together and criticise, nursing a sense of wrong; some burying themselves in theological or other deep, dry study; but more than would own it, perhaps, echoing in their secret hearts the bitter cry of one of their number, bemoaning the restricted opportunities of a Welshman—

'I sometimes wish the Welsh language had died before my mother had dropped its charm into my heart in hymn and verse! Will there be a chance for a Welshman in the next world, with no restrictions of language – worse than restrictions of sect?'

Elwyn loved his country – in Cordelia's way – according to his bond, nor more nor less. It was always 'Hail fellow, well met!' with him and his Welsh Oxford acquaintance. But he owned no previous intimates among them, and all his newly formed intimacies were beyond the pale. His social relations had been decided for him mainly by his own personality, and the little difficulties that beset some – the miseries of self-consciousness – for him did not exist. Men – the best sort of many sorts – the men he liked, sought his company for its own sake. Even scarcity of ready cash hampered him less than most. He was constitutionally careful and fastidious in the important matter of attire; and it was not wholly due to a way Rosser had of wearing his clothes that these, as his friends remarked, though not coming from the master tailor's shop, never drew attention to the fact or incited criticism.

That the power of suiting yourself to circumstances as they arise makes for success in this world is a commonplace. Or was it merely that chance here had favoured him? For say that reverses had forced Mrs Rosser to emigrate to Colorado or Dakota, as a ranchman he might have proved a failure. Or had Katie and Mary been bold, bad girls, of evil and designing knowledge, instead of just love-lorn little girl students, his life might have been misshapen, and its upward course checked at the outset.

'It is good for us to be here!' So his soul kept telling him night and day. To him it was an ideally happy life, and the place a ground of delights. He revelled in its natural and artistic beauties, welcomed the absence of bother about details, the supply of those amenities of life so congenial to his temperament. But above all he felt free – free to explore, observe, enthuse, abuse, exercise to the full and continually the interplay of ideas with those starting on the same lines and like-minded – young, eager, and unafraid; able to indulge to his heart's content that passion for varied knowledge that was rapidly and irretrievably alienating him from his next of kin. And whether the life he was leading was one calculated to enable him to earn a living as quickly as possible, he was much too in love with that life just now to consider.

In matters of religion he had always been reserved. For him, it was a very intimate thing, and his mother had sufficient perception to know that his silence on this head did not imply indifference, let alone unbelief. Besides, thanks to his early acquired thorough familiarity with Holy Scripture (rarer now than in her younger days), as also with the best works on divinity, he always came out well in these subjects, a solace to which she clung. Not the most sinister imagination, she must now own, could conceive of Elwyn as roistering with boon companions or consorting with Jezebels. Thus as time wore on, and the winter and the summer were the second year, she came to rest satisfied that he was using the dangerous freedom of opportunity allowed him for self-improvement and not for self-destruction. Another twelvemonth or so – a mere watch in the night at her time of life – and he would 'have done with Oxford'. With the end thus in sight she ceased to be troubled by baseless fears, while vaguer, dimmer presentiments were lulled or stifled.

The accidental trove among his belongings during one of his visits home of a cabinet portrait of a young lady, indisputably pretty and very well dressed, caused a family flutter, in no wise allayed by his exclamation when interrogated—

'Gerty King's photo. Oh, how shockingly careless of me!'

'Gerty – King! What – who is this?' Mrs Rosser demanded, aghast, and the sisters agog with curiosity.

'Oh, some people I know a little,' Elwyn explained quickly. 'Mrs King is the widow of a half-pay officer, with one daughter at home. They have a house just outside Oxford. Brownjohn knows them; they are very kind to undergraduates, and I – we – go there to tea sometimes.'

Mrs Rosser was scanning the photo with ruthless eyes. A small, slightly-made personage, faintly aquiline in feature – dangerously feline-looking to her thinking.

'And pray, do you call her "Gerty"?'

'Everybody calls her Gerty,' said Elwyn, shrugging his shoulders. 'Not to her face, of course. Although,' he let fall aloud as to himself, 'upon my honour I don't think she would mind it.'

His manner seemed to imply a certain indifference, and when Mrs Rosser, after searching inspection of the photograph, exclaimed, 'Impudent little puss!' he laughed outright, but said quickly, as though aware he had been unmannerly:

'She's a very clever young lady, very amusing, a capital talker. She told me she collects the photos of her men friends, and asked for mine, then very kindly gave me her own. I should never have made so bold as to ask for it.'

Except for a short Christmas visit this third year, they scarcely saw him. The Easter vacation he spent, by special invitation, with Brownjohn and his aunts in London; the Long, in studying for the Honour Schools with Old Mac! He must make a push for it if he meant to make a splash. It was given him to understand that cash was not forthcoming to keep him much longer where he was. But weighing his chances of coming through with such credit as might hasten his obtaining a good post and fixed income, Mrs Rosser decided that they were good. Thus she soothed her idle hours with fond imaginings! Again and again she heard his voice in the reading desk at

Llanffelix Church; many a time she preached his first sermon for him. By and by they would have him settled; if not close at hand, somewhere in the same pleasant shire. They would share his interests, social, professional, and domestic, and he theirs. Mere ambition, she knew, though she did not know why, would never be his ruling passion. He desired happiness and usefulness; but his was the divine content of one who can find a mint of satisfaction in this despised world without losing himself in vain and impossible aspirations.

What a winter, what a spring, would be theirs! Really Gwladys must postpone her wedding with Joseph Lloyd Jones Harris till Elwyn was ordained and qualified to assist the ceremony.

So she mused, while adding to her garden produce, devising improvements in the dairy, and generally upholding the standard of efficiency in housekeeping and the farming industry.

PART II

Daughters of Heth

I

'Finals' were over. Elwyn sat alone in his rooms, his home of happiness this long time, abject, miserable, sunk into the depths by a load of black and dire dejection.

It had sprung on him yesterday, out of nowhere, like one of the quick weather metamorphoses of his native land that claim so many human lives annually – reversing the face of things, turning all previous brightness into a mocking show, and proclaiming itself, the destroyer, the abiding reality.

His eyes were opened, and he knew he had been living in a

dream these three glorious years, pursuing his explorer's path, every turn of which revealed new and delectable lands, but ending for him abruptly and, as it were, in a sheer precipice.

The dupe of a huge educational mistake! The true account now rendered of his scholarship was that it had unfitted him past redemption for the life that lay before him. Never could he again be understanded of his own people, never be at home in his real home again. Here he had made many friends, but with those among whom he had no ties. All were leaving, like himself, but it was to start their young lives – lives of action or of enjoyment according to their character and circumstances – on approved lines, chosen or accepted by themselves and prepared for them by their relatives. He would lose sight of, lose touch with them all, one by one.

While in his own case sacrifices had been made, prejudices waived, separation borne, all to the intent that he should take orders. "From plough to pulpit in two years," as the saying runs in his own country. Here now was he, the finished product, as disqualified for the one as for the other, and for reasons that would never seem reasons to those of his own household. Warning glimmerings of the coming crash had visited him already, but, in the stress of study, been thrust out of sight. Face to face now with the prospect he was overcome by its dreary nakedness. He was here in the world as one without home or ties or the least belongings. No way back, no way on, no way out! Many a youth has gone and hanged himself for less.

Brownjohn came capering boy-like into the room, waving a news sheet.

'I say! The Jessamy Bride's won the Manydown Cup!'

'No, *has* she?' responded Elwyn, momentarily galvanised into life and interest. 'How did that happen? And the favourite? And Black Robin?'

'Black Robin lost ground at the start. Scramble-Jack showed

the way to Invasion, Ox-eye, Knuckle-duster, and Jessamy Bride, the first leading, and in this order they raced for a mile, when Knuckle-duster broke down. Six furlongs from home, Scramble-Jack was beaten, Ox-eye going on second. At the bushes Jessamy Bride dashed to the front just clear of Ox-eye, but could not quite get on terms with Jessamy Bride, who got the better by a fine finish. Won by a short head,' the reader rattled off from his paper: 'And she was without friends at 20 to 1!' Here Brownjohn, in whom the relief from the pressure of examinations had induced a fit of wild spirits, went waltzing round the room singing out, 'And I've won Gerty King's sweepstakes – thirty shillings – if she can make her friends pay up. Well, are you ready now? Come on! It's time we were off to that garden-party. We'll have to scorch it as it is; but I've got the car waiting at the gates. Fitzisaacs will trust me with it, he says, it being heavily insured.' He stopped short, now first noting his friend's strangely listless attitude and bearing. 'Hullo!' he said, 'What's up? Something the matter?'

Elwyn laughed nervously. 'To say the truth, I'd clean forgotten that you were taking me out.' He would have given ten pounds, had he got them, to stop where he was; but the alternative – to unburden his mind to his comrade – was out of the question just at that moment.

So out and away now from town and gown far into the next county. The darting motion was as good as an anaesthetic for annulling thought and feeling, while conducing to agreeable physical ease and content. How swiftly, gracefully that curve was rushed! though all but at the cost of suicide or murder or both, through a barely averted collision with a pony-cart.

'They were on the wrong side,' said Elwyn's companion triumphantly, who, while opposed to capital punishment, held it to be the legitimate and just due for this particular offence.

The shave had been a narrow one. Thanks mainly to old Dobbin's prompt and independent action nothing happened.

Somehow that moment had brought home to Elwyn that, after all, he would rather be in this troublesome world than out of it.

'Where are we off to, and what for?' he asked presently. 'These exams have left my brain a blank – a clean slate.'

'The Vicarage, Yewdene, Berks – garden-party,' his amateur chauffeur reminded him. 'Sort of bridal house-warming or reception, by the Honourable and Reverend Archibald Praed, thirty years vicar of the parish.'

'Thirty years vicar – and a bridegroom today? Silver wedding, I suppose?'

'Not a bit of it. His first wife has been dead for some years. The new one is about of an age with his youngest daughter. I believe the bride's mother schemed to bring out the match, and he was always a wax in the hands of the ladies. He's a fine old boy, and a good old boy. Ought to have been a bishop. Has high connections in Church and State. Might be of use to you when you are ordained.'

'I shall never be ordained,' said Elwyn loudly. 'Never!'

'Oho!' His friend eyed him wonderingly for a moment; then after a pause put the question delicately, 'Doubting Castle? The Thirty-nine, is it?'

Elwyn told him 'No'. As a fact, the dogmatic troubles to which so many fall an easy prey had no tight grip on him, an imaginative thinker. 'But it is a vocation no man is justified in committing himself to with the disinclination I perceive in myself towards it – implying unfitness, to say the least,' he explained.

'What, then, would you prefer?' inquired his friend cautiously by and by.

'The Army,' returned Elwyn promptly. 'Not to be thought of, that, of course. Teaching? But I want to learn. Life is too short, even for that.'

He was seeing blue again, as they neared Yewdene, slowed down, and snaked up the drive to the pleasant-looking,

gardened Vicarage, so peculiarly Anglican in its happy
blend of sedate, other-worldly seclusion, with genial social
kindliness and domestic ease. The Hon. and Rev. Archibald,
a fine and courteous old-school specimen, was a picture, just
the right one to fill the frame. But both he and the bride – an
auburn-haired, well-favoured, though rather wooden-faced
girl – behaved today like nervous dèbutants, hiding secret
flurry under an exaggerated ease and artificial volubility of
manner that became neither him nor her. Moreover, the showy
display of wedding presents sensibly marred the dignity of the
simple home. So felt Elwyn, as he stood apart, a stranger in
the crowd taking notes.

Yes, the tallest, the most striking-looking man in the
house was unquestionably the master of the house. The next
conspicuous was a military-looking fellow, with command in
his stature at all events, thought Elwyn, faintly envious.

The man of war was looking down on and discoursing to
some one upon whom Elwyn's glance, once drawn, dwelt;
held, fixed, as by some treasure trove of a jewel, spied of a
sudden lying there in your path.

She might or might not be beautiful, but, if not – well, then
beauty was a thing of naught and a fraud. The effect on him of
the sight of her was that of a fine piece of music that takes hold
of you before you have time to think, or perceive separately a
single one of the innumerable touches that go to make up the
incomparable whole. As here, the slender grace of figure, the
fine skin and pure tones of her complexion, soft, rather dark,
and abundant hair shading a perfect forehead. There was
natural distinction in her every movement – nothing forced
nor feverish in the life that her whole person seemed to radiate.
Beside her the bride, who had come up to ask her something,
appeared suddenly to him as inanimate and unintelligent-
looking as a rather clumsily made doll.

The delighted Elwyn, regarding her admiringly, entirely lost
the forlorn sense of a stranger guest set down in a room full

of people, among whom he had descried but a single familiar face – that of the Oxford girl, Gerty King, who just at this point came to accost him and carry him off to play some nice, foolish garden game, saying she wanted him for her partner.

She was a maiden he was persuaded he disliked, not withstanding that he found her good company. Her rather shrewish style of prettiness did not appeal to him, and her dauntless manners and outspokenness jarred on his taste; which was ungrateful on his part, since she not only liked but thoroughly appreciated him. An expert little schemer, who could get round most men and all women. Sharp as a needle, cool as a cucumber, and hard as nails.

Having played and won their round, the two joined the tea-drinking groups on the lawn. There was the tall officer, still with the lady who had arrested Elwyn's attention, handing her a cup with a privileged expression, as well he might, thought Elwyn, now watching her with an air that Gerty, who never stopped talking for a moment, marked instantly, as one besotted.

'Mr Rosser, Mr Rosser! I did not know you could be so rude.'

'Rude! I?' cried the shocked Elwyn, recalled of a sudden from the clouds.

'Pretending to attend me, while taken up with watching Captain Soanes and Aline there.'

'Aline, Aline! Who is Aline?' Elwyn flushed as he spoke, innocently.

'You don't know?' She saw he did not. 'Why, the daughter of the house, to be sure, and its mistress since she was sixteen.'

Elwyn was listening now, acutely, as Gerty went on.

'Rather hard lines for her to have to stand aside to make room for a young stepmother,' – lowering her voice – ' who isn't fit to mend her clothes for her. You have taste, Mr Rosser. But none of us have a chance where Aline comes in. Look at

poor Captain Soanes, over head and ears, and she doesn't care
for him, not a snap, and he knows it. Shall I introduce you?
Aline, dear, do let me present to you your distinguished guest,
as no one else appears to have done so. Mr Elwyn Rosser,
winner of the Flat Mile race.'

The girl held out her hand smilingly as Elwyn named the
friend who was responsible for his presence on the lawn.

'It was as the holder of the Gamaliel scholarship that Mr
Brownjohn spoke to us of Mr Rosser,' she said; and thus
playfully, as in some sort a double honours man already,
Elwyn was next presented to Captain Soanes.

'Man of Thought and Man of Action, too,' quoth the Captain
facetiously.

'Oh, no, no! Only a poor Welsh scholar, at your service,'
returned Elwyn gaily. 'In old times I should have been a
servitor and blacked the other fellows' boots. And I'll engage,'
he continued, with a thoughtful, critical look down at his own
shoe leather, 'I'd have done that better than my scout or his
boy.'

'Man of many parts, evidently,' said the Captain, with
supercilious amusement. 'Universal genius, shall we say?'

'Not so bad as that,' responded Elwyn, catching his tone of
mock gravity; 'for I must specialise.'

'What is it to be? Law? Medicine?'

'Divinity, it should be,' Elwyn answered quickly. 'But
the lists won't be out yet; and if they put me at the bottom I
may yet have to turn my hand to shoe-blacking or some other
useful industry.'

There the conversation ended, Gerty intervening to spirit
the Captain away in his turn, to play the return game, and he
went, testifying his approval of Elwyn's readiness and good-
humour by a half-jesting, courteously worded desire for the
better acquaintance of so notable a character, and willingness
to see him to dine at the officers' mess at Brackenbury, his
present quarters.

The elation that had momentarily loosened Elwyn's tongue now forsook him completely. Left standing there alone – aloof as a ghost with one whom they call Aline! One he might never see again, and whom merely to stay regarding, as he was now, seemed to him the highest happiness he was capable of receiving. A very few sentences were interchanged, in themselves of no import; but the voice, the words, the sense, instead of breaking, as they might, only perfected the spell.

'Was he leaving Oxford,' she asked presently, 'now his course there was finished?'

'Not yet; not immediately.' Ah, he thanked heaven for that. Chance that had brought him hither, might bless him once more. All else had of a sudden become relatively unimportant. And now there was Brownjohn taking leave of the host and hostess, and beckoning to him, and the garden-party, so reluctantly attended, was ending, and all in life that for him was worth living might be ending too!

It was a changed Elwyn that Brownjohn drove back to Oxford, companionable and self-possessed again outwardly, inwardly exultant, and uplifted above the world of common things. Before him floated the delighting image of something – of one – his imagination must for long have been unconsciously seeking. For, though never beheld in fancy or in human shape till this afternoon, he felt that, in her slightest service, he could readily have thrown himself under the wheels of that car!

II

Dear Mr Rosser, – Mother is asking a lot of dull people to tea on Saturday. I am beseeching the few superior yet unselfish souls that I know to come and help me bear it. Aline – you know who I mean – is spending the weekend with friends in Oxford, and has promised. Will you be as noble? If unsupported I shall succumb;

> *and you, believe me, will lose a friend.*
> *Yours, for the present,*
> *GERTY KING.*

'Stupendous luck!' thought Elwyn as he read, and kept re-exclaiming to himself when on the appointed afternoon he bent his willing steps towards the Kings' little villa, surnamed "The Doll's House" by Gerty, on the edge of one of the town's newer garden suburbs. 'What have I done to deserve this?' he asked himself naively, stone blind to it that Gerty was pulling the wires that controlled his movements, among others.

A fairly frequent visitor at the house, he was no stranger to Mrs King's set, so cruelly disparaged by Gerty. She, however, was not going to let him be button-holed by one of these. She had laid hold of him at once, rattling on in a way she had, while carrying out her most deeply laid purposes, of seeming to speak and to act entirely on the spur of the moment.

'So nice of you, Mr Rosser, to like to come!' Thus she greeted him gushingly. 'I was feeling surly – suicidal, I vow. Aline turned up just in time to save my life. And now that you are here I feel a little less inhospitable, and shall presently begin to think all these old fossils and parrots entertaining creatures after all. Don't you want to go and talk to her, my preserver – to Aline?' airily. 'So you shall presently.'

Elwyn hardly knew if he wanted to. The mere presence of this being, whom he felt, mysteriously, to be built spiritually and externally on what, to him, were perfect lines, filled him with absolute content. Gerty ran on, changing her voice – she had a trick of making all she said, without lowering it, audible to one alone.

'Men are fools! Don't you think so, Mr Rosser? That old father of hers, letting Mrs Markham catch him for Conny, the eldest of her three dowerless daughters, walking into the snare spread in his very sight.'

Elwyn's chivalrous instincts revolted and protested. Mrs

Praed seemed a pleasant-faced young lady,' he remarked.

'Oh, she may pass – in a common way – and looks the parson's wife all over, I grant you. But, to think of choosing her to sit opposite him at a table for the remainder of his days; displacing that – that adorable daughter!'

Elwyn had a motion of surprise; glanced sharply at her, and saw that she spoke from her heart.

'She's too good for such a parent. No, no, I didn't mean that. The Vicar is an old darling whom we all love – but for such a stepmother. Conny is as Audrey to her Rosalind. However,' she chattered on, 'Aline isn't tied down to that hearth, as it happens. She has money of her own now she's of age – inherited from her mother. Three or four hundred a year, I believe. *I'd* not stay to have my home, my garden, my household all spoilt and made up-to-date – that is, gaudy and vulgar – hot and strong. Their tastes are as different as their selves.'

Here the tall form of Captain Soanes, just announced, appeared, threading his way towards them.

'Now you go and speak to Aline,' Gerty concluded, in her off-hand way. 'She's there by the window. I wish you'd open it for me. Ask her if she doesn't mind. Captain Soanes will take care of me.'

A summary order, but one which she to whose side he was dispatched made it easy for him to obey. And forthwith Elwyn had entered a region of bliss pure and simple. For to the lover where, from the very first, the quest – the very dream – of requital is ruled out as inconceivable, sufficient unto the flying instant is the delight thereof.

They talked of Oxford, which she seemed to know well, and love as fondly as he did. It was at Elwyn's college, he now learnt, that her father, the Yewdene Vicar, in days that are no more, had run his not undistinguished course. Matter-of-fact, mere company talk on the face of it, thus far, only with now and again for Elwyn a thrill of exquisite surprise at meeting here, in the unknown, with what he knew best of all – or its counterpart – the counterpart of his inward spiritual self; his fervent eyes meanwhile acquainting themselves and memorising the features of her uncommon grace and beauty.

In the prime of young girlhood was Aline; her refined cast of face and figure had not, as with too many, its source in delicate or impaired health. No sounder blood can run in women's veins than that which coloured her cheek. Her onyx-brown, well-grown hair set of the white and well formed brow. The eyes did not reveal themselves fully, and left you wondering what yet might be there for them to tell you. Yes, good was the mould; yet the beautifying power lay in the being that animated it. A vivid, vital beauty with power to redeem, to transform the outside shape by its compelling working. No glamour, nothing fantastic, fairylike, witchlike or even angelic, but deliciously human. Could the world, for him, ever hold anything better?

Gerty King came slithering through the crowd like a lizard towards them, in seeming dismay, to give one of her masterly asides. 'Mother has asked *all* the stupid people in Oxford; *and they've all come!* Our jerry-built room will burst. Professor Palaver has just thrust his arm through the middle wall of partition into the dining room! Do, pray, Aline – you and Mr Rosser – lead the way into the garden. Ours is not much more than a horticultural expression, I know; but it will relieve the pressure and avert a catastrophe. The sheep will follow you.'

From the open window by which they were standing, a little spiral iron stair led down to a brick-walled enclosure. Obeying the order, they saw a stream of people follow in their wake till the little turfed oblong center and strips of gravel walk began to to be as crowded as the room they had left.

They two stood aside. Close by was a door in the wall, ajar, opening into the lane beyond.

'Emergency Exit,' Elwyn suggested jokingly.

'Room for an overflow meeting outside,' she responded

likewise.

'Let us see.'

Just for fun they slipped through into the open: a stretch of lane – grass-grown, neglected, ragged-hedged, uninviting-looking and leading nowhere; land "ripening" for building purposes. But the fresher air, ampler space, and hush of tongues gave to their mild truancy the flavour of an escapade, as by tacit consent they put more and more of that lane between them and the "Doll's House." 'Oh that it were longer still!' thought Elwyn in his soul. He did not know it, but his heart was beating as after the Mile Race, though he preserved his even tone and natural ease of manner.

She asked if he was returning to Wales before a certain important local musical event – the Choral Festival at St. Primus's Church – a week or two hence.

'I do not know,' he told her. 'It all depends on the Working Man.'

'How can that be?'

'Dr Golightly is prevented by laryngitis from delivering his lecture on Social Reform at the Working Men's Innovation Institute at Yokelham next Friday. They have asked me to take his place on this occasion, and, should they approve of me, on the Friday following.'

'You are going to lecture on Social Reform?'

'Oh, no! What should I, a beginner in human society, know about it – high or low – that I should presume, should pretend to teach?' exclaimed Elwyn. 'They let me choose my own subject.'

'And you chose?'

'Aristotle.'

'Aristotle?'

'Well, you see I ought to know something about him – perhaps a little more than they. While as to the other subject, I suspect I have more to learn from them than they from me.'

Aline looked up at him, as in sympathetic welcome to an

unexpected admission. 'But Aristotle. How will they like that?'

'That will depend on me. It will be my fault if they do not find him amusing, and – and that perhaps he knew as much about Social Reform as I do or they.'

Lecture – Aristotle – Working Man – Social Reform – hitherto matters of weight, pressing realities inciting to serious consideration, had become airy nothings to him, or mere words and phrases of no active interest. Yet it seemed the most natural thing in the world – no wonder at all – that this girl on whom he had chanced should suddenly stand revealed to him as the supreme fact of his existence. Of course it was only her innate good manners and tact that explained the semblance of interest she showed in his proceedings. But every turn up and down that lane – and they took several – was a turn of the screw that held him, as her personality, slowly, subtly declared itself, in look, voice, speech, and the most unconsidered, trifling touches of self-expression.

'Suppose the Emergency Exit is closed. Shall we have to go round to the front door, ring, and be readmitted and reannounced?' they laughingly asked each other when recalled to the "Doll's House" by a sense of social duty. 'How foolish we should look!' they mentally added. But the door was as they had left it; they re-entered the garden and went in to tea.

None had missed them, nor – unless it were that sly puss Gerty – had a suspicion of the tête-à-tête that, perhaps, determined Elwyn's future path for him.

They now got parted in the crowd, and he saw her no more, not even to take leave.

Back in his rooms, he must acknowledge to himself that something had happened – was happening to, and had not yet done with him. What was this rising force, overruling all other considerations?

'Well, well,' he reasoned convincingly, 'since nothing whatever can ever possibly come of it, I need not disturb myself or look ahead, or resist, or run away from this, whatever it means.' And he tried to pass it off with feint levity and a quotation:

'Though dog-rose and anemone are fair in their degree,
The rose that blooms on garden-walls is still the rose
for me!'

Then having soothed himself thus he sat down and wrote notes for his lecture, his brain working with surprising facility and ease.

III

'Well done, Mr Rosser! Upon my word there seems to be no end to your accomplishments. How many more may you have got up your sleeve, pray?'

'I don't know, I haven't looked!' So Elwyn sportively replied to Gerty King's flattering comment after his first lecture. This had certainly "gone down" at the Village Institute with the mixed audience, compelling a pleasant attention while it lasted, and sending everyone away with an agreeable sense of something in a mental pocket that had been empty beforehand.

'I can't speak for the Working Men,' continued Gerty, who had pressed to the front to compliment him. 'But since a good half of those present seemed to be ladies of leisure and independent means like my humble self, I suppose we do count. I wouldn't have believed Aristotle could have been made so amusing. But was he really as up-to-date as that? Is it true, all you told us? And the quotations, were they genuine? You didn't fake them, or play free with the words, just so make us laugh or wonder? Say!'

'Honour bright, no. Jowett's translation. My solemn word for that.'

'Well, you kept us all on the tip-toe of pleasant expectation for an hour and a half. And I came prepared to be bored, oh, awfully!'

'Why then did you attend?' asked Elwyn naturally.

'Oh, because of Aline,' Gerty, whose prattle so far had been quite spontaneous, let slip unthinkingly. 'She's staying with us. She wanted so to come and hear you. It was on her account. I sacrificed myself, as I thought.'

Elwyn now first caught sight of Aline among a knot of lady folk at the farther end of the room. No previous inkling of her presence there had he had. Gerty's words thrilled him with an inward shock. The dart had penetrated his soul. The serpent had entered his paradise.

The bare possibility that he could count for anything in that quarter had hitherto seemed absolutely inadmissible. The bare idea that she should distinguish him or take interest in his doings was too absurd to contemplate or even indulge in wistfully as a dream. Was Gerty laughing at him now?

At this point he was forcibly taken possession of by some Ruskin students, and saw no more on that occasion of his lady friends.

Henceforward it seemed to him that there were two Elwyns. The one the young Oxonian of distinction, finishing his course with good report, in more lines than one. He had been pressed to repeat his first lecture at another village hall or club, and was to deliver a second shortly at Brackenbury, with free choice of theme.

The other self was an insensate lover, cherishing desires, dreams, – hopes, even, at the bottom of his heart – while convinced that they were born only to be destroyed. It was rapture, then torture, when the sense came uppermost that it led to nothing, but must end – and that soon.

Aline stayed on at the villa, and they met fairly often.

'She has never honoured us for so long before,' Gerty was careful to inform him in a casual-seeming way. 'Ah, her own home was a better place when she was in it. *I* couldn't stay there, I know, and look on and see Conny undo all my work, remodel my garden, refurnish my house, and mismanage my servants.'

Another besides Elwyn hovered around the "Doll's House" at that time – namely, Captain Soanes. Too politic to risk a refusal by importunity in his suit, his courtship of Aline though open was undeclared; his best chance of success lying, as his masculine intellect told him, in protracting it – unwitting that Gerty was ending it for him in her own way.

Letters from home Elwyn would read and then put aside for future attention. 'For this can never last,' he reminded himself daily. 'I must go back, I will, so soon as I have done with these lectures.' The next and last, on the Odyssey, he had found as good as ready composed in his head. It so delighted the audience that its renown spread to the University and caused the anti-Greek party a passing annoyance.

But this over, he faced the facts of the situation in a dry light and without blinking.

It was as Elwyn the first that he went to pay his farewell call at the "Doll's House." He had yesterday written to his mother, announcing his return to Trearavon next week. That absolved him from the immediate necessity of saying more. On that step he felt there was no going back.

Mrs King was laid up with a cold. Aline was not there. Gerty, presiding, contrived to detain Elwyn after her other visitors had all left.

Then she stood up and let fall in a level tone, unconcernedly, 'Aline, who is still with us, is attending the rehearsal for the choral performance at St. Primus's Church. It should be nearly over now. I promised to go there and meet her. You might come with me so far.'

Elwyn submitted silently, willingly. He was not fond of Gerty, but to shake her off at this moment would be to break the last link with his idol.

She chose a circuitous, quiet way through the open park surround, where so few were passing that they two were as good as alone, as unobserved and unobservable as in her own garden.

In reply to a curt question, Elwyn curtly repeated the date of his pending departure to his own country.

'And when shall we see you here again, Mr Rosser?'

'I do not know that you ever will.'

'So you are going home – and for good?'

'Leaving here – yes – and for good.'

'And Aline?'

'Aline?' he echoed mechanically. Then, after a pause, 'What do you mean?'

Gerty did not answer at once. Already the church was in sight. She seated herself on a park bench for a few moments, just to prolong the walk and the conversation. When she spoke it was gravely, firmly. Her usual tone of *badinage* had changed to one of straightforward insistence.

'Please understand I ask this on my own account. I am not in Aline's confidence. We are friends but not intimates. She has none. She is the one who has learnt not to lean on others. But what I ask in my own behalf, as her friend, you need not refuse to tell me. Saying goodbye to Oxford means more for you than … for your friend, Mr Brownjohn, for instance? In a word, do you mean to tell me you don't want to see her again … to see a little more of her before that happens?'

There was a mocking ring in her tone now. Elwyn looked at her imploringly. Oh that she would stop – would spare him! Inexorable was Gerty.

'Is it a matter of indifference to you whether you meet again or not?'

Elwyn, overridden by her persistence, hid his face in his hands for a moment, worsted, defenceless, silent.

'Now Mr Rosser,' began Gerty, seizing her advantage, 'I have nothing much to lose in making you dislike me a little more than you do already; and speak I must. Of course you admire and adore Aline, as do I and every one else who is worth counting. Of course you will remember her. But will that be as an adoring friend or brother remembers?'

Elwyn stood confessed; his involuntary negative gesture did not escape his deadly cross-questioner. 'If that is so and I am mistaken,' Gerty went on, 'try to think and let it be as though I had never spoken. But if, as I believe, she is all, and more than all the world to you, why will you not tell her so?'

'Don't torment me,' cried Elwyn helplessly. 'Why? It stares you in the face. The difference in our place in the world, our positions, forbids me to dream of it. I a poor Welsh student – with all the ladder to climb, nothing to offer! Do you not see the thing is monstrous, unthinkable!'

'I respect your view, Mr Rosser, and against all that you urge I have only one thing to say: I am certain you have it in your power to make Aline very happy, as no one else could do. Must those hindrances you have just named prevail? You won't take my word that it is so? But she can't come and tell you herself what you are to her. Would you like her better if she did that sort of thing? Oh, it is hard that, because a girl happens to have a little of her own, when *for once* "the time and the place and" – you know the rest – chance together, there must be a deadlock!'

They were nearing St Primus's Church, whence came to them the peals of the organ, and broken snatches of the strains of the choir, rehearsing Brahms's "Song of Destiny":

> Ye dwell on high in the light,
> Soft-treading, wandering,
> Spirits celestial,
> Radiant, divine,
> Gentle airs stir around
> As the lute-strings are touched by
> The hand of the minstrel.

To which solemn music Gerty finished her say.

'Yours will be the blame if she misses that chance – the chance of a lifetime.'

Thus spake Gerty the prophetess.

Into the porch and through into the body of the church the magnetised man followed her lead, dazed and faltering in will as they stood waiting for the end, and the choir sang on:

> Free from Fate
> As a slumbering infant
> Breathe they – the host of heaven.
> Ever pure-kept, enfolded, unfading
> Bloom shall rest on their souls,
> And the eyes of the blessed
> Look upon tranquil
> Life everlasting.

There the music stopped, the practise ending abruptly, and the singers dispersing. Gerty ran off, saying hurriedly, 'I must just catch and say a word to Jerry – to Geraldine Skipwither. Wait for me, please, Mr Rosser.'

Presently Aline, whom he saw talking to the organist in the chancel, came walking down the aisle, and was confronted with Elwyn standing there solitary, as it were at a loss.

Her involuntary start, the sudden light in her countenance, bore a message to the eyes unsealed by Gerty.

Their hands met. The organ-player had started a little recital on his own account. They two lingered, talking mirthfully to solemn music in the aisle, and waiting for Gerty. The caretaker coming to lock up, they waited in the churchyard, then in silent, lonely park gardens beyond. No Gerty! Dusk fell, and later on two shadows wended their way slowly, by outlying pathways, back to the "Doll's House" gates, where they were met by the sound of Gerty's voice giving orders on the doorstep to the gardener. Aline went in alone.

'I felt sure you must have given me up long ago and gone home,' said Gerty, so unaffectedly that Aline believed her.

Elwyn walked back to his rooms scarcely able to bear the weight of his sudden happiness, afraid to believe in the gift that had fallen on him straight from heaven; that "love of one" to which the "love of many" is so small a thing.

Love, the perfect love that casteth out fear – fear of anything and everything the future may have in store.

How, by what miracle, words had come to him to express his own was utterly forgotten, swallowed up in, eclipsed by, the greater after-wonder, the revelation of hers for him, won thus unawares, without playing for it, which he would never have dared to do. He felt lifted on to a higher plane of existence by the astounding discovery.

He must be left alone, he felt. Then it seemed to him he was going off his head with joy, and he made for the club, for a shower-bath of common talk; but finding his distraction beyond concealment or control, sought the solitude and protection of the college walls again.

IV

Mrs Rosser sat in the old family chair – an Eisteddfod prize and heirloom that might itself be imbued with the spirit of vanished generations – looking more like an avenging deity than a fond mother awaiting the return of her only and well-beloved son.

Forgive her! Last week had brought her, instead of the expected Elwyn, two knock-down blows. First, the intelligence that he was about to take himself a wife – of an alien nation and class, a class somewhat higher than their own; secondly, the revocation of his intention, or passive acceptance of other people's intentions for him, that he should enter the ministry.

'I said so! I knew when they made me let him go how it would be with him!' she exclaimed passionately, rocking to and fro and flinging the letter across to her daughters, who read and wondered in a different key.

'But he is coming back, coming next week for certain, he says – coming here,' stammered Gwen.

Silently, helplessly, Mrs Rosser shook her head. Coming, yes, but as one lost, one who has suffered himself to be doubly enticed away, his feet well set on the primrose path that leadeth to the service of Mammon.

The worst was that the engagement, which, though she would not have owned it, was to her unkindest cut of the two, sounded so plausible. She would be receiving congratulations from every quarter. Had Elwyn been entrapped into early matrimony by some girl of doubtful repute, or designing woman twenty years his senior, parental authority might have intervened, or she have had at least sympathy and support from her neighbours in her vehement disapproval.

'Marrying at two-and-twenty, with no occupation, no prospect of any means! What will they live on? He should know I can give them nothing.'

'Perhaps the young lady has money of her own.'

At that she almost wept. 'That Elwyn, my Elwyn, should marry for greed! No good ever came of that. At his age, too! Who would have thought it? Never once has he so much as mentioned her name to us before.'

'He says here that they have only lately become acquainted.'

'So men marry, to spend their life in repenting.'

'Why should he repent? Why shouldn't they be as happy as Joseph Harris and I are going to be?' said the engaged sister.

'Never! I know what these English society girls are like nowadays. She will look down on us as food for amusement. This I know, I will never see her here – never!'

A snail and its shell are not harder to part than a woman and a grievance. 'It will be alright as soon as Elwyn comes,' the girls kept reassuring each other cheerfully confident. But it was not.

To mark her displeasure she would not have him met at the station, a hint which Elwyn arrived in too blissfully elated a condition to take. Consigning his trunk to the porter, an old friend, he walked on home, presenting himself at the door such a picture of innocence and beaming amiability that the girls who had rushed to meet him in the porch straightway let themselves go to the natural affections. Alarmed by his obvious insensibility to the fact that here he was in disgrace, they warned him.

'Mother is terribly upset and cast down. It was such a shock to her; and so sudden.'

'I couldn't help that.'

Had it not come suddenly on him too? Refusing to be intimidated, he walked in upon his parent in the state apartment, and broke the embarrassment of the first constrained, formalised greetings by remarking on some trivial alterations that struck his eye.

'I see you've shifted the old china cupboard. An improvement, that; and set that old clock going at last.'

'Have you nothing to say to me, Elwyn?' she asked presently, in a tone that was as freezing as she meant it to be.

'All that there is to tell was in my letter,' he answered, effectually repulsed, in his present super-sensitive mood, by her peculiar tone and manner. Nervously he added, trying to laugh, 'Even for me, that is enough for the present. What more do you want?'

'How do you render account of your conduct? Is it possible you do not see that it needs excuse – is, in fact, inexcusable?'

Elwyn, chafing inwardly at his inability to meet this unmerited displeasure, made a movement of impatience, but remained silent.

'Who, pray, is this Aline Praed whom you propose to bring

into the family, and whose very name is strange to us all?'

His soul rose in him at her disparaging tone, but controlling himself he replied quietly, 'Her father is Vicar of Yewdene in Berkshire. She has kept his house for seven years.'

'Much older than you, then. Just as I thought.'

'No; we were born in the same year.'

'And she is forsaking her widowed father for a rash marriage with a boy like you?'

'It is her father who they say has done rashly. But I know nothing about that. He married not long ago. His present wife is a girl very little older than his daughter. Thus she is now not wanted at home. She is quite free, having independent means.'

'Is it that that is influencing you, Elwyn?'

At this he made a movement of the direst indignation, wounded to the quick, and cried out. But she persisted the more.

'Some side motive you must have, for rushing head-long and prematurely into this life connection, out of your own country, your natural circle, and your station. Your behavior pains me very deeply.' Then, mistaking Elwyn's writhing under the harrow of her taunts for guilty self-avowal, she concluded, 'I should hardly have believed that my son could act so.'

Hereupon Elwyn, in desperation, feeling goaded beyond endurance, got up and left the room abruptly.

'I knew it,' she cried to herself, with a sense of bitter triumph at having struck home. So she certainly had, though not as she imagined.

A turn or two in the garden restored to him his balance and outward equanimity, not again to suffer disturbance. The mischief, done in a few moments, was irreparable. He was perfectly good-tempered, patient and self-possessed, but his reserve on the one subject – the subject of his betrothed – henceforward was absolute.

How should he convince them, against their will, of what he

himself knew only as by intuition, that he had chanced upon a rarity and thing of worth, no mere fair and drifting weed; and that in yielding to the outward charm and assuming, as lightly as ever man before him, its connection with some inward spiritual grace, though enslaved, he had not been duped.

He had been drawn – little though he dreamt it – by proved metal. She had passed no fancy girlhood, reared in a make-believe pleasure-garden or forcing-house, with the worser half of life's weather shut out, even from view, and its lessons unlearnt or unfelt. Young, she had looked death in the face; tender-hearted and unforgetting, she had known sorrow, loss, and strife. It had gone ill with a being less happy adjusted; yet there was she, unalloyed, unembittered, her outlook on life unmarred, still keenly sensitive to life's joys as to its sorrows.

Of all this Elwyn then knew nothing. But he knew that for him the peace of strength was in those eyes, and that merely to recall that image of quiet animation, of serenity, which signifies not apathy but a perfect balance of the natural powers, and to dwell upon it restored him to his rightful self, when for some passing cloud of gloom or petty present torment, his heart and his temper played him false or failed him.

Elwyn and Aline were married in April, very quietly, he remaining in Oxford during the months that intervened.

I must have more pomp and circumstance when my turn comes up, so wrote Gerty King to her most intimate friend, Mrs Skipwither, *if only to impress upon me that I am married at all, and that the ceremony is binding. But for those two it seemed an all but superfluous acknowledgment of what the dullest-witted wedding-guest must have felt as they stood there together – that they were made for each other, and for no one else. None of the lovely women or charming men they may meet hereafter will be able to give to one or the other just that. "Children of the King" – you know the old fairy story. I thought of it that day in the church. He was nervous, and showed it, but one look at Aline would have steadied an aspen leaf. She bears happiness well, as she has borne – the other thing.*

Her parent, the Honourable and Reverend Archibald, made a good third with them in the altar-rail group. After the first surprise of it, he accepted most good-humouredly, in his easy-going way, this stranger son-in-law, dropped on him abruptly, but out of the Honours List, First Class in Classics and History. The Vicar is a staunch Oxonian in the first place, and everything else afterwards. To him the University is as Nebuchadnezzar's golden image, before which all people, nations, and languages should bow down. Besides, after his own recent matrimonial freak, he couldn't decently refuse them his blessing. Oh, my dear, such a fatal mistake she – Connie Praed, nèe Markham – made in wearing her own bridal gown, slightly disguised, at Aline's wedding. You never saw such a lump as she looked, with her plaster-cast face – the image of unintelligent obstinacy. I should have felt sorry for her had she the faintest sense, which she hasn't, that the comparison could go against her. There's something wrong about her too – about all the Markham girls, "nerve-storms" and that sort of thing; and I fancy the poor dear old Vicar got caught in that affair, laying up fresh trouble for his old age. He was broken-hearted when his first wife died, and so was Aline, who can never speak of it to this day. They say she was a perfect creature, something like Aline; but I don't believe in two such adorable beings in one family. Nature is not so unfair.

Rosser's own people did not show up. I can't quite make out where to put them in the social order; they seem simple but not common folk. I should think hobereau *would be the French for his late father, a genus that may thrive down in Wales, but almost unknown among us here. The mother, from her portrait, seems one of those fine-featured, large-framed old ladies, who might be a man in disguise. She was afraid of the long journey for her health, she said, but she looks as if she*

*could stand anything. They don't seem very keen on this new
connection. Now it might have been said it was Aline who was
making the* mèsalliance, *but, glory be to Elwyn Rosser and
to Wales! no one has said that. The Vicar has grown quickly
quite fond of him. He lost his own son, you know, through a
gun accident, and his daughter, the elder one,* would *marry
that clever amateur artist, Jack Dalleyn, whom he detested,
and who, as everybody knows, drinks. But Elwyn Rosser and
the pater got on famously from the start. They are always
making Greek and Latin quotations and nonsensical classical
jokes to each other. I don't know if Aline understands them;
Conny doesn't, and it annoys her to be left out – makes her
quite cross. Oh, wasn't she delighted to see the happy pair
depart! They are off to spend a long honeymoon in Italy; the
father's wedding present to the bride.*

*Ha, ha! And here am I left exulting – I, their unknown
benefactress. Never will they know what they owe to the
present writer; for "alone I did it," Jerry, I —*

                    GERTY KING.

*P.S. Captain Soanes is so miserable that he comes to me
for consolation.*

'Which you, Gerty, are ready waiting to supply.'

Such was the reader, Geraldine Skipwither's, comment.
And she forthwith laid a wager with her husband what would
be the next engagement they would hear of, and in due time
she won it.

PART III

Back to the Land

I

Never were there two people less wishful to attract notice, however flattering, than Elwyn Rosser and Aline. Yet, wherever they passed, it was theirs to compel, as by some natural law, a singular passing attention.

Remarkable separately, seen together their personalities in their harmonious dissimilarity presented a blend of rare distinction, the mere sight of which woke a lively interest – as of a new discovery.

'Children of the King.' Gerty had said it; and it brought this disadvantage, that, to them, their fellow creatures for the most part showed themselves in disguise. Even the drunken peasant instinctively stopped beating his donkey at their approach. The worst felt impelled to put a beautifying halo round their unlovely heads; while the merely petty and vulgar, fain when in their company to seem even as they – better than they had it in them really to be – kept on the stretch – with their little spites and jealousies, low motive impulses, corrupt opinions, coarse or malicious leanings in abeyance. It was elevating; but like pygmies kept standing on tip-toe, there came a latent sense of relief when, on the removal of the constraining raising influence, things reverted to their normal spiritual level.

Never a thought had those two to give to the impression they might be making. Far too happily occupied in those days were they both; the causes above-mentioned helping still further to preserve the serenity of their outlook, the felicity of their mood, unbroken. The jewel of their own happiness was their own secret – untarnished and inviolate. Lovers' joys, friendships' joys, travellers' joys – life's three best gifts united were theirs in full measure as they roamed from one of Italy's many unique cities to another.

Pisa, a little one, though unmatched as a picture-effect, afforded to you who pass by – and at a single, even transient glance – of present poetic loneliness, of greatness that has passed away, and of human power, quick and not dead, lastly conserved in noble fanes of marble composing that monumental group – Cathedral, Baptistery, and Bell-Tower – that dominates the dwindling city, whether viewed from far or near.

By the Arno's sluggish stream they lingered at evening, where, as one wrote, close on a century ago:

> 'Within the surface of the wrinkled river
> The fleeting image of the city lay;
> Immovably unquiet, and forever
> It trembles but it never fades away.'

Though "Ponte al Mare", the name by which we know those haunting lines, has disappeared long since, the scene has not changed, the poet's part in which remains imperishable:

> 'The sun is set, the swallows are asleep;
> The bats are flitting past in the grey air;
> The slow soft toads out of the dark corners creep;
> And evening's breath, wandering here and there
> Over the quivering surface of the stream
> Wakes not one ripple from its summer dream.'

Florence – aptly so-called – the garden-ground of Italian art, blossoming there since a thousand years, and seeding and blossoming still – for whatever it may prove to be worth. Florence the felicitous, the amateur's *plaisance*. There, in the shadow of her tall, proud towers and palaces you go your own way from one thing of beauty to another, joying in master creations of poesy and prose, of statuary, painting, and superfine arts and crafts of infinite variety and value; your pleasure undistracted by the hurly-burly of a modern capital – the blatant self-assertion of industrialism triumphant.

Florence – ever charming, ever slowly renewing itself with changing times; thus ever cheerful, in its old-standing beauties and modern additions (for good or ill) alike.

The site itself makes for sanity and mental health. Though your Florentine refuse ever to set foot out of town, he can never forget or lose touch with the country. In the busiest streets he is met, up and down by a vista of the circlet of wild and not distant hills, with rural valleys, olive gardens and villas walled in with roses and peaceful cypress groves.

Twice dear to all English-speaking comers, as the second home of certain of their own great ones; the scene from whose magic-working suggestion have sprung some of the choicest flowers of English imaginative art and literature.

As a harmonious whole, alone among cities and art centres. Even classic art, as figured here, seems touched with the modern spirit, so that we are never quite taken away from ourselves. Until we stumble on some remnant of Etruria and the Etruscans. That, indeed, is another story!

Rome the incomparable – a name the mere sound or sight of which signifies more than any other; the power-house of the forces, temporal and spiritual, that have determined the progress of mankind – the trend of life, throughout the Western world. She has more to give than you are able to receive, of mighty impressions, each a separate onslaught on your senses, and startling as a blow.

The magnificent human energy of ancient Rome, taking tangible, indestructible shape in buildings which, whether for use or ornament, serve us as models to this day; her galleries with their priceless jewels of Grecian art – emanations of the beauty-worship that inspired it – the art of which her own was the offspring; her pagan temples – imposing, to the latest unearthed fragment; her fanes of Christendom passing quickly from its mystic, obscure beginnings to predominance among the Powers; everywhere the same stamp of audacious, intelligent enterprise, of might and magnitude, dwarfing and defying what may lie outside its realm. Not the least learned, the merest babe among travellers can miss Rome's message; nor then greatest wiseacre, the keenest most comprehensive mind feel or say truly of her, "I have seen the whole".

Can any city contain anything to move us deeply after this?

One – Ravenna – one that has known more violent outward changes than perhaps any other; a chequered past which has left little or no trace behind. It is here, and here alone, that an inestimable something awaits all those whom it may concern – nothing less than an initiation offered – as by illuminating glimpses, into the heart of the mysterious origin of the profoundest, most powerful, and widest spread spiritual influence the world has ever known.

Ravenna. As you pass from one to another of her many grandly impressive basilicas, all undecayed nor ever diverted from the purpose for which, as places of Christian worship, they were erected – when, in the fifth and sixth centuries, the new movement already held sway in the seats of the mighty – the very much earlier life and spirit of that worship are perceptible, as shadowed darkly but imperishably in the mosaic pictures that hallow certain of these walls. Face to face we seem with the sincere, direct artistic expression of the new and rising faith, as soon as art began to exist among Christian men. As a flashlight thrown on dark places is this half-veiled, semi-allegorical presentment of its oriental-born miracle-working secrets. A nearer approach to the most elusive of mysteries, a strange, remote-seeming emotion stirred, a sense as of a faint clue to things undiscoverable – an incomplete revelation – this is Ravenna!

Enough of cities and men. Go southward, and southward still, pushing far into the wilderness and desert places, by the loneliest of lone sea shores. Here too was once a city, built and rebuilt and peopled in turn by the dominant race and nation of the age; centuries of active life that has left no trace. Yet, come here for what, to some, remains perhaps the best, the most unforgettable moment of all: the first sight of the Temples of Paestum. 'There is nothing like it on this wide earth!' So spoke one fervent traveller; and he spoke for many.

Only the Grecian migrants, who held the city in possession in her days of greatness, have set here their abiding mark, with its message to all those who can read it.

How far the wild melancholy of the spot – the tideless sea, the near background of rugged mountains, and between these the wide stretch of shore, all tangled thickets of weed and wild flower growth, where the temples, standing there quietly, strike like living presences – how far the poets, classic and modern, that have sung of the scene count for in the spell it continues to exercise, no need to inquire. Long may they stand, telling their wordless tale – of Greece and its overpowering significance.

Sad, yet not utterly. It is their preservation, not their decay – their undying influence even as mere mementoes that is the speaking fact here. Not the most careless observer can escape the wonder of it.

II

'We must go back!'

It was Aline speaking; but Aline, though more loth even than he to end his little lifetime of delight, felt her heart give assent. The moment of reaction that waits upon the most enchanting pleasure-travel had come, with its warning homeward tug. You feel your roots are being tampered with, and the dweller in the innermost says, 'It is enough. Back to where you came from – and to the Day's Work!'

One week more they lingered in South Italy. Then Elwyn sickened suddenly from a chill, with a disquieting touch of the local malarial fever. He was not particularly ill, but it seemed as though at any moment he might become so. They were in a desolate, though to them enchanting region in Calabria, alive with memories of Greek and Roman poets, and names great in later story, martial and romantic, of vanished Goth and Norman. From the heights above the little town you could view the Ionian and the Tyrrhenian Seas; on the hill slopes and in the valleys of those parts, watch the goatherds tending and piping to their flocks; foxes creeping down the fences to purloin the grapes; children weaving cricket-traps with corn-stalks; and other pictures unchanged since the idyllists sang of these things two thousand years ago. But the rough accommodation and sorry fare of sour goat's milk, pork, and nondescript sausage – a laughing matter hitherto – were turned to a grievance amounting to danger. He weakened sensibly under the local medical treatment, and while improvement in such circumstances was hardly to be looked for, he was quite unfit to travel without grave peril; so the doctor gave assurance. Was Calabria going to prove the death of him, Elwyn half-sportively wondered, as among others, of his favourite poet, Virgil; and oughtn't he to be proud of the honour of sharing the fate of that immortal among the bards? To poor Aline, beset by sudden horrible terrors, it seemed a special intervention of Providence that sent help to them in this pass.

A retired English army doctor, on his return journey from a Sicilian tour with his daughters, was reported staying at Sta. Chionia, a post-town with which, though remote, there was communication. He came over willingly to the aid of his countrymen in distress, and gave cheering advice. For though he looked a little grave at first, and asked perplexing questions, his opinion was that there was not much the matter yet, but that they must leave the place at once, as a lesser risk than to stay on. He would procure to send over from Sta Chionia some sort of carriage to convey them to the station there. 'Get him to Naples; to more comfortable quarters. Then – you are homeward bound, you say. So much the better. The late season in these parts is unhealthy, and, for foreigners, dangerous.'

There must be some virtue in Nationality in Medicine, they decided. For, starting as an invalid and prostrate, Elwyn reached Naples, shaky, exhausted, but already convalescent, and picked up so rapidly that when a few days later they set off towards England, all traces of his recent malady had disappeared. And the first sight of the Dover cliffs surprised them in mid-Channel in animated discussion whither their steps should lead them next.

Even the most unwilling home-comers know the singular mysterious attraction it is the property of that austerely-attractive coast line to inspire – its immemorial message to seafarers: 'You, passing by, whoever you are, and be your purpose what it may, to move the world, or to plant cabbages, you must find or choose a place to stand upon. Land you here!'

The point – their next move – was one in dispute between them.

For there was Elwyn, on the one hand, in a wild hurry to find some fixed paid employment, and ready to snatch at the first that should offer. What need for such impatience? urged Aline, perhaps instinctively aware that whatever he undertook, he, no idler, would give himself away there; it would absorb, exploit, retain him. She advised waiting to look about and hit on the rightful, worthy field for his abilities. Elwyn assured her that she overrated these absurdly; that he owed his brilliant college successes to Macpherson; that he might have a poet inside him, but wasn't what she thought him – a poet – which is quite another thing; and that he would never set the Thames on fire; but that he might – indeed he really must – gratify this modest ambition: to contribute what he could to their yearly income.

The matter was compromised for the time being by his acceptance of an offer he found awaiting him, of temporary tutorial work at Oxford as another man's deputy for the Michaelmas term. There, too, they would be near Aline's home, where things were not going smoothly, the young stepmother's health becoming a source of ominous anxiety. 'A complete nervous breakdown' – 'Her own mother there in attendance on her.' They might be wanted there at any moment, and would be for certain at Christmas to make things cheerful.

One month of summer – one little holiday month – still lay before them; and Elwyn had yielded to Aline's entreaties to spend it in Wales. She had even wrung from him his half-promise to conclude with a few – just a very few – days at Trearavon.

His baffling reserve on the subject of native land and circle Aline longed, but had utterly failed, to break through. It seemed perverse, almost unnatural, and was, in fact, a thing inexplicable to any rational English-woman. Probably he could hardly have clearly accounted for it himself. Things were as they were, and unalterable. So much he knew, but not why.

True, he had been drawn out of his native medium, charmed into a vaster nationality and a still vaster world, a world where there are glories of many sorts and of all scales, and he had become in it and of it too, till the glory of a small, however peculiar nationality, was to him a thing ridiculously unsufficing. But a remnant of him was there, and its clutch on the secret places of his heart he could not altogether escape. He had never thought much about Welsh patriotism, and would never have any thought to give to it now. Still, that ancient, traditional virtue of a cherished, indestructible nationality, of which none outside the fold, whether scoffer or admirer, can appreciate the peculiar sanctity and importance to insiders, its indirect or cross-working on Elwyn showed itself thus;

prohibiting the shaping or thinking out of his own sentiments to himself. How, then, should he word them to another? His intercourse with his kith and kin remained strictly amicable, but limited to trivial passing matters. No communion nor desire for it, on either side, regarding the things filling their minds – the things next their hearts. It was silence. The door was shut.

III

They had come to Port Alba for a three days' stay, extended it to a week, and the week's end found them with no mind to go farther. And as the time lengthened the hold on them strengthened of a place they had dropped on well nigh by chance.

For they had set out on an orthodox Welsh tour that was to have shown them all the famed beauties of Elwyn's country, of which, out of his native valley, he knew little. They would be conveyed in snug railway carriages to smart hotels on snowy mountain tops; motor *chars-à-bancs* would rush them through the best advertised river, lake, mountain, and coast scenery, all the desolate places of romance. Instead, Port Alba, dismissed with a few lines in the guide-books, held them and would not let them go.

A little land-locked haven, formed on one side by the inwards curve of a shore line of low cliffs, evergreen with ivy and overhanging woodland, and fronting a wide sea, with a foreshore miles in extent of firm white sand. Westward a jutting headland parts the estuaries of two rivers that lose themselves in the shallows at low tide; the sand-flats affording an inexhaustible hunting ground to cockle fishers, whose toy-like punts, ferries, and sailing boats dot the little creeks and inlets.

Here round about was no Sleepy Hollow either, but a treasure-land of fine things, if not famous, to be found without going

far. Such as a mountain range rising to 2,000 feet; elsewhere
a paradise of forest scenery; haunts still free from man's
meddling, and where you may yet surprise some lost secret
of Nature to set fancy playing, creating. Survivals strange,
prehistoric – tokens both of the world we are in, and of the
world before it – known to us by these flashlights only – the
Wales of the mammoth, elephant, rhinoceros, hyena – remote
and inconceivable, only that there was the ocular proof, the
monster skeletons in the county museum, transferred thither
from the sea-cavern where these creatures slept their last
sleep.

Riddles – these memorials all! – as that gigantic, that
impressive stone structure, so unquestionably a Roman camp
to one generation, to another a British sheepfold, and to the
scoffer of all ages a casual heap of boulders merely. Weird,
upright stones, marking a giant's grave, according to the old
women; a battlefield, said the old men. Cromlechs, tumuli,
barrows, stone circles, tombs or altars; who knows? Whose
mystery attracts the antiquity-man and the artist-dreamer alike.
Castles in every stage of life, from the vanishing stronghold
on the headland across the estuary – only preserved from
disparition by the careful attentions of the mason of the lord
of the manor – to such a one as they faced from the windows
of their farm lodgings, proud in its eight hundred years of
continuous occupation, and of watch and ward over the little
sea port and settlement grown up under its protection and
shelter. Authority in being – keeping guard over the rivers
and rocky islets, with their attendant dangers, initiating and
directing works, improvements, innovations, the motor spirit
of the little settlement; as things have been and will be as long
as the moon endureth.

Aline found but one fault with the place; that on the face of
it, it didn't seem very Welsh. The language was seldom heard;
the names, types, manners and address of these fisher-farmers
and others in and about Port Alba were too like Wessex. They

were just as far from the English border as they could get,
Elwyn represented, and said something about "Little England
beyond Wales" (of which Aline had never heard), and that
he supposed they must have got there. It wasn't his fault.
He really couldn't help it if some little foreign settlement
as to whose exact origin opinions still differ had, like this,
refused to be utterly absorbed by the Cambrians. And though
Newfoundland Farm, their present habitation, sounded
colonial, the present fisher-farmer occupier, with his stalwart
son and daughter, Pat and Ellin, were as thoroughgoing, fine
old-fashioned specimens of the Welsh breed as she could
wish to come across. Pam the father and Pat the son. No
connection with English statesman or Irish saint; Pat being
short for Patagonia, site of that successful Welsh colony which
is not the least of the national glories; Pam a contraction of
Padan-aram, a chance word caught from the Book of Genesis
and bestowed on him as a luck-bearing appellation by his
forefathers.

So much for Port Alba; a place of peace and of beauty,
in itself complete, a place where you had time – time to be
happy.

Supremely happy both, yet most differently!

Elwyn, now that the miracle was accomplished, the incredible
thing made fact, that he was loved, loved by Aline with all the
powers of her being, was accepting the gift most thankfully,
but serenely, an inherent blessing of his daily life, precious,
but as natural as sunlight and fresh air, a gift of which death
only should deprive him.

To Aline it meant more, of even greater worth. She had not,
like Elwyn, grown up unacquainted with grief. Home troubles,
desperate home sorrows, had wrung her affectionate nature.
Things so deep, so intimate, she could not speak of them, even
to Elwyn. While too young to be crushed by sorrow, though of
the sharpest, once, twice, thrice, had her broken-winged spirit
cried out within her, 'What good shall my life do me?'

Nevermore, nevermore! For Elwyn, there, was the answer.

The love that had shone suddenly in the night of pain-fraught memories, lifting their weight, teaching hope by its perfection, touching past, present, and future by its sweet revelation. At its approach the shadows in her soul drew back. In its fulfilment joy asserted its creative powers. So she loved, she gave thanks, she was glad, though tremblingly and fate-fearing, as are those who have suffered loss.

IV

The day's walk had taken them to Newslade Head. There they rested, Elwyn lying sunning himself on the short turf, Aline seated by, watching the rocks out at sea become islets as the tide rose.

Talking of matters grave and light, untiringly and with the zest that mostly denotes quarrelling, but that here meant that two lonely, kindred souls had met and were exulting in being alone no more – two minds travelling wing to wing, feelings confidently interchanged, sure of easy, rapid, mutual comprehension, taking and giving freely and equally with a rare and perfect interplay. So far things of the mind. Never had Aline seemed fairer in Elwyn's eyes, nor her fairness so precious to his soul and sense. A face that was like balm if you were sore, a cordial to the faint-hearted, an upholding force to keep you or to set you on your way rejoicing.

He was playfully narrating how once when he was a schoolboy at Llanwastad his people, "having nothing particular just then to fuss about", had made him submit to a medical examination by a local celebrity, whom some called a quack.

'A fellow with a cure for all incurable ills – from consumption to chilblains. He pommelled, poked, and punched me till I felt like punching his old head: then let me go, saying, "It's early to pronounce, madam. If he goes on the farm, he may be there still, hale and hearty, at eighty. If it's a professional gentleman's life he's to lead, buried in books and afraid of soiling his fingers, well – he must just take his chance with the rest."'

Trearavon! His thoughts went back there. 'Just fancy, Aline, if I settled down at home I might now be a herdsman coming out of the copse with my arms full of bracken, or, "leading my jocund team afield", "the horned herd my care", and milking them in the gloaming.'

And never, never the one at his side, whose presence there, though he closed his eyes, remained a felt delight!

'Are you repenting?' she asked him in play.

Elwyn made a negative sign.

'Sure?' She bent over where he lay outstretched, and looked into his face.

'Though he slay me – no!'

Only the sea-birds saw that kiss. A moment that thrilled their heartstrings with a joy that is not of this earth – such joy as makes you afraid.

Just then Neptune, or Nature, interposed, as if minded to play them a trick.

The precipitous sea cliff they were on stands some two hundred feet high, and overhanging an ocean smooth and motionless that afternoon as a mirror. Of a sudden a volume of water thrown up rose above the cliff's brink, curled over, and descended in a shower close to where they sat, startling them to their feet.

'What next?' wondered Aline aloud, as they stood regarding the face of the waters.

Not a ripple to be seen; not a breath stirring. 'Do that again!' shouted Elwyn to the sea-god. And presently, as in answer to the challenge, the joke was repeated. They saw the vast sheet of water surge up the wall of rock, and break in a fountain almost over their heads.

'Now I remember, Pat was telling me of this the other day, that it happens here sometimes,' Elwyn remarked. 'The sailors account for it by the meeting of the two undercurrents. They say it heralds rough weather.'

V

But the morrow broke bright and clear. That day they were to spend with Pat and Ellin out cockle-gathering from the punt on the sand-flats. For whatever our love for Nature we must always, it is said, invent some excuse for trusting ourselves alone to her – some definite pursuit – a rod, or a gun, or as now, for Elwyn and Aline Rosser, lending a hand in the local marine industry.

With Pat for their ferryman they left the tiny harbour of Port Alba, crossed the first broad estuary, and rounding the headland passed through the second, halting at suitable selected spots to paddle and glean their harvest of cockles from the rippled sands. Farther and farther they pushed on. Pat knew every inch of the grounds, could gauge the exact position and depth of every channel, tell to a nicety just where he could get the tub through and where it would stick, and the likeliest places for fishers to fill sack, net, apron, and basket with the treasures of the deep.

The treasure sands seemed limitless. The pastime proved beguiling, and the zeal and energy with which the visitors worked was highly amusing to Pat and Ellin, the professionals. And when the afternoon weather turned very wild, the strange cloud effects and changing skies served merely to enliven an employment rather tame and same on the face of it.

Evening brought promise of more than fulfilment on the portent witnessed yesterday.

'You'd say the heavens was moving in a body,' ejaculated Ellin, as, emptying her apron full of shell-fish into the basket, she stepped into the punt and looked up.

'Yes, sure,' said Pat, deftly poleing them away from the sandbank and facing homewards at last. 'If we'd be up there we'd be wishing ourselves down here again pretty soon.'

Now Pat was an expert at punt-handling, and each fresh obstacle encountered was welcomed as an invitation to show off his skill.

Now the time-honoured pleasure of contemplating from a place of security – the landlocked bay where their route lay – the perils and discomforts of the less fortunate, any luckless herring or mackerel boats outside it, was offered to the part in full.

'What with rain and thunder and fire-flying it's fearsome to look at,' said Ellin. 'Ah, the new moon was last Wednesday, and the seamans they do say that one Wednesday moon in seven years is enough. There's glad I am it's a safe place we are in!' she concluded complacently.

To the novices the safety was becoming less obvious. The riot appeared to be spreading, and threatening to overrun the barricade. It cost them some trouble to get across the first estuary; but Pat must know, Pat the pilot, who, absolutely untroubled and undoubting, kept reiterating that it was "all right".

The sea, roaring and running high outside the bay, could not hurt them, he represented, nor the wind, unless it shifted suddenly. There was only the tide, which never – or hardly ever – rose above a certain height to such as might impede their progress.

Even when the gale declared itself as one of the annual "worst within living memory", so short-lived is human memory, and the punt was jerked and bumped about mercilessly in the lopping waters, and an elderly craven on the bank shouted his advice to the party to land here, and not attempt the crossing of the second estuary, such timorous fancies were scouted by brother and sister alike.

'Why, we should have to stay here overnight!' Pat ejaculated. Oh, they would get across the river's mouth, and round the point into Port Alba right enough.

It might have been, only they must stay to help an infirm old brother punt in difficulties, stuck fast on a sandbank; a boat whose occupants – mere children – failed utterly to push her off. They floated and started them, and saw them safe ashore; but meanwhile thickening clouds and dark curtains of rain descending had brought about an untimely darkness that would be black night before long. Still, neither brother nor sister felt or showed the faintest discomposure. Pat knew the cross-passage, the way home, so well, he could find it blindfold, they protested.

But how if he found the way impassable?

That which had never happened to him before, and might never happen to him again, happened to happen now.

The perilous predicament that had been preparing before their eyes these two hours, and given one warning sign after another of its approach, was sprung on them actually all in a moment. Flung headlong into the heart of an extraordinary, an exciting adventure. The punting-hole, from awkward and unmanageable, became utterly useless; the darkness impenetrable. The wind, slightly shifted, was blowing straight up the estuary with a wild violence that had turned the usual lake-like surface to a whirling, surging sea. The tide (which had never risen so high or run so strong before, according to Pat), was sweeping them up the broad river, strive how they might with the two little oars they carried.

The worst was that the swirl of the lopping waves, breaking over the punt, was filling it with water faster than they could bail it out; the flood kept rising still, and roughening every instant. There were they helpless in the midst of it, unable to make for the bank, wherever it might lie.

There was no room for fear, even now that the crisis had come and the danger was imminent. There was just one moment for action, and only one thing to be done – jump into the river, abandoning the boat, and wade to the bank. The water would be over their heads if they waited longer. With one accord they plunged in.

It was a supreme struggle with warring elements – wind, flood, and outer darkness. Some sixth sense in Pat made of him no blind guide even now. They must wade further up stream before trying to land. It wasn't far. But in such emergencies our scale of time and space ceases to apply.

Holding on to each other, lest one of them should lose footing and be swept off by the cross-currents, they wrestled on in the dark. The tremendous struggle, the preternatural effort, made possible by the exciting risks of the moment, had a certain wild physical relish. Fear, cold, fatigue were as unfelt as wounds by soldiers while still fighting, or, by huntsmen, the grip of a beast of prey at a crucial moment.

Step by step, strain by strain, they fought on, and just as the strain had touched breaking point, they found themselves in shallower and rather calmer waters, and Pat struck for the shore, his convoy dragging along in his wake, and half scrambling, half washed up by the flood, got out of it on to the marshy bank, and fumbling, stumbling father, reached firm ground. And there was Pat bemoaning the abandoned punt, and Ellin the lost loot of cockles!

The hardest tussle, as they afterwards agreed, was the one that came now. A certain farmhouse Pat knew of, and pronounced to be close at hand, was reached only after a tramp of several miles, in a tempest of rain, along rough and hilly highways and byways. They got there at last, a drenched and shipwrecked crew, to be most hospitably received, accommodated for the night in tolerable comfort, and driven back in the morning to Port Alba and Newfoundland Farm, where Pam, smoking his pipe in the yard, had never suffered a moment's anxiety on their account, making sure they had stopped at one of the coast villages. The loss of the punt now troubled him sorely. He and Pat started at once in search. It was found in due time, bottom upward, in a backwater, much damaged, yet not beyond repair; and they smiled again.

And Ellin, still mourning for her cockles, went about her baking as usual; and Elwyn sat down and dashed off a vivid, wittily jocular letter to Trearavon, descriptive of their adventure and narrow escape – one of those inimitable happy effusions of the moment, things of perfect though ephemeral worth. It was fine today, with a stiff breeze, and he wanted to go for a sail, but Aline begged off, and he would not leave her. She owned that last evening's experience was one she would not have been sorry to have missed, and felt thankful to sit quiet.

In Elwyn, over-exertion had induced such a fit of unappeasable activity and high spirits as made silence or stillness a sheer impossibility. He chatted on humorously and incessantly, devising fantastic excursions by land and by water, picturing grotesque incidents and tragi-comic dilemmas, and running these into clever nonsense rhymes to make her laugh – till a storm-belated post brought letters that recalled him to things and troubles of everyday and common life.

VI

The news was from Aline's home, and it was not good. The poor little stepmother, now admitted to be suffering from a bad form of hysteria, was in a Nursing Home, by stringent medical order, undergoing a "cure". The distressed, half-broken Vicar was clearly in terrible need of moral support and some cheering presence. Aline at the moment was feeling too tired out even to make plans for tomorrow, but Elwyn brimmed over with ideas and suggestions for the arranging of their future.

There followed for him the queerest of nights: snatches of sleep, of waking dreams, and of wide-awake thoughts alternating and mixed indistinguishably. Bands of music don't pass in the night at Port Alba; yet he could have sworn to have heard one go by slowly, playing some tune he did not know, but the last phrase of which rang in his ears after the sounds got lost in the distance. Then it was a series of

pictures floating before his closed eyes – scenes unconnected
and unaccountable as dreams; yet here was he not even drowsy.
Had the storms of yesternight got into his head to vex it into
this visionary state? he wondered.

By the morning it was clear he was not going to get off scot
free. There was fever and chest affection. But Port Alba,
though secluded, was at least within reach of the resources of
science. Pat strode straight off nine miles to a certain favourite
wateringplace and fetched thence its leading practitioner.

Yes; a touch of pneumonia – slight, nothing to alarm. Still,
when Aline mentioned the Calabrian episode, he enjoined the
same vigilance and care as though the case were a serious one.
And she – alert and rested today – knew how to render these.
Custom had made it an easy thing for her to cope with illness.
The direst anxiety would not paralyse the ministering hand or
head; and into the slips of ignorance she could not fall. It was
a treat to be nursed by her, Elwyn declared; he would presently
be shamming – malingering – to enjoy it the longer.

The next day brought amendment of the local symptoms; and
his unflagging good, gay-seeming spirits proved communicative
to both doctor and nurse. Trearavon was mentioned, but he did
not write or let her write there for him. He did not want them
to know of his indisposition till it was past. 'They might come
bearing down upon us, and insist on it that I'm in a consumption
and want to pack me off to a Sanatorium.'

But as soon as he got well, to Trearavon they would go.
He talked of it freely, as never before, seemed smitten with a
sudden fancy to show her this and that: the nook on the river
that had been his bathing-place; the spot where he had shot his
first rabbit; the pool where he once hooked a salmon; above
all, certain mountain passes and views they had not seen the
like of in their recent crossings of the Alps. And that weird
little lake, haunted-looking, high up on the highest mountain,
and its overhanging crest of rock, which once when a little lad
he climbed for a freak, which nearly proved his last – as half-

way up he found himself hanging on to a ledge unable to get forward or back, but was rescued by a heaven-sent bracken-mower. A fairy lake whereby hangs many a legendary tale.

Over all this eager activity in looking onward was a mist of unreality. The talker was not his usual self. In Aline there stirred a foreboding – dim, profound, abiding; a thing to be driven back, unshaped, lest heart and power to act should faint utterly.

He had seemed to get better so quickly – was allowed up. Ah, why did she let him stay about the room so long and tire himself with talking? Just a touch of fever recurred, which yielded to treatment, forewarned and forearmed as they were against every likely contingency, so far as human resources go. Inept and unavailing, every one, to repel this overwhelming, this mortal weakness stealing over him, till speech died on his lips, thoughts as soon as born.

Like one of those mysterious, invincible ills that strike and slay a man in the street, the market-place, at his work. Before it he went down – went out – like a flame that is spent.

No pain – but the strangest slackening of his hold on life. The known world seemed sailing away from him. Gone were the strength, even the will to resist or regret this loosening of his hold on all – all but her, his beloved – the more dear as the rest – the world that was – faded into utter insignificance, till it was as good as wiped out for him.

That fairy lake they were never to see.

Whether from some still-lurking poison from Calabrian river swamp, or inherent, unsuspected frailty – something slender and transitory in the very intensity of life that was in him – there was no rally. The slackened silver cord was giving way, the golden bowl breaking, quickly – as man's time measurements go.

Still the narrowing horizon brought no blurring of what lay within it. Rather the fullest revelation, the most poignant sense of a half-known thing – such a treasure of happiness bestowed as left them Fate's debtors, whatever befall. The Blue Bird was taking wing. But they had found it.

'Woe – woe to the living!' Aline put that thought back – the destroyer. She even felt calm – as Elwyn was calm – their communion unbroken. Ah, might not, should not, such love as hers fetch him back, from the very brink?

It was not to be.

'Nearer – nearer,' he whispered, drawing closer to him the face of his own – never more his own than at the moment when he was leaving her for ever.

'For mine eyes have seen,' he said suddenly – solemnly – but distantly now, and the voice was as it were of one speaking already from the Other Side.

VII

The havoc wrought by rough weather on roads and bridges had delayed Elwyn's letter home, which came to his mother's hands together with one from Aline, written without his knowledge, two days later, not worded so as to alarm – for that note had not then been struck, but transmitting, unintentionally and unexpressed, a dread intuition. Unsummoned, Mrs Rosser determined to start for Port Alba, and was now on her way thither, her heart wild with bitterness, anger, and desperate sorrow.

So sure she felt of that which was before her that, when she got there, what she heard brought no fresh shock. Had she not known, when she set forth, and as certainly as by special revelation, that she would not find her son alive?

Thought and feeling had travelled even farther, saying fiercely, 'He could not be more lost to me than he is – than he was before.'

Pity for the one left – the one who had taken him from them – was numb – unwilling; long pent-up jealous animosity was loosed, and well nigh uncontrollable even at this, their first meeting. Her heart, in savage maternity, was crying out to her in relentless exultation that Elwyn was hers again at last – hers, now that he lay dead.

For death, that cancels many a feud and real or fancied wrong, worked contrariwise here. The unwelcome link between her and the stranger-wife broken, it mattered not at all to Mrs Rosser what Aline thought of her. No motive now for self-restraint or disguise. Beyond preserving the outward forms of propriety which habit and self-respect made a second nature to her, she cared little what irrational hostility or injustice she might betray. She would have shunned the meeting altogether had that been possible. It was Elwyn she wanted to see; now that he was hers again. Only let her be alone with him once more!

But the message of that Silent Voice was to another effect.

That was Elwyn – yes – but not her Elwyn – not the son she had known. Elwyn lifted on to a higher plane, and not by death, but by life, and by love – the love of Aline.

Just one instant of awe and reverence, then came quick revulsion, then a passion of jealous resentment, repressed but inextinguishable.

She, that Daughter of Heth, with her superfine attainments – she had taken him for her own, changed him so that hers, even in the grave, he would remain.

The grave – at Llanffelix, by the mother's decree, as against Aline's wistful supplication. She, the survivor, was still in the half trance-like state of one overstrung, uplifted – still out of touch with earthly things – the lingering sense of communion with Elwyn so strong and real, seeming that the loss was the unreal, the unrealised thing.

But Llanffelix – a strange place to her – one where he and she had never been together – never would be, now! She would have pleaded for Yewdene, where they first met – or even for Port Alba, in whose shady, sequestered, ancient churchyard, ah, only the other day, he and she had agreed one might contentedly find one's last resting-place.

The mother rose and burst out with an exceeding bitter cry: 'You have taken his soul – his immortal soul – from me and mine. These, at last – these mortal remains – let me keep!'

So Aline came to Trearavon.

It had been forced in upon Mrs Rosser how all her judgements and estimates of her had been wrong – and wronging to Elwyn as well as to his choice. She, the Englishwoman, had conquered at the last – too late.

For just to her now she could never be – the will was wanting. That the love she had withstood with might and main was worthy of the dead, her clear head and fair mind must recognise. But the sense of mistake, the breaking down of her magnificent disdain, brought no repentance, no relenting. The distance, the stern and solemn calm of her attitude, remained unbroken.

The sisters – Aline felt she might have loved them, and they her; but the moment was none for the nearer, familiar approach of perfect strangers.

The girl-widow's present path was marked out for her, destiny mercifully sparing her in this hour the burden of choice. More than ever in his life her father now wanted a stand-by; his luckless bridal having brought with it dire tribulation, and boding nothing else.

'To you he is not lost – not utterly!' These, Mrs Rosser's last words to Aline, were cried out suddenly, painfully. They startled her as breathing of remorseful pleading; they bespoke something more – earnest aspiration. They rang in the ears of the one departing, unforgettable in their impetuosity and conviction.

Memory is life. Not all of us can accept this saying; and to Aline there had come a certain hope – a hope not unmixed with fear of its fulfilment. Yet in that hope lay life; if but that hope might be!

An Undesirable Alien

In the morning it was merely a labourer's roughcast, two-roomed thatched cottage, and one that you, in passing, would have condemned because of its narrow window-space and lack of water supply.

But no sooner did the western sun come shining through the group of trees facing which it stood – looking like a beehive in a grove, sheltered and shadowed by a semicircle of fir and ash springing from the low bank beside it – than the spirit of the place came out and worked a magic. There stood, as it were, the witch cottage of a fairy tale, or the dwelling of some hermit of old, where the Knight Errant of Romance, riding up one of the five crossroads that here meet in the shade, would reign in and sue for rest and refreshment.

Then, to complete the illusion, an ancient, white-bearded figure would stand forth, as it might be some old harper of King Arthur's halls, fallen upon evil days but moving nobly in his shredded and patched raiment. His face, with its blanched, elegantly cut features and contemplative air, was the face of a bard; but that dreamy blue eye could wake to the sharpness of a weasel's at the mere mention of mole-catching or other sport. His name was Rhydderch Morris, his wife's was Martha, and their habitation The Lodge, Bryncennin, near Llanffelix, South Wales.

Never was a more harmonious contrast than that presented by Martha, shrewd of face, solid of build and grown stout, and her frail, almost ethereal looking partner. Rhydderch, trailing firewood home from the pine grove, or seated shelling a heap of nuts on the mossy bank beside his cottage door, or weaving willow baskets on the winter hearth, Martha sitting by, knitting steadily, made pictures not to be forgotten. Guests at Bryncennin never failed to be charmed by the old couple. They were sketched by an English artist of note for his Academy picture of 'Philemon and Baucis' concluding their long and peaceful lives in the Arcady where, together, they had been spent.

The lady of Bryncennin did not undeceive the painter; but, when a minor poet began versifying the same idea in her Visitors' Book, she spoke:

'Only this "Philemon" has been a collier all his life.'

'A collier?' gasped the idyllist. 'Why, he was talking to me yesterday of his boyhood here forty or fifty years since, and his birthplace – Pontyclerc Cottage, somewhere down the old coach road by the Lodge.'

'Yes. It's a heap of ruins now. He went from here when a mere lad to work in the Rhondda Valley. "Baucis" is his second wife. She too had a past when they married: a grown-up family by her first husband, who was English. She comes from a distant border county.'

Yes, the peasant pair had seen life and knew more of it than Miss Durden or the minor poet were ever likely to know. But we have only to do with the former in their days of dignified retirement at the Lodge; days of work, unhasting, unresting, in their garden – a rood or so of highly cultivated ground behind the hedgerow at a stone's cast from their door.

Here on chill October morning Rhydderch was 'lifting' potatoes when Martha, staggering with a sackful across to the cottage, espied a figure moving up the three miles' hill of a high road leading down to Llanffelix. A tramp, out of doubt; so a devious something in his gait, air, and way of wearing his clothes, while yet a great way off proclaimed him. Her attitude to such too common objects of this country was kindlilly discreet. A drink of water – or milk if there was any – might be theirs for the asking. If alms were begged urgently, she would bestow a halfpenny with a solemn, sacrificial, widow's-mite gesture. There was nothing, indeed, about the Morrises – faring roughly and toiling hard, and in half-patched clothing – to suggest anything but poverty and a certain struggle to make the two ends meet.

She watched the wanderer as he approached: a strong-looking, roughly-built fellow, with no fool's face under his slouched cap.

'May an Englishman speak to you, ma'am?' The tone of offhand freedom and cheerful pleasantry with which he accosted her took her by surprise.

'You are English?' she said inquiringly.

'Blame the mother who bore me and the father she chose for me (poor souls! They lie in their graves) for that,' he retorted. 'To be Welsh born would have pleased Tim Brady – would have pleased me better. That is – you are Welsh yourself, ma'am?'

She nodded.

'It's not from your speech, then, I'd have known it. Why, you might be native-born English. I've met few here of whom I could say that.'

Mrs Morris was so used to compliments on her familiarity with this foreign tongue that she accepted this one as genuine, never bethinking her that she had scarcely spoken three words to this man.

Here old Rhydderch showed himself at the garden gate. Who was discoursing thus lightly with his Martha?

'Your goodman?' asked the stranger. Then as Martha assented, 'May a poor man wish you good-day, sir?' he said doffing his cap.

'A poor man myself,' said Rhydderch, with a grace and a wave of the hand worthy of a king in exile. 'What can I do for you?'

'How much farther to Llandarren?'

'For myself two hours at the least; for you rather less. Have you work there?'

'I go to look for it. Unless,' he hesitated, 'you or some other gentleman could put me up to a job nearer. I'm weary and footsore with walking all the way from Swansea.'

'No,' Rhyddarch shook his fine head, surveying this stalwart, well-spoken gentleman of the road with some interest. 'Except,' he added doubtfully, but struck by an idea, 'you had a mind to lend a hand with the potatoes for a trifle. I'm not the man I was once, and my good wife there is getting on. What, now, would you ask?'

After some palaver they were agreed; and until nightfall three worked together briskly in the patch. Certainly the labourer proved worthy of his hire, which included board and lodging for the night. With mournful envy did old Rhydderch, forced in his declining years to hoard and carefully eke out the shrinking remnant of his strength, behold this splendid hireling fling his physical energy about with a 'plenty more where that came from' air. Such a one should be doing better in the world than seemed to be his case.

'To think, now, that a strong, smart young fellow like you should be working as a journeyman for one like me!' he wondered inquisitively aloud.

'My own fault – my own doing!' owned the other frankly. 'A quarrel I had with my employer – a good employer too! And all for a shilling! I'm sorry now I stood out. But there, they drive us to it, these masters. We've to teach them they can't have everything their own way with us as they expect.'

This sentiment was approved and agreed to.

Yes, it was Swansea he came from last. Oh, Swansea was a big place. And a bad one! All towns were wicked. It was in the country – country like this – that he, Tim Brady, would choose to live. Only – was there any money to be made there?

'*No*,' man and wife hastily affirmed in a breath. A bare living at the utmost, and for that you must work hard – too hard.

America was the place, rejoined their new friend. It was there he would go if he had the passage money. He knew men who had gone. Men grew rich there; but how?

And that evening, by the wide hearth, Brady treated them to tales of the West – tales wondrous and wicked; the more wicked the more keenly relished by the dear old people, who listened greedily, pleasantly agitated as by thrilling fiction, which perhaps it all was. Miss Durden, of Bryncennin, passing in at the gate of her grounds, heard the story-teller's voice and caught a glimpse of the trio through the open door. Who on earth, she wondered, was this 'Englishman from the Emerald Isle' (as some here put it) who was the night's guest at the Lodge?

Sleep? He? Just wherever they chose to put him. Tim Brady wasn't one to lie awake. On the oak settle here in the kitchen he'd be snug – snug as a rabbit, nor envy them their bed-chamber – fit for a lady born though it was. An admiring peep showed him the door and front wall inside draped with yards and yards of art muslin; a piece begged of Miss Durden to hide discoloured wall paper. Now weren't those hangings a bit comestible? Combustible, he meant, but somehow they understood, and Morris quite agreed with him. 'Only my wife says, since we never strike a light in here we are safe.' 'What do you want with a light to go to bed by?' said Martha scornfully. 'Good night, now.' So they went in, drawing the bolt.

Morning saw them busy again in the potato patch. The day was warm, and after the midday meal by general consent there was a lengthy halt. Outside the cottage door they sat; the hireling stretched himself at full length on the mossy bank, and presently fell sound asleep; when the old people dropped naturally into their native Welsh.

'How he sleeps!' sighed Rhydderch, pointing with his pipe to the recumbent brawny form.

'Like a child.'

'Ah, he is light-hearted, though penniless.' Morris spoke feelingly with a regretful backward glance at his own light youth. Drawing a tattered newspaper from his pocket he began to read aloud the day's chronicle of battle, murder, and sudden death all the world over, compounded for the individual interest of the average reader. The worst horrors exhausted, there followed the grave item: "*Failure of the Bethesda Bank!*"

'There!' said his wife, triumphantly. 'What did I tell you? Now, but for me, Rhydderch, our money might have gone with that bank (or some other – they are all alike, unsafe) instead of lying as it does snug and sure between the mattress.'

'Hush, hush you!' prayed old Morris in terror. True, the stranger there was fast asleep. Besides, they were speaking Welsh, of which he professed ignorance. Still, stones – trees – have ears when you talk secrets. But the solitude and stillness around were unbroken, and Rhydderch quietly resumed his pipe and his tranquility.

'Keep out of banks,' Martha insisted. 'The clerks they gossip; people get to know you have two – three hundred pounds or more lying there. You are rich, they say. Then they will be coming – the minister, the spendthrift, the beggar – asking; the shopkeeper puts up his prices, the landlord raises the rent – they make it hard for you to keep your own. You are going to your pocket till it is empty.'

He could not contradict her, but his attention was now fastened on the column devoted to poetry, of which he was fond, and which interested her less. Her roving eye rested by chance on the somnolent hireling's head, and under the cap she caught a gleam – a sunlight glint, was it, or an astutely open eye? Something that begat in her a moment's uneasiness. Was the sleeper shamming, and at this moment awake, alert, and listening? Nay, the sparkle went out, the figure never stirred; the uncomfortable idea was dismissed. But it had given her a turn.

'I am thirsty,' said old Morris. 'Fetch me a drink, wife.'

She crossed to the cottage for some water. When she returned the shutting of the gate roused the sleeper, who sat up dazedly, as one abruptly wakened.

That was a snooze he had had! Well, he was going to make up for it now. The weather threatened a change. They must finish that night; but it was past seven before, the last load lifted, they were about to shut themselves in for a hearth chat, when a child messenger came hurrying up breathlessly from the hill.

'Morris, you're wanted at Pen Draw. Your brother is very much worse. The doctor says he will hardly pass the night. They want you to come to him at once.'

This summons to the bedside of his long invalided relative flurried but scarcely startled the old man. Oh, yes, he must go, after settling accounts with Brady. But a second night's lodging had been promised him, and Rhydderch Morris felt embarrassed. To turn him out would have been the act of a churl, suggesting a distrust he did not feel. Martha, too, had all but forgotten her momentary fears. She was cheerful and accommodating, and Brady made things easy for both. He would not incommode them, not he; not for the whole world. All he wanted was few hours' sleep on a kitchen bench. He would be off before daybreak so as to catch the early worm at Llandarren. 'But I shall carry you both in my heart,' he affirmed, shaking hands with the host with unaffected cordiality. So Morris hurried off to Llanffelix; his wife hung about the kitchen awhile, talking of the sick brother-in-law, his symptoms, and above all, of his spiritual condition, which preoccupied her sadly, and which she seemed to know as intimately as the bread of last week's baking, while entertaining thereof a less favourable opinion. Small blame to Tim Brady if he could neither feel nor feign much concern in the matter. He was drowsy, too, after a hot day's toil.

'Well, friend,' said Mrs Morris presently, 'you want rest and so, I think, do I. There's fire on the hearth still. I leave you to finish your pipe. Goodbye and good-night to you.'

So out went Martha into the bedchamber, bolting herself in.

She got to bed, but not to sleep as quickly as was her wont. Her brain, fevered by the strain of muscular exertion, ran restlessly on the trouble of this brother-in-law. He had had as alarming attacks before and rallied from them. But supposing this time he did not. Dead or dying, he, no special friend of hers otherwise, became an object of sudden and surpassing interest. What sort of fate was in store for him in the other world? The fascination of the horrible, to which most of us are prone in some form, took full possession of her, and lurid depths opened to her imagination run wild. Actual nightmare was not unknown to Martha Morris, but, firm believer and devout chapel-goer though she was, it seldom took a religious form. Tonight it did so; and when at last she slept, the waking dream, unchecked, became ten times more vivid, more terrifying. Flames – a pit of fire – the fire everlasting, flames tormenting, never to be quenched, whose illuminating blaze showed awful shapes, monstrous demons grinning fiercely. Martha, Martha, what ails your honest, childlike, innocent head? And now the flames roar, the tongues of fire shoot out and curl and hiss, and the devil-adversary, incarnate, bursts out of the furnace and glares at her, seeking whom he may devour...

Martha was siting up in bed, with a circle of roaring flames encompassing here. Then came a frightful crash, with a shock that was like a blow on the head. The Last Day had come, out of doubt. She had secretly hoped that she was prepared. But what had it brought to her, Martha Morris, for her portion? Hell-fire, with the devil and his angels. An evil face met hers in the fiery glare; a look of desperate, determined greed and lawless violence, that burnt itself in her memory for ever. And yet there was something not quite unfamiliar to her about this Satan. Now he spoke in a human voice that awoke recent echoes in her ears.

'Mrs Morris, get up – come out! Make haste! Fire! The house is burning!'

'Fire! The house is burning!' her lips moved feebly, as if repeating his words like a child; but no sound came. Panic-struck, she seemed turned to stone.

Brady, for it was he, dragged her out of bed and from the room out of doors, where she sank in a helpless heap on the bank. Satan rushed back into the cottage and presently brought out the blanket she had given him for a coverlet, and threw it round her.

'There, you are safe here. Wait while I run to the big house – to Bryncennin – for help.' And he disappeared in the darkness through the white gate that led into Miss Durden's grounds.

How long Martha "waited" she could never have told. Slowly, yet gradually, she came to her senses. Her brain cleared a little; she understood that the end of the world was not yet; that "Satan" had come to save, not to destroy; thus she had not been called to account or lost hope of salvation. But, this nightmare removed, other minor griefs assailed her, under whose weight she sank, as she sat there, her head buried in her hands. Here was her home, her chosen cottage on the hill, where she and Rhydderch meant to live on till they died – in flames, burnt out. Brady had said so. A thatched roof, unceiled underneath, old wooden rafters exposed everywhere, in kitchen and bedchamber-ceilings below. Not Miss Durden and her menservants and maidservants all could help to stop it. Tomorrow she and her old man would be homeless, roofless, as the tramp they had harboured. Still too overcome by the shocks undergone to look up or to stir, she was brooding over their plight when the sound of footsteps roused her, and broke her lethargy of woe. Doubtless Tim Brady at last returning with help from Bryncennin.

Strange that the footsteps approaching seemed so deliberate

and slow, and from the opposite direction. Daybreak had come, and the sight of old Morris, for it was he, trudging up the hill from Llanffelix brought her suddenly to herself. He looked pale but placid; the sick man having taken a more favourable turn, all the immediate danger had passed over, and he had come home, but to find his wife, a half-crazed, half-dressed creature, cowering on the cold ground in a blanket.

'The house – our house is on fire,' she managed to tell him.

'What? Brady – where is he?'

'The Lodge is burnt; burning still' – she had not yet ventured to look that way.

'But the Englishman? Why is he not here?'

'He has run off to Bryncennin for help.'

The old man, half mazed, stood staring at the four cottage walls and thatch, apparently intact. Was she demented? He peered cautiously through the wide-open house door and was met by a strong smell of burning, but taking courage, in he went.

The fire had consumed the bedroom hangings to the last shred, but had quickly burnt itself out and wreaked no further havoc. Even the bedclothes, though scorched and damaged here and there, had never been aflame. He hastened back to reassure Martha as to the extent of the mischief; and she, her mind helped by his familiar presence to recover its balance, related as much as she knew of what had taken place.

A sudden terrible suspicion seized on old Ryhdderch at once. He rushed back into the bedroom and came out again all of a tremble, hair and beard dishevelled, eyes wild with anger.

'He has done it! That tramp, that thief! The bag with the money has gone! He has taken it. He made the fire; a pretence for bursting open the bedroom door. Martha, he has gone off with our all! He trusted the flames would destroy all proof of his guilt. It is all gone! The savings of our whole lives! We shall die paupers – as was he.'

He was sobbing hysterically, carried away by the passion of

his sudden grief. The next moment he repented the outburst. Mrs Morris's heart was set on their savings; this fresh shock, after all she had just undergone, might be her death. But the words had gone forth.

To his surprise she showed no emotion, which only frightened him the more, as unnatural. She fixed her eyes on his with a strange and unaccountable serenity, more perturbing than mourning and woe. It was clean out of her mind she must have gone. It would be no wonder.

Rising, she took his hand and led him slowly, solemnly, to a spot at the back of the cottage where, under a large, flat, inconspicuous stone, they were used on occasion to deposit the door key. At a sign from her he lifted it. Here beneath lay, not, indeed, the bag, but its main contents, a flat parcel of £10 notes that crackled reassuringly.

'This afternoon I had a moment's suspicion of him,' she explained. 'For an instant his eyes seemed open and he to be listening to our talk. Talking we had been of the money and where it lay. I went in to get you some water, and I said to myself, 'Who knows? He may understand Welsh, though he doesn't speak it. Well, if I move the money from where it is, it is no harm, and I shall sleep better.' (Oh, but there I was wrong! I could not live through another such a night.) Afterwards I felt so sure I had been mistaken in distrusting him, I put the thought from me that I had ever done so. Oh, the traitor, the evil doer! He has the empty bag for his pains!'

'Well, sure!' The old man was quaking still from the triple scare; of incendiarism, robbery, and his wife's loss of her reason; empty fears though they all had proved. Together the pair tottered over to Bryncennin, in whose warm and hospitable kitchen they gave soothing vent to their agitation by recounting their adventures; and gradually a sense of better being was established. The Lodge was unconsumed, the money safe in Rhydderch's pocket; they were quit for the loss of the presentation art-muslin, fired by the vagabond – turned to a ruffian by opportunity and greed – by means of a red-hot wire thrust through the keyhole. Closer examination, however, revealed that one bank note was missing, a fiver, recently added to the store; and thrust hastily into the bag, unenclosed in the parcel with the rest. Neither it nor the delinquent were ever heard of again in the Principality, the one having probably enabled the other to ship to parts of the earth where Rhydderch and Martha Morris, though the loss rankles, think it vain to prosecute inquiries.

But they have agreed to bank the remainder.

Comic Objects of the Country

Being the Impressions of an Industrial Schoolboy

What had I done for to get clapped into a 'Dustrial school? Say, what hadn't I, rather?

There's fool-chaps get put away there all along of askin' of a kind lady to give 'em a cup o' tea. U.S. – short for Eustace Smart – (that's me) ain't one of they. Beggin' bein' a criminal offence, better get took for burglary at once, sure*ly*! 'Tain't as I holds with Burglary for Boys. Smacks o' playgame, which lowers the business to my eye. No. Burglary never was my form.

Sneakin' o' stamps and halfpence don't count. Lord! I've known gentlemen-father of a family as was forced to start a penny-in-the-slot thing in his hall to stop the lot of his genteel household from a-makin' free with his King's heads. As to gents as leaves coppers in pockets of coats as they gives you to brush – well, I take it that's their genteel way of tippin' of the little lad. Ah, I was a house-boy once! My House people were very kind to me; but you know what SERVANTS are! Six months of that, and I chucked it.

'Twas then I had the time of my life; the roarin' good time no man but the street boy quite beyond parental control (mine were poor creatures both) ever gets. Nothing nor nobody to fear. The Force, a-mopin' there round the street corner, why, we takes no more heed of he nor of the pillar-box. Nor him of us. He can't stop us, *he* knows. The lor can't get no fines outer we children; it won't thrash us, and prison's no fit place for young innercents same as we. Safe, at worst, to be bound over under the First 'Fenders Acts, it's free as birds we is to go and do whatever we've a mind to.

And that was Loot. Bell-pulls, plates, knobs – brass fittin's ginerally. Lord, how we raided Maida Vale and St. John's Wood in a single victorious happy an' glorious night! There was a toff a-residin' in Grandcourt Gardens near by as give us three farthin's each for the stuff. But the joy was in the work and dodgin' of the enemy. Ah, your London slum boy, *he* lives. Your young gentleman, he merely exists.

But it was too fond of book-learnin' was U.S. That an' school was my undoin'. Had I been Smart by natur as by name, and shammed stupid, the master mightn't a' missed me so sore. But no chance for a promisin' scholar like I was; and it's had up before the magistrate I got at last as an uncorrigible truant. I tried a whole box o' tricks on his Honor: Led away by older boys; been readin' "Raffles"; watchin' of a movin'-show – "Life and Death of a Grand Old Cracksman"; suff'rin' from delusions takin' the form an unresistable desire to steal somethink; they wouldn't go off – not even a-cryin' and a-callin' for mother. Three years in a 'Dustrial School he gave me. Yah, he oughter go through it himself; and so I told him, causin' loud laughter in court.

Havin' told you as how I got in, as how I got out is told in two words: Exemplairy behaviour. There's fool-chaps tries scalin' walls an' winders, an' gets their bones broke, or a thrashin' for their reward. To such I say, 'Be a hangel an' the wings'll grow an' carry yer away, no man a-forbiddin' yer.' Which was figur of speech. But so it come to pass.

It was just no blamed use fussin' an' spendin' any more on reformin' such a pattern of virtue an' forward schoolin' as U.S. becomed, and pretty quick, hey. So soon as fit and proper, I was drafted off for farm service in the country. 'Ence these pages.

Wales, where I was took, is very much country indeed. Sorter place we London people knows no more of than life on a Chinese junk. I've heard that it was chose as a startin' ground for the Boy Farming-out Scheme as dumping us down at a safe distance from bad company, and as hoping we might there strike root. There's chaps as has; but mostly speakin' it's too late to begin. Guess U.S. should have been dumped earlier.

Now though I holds as the newspaper gents as writes books overrates the country that shockin', there's amusin' sights there to see, as you shall hear. Only take warnin': if like U.S. you come from John Street, East London, you'll find it cruel hard to put up with the dirt an' bad smells outer doors; used as we been to streets as is washed an' swept regular; flushed o' nights too an' all made sweet an' clean by the mornin'. Why, I seen a troop o' Boro' scavenger men a-lollin' away the whole of a sunny afternoon a-flickin' and a-brushin' just a sprinklin' of dust from a London by-road. Nor has we known what 'tis like to be without a clean dry pavement to walk on, with shelter from the beggarly elements in archways an' shop doors always handy, and lighted proper; while here, though you're out in all weathers, it's through all the muck and the dark you must go. No boots fit for civilised lads' wear would stand it. And it's goodbye now to the fresh and sanitary sniff o' the asphalte, an' the petrol, an' them infectants they paints the drains red with. (Here they uses it on the sheep, but they smell bad all the same!) The reek of the cheese-room is fit to knock you down, but that's nothin' to what's lyin' in wait for you in wood-lands, fields, and hedges. 'Tom, there's a corpse somewhere. Is it a sheep or a man, d'ye think?' says I to my mate – a Welsh lad – my first day in the open. 'Bless you,' says he, 'why 'tis only one o' they bad mushrooms – fungus you say in English. Here we calls them "everlasting potatoes."' 'And right you are,' says I, 'for there's no end to their stink.' Soon as you're outer that comes the stench of burnin' muck, or them fertilisers, chimerical and natural, which it is simply appallin'. Pig-sties – gosh! – is nasty things as the lor didn't oughter allow to exist. Duckponds and watercourses, too – pah! I'd sooner be a snipe of our John Street gutter nor o' they. Country noses takes these things for granted, you see. Same with funny sights, they don't tickle 'em. Cows now.

See'd for the first time outer a picture, or in partitions like, a hangin' at the butcher's, it kep' me on the full grin it did, that monster babby on four short legs it never learns how to use proper. Whatever your cow's a-doin' of, gettin' on her feet, jumpin', runnin', buttin', you'd swear it was for the first time. Dogs – why, even cats – along of movin' in human society, gets to catch the jist so of what you says to them. But cows has no sense, no mind but to go contrairy to what you want. Comes of their bein' all females, I suppose, as is milk maids an' dairymaids mostly.

One there was – an' a wicked old witch of a cow was she – but she knew a thing or two. As how to open gates an' get outer wheresoever she was put into where she didn't ought for to be. She'd watch you outer the corner of her wicked old eye by the hour for her chance of the mischief on which her heart was set. Pure love of sin 'twas, I'll swear. My mate Tom, a-coercin' of that old cow to Llanffelix market was a sight to make hangels weep – for laughin'.

Country hosses runs to bulk, same as the elephant at the Zoo, only not baggy-hided like he, but fit to burst their fat old skins. How they can carry more nor their own size or be worth their stable-room, let alone their upkeep, I wonder! But if "Boy,"our biggest, belonged to me *I'd* not waste all that space and throw away such a good blackboard for advertisements. I'd just plaster him all over from mane to tail with Beecham's Pills or Colman's Mustard, an' lead him, a walkin' hoardin' a processin' round the country. I put the notion before my boss, told him there was money in it; but he went wild with rage and I had to run, though innercent of meanin' offence. They takes their live-stock very seriously here down in Wales. Yet I haven't clapped eyes on a horse you'd put a bet on, nor so much as a dog worth stealin'.

Your grand Country Comique is the goose; and it's my belief

that he knows it, same as any playboy in the music-halls. I've seen him, G. Gander, Esq., go through it, time and again, fixed an' regular. Up he starts, a-breathin' out threatenins an' slaughter like the jealous mad husband in a mellow-drama. Flaps wings fit to break your arm, a-screechin' "I'll peck your eyes out if you dare look my wife's way again"; then makes believe to rush you, who just winks an' waggles your stick, whereon he rights about an' waddles, slow-march, back to his goosey, a-chantin', soothin'-like and low, "Only my fun, stranger! It's all in the part, see?"

Pigs? A standin' joke is pigs; savin' always the killin' of 'em. It's the day of the year here, sorter solemn feast day. Oh, grand! *That* tit-bit I'll keep over for another story, fearin' for to shock my lady readers. But the joke of it, that makes the tend'rest hearted smile, is the amazin' quick change from the fussy gruntin', squealin', wallowin' swine of the early mornin' into clean an' tidy pork sections, an' prime cuts of bacon for table consumption, of the afternoon. I know at Chicago Piggy trots in one end of a tube an' comes out as sausage at the other. But you spoils the effect of a thing by overdoin' of it, and so quick as your wits can't keep up with it.

Lambs, calves, colts, I skips. To name 'em is to grin. Why the infant four-legger should thus be born unproportionate an' out of gear, an' with no sense of the ridiclus, I wonder – unless 'tis to divert us with their antics. But another smart notion of mine I daren't put before my boss is a Truant School for live-stock. 'Tis a cryin' need here. And 'taint that they're treated rough, by shyin' stones and sticks after 'em as they deserves, and as I should do if I was let. Yet they wanders shockin', and half the hands' time is swallered up with a-huntin' of 'em up and a-runnin' of 'em in. An' comical though they shows at home, they's screamin' farce when broken loose. From the biggest bull to the littlest ducklin' they all does it. Guess they can't help it, bein' Welsh, an' longin' for to show their independence. But I do wish the brutes' instincts was a bit more slavish. 'Twould save a lot of wear an' tear.

Houses? There's fine talkin' an' writin' of them solid old farm-houses. Solid, you bet, as suet puddin'; but for 'fficiency, and things requisite an' necessary for the body as for the soul, give me your jerry-built artisans' up-to-date dwellin' or lodgin'-house, with gas an' water, sinks an' taps proper, to name but a few. Why there's mansions here without so much as a door-bell or knocker for little chaps to ring or rat-tat an' run away – same as I used; an' letter-boxes, as fittin's, seems unknown. Some of these old solids has a ladder does dooty for a staircase; and it ain't my granny or grandad could scramble up an' down nimble, like the old folks here – that it's a treat to behold. But 'twould be poor fun for Londoners, used to the business-house lift.

Scenery? You sees a long way in the country, but there's no more to look at, like, in a single tram-top ride along Commercial Road than from the highest of these here hills. The views so fine I tells Tom I seen 'em all on the Mountain Railway, Shepherd's Bush. Rainbows now – and Wales is strong in such, my word for that! – never a one to beat the sample I mind once of an evenin' in Leicester Square – a-spannin' of the Alhambra Music Hall, as though made to special measurements. A party-coloured Elevated Foot-Bridge for sky traffic. And oh Lord, the hootin' taxis, roarin' busses, the hustlin', bustlin', cussin' crowd underneath! They set it off. All these Nature beauties wants the town, like, for to give 'em a relish.

Song-birds? Then strange twitterations birds makes, they calls music. I wonder why. If you or I was to make the like where'd the music be, I ask you? When, like U.S., you've heard Melba, Tetrazzini, an' Cruso on the gramophone, you'd be ashamed not to know better. Music's a thing you do miss cruel in the country. Once, a-returnin' from taking of a pig to Llanffelix market, I heards sounds as made my heart jump. A barrel-organ 'twas. And a right comic object it did look, far,

far away from its John Street home, a-grindin' of my pet piece, "Cavil, Area, Rusty, Karna," at a roadside pub. My, at the thrill of it, back I was in the old slum, with the little wee shops I knows so well. First and chiefest the gin-shop; next, a lovely winderful of artificial teeth like dead men's jaws; Moses, the pawnbroker, then the baccy store with posters outside tellin' of the awful crimes an' fatal smashes we misses worse nor our daily bread, if so be as they don't occur. Next, ever such a smart set-out o' flash joolery, an' every passin' gal a-stoppin' for a stare. Last, the new store with its grand front round the corner, packed close with tasty tinned food-stuffs. Chicago! It made my mouth water to think of them things. Pity the poor country kiddies as grows up with never a sight of town and its amusements.

Folks? Folks in the country is so few an' so far between they all counts. Now though country air don't by any means come up to its reputation, country *airs* is superior to anything we can do in the metropolis. Why, there I seen dukes, princes – Kings as is now – a-walkin' down to business (the House of Lords that is), or a-doin' of their shoppin' humble-like, just as if they was no one in particular, and a thankin' of the public not to notice them. Duffers! Here, now, the King ain't in it, for side! One or two big men sets the copy, and every other man, great an' small, gets as near it as he can, each a-mindin' to give himself airs over the next below. As I'll do, soon as I get a rise!

Second to none in his airs is the Country Constable. Seldom seen, but then a-loungin' 'long the road, with nothing to mind or take notice of but his blessed self. As outer place, he looks, as a camel or a cassowary astray from a circus. 'Lord, man, however did you come here and whatever are you a-doin' of in this Garden of Eden?' was on my tongue to ask him. But the police is so dull and so ill-read, you can't talk to them at all.

There's just one country sight beats the town shows holler; the exception as proves the rule. One cold an' frosty mornin' as

my boss an' I was a-muckin' and a-manicurin' of his old field,
lazy-like – one as stands on end facin' Jones's land t'other side
of the valley – we heard sounds as you don't hear every day
of your life; sounds like comin' from the earth and air at once.
We stops an' looks up, and afore you could say 'bang,' see
if there ain't the Hunt a-goin' by in full blast along the ridge
opposite where Jones's man was a-ploughin'. Hounds yellin',
hoofs clatterin', riders in pink coats racin' – aha, that waked
us up, it did! My boss, he's no respecter of foxes (as to which
I could tell tales), he holds huntin', as damages his fences an'
his crops, in contempt – or a sin as should be put down by the
lor. All same, his face lit up at sight of that like a sky sign, an'
his looks was catched and hung on to them hounds same as
mine. They was on Jones's land, as farms under Sir Meuric
Williams, you see, not my boss's. I never wished myself a dog
but that once, but then I did. Oh, 'twas life to watch 'em, an'
the hosses, an' the gents, some o' them ladies, a-sprintin' over
hill an' dale! *All* life's wasted as ain't spent huntin', say some.
I guess 'tis – in the country.

Then a strange thing happened, as they put in books. Them
two horses as Jones's man was ploughin' with gets excited,
starts snortin' an' prancin' as though gone stark mad. 'Look
at that,' says my boss. 'It's two of Sir Meuric's old hunters.
He can't hold them. Lord, mercy, what will become of plough
and man?'

Well, the man was "left lamentin'," as I've heard sing. But
the hosses – off and away they gallops, a-draggin' the plough
after them as though 'twere their tails, tearin' through an
opening in the hedge, a-neighin' out "Back to the Hunt," and
follers, plough and all, in the rear of the pack. 'Twas a queer
sight. But, oh, and I'd a feller-feelin' for those two old gees,
just as though I'd been a huntin' man myself.

Girls? Girls is girls an' funny everywheres, same town as
country. If ever I could think myself back in the street-land

I love so dear 'twas in Llanffelix, early closin', servants' holiday-out afternoon. All over the place was girls. Stuck up things! All hats, an' gigglin' at us boys as though we were there by mistake, an' they could do everything by lookin' an' talkin'. I hate girls!

One I didn't. Ethel her name was; a daughter at the farm next door – across the hill, I mean. I could sight her three fields away. She never wore no hat in the open. Tall-lookin' she was, an' her hair that thick an' soft! If I shuts my eyes I see her now, a-watchin' the hay-cart pitch down the hilly field, or a-feedin' of her lamb; mindin' me of pictures I seen in shop winders in the Strand.

Once I remember a-comin' on her by surprise like, as she was leavin' an old wool-shed, with her arms chock full o' fleeces of her father's sheep – an' lookin' that pretty – prettier nor any picture. It knocked me clean silly.

'Why, Jim' (so they calls me on the farm), 'what's the matter?' she says, wondering like, but grave an' gentle as she always was.

There was I standin' starin' owl-stupid at her, feelin' as only half awake an' dreamin' hard.

'Well, it's just *you*,' I told her, and all I could do to speak it, with voice and eyes gone queer of a sudden.

'*Me?*' she said, struck like. She didn't understand, no more did I. One minute we stood so, facin' one another – I and she. Then I turned away.

An' when we London lads gets together and makes fun of Wales an' the Welsh, I see her sometimes as she looked and was. And the laugh goes outer the fun, an' the jokes sounds dead stupid.

Miss Durden of Bryncennin, as owns my boss's land, is a lady as takes int'rest in literature. So it happened I showed her these pages, askin' if she thought the Charity Organisation or Salvation Army would publish them for me. She said she didn't think it was quite in her line, but she'd see to it herself, if I'd let her.

I didn't mind, I told her, provided she'd put my name an' didn't alter my work. I know the spellin' an' grammer isn't right or regular all through, but once she started meddlin' 'twouldn't be mine no longer, see?

She asked me if I didn't feel cruel lonesome among a strange people speakin' a strange tongue. I told her no. These farmers they treats us well accordin' to their lights, though they're a bit stodgy, an' don't afford much laughin' matter. I said I thought I'd get used to Welsh folk in time, an' pointed out as I'd learnt more of their lingo in six months than she in as many years. But what I'd never do with, as a Bermondsey boy born and bred, is the country – lag-behind an' stationary in it's fashions as it's bound to be. 'You can't put the clock back, Miss; and I'd sooner be a cab-runner in the Great Metropolis, where I was born, nor any thrivin' husband-man or rooral artisan in England and Wales.'

A House that Was

> . . . Where we sang
> The mole now labours, and spiders hang.

> T. HARDY

It was Ivy Harvey, a girl from Kansas, aged two-and-twenty, just disembarked on European shores.

Her parents had treated her to a trip to England, and she was taking it, alone and as unconcernedly as though it were a mere run from London to the Isle of Wight.

The liner *Recordiana* set her down at Fishguard, South Wales. 'Land of a hundred castles,' read Ivy from her guide book. 'Say, I'll stop and sample one or two of these before I jog on.'

Now Ivy had never seen any ancient thing in her life.

But before she was two days older she had viewed a cathedral whose bells were ringing in King John's time, a palace where men feasted in the days of the Black Prince, mysterious carved stone wayside crosses of untold antiquity, and castles such as made of all the wildest romances she had ever read and laughed at so many bits of real life.

On the third afternoon – the morning had added a Merlin's cave and an Arthur's Stone to her Welsh records – she stood on the ramparts of Carreg Cenen, a ruined fortress great in story, back to the legendary days of the Wizard and the Warrior King, and looking as though sprung by magic from the precipitous rocky steep whence, from miles afar, it arrests the attention.

Such tokens of things that have lasted – of continuous

life and action unbroken from generation to generation – to
the Britisher mere common objects of his country – were
fascinating novelties to Ivy, half-mazing her with wonder and
enjoyment.

'I must grab on to that London express before breakfast
tomorrow,' she said, contemplating the rare and splendid
panorama of mountain crags and evergreen pastures looking
as if they were just created, 'or I'll be staying here till I die! I
just can't believe these things have been round here all these
ages – and I never dreamt!'

Now to get back to the Glendower Arms, Llanffelix, five
miles by the high road. Striking a bee-line across country, Ivy
walked for two hours up and down deep land dips, numerous
and undiscernible till you came upon them as crevasses in a
glacier; then followed a fisherman's path by an alder-fringed
brook to its full stop near a cottage farm, buried like a hermit's
cell in a shady, sleepy hollow.

'Well, I've loafed about a might sight,' she sighed, 'and all
to end up with this shallow! Hey, my dear boy in the barn
there! I want the way to Llanffelix – if there is one.'

The dear boy carefully shut all of him but his head and
scowling face into the barn. But Ivy was not to be taken in
by that scowl. 'It just yells at you, "There's a stranger and an
enemy coming along. Shoot or hide!" But it means, "This
young lady is about to address me in English, a foreign tongue
with which circumstances have prevented my becoming
sufficiently acquainted to enable me to reply with suitable
fluency and ease."'

So Ivy smiled her winningest, and cooed entreaty, 'Llanffelix
– where?'

He pointed to the setting sun, bawled something uncatchable,
and bolted himself securely into the barn.

Facing westward, Ivy explored two hilly fields, with no
discoverable outlet till a kink in the hedge disclosed a little
spiked iron gateway, as it were, into private grounds, and

alongside a brick-walled enclosure.

'That there's a large cabbage-patch,' reasoned Ivy. 'Should belong to a white man with an English tongue in his head.'

She broke through into the grass-grown glade – ringed with forest trees, gay underfoot with yellow Turk's-cap lilies, and blue wild hyacinths – and stopped short, met by something more beautiful than the loveliest dream.

A tiny path slanting steeply and straightly upward, between two thin files of over-shadowing fir, ash, and sycamore, with an undergrowth of rich-flowering laburnum, whose branches, meeting overhead, formed a complete golden avenue, radiant, dazzling, for as far onward as eye could reach.

'Oh, but this is Fairyland!' exclaimed Ivy. 'Fairyland, saying, "Come and find me." Wait, I'm coming.'

She wanted a peep through the dilapidated doorway into the herb-garden. Paradise forsaken and run wild. A hedgehog was sunning itself on a low stone bank; a snake and a lizard slithered away at her tread. 'Impish elves in disguise,' her roused fancy suggested. Or spirits of departed presences revisiting, in these lowly shapes, their old haunts. Who knows?

'I'm just gone silly,' she told herself. 'But don't tell me I'm here in one and the same world as the Kansas Cowboys' Club, at the Crack Ball Splitters.'

Onward she climbed under that golden arcade. The laburnum clusters, hanging thick as grapes in an Italian vineyard, almost touched her head, half intoxicating her with their fragrance, mingled with scents of hawthorn hedges in the fields beyond. A slit in the leafy screen startled her with a sudden passing glimpse of Carreg Cenen Castle, looking, by some trick of atmosphere, thirty miles off instead of three – dark, rugged, angular, like some mighty monster couched there and waiting to spring.

Atop she found a little shrubbery gate. Close before her loomed the rough-cast walls and gables of a house, ancient looking and grey.

Turning to say goodbye to the golden avenue, Ivy distinctly saw, or thought she saw, an ugly, hobgoblin-like thing – black monkey or mannikin – picking his way upward in her wake. Fancy, at her tricks again! Nothing but the wriggling shadow of a dark bush in the breeze. 'Git! You bogey man!' quoth Ivy, indignant though half scared by an illusion born, perhaps, of that sheer craving for crude contrast that drove court-beauties of old to keep apes and black dwarfs at their sides as a set-off to their charms.

Past a shrubbery that was all blossom and no shrub, she slipped furtively by the veranda front, and round the angle to the drive and entrance door of solid oak under a pointed wooden porch. Ivy pulled at the old bell knob. But none answered.

Glancing up at the chimneys, 'Smoke means fire,' she said hopefully. 'Fire means man,' and rang again. Still nothing happened.

Came a faint shuffling as of slippered feet; a hand groped at the latch, and the door was opened to her.

II

By a dead woman! So it struck her. A corpse-thing. Ivy stood aghast, spellbound with horror, or she would have turned and fled from the shrivelled, vanishing-looking shape, huddled in a loose wrapper, the parched, blanched features, sunken eyes, and dishevelled hair, as it were, of a death's head, hastily enveloped in an old woollen shawl.

Then, as she stood her ground, she perceived that those eyes were regarding her intelligently. She there was still living, though perhaps dying. Anyway, she looked at it; and compassion forbade Ivy to flee.

'Oh, please excuse,' she stammered out, 'I've missed my way from Carreg Cenen, and thought to ask it. It's a long distance from over there. I've disturbed you... I never meant...' Voice and nerve failed her to go on.

'What! Have you walked from Carreg Cenen?' said the Grey Lady kindly. 'You must be very tired. Would you not like to rest yourself for a few minutes? Will you come in?'

Ivy, who was quick-witted, had recovered herself. "I was a sheep to be scared so just because she looks a bit ill." 'Oh, I'll be pleased to,' she responded aloud. There was nothing so terrifying here after all when you came to look. The wasted features were delicate, the eyes came to life as the lips spoke. And Ivy had caught a glimpse of the old-world house interior. 'I'm raging to see inside,' she thought. 'Just the quaintest old tenement! With the dearest old lady ghost hanging on to it!' For that it was the lady speaking was as obvious to her as, to the lady, that Ivy was an American girl on her travels. Such mutual introduction seemed enough, and she stepped into the little hall.

Ravishing to Ivy beyond any millionaire's palace was the simple, sober symmetry of a Welsh country house – the old oak flooring, settle, chest, and woodwork. 'Those fixings were sawn before ever the *Mayflower* set sail,' she thought enviously. 'And that oak staircase I'd love to carry straight off to Kansas City. Ho! The lady ghost has a flesh-and-blood maid, at all events,' as a female domestic showed herself at a doorway in the passage, eyeing Ivy unpleasantly.

A handsome but evil and insolent face that gave her a turn, like the scarecrow her imagination had conjured up in the Golden Avenue. Better the Grey Ghost by far, Ivy felt, shut in with her now in the sitting-room opening on the veranda, a room whose faded, decaying upholstery and tottering furniture seemed, like its occupant, perilously nearing its end.

Like to like! Ivy's young eyes flew straight to the one thing bright and beautiful here visible. A vignette portrait in pastels of a young girl that hung over the fireplace.

Such a girl! Coils of Italian-like dark hair crowning a brilliant young face, vivid-complexioned and of thrilling vivacity. It shone there like a jewel in a vault. What was it sent the visitor's eye rebounding to the withered visage beneath the shawl, wondering doubtfully? The Grey Lady shook her head.

'My sister Julie,' she said, 'who died in May.' Lingeringly, as to herself, she added, 'The May after that likeness was painted.'

'What eyes!' murmured the fascinated Ivy. 'They dance, they sing. Yet – she died?'

The grey face smiled wistfully, the white lips let fall:

'Here where we were born and brought up – so suddenly – as by the visitation of God – she was taken. . . . Over forty years gone by.'

"And you, you poor old dear, have you been mouldering here ever since?" Ivy wondered on silently. But she said, regarding the lovely hill-and-dale prospect from the windows, 'What a beautiful place this is, and how happy you must be to live here and have all these enjoyments without the seeking!'

'While I,' the other resumed unheedingly, 'who had gone hence to be married at the New Year, was never to set foot in the old home again till . . . yesterday, was it? No, longer ago than that, but not much. One forgets. Few here now remember me or my dear – my lost husband.'

'A widow, then,' thought Ivy pondering. 'And she – Julie?'

'Never a bride!'

Ivy, startled at the prompt reply, perceived she had been thinking aloud.

'Forgive me if I seem impertinent,' she said. 'But when people are nice to me as you have been I get interested in them, forget my play talk and company manners, and long to know what their lives are and all that they do and have done.'

She could not keep her eyes from that face on the wall there – 'So fair and morning-eyed!' 'She is beautiful,' she let fall.

'I was not,' said the Grey Woman. 'And yet—'

'It was you he preferred.' The words sprang spontaneously from Ivy's lips.

The strangeness of it, that they two, only just met together, two with half a century and the ocean between their ages and their homes, and who did not know so much as one another's names, should be discoursing thus, was unfelt by both, as though mutually hypnotised. Ivy's sympathetic little soul went out to the lonely invalid. While to her, the native born, the Spirit of Place was calling back the remote facts that had determined her life's course, and moving her to relate them to this eager and attractive listener who had dropped, as it were, from the clouds.

'We were not brought up orderly – not like other girls. Father and mother had poor health, and lived in a way of their own to humour it. Their dress and habits were peculiar; they kept odd hours, paid no visits and received none. My Frankie and I used to meet by the stealth in the lanes after dusk, till the whole countryside rang with our romance, shocked out of measure.'

'Why?' asked the New World maiden naively.

'Well, it was not customary,' her hostess explained with a passing smile. 'Only farmers' or labourers' daughters did such things, and it was many generations since our husbandmen ancestors had struggled up into the ranks of the gentry. People wrote to tell my mother of the scandal. It had to be stopped, and we were forbidden to meet. Frankie and I stopped it. We ran away.'

'Oh, well done!' came from the impulsive Ivy. She thought a good deal. The narrator pursued.

'Julie was against it. She said, "He is delightful, but he will make you miserable. He must. He was known for a waster and a free-liver." I said, "You wait here for your saint and prince. He loves me. And I? By him I stand or fall. But I think… I believe… that together we shall stand." Then she helped us. Had she lived she would have agreed that I was right. And yet,' in an undertone, distantly, 'Julie was not quite wrong.'

Ivy felt as if between two phantom-like presences. For Julie there opposite, so fair and free-hearted in her unspent youth, radiant with energy and the joy of life, seemed every bit as real to her as the shadow-woman in the chair, the woman with the shrunken, marred visage, stamped with the wear and tear of a long and chequered life – joys of the sweetest, sorrows of the sharpest, the tribulations and ups and down of a life lived out bravely to its desolate end. "Game to the last bunch of feathers!" thought Ivy, admiring the spark of Julie-like animation smouldering in those dimmed and dimming eyes. Sister souls, Julie and she. But what an unspeakable gap between their destinies! Which, now, was the more blessed?

III

Here a piece of buxom humanity – the sinister-looking maid-servant Ivy had caught sight of in the passage – came sauntering past the veranda. Her watchful stare inside was as purposely insolent as a grimace. The lady rose sharply, opened the window and stepped out to give some peremptory order. The reply it provoked Ivy did not catch, but it seemed of the box-on-the-ear, slap-in-the-face temper. A moment's altercation followed, then the maid walked away, but the little passage-at-arms had upset the old lady. With difficulty she got back into the room, a ghastly pallor on her cheek, a glassy look in her eyes. She staggered and fell. Ivy caught her in her arms and lifted her on to the sofa, shocked at finding but a mere featherweight to lift.

"Fainted. Now if I yell for help," Ivy reflected, "it will only bring back that devil of a woman – enough to kill her outright." Without an instant's hesitation she went into the passage and through a door into the servant's quarters, and faced the demon in her kitchen den.

'Some water for your mistress,' she demanded. 'She has

fainted.'

'My mistress, indeed!' came the answer. 'I take no orders from her – nor from you – whoever you may be.'

'I give no orders,' said Ivy, promptly. Her sharp eyes had immediately detected a brandy bottle half full on the dresser.

'But a thimbleful of that – *if you can spare it* – with some water, will bring her round. I would save you the trouble.'

She had scored – got what she wanted; and in a few minutes had revived the prostrate invalid, who struggled to a sitting posture with a bewildered look round. 'You were taken bad,' said Ivy soothingly, 'and just toppling over when I caught you. I thought if I called your servant you might be annoyed.'

The lady shuddered. All that was left of her seemed to cling to the kindly girl. "Appallingly weak and just terrified of that woman," thought Ivy, perplexed and concerned.

'Not my servant,' she was told. 'She and her husband stayed on in charge here after the last owner's death, and my coming displeased her, for good reasons of her own. A strange breed too; no native here.'

'Well, I tell you our home helps in Kansas don't spoil us,' said Ivy feelingly, 'but that type makes me feel boiling inside.'

The Grey Ghost smiled. The eye-spark flickered again, and in a few minutes she seemed to Ivy about as much alive as before. Presently, to their mutual surprise, the maid-demon brought in the tea, for which previous order had been given.

"Brazen thing!" thought Ivy; "she just wanted to know what we were doing. She can't look me in the face, though. I'd give anything to see the inside of her head."

Recalling that tea with the Grey Ghost, Ivy could think herself the dupe of false memory, though every detail of it is as clear to her mind's eye as a Dutch picture seen under a triplex American arc.

'She who had just now seemed utterly broke in spirit and body seemed to grow almost fit again,' so Ivy afterwards described the scene, 'as she went chattering on at a great rate, telling me heaps and stacks of things – her life's tale, but all in scraps, like nuggets. A grey bundle of energy, sunk in the chair, she held me fast by a moving show of pictures in the web of her life.'

"A web of tangled yarn," from the leaving of her home, with one irrevocably dear, chronically undeserving. One with lofty ideals, good gifts, and right intuitions, yet in conduct falling often below the level of the despised Philistine. One to wreck the life of a feebler partner – their life's voyage together a twenty years' venture – but whose bark her unflagging spirit and resource had kept afloat to the last. Children born and reared to become fresh springs of joy and of anguish; bright hopes gleaming and ending like rockets; poverty that failed to depress, windfalls that failed to enrich; a haphazard existence spent chiefly abroad – for cheapness – births, sicknesses, deaths; a troubled sea out of which in her widowhood she had drifted into a quiet backwater in a foreign town with a beloved son, the last survivor of her offspring, not one of whom were built for a long span, alas!

If, after losing him, she had gone on living, it was from habit only.

And now the old home, passed long ago into the hands of distant kinsmen, had reverted to her ownership, heavily mortgaged and valueless, a prey to be handed over to the speculative builder – a mock heritage that had brought her hither from the little German capital where she still sat mourning for her best beloved. She was wanted here to order and to rule, but had arrived to succumb only, and to vanish.

Every once in a while the graveyard shadow crept over her countenance, wiping out the life therein. She thrilled it back till the thread of reminiscence was ended, leading her on to where Julie had lain these many years.

IV

For it was only a flare-up after all. Back came that mortal pallor, never more to be driven away. The maid-devil re-entered stealthily. 'Oh mercy!' moaned poor Ivy, to whom the room seemed full of shudders. When that hard, cruel, handsome face had removed itself, together with the tea-things, the invalid, with a final effort to rally, said feebly:

'It's poor hospitality I've shown you, young lady!'

'Why no – quite a flourish tea, you mean,' said Ivy cheerfully. 'But I'm troubling you.' The Grey Ghost rose totteringly; Ivy helped her back to the sofa, where she lay unable to speak or to stir, Ivy now fully alive to her own predicament. Alone in a strange house with its dying mistress, an utter stranger. Ought she not properly to withdraw her interloping presence? 'And leave her with that she-devil?' her nominal servant, the real mistress and tormentor of the moribund lady of the manor. 'The idea makes me sick. But I must call someone.' She moved, but the quick, appealing, detaining hold taken of the little dainty hand was heart-rending. 'Hark you,' said Ivy, steadily. 'Strike me dead if I leave you alone with her! Let me go. I'll polish her off, that I swear.' Gently disengaging herself she went quickly back to the dragon's den and asked her:

'Where is your husband?'

'And what do you want with him, pray?' demanded the woman, incensed.

'I want you,' said Ivy, 'to tell him to go straight to Llanffelix for the doctor, and not to come back without him. The lady here is perilously ill – dying, I fear.'

'Oh these old people!' was the rejoinder. 'They give a lot of trouble! Why can't she die and have done with it?'

'Mind you,' said Ivy, restraining herself, 'I am staying at the Glendower Arms in the town. If you refuse to take my warning and my advice – well, it shall be known there; and you will be blamed, should this poor lady die unattended.'

The shot had told. The hostelry was one of standing. County families stayed there. Ivy might belong to one of these for all that the house-servant could tell. She went out into the yard. 'Nat!' she shouted peremptorily. An absent-minded, subdued-looking Welshman emerged from the shed where he was chopping wood. Ivy stayed to hear the message given and see the man start, nothing loth, on his errand to the town. 'Urgent mind!' she called out after him, and turning her back on the wife flew back to the faded parlour where the lady lay in a stupor. But she stirred faintly, and her eyes glimmered consciousness at the girl's approach. 'I don't know who you are,' she said, 'but it seems to me I have been entertaining an angel unawares.'

'She's slipped back a few paces since I left the room,' poor Ivy observed, dismayed. She was sinking fast now. Restoratives avail not where nothing is left to restore. Immeasurable to Ivy was the hour and a half that she sat there, by the light of a solitary candle, watching the departing spirit, herself on the verge of collapse under the nerve tension of the closing scene of that strange afternoon. Only Julie, who could never grow old, seemed to become more living, beaming joy and welcome down on the sister, worn and widowed, who was coming to meet her. This that was happening was not a calamity or a tragedy, but a change. So felt the looker-on.

At intervals she spoke, in broken accents; but through those disconnected utterances ran a traceable thread. Not death, but life taking lingering leave of her; the latter years the first to slip away – widowhood, motherhood, wifehood – as a tale that is told. Then the love romance of half a century away.

"He says there's none he'd rather meet 'neath moon
or star,

Than me – of all that are!"

she said slowly, not loudly, with an emphasis that rings in the girl's ears to this day.

Lastly, the old home life with Julie in the House that Was – things from the very Back of Beyond of memory; snatches of talk and jest. She saw Julie everywhere – in Ivy – in the picture, fitfully recalling little happenings, follies, drolleries, things childish, even babyish, trifles every one, yet undying, as are things felt in the beginning, when God created the heavens and the earth; and those young things questioned not but that for themselves and their pleasure they are and were created.

At length, when Ivy was feeling almost as old as her charge, came the relieving sound of wheels on the drive – and an arrival. The Satanic servant woman, in the guise of a pattern parlourmaid and with the mien of a ministering angel, announced, 'Dr Edwards.'

At the sight of the strong, benignant, prosperous, and fatherly looking professional man, Ivy was herself again at once.

In a word or two she explained her position. A stranger to the patient, she was none – little though she suspected it – to the Llanffelix medical magnate. The pretty little American girl staying at the Glendower Arms had been the three days' wonder and talk of the town, and he accepted her accidental presence here without surprise. Then he looked at the inanimate form on the sofa, put his finger on the flickering pulse and shook his head, saying:

'Her life is over. Only her wonderful spirit has kept her here in this world so long. There is nothing to be done – nothing.'

He seemed at least concerned for the young lady herself, nerve-worn and wearied out. 'You must get home,' he told her. She hesitated, then came out with it:

'I have vowed not to leave her alone with that – that creature; I mean with nobody to moan to but that servant-woman. They had a little wrestling-match a while ago that ended disastrously, in a faint.' She looked at him significantly, and saw he understood.

'We feared as much,' he sighed. 'But it was difficult; it seemed that it needed a stranger and a foreigner like yourself to interfere to protect her. But the man Nat, though a booby and a chicken-heart, is a good fellow, and I got enough out of him to make me bring a nurse along with me – one who knew her and whom once she knew – Ruth Harris, the daughter of old Betty who nursed them both.'

'Both?'

'Both.'

He was looking at Julie's face in the portrait, fixedly, intently, as though it meant something to him. Might his boyhood's romance, perhaps, lie buried in the grave with her? – a student lad's adoration – a mere jest, perhaps, to the beauty there in the pride of her youth? Ivy wondered, but she never knew.

'I am sending my servant back to Llanffelix with an order,' he said. 'He shall drive you to the Glendower Arms.'

'If I am of no service here,' Ivy assented. 'Only . . . that serpent – that hateful woman. . . .'

'Shall not come near her. You may trust Ruth not to leave her for a moment, and I myself shall stay on for as long as may be necessary.'

Ivy bent down and kissed the pale, fine forehead, then turned to go. The doctor shook hands with her, saying emphatically:

'You have done a beautiful thing, young lady – a thing for which I would thank you, as would not a few others that are left, right heartily, did they but know – softened the last hours of one of the cleverest and most charming women that they ever knew.'

Ivy drove from the door, her memory indelibly impressed by the image of the Lady of the House that Was.

She never recovered consciousness, Ivy heard on the morrow, but died at dawn, so quietly that to the watchers the moment was all but imperceptible when she crossed the border into the Land of Memory.

The Courtship of "Ragged Robin"

That was not his name, nor yet his nickname.

In a lawyer's deed he would figure as Robert John David Morgan Lloyd, of Penglas. "Ragged Robin" was a fancy pet-name privately bestowed upon him by Miss Durden, of Bryncennin, the lady-owner of the substantial Welsh farm holding whereon, so far as in him lay, he flourished.

He had nephews and nieces occupying good positions in the service of Church and State, as did their photographs in Penglas farm parlour. Himself a son of the soil, he had been faithful, all his fifty years, to his Mother Earth. His only resemblance to the above-named pretty pink flower of his hayfields lay in a sort of naturally dilapidated cut; a jagged negligence of hair, beard, gait, attitude, and attire. He might not be the most reputable figure on the Bryncennin estate, but he was far and away the most picturesque.

See him aslouch in the tedder, supplying the human touch to an exquisite pastoral! Stand in the adjacent upland meadow and watch the cart as it crosses the skyline, dimly seen between the three lights – daylight, twilight, and moonlight contending. Rose-colour in the west; across the valley a wavy line of distant hills; and a pale crescent moon hanging low, just over Robin's head as he and his equipage draw by, with a whirligig of hay in their wake.

Or see him posed, leaning on his pitchfork, in a winter-bound wood, looking like an untidy Faun, or some higher deity in sylvan disguise; his garb all run to fringe, as usual; his face – well, if unclean, it was certainly not common, but it had never had fair play nor good treatment. How far the

divine fire in his eyes was due to genius, and not to gin, it were
ungracious to inquire. Hear him discourse slowly, solemnly,
of the frozen earth, undergoing a rest-cure, he considered, of
fruitful promise for the coming May – as a man talks of his
own. The inwardness of these things was in his utterances.
He was nearer, more one with nature than the smart young
farmers, with their spruce neckties and music-hall whistlings.
Between Robert John David Morgan Lloyd and the sheep and
kine he tended there was a truer understanding. He did not
expect more of them than they could easily give. Nothing like
a sense of our own limitations to make us tolerant of incapacity
in others.

Still, it was only from the artistic point of view that he could
command unqualified approval. His "habits" were tacitly
accepted by his kindred as unalterable. There were things in
this world you had to put up with, and Robert was one. But
one shudders to think of his inevitable, his gruesome fate, had
the lot fallen to him in a town. In the home of his forefathers
he just managed to hold up his unkempt head. A place on the
hearth and at the board would be vouchsafed him up to the
end. He might chafe under his subordination, he who should
have been master and lord there, yet scarcely dared lift up his
voice, much less overrule the decisions of his orderly sister
and brother-in-law, who ran the farm. Still, he was sensible
of where the blame lay; and his attitude towards himself was,
like theirs, one of faintly sentimental pity for the backslider.

But if "Ragged Robin" was harmless, as mere man goes,
agriculturally useful, and appealed pleasantly to idle poetic
instincts, he suddenly became a haunting terror to Miss
Durden, when it transpired that he was paying his addresses to
Lois Roy, these many years the family housemaid, and become
the treasure, the very pivot, of the household.

No ordinary housemaid was Lois, but a personage, and
a favourite wherever she showed her handsome, cheerful,
buxom, bouncing self. I should weary you with a list of her

many excellences. She combined the fine physique of the country-bred (which she was not) with the brisk wits and ways of the trained Londoner. Her age? Pedantic to inquire. Lois was, and always had been, in the prime of life. Her faults? Well, never were faults and virtues more interdependent than in her temperament. Her splendid vitality enabled her perpetually to defy the truths of logic, science, prudence – so far without dire disaster. Transported recently of a sudden from a London suburban residence to a wild Welsh mountain side, remote from the numberless household conveniences and appliances she was used to see come penny-in-the-slot fashion, and to regard as indispensable as shoes and stockings, she was not disconcerted – not seriously. Nor was she a woman to depart one inch from her standard, or her style of dress, at the beck and call of a half-fashioned country with an ill-regulated climate. The mountain gales might blow the birds' nests out of the bushes, but seemed powerless to rumple her edifice of hair. Her smart gowns and hats withstood the naughtiest pranks of the most abandoned weather. Order and symmetry were the gods of her idolatry; and though not so weak a vessel as to break down under rough-and-tumble, makeshift conditions, look tolerantly on such things she would not. How she would have liked to tell these proud Celts in their own tongue what she thought of their manners and customs! Much of her eloquent King's English was, she found, as a tinkling cymbal in their ears. But she interested them as a phenomenal person, too remote from themselves for them even to fancy they understood her, and she was good friends with all.

When first "Ragged Robin," going farther, openly singled her out as a "tidy young woman" to admire, his little Welsh world laughed at the old bachelor. Nay, even after it had come to an offer of marriage, casually made at the kitchen door, the affair seemed but an airy jest. Wicked Welsh lads egged him on, for the fun of the thing, hinting at Lois's possible savings – while not for a twinkling second would Lois's English fellow-servants treat the matter as earnest. What! Lois – *Lois* go with that *tramp*! Judged by appearances, indeed, you would have sworn that Robert John David Morgan Lloyd was quite out of the question.

But the eyes of experience, in Miss Durden, saw yawning depths beyond, and that there was trouble, sore and terrible, ahead.

Friends gave facile advice. "Women of Lois's age are susceptible to flattery. Do not let her tie herself to a man of that sort." And how to prevent it, pray? Here was a life-problem, common enough, but as fateful as any that Ibsen or Sudermann ever handled. Certainly Lois was human, and her Welsh conquest surprised and did not displease her. But Robin's real chance lay in his wholly unintentional and unconscious appeal to her ultra-compassionate impulses. Now, against these, if mistress or menial had ever the inhumanity to argue, they succeeded only in sinking themselves in her esteem. Her rule was to give to those in want, nor look beyond – a magnificent principle, that made of Bryncennin a paradise for all the undesirable dogs, cats, fowls, in the vicinity – to poor, meek Miss Durden's untold discomfort and the destruction of her beloved garden. Well did those cunning animals – like beggars in the street – know how to impose on the kindly almoner at the back door by a theatrical display of woe. It was not difficult.

Now "Ragged Robin" had obviously fallen somewhat from the estate to which Robert John David Morgan Lloyd was born; he lived and moved under a cloud, sometimes unfairly depreciated or put upon. Now the merest molehill of injustice could raise mountains of generous indignation in Lois. She was one heedlessly to race down the road to ruin, to remedy some trifling wrong.

The illusions of reason are more obdurate than those of sentiment. Speak to her? As sensibly might the Dean "speak" to the dome of St. Paul's. Without jumping at the offer, she had taken it in good part, and was kind and civil-tongued to her suitor. Henceforth he would waylay her as she went to the post, staring out suddenly from behind a hedge to renew his addresses, or call in on some pretext when the highly superior cook and housekeeper – whose steady glance he never could meet – was out of the way. In short, the pair were drifting steadily, cheerily on to Hymen and hopeless ruin of mind, body, and estate.

High-handed interference with "servant" or "tenant" is obsolete as the feudal system. Moreover, Robert Lloyd was the scion of ancient tenantry, and had many a time enlarged to Miss Durden on his heart's desire to live and die on the old estate. How could even an English lady be so brutal as to hint to such a one that he would be a *mèsalliance* for her housemaid? Lois, for her long and faithful service, was near to that lady's heart, and when informed that she had given her word in favour of Mr Lloyd, of Penglas, for three whole nights Miss Durden never slept a wink.

For "Ragged Robin's" "habits" were, alas! notorious. His own kindred might have their reasons for bearing with them philosophically – for them the thing was possible; but they meant misery and something more to a wife like Lois. Regularity was the soul of her existence, and there *was* a point where her tolerance came to a full stop. She would be wretched first, and come to hate him at last. She was excitable, had short patience with wrong, and was recklessly ready with boomerang-like repartee. Robert Lloyd was a mild man on the face of him, but every Cymro has a wildfire within him, to be reckoned with when incensed. Unable to retaliate adequately in a foreign language, he might – what might he not? But Lois's face was set as a flint. There was nothing to do but to speculate, grimly, on the precise form the coming Village Tragedy would take.

The matter had been kept quiet by the parties concerned, who disrelished the jocularity of the local wags. Miss Durden was just going back to her London flat for a week or two, taking Lois. Forthwith Mr Lloyd announced his intention of visiting the metropolis. He had relations there who would house him, and he wanted Lois, in her leisure hours, to show him round. She was as willing as she was competent. What sort of figure, Miss Durden wondered, would "Ragged Robin" cut in the streets of the great city?

Nothing less like a husbandman in Sunday clothes was ever seen! A smart journalist would have classed him, off-hand, as a decayed gentleman – one of the failures of our University system. He might be the legendary shabby-genteel baronet who has come down to driving a cab or turning a street-organ. He and Lois (looking as though she had unearthed some strange old uncle) went the round of the favourite entertainments, as orderly and soberly as you please. Any forlorn though fiendish hope in Lois's friends that his bacchic failing would loom large under the temptations of the big Babylon were very properly disappointed. Then he went home. Lois saw him off at Paddington. Three days later she came to Miss Durden in tears.

Tears, with Lois, were no melting mood, but tantamount to a positive announcement: to wit, that she had thrown up the sponge, and would not be responsible for whatever was going to happen now. She could not be miserable – no more than anything else – by halves. Miss Durden nerved herself, beset by distressful imaginings. 'What is it, Lois?' she asked, with the calm of despair.

'Oh, Miss Durden!' – Lois's speech was punctuated with sobs – 'it's Robert... Mr Lloyd. I feel... I am afraid... I cannot marry him after all!'

'Praise Heaven for that!' Miss Durden sang in her soul, and felt ten years younger on the spot. But she merely said, gravely, 'Why is it? You told me your mind was made up. What has he done?'

'Nothing – oh, nothing, poor man! That's what's so

dreadful!' Her utterances after this were unintelligible unless
you had known her for years. Well, there are awful mistakes
in life you can never view as such, until perpetrated. Lois's
engagement was one. But companionship in London – her real
medium – had somehow brought home to her (she did not for
the life of her know why, nor would even for a moment have
admitted) that mutual fellowship was out of the question, and
that partnership would be her ruin.

'Have you told him of your altered mind?'

'I don't dare,' she said shudderingly, 'for fear of how he
might take it. He's told me again and again I'm the one bright
star in his unhappy life! I'm ever so sorry for him, poor dear!
If he thought I could forsake him I know it would drive him
wild – or to drink – or to make away with himself. Oh miss,
what am I to do?'

Miss Durden preserved a thoughtful silence.

'Perhaps,' Lois sobbed, 'I thought perhaps… *you* could tell
him… break it to him… and see how he bears it.'

Of course Miss Durden undertook the task, but it was with
dire forebodings that she returned to Bryncennin. Crimes of
violence had hitherto been absent in that Arcadia. Probably no
one there, so far as was known, had died other than a natural
death, or furnished a lethal horror-paragraph for local papers.
But the columns of the latter were never short of such blood-
curdling events. A dispute about the rival merits of the English
or Welsh languages had ended fatally only the other day. A
brawl about a watercourse, or an open gate, leads frequently
to assault and battery. So she kept deferring the dread ordeal,
saying to herself daily she would send for him "tomorrow."
Then one "tomorrow," as she was leaving the house, she
met him at the gate – demanding an interview – which she
granted then and there, in unspeakable fear and trembling.
Did he know? Did he suspect? Was he sober? Would his
wrath, his vengeance, fall on her – suspecting her meddling

interference?

A weird presence, in characteristically ragged trousers, coat, comforter, and hat, he sat, confronting her. Sober he was, out of doubt, but that eye was like the disturbed and disturbing eye of a madman with some fell purpose. Furtively she bethought her of how to flee, in the event of a "brain-storm" coming on. Had he, apprised of Lois's fickleness, murdered her, or another – seized by an "uncontrollable impulse" to do something shocking? It seemed written in his face: *Bryncennin Horror! Girl Shot! Suicide of the Assailant.*

'I have a confession I wish to make to you,' he said in a muffled, measured tone of ominous import, 'but it must be a secret between you and me. Give me your promise.' And she gave it, as you humour the mentally afflicted.

Half an hour later "Ragged Robin" had gone and Miss Durden sat shaking with joyous, half-hysterical laughter – laughter at her apprehensions that now seemed grotesque, and amusement at their complete removal and the manner of it.

For the "confession" was to the effect that closer contact with his fiancée's position, walk in life, circle of friends of her own class, and social ideas, had brought it to him sorrowfully to see that he, the rightful, if dethroned tenant-king of Penglas, would lose caste seriously by such a marriage.

He might demean himself so far for love's sake. But such a match could never command the complete approval of his relatives. It would expose Lois to slights and slurs, which would pain him and make her uncomfortable.

'I couldn't tell her this – I wouldn't wound her feelings – not for the whole world. But – I fear me – she would feel out of place amongst us…'

Undoubtedly she would! Here Miss Durden had chimed in with a sigh of sympathy.

Could she get him out of it? he wanted to know. Could she persuade Miss Roy that for both their sakes it were better they should be content to remain friends, and friends only?

Yes, she thought she could. He himself had furnished her with the word: "She would feel out of place among us!" and in due course he learnt that Lois owned he and she were no proper match for one another, and that he was free.

It is many moons since these events. Lois's honeymoon was amongst them. For she made a glorious love-match just a twelvemonth later, with an Admirable Crichton of an ex-butler – now a state official in a London Museum – and finds perfect felicity with him, at Peckham.

"Ragged Robin" still adorns the green pastures and oaken groves of his birthplace, and is likely to do so for the best part of another half-century, the picture of a homekeeping vagabond – immovable, irreclaimable. But he has his innocent enjoyments, and among them is the deploring of what has really been his salvation: the dependence – the limitations of his lot.

The Castle of Sleep

He came upon it late one afternoon, worn, wet, and wearied by a fifty mile fight with foul weather. The cycle gave out first, vanquished, then the man. Instantly, as at a signal shot, the victor relented. The scenery shifted, the clouds vanished, and the sunset glory – enhanced by a magnificent rainbow arch – irradiated yonder, in the desert place alongside, the shape of a mighty ruin.

A long, irregular frontage, broken by turrets and projections, scarred and wrinkled, but palatial and imposing even in utter decay, it rose, a giant monument of history and romance.

'Oh, let's see this!' gasped the cyclist, and spent his last breath, or next to it, in dragging himself and his machine across to the castle gatehouse, in whose shelter, from sheer exhaustion, he dropped, and went dead asleep.

Alan Johns, journalist – his name and trade – travelled in literary work. A commission from a London syndicate had brought him hither, to furnish a series of popular articles on the chain of Norman castles that once guarded the coast of West Wales.

Here indeed, on the jagged sea-board of two counties – all creeks, bays, and estuaries, offering rich choice of landing-places to pirates and invaders – these strongholds were essential to the continued existence of their lords. Themselves but a handful of stranger settlers planted there between the furtive hostility of the common people and the quarrelsome friendship and sometimes treacherous alliance of the Welsh nobility and gentry, their lot was at all times a busy one. Witness these edifices – remarkable – nay, unique. Legion is their name. As

"The Castle of Sleep" – for reasons that will presently appear – this one abides in the memory of Alan Johns. A proper name it has, but its origin and early history, curiously enough, are lost, irrevocably, as the hues of the rainbow itself.

When the sleeper awoke, refreshed, night was impending. All that was visible was seen as through a veil, dimly.

Marshlands below – to seaward; grass-wastes to landward, with a single roadway stretching far and straight onward to its apparent termination – the sea. "The Back of Beyond", so another bewildered traveller has nicknamed the spot.

'I am out of humanity's reach,' this one would have said, had he not known otherwise.

'I shall lose my way if I attempt to pursue it,' he reflected. 'Well, provender and a pipe I have with me. Perfect shelter these stout walls afford. I shall sleep out. Constables don't trouble the Back of Beyond.'

The moon rose, a silver glory, mirrored in each white, reed-fringed pool, turning it to a fancy picture. Night brought the traveller what had failed him all day – light to restudy his map and guide-book comfortably.

But first to explore the ruins. Their extent and well-preserved features astonished him.

Fairly perfect in outline was that lordly dwelling house, the chapel with vestry and clerestory, the mural towers at the angles, the winding staircase leading to the gatehouse chamber which the cyclist was going to occupy tonight. These walls had outlasted the many noble dames and brave men they had sheltered aforetime. Their loves, hatreds, jealousies – the most poignant – had passed into nothingness, leaving no trace.

Can this be? Is it folly or latent insight in us that craves and calls for *some* remaining essence, some haunting emanation, which, meeting and striking some chance wandering kindred force, shall create a dim communion?

Freed from workaday external realities and distractions, the explorer's fancy, all agog, would fain have wormed out of those indestructible old walls, whose hospitality he had accepted, some one page of their forgotten history.

'Wouldn't you like to know the things we have seen and heard?' they seemed silently to be asking him.

'I believe in my soul you are longing to tell them,' Alan Johns retorted mentally. 'In the old fable,' so he mused on, 'the man who had tasted dragon's blood understood at once what the birds were saying. What should a man do? how should he try to steal here some glimpse of an unrecorded past?'

Well, precisely what he was doing now. Let the surroundings fill his eye and his mind with their mysterious significance – expel all else from that mind – then wait passively for some dim revelation.

Some such vague surmise was the traveller's last waking thought as he settled for the night in the roofless chamber.

What the moon saw was a benighted cyclist, sound asleep in the castle ruins.

But the sleeper, Alan Johns, was contemplating a drama whose scenery, plot, and personages were clearer and more living to him than those of any stage play.

Nay, more so than in real life as we know it. For, as he heard their lips' speech he saw into their hearts, and their thoughts became plainer to him than words, spoken or written, could have made them.

He and the ghostly presences he had invoked had changed places. His now was the merely spiritual presence, while figures long ago turned to dust had re-arisen in their persons, as they lived, to re-enact for him a scene here beheld at some period to which the dress and speech of the actors gave no more definite clue than that it was somewhat remote.

SCENE 1

Martin, sometime Lord of this castle, and Olwen, his beautiful wife. A man in the flower of his years, of commanding aspect, subtle-headed, tender-hearted, on the face of him, and his countenance alive with the immense, the unspeakable joy of a home-comer after years of absence on hard service. It rang in his voice as he spoke.

'Sit nearer; sit where I can see you Olwen. I may not look away, or sleep, or lose sense that this hour, so longed for, so often utterly despaired of, is mine at last.'

'I too have lived for it,' she told him. 'If sometimes a voice said, 'You are feeding on air,' I would not listen. But of the ill that might have been what need to think, now that you are here and all well?'

'Nay, dear heart! Too often, these three years, has this safe return to my hearth mocked me as the mad dream of a dotard. Without were fightings – within were fears.'

'What fears?'

'Of the arrow that flieth by night; the pestilence that destroyeth in the noonday. Not least, misorder and disaffection in my good men. Of mercenaries – of our Welsh levies – what leader can ever be utterly sure?'

'They behaved?'

'Like children in matters of reason; in fighting like one man, and he of the best. In time of peace never at peace with one another.'

Olwen smiled.

'There I know my countrymen. But you have brought them back with good and brave renown, and scarce a man missing.'

'Save Maelwas the Northman – expelled. He would have slain a sleeping comrade for some petty grudge he owed him. So a man who values not his own life has that of others in his keeping.'

'Another ill-deed prevented,' said Olwen gently.

'Ay! But I am weary – pray to be delivered awhile from court and camp alike. Is it the long sickness of hope deferred? Now the desire – the tree of life that should be – has come, I could weep like a woman.'

His brow contracted with the persistent after-sense of pains endured. Olwen, with a sweet intuitive movement, bent down and kissed it lightly.

'Beloved!' he murmured inaudibly; then, mastering himself, 'Life means strife, wherever you tread. But thank God we are one again. Our wedding-night, as it were, Olwen.'

A child cried out from the inner room. Olwen went to the plaintive call, which hushed quickly; then she came again, saying:

'Since I first spoke to Cecil of your return I can hardly still him to sleep.'

'Poor babe! I wonder, Olwen that you have kept remembrance alive in him so long – in one so young. He knew me when I came, I think for he kissed me.'

'He was dreaming of you just now. Babbling, just as though in his sleep he had overheard our talk, of the strange dangers from which he would save you.'

'I, too, dreamt strangely last night, where we camped last,' Martin said presently, musing, 'of returning here to find the Dogs of Death, the White Hounds of the Underworld Ivor tells us of, waiting for me, crouched on the threshold.'

'A folk-tale only,' laughed Olwen who was not superstitious. 'Instead, it was only Jestyn you met there, on the watch.'

'Dog-like indeed is our steward in patience and fidelity. He said that in the stars, which he was studying, he had read of my return, appointed before I knew of it myself – to the very day almost.'

'These many months he has fallen to such studies. His talk, when at times he tries to tell me of them, is but a strange jargon. He is persuaded that in his asterisms and signs and constellations he can foreknow the destinies of whom he will, and the fortunes or infortunes that will come to pass.'

'I have heard there are those who hold it. Think you, Olwen, there be any verity in the art – some spice of truth?'

'Be there or not,' answered Olwen, 'it is not he – Jestyn – who will unfold their mystery. I saw him once, out on the plain, tracing quaint signs and figures on the sand with his stick, and talking low to himself of prognostics, significations, and consignifications, ascensions – deeply rapt in these fancies – as one distraught.'

'For him, who grows old, it serves as a pastime; as for the young, song or sport,' Martin said carelessly, resuming, after a pause:

'And the boy Ivor, how does he, now he is grown into more years? Is it with him as ever? Still loitering his way through life in the lazy-going Welsh fashion? A little hunting, a little hawking, a little fishing and shooting of wild-fowl over tarns, not a little harping and song-singing, and much dreaming over things that have been, and things that will be, in days never to come to pass?'

'As ever.' Olwen averted her face, visibly troubled.

'I would he were here now,' said Martin heartily, 'with some song of Wales to charm away melancholy and silence ill foreboding. There was one I liked – you rendered the words for me in English – do you remember, Olwen?' – and Martin sang out in a resonant if untutored voice,

> 'By the salt waves walking I saw alight
> A wild sea-mew. It was lily-white;
> Wet with the ocean-foam that clings,
> On the warm sand drying its underwings.
>
> I wept for the one I might not meet;
> The sea-bird fluttered to my feet –
> I gave to its white wing, to bear afar,
> A love-sign to her – my guiding star.'

'How often has that come back to me in my exile! Only the carrier-bird I could not trust. What troubles you, Olwen?'

'Nothing – nothing.'

'Something there was?'

'Just a thought that passed – a thought only.'

'Away with it – for tonight! You shall tell it me tomorrow.'

'Child that you are! I think, Martin, all men are children. In that they are happier, lighter-hearted than we.'

As she spoke there appeared standing in the doorway, his approach as unheard as a phantom, a figure whose garb and demeanour denoted a high-placed, trusted house-servant or steward. He carried a salver with refreshments.

Not an ill-looking knave, but a certain disjointedness of limb and movements, and disproportion of features well-shapen separately, gave a crooked singularity to his aspect, as it were the travesty of a human being.

'Thanks, Jestyn,' said Martin, taking the win-cup from him with a courteous grace. 'What of the soldiery, come home to beat their swords into ploughshares and their spears into pruning-hooks? Feasting still? or fallen out over some grave matter of song or of supper?'

'They are giving your good health,' the man answered, 'in the barn over the hill that I appointed for their riot, for fear lest their noise should vex you and my lady. When I left them they were wishing you might live for ever.'

''Tis well, so that their potations be not prolonged in equal measure. My thanks to them! Do you not join the revels, Jestyn?'

The man made a negative sign. 'I have other, graver work appointed for me tonight, and would keep sober,' he said.

'Reading of the planets, is it? How stand they configurated at this hour? Are the aspects favourable?'

'Unto some of us.' He smiled wryly.

'How of my lady Olwen here?'

'The Sun and the Moon, as rulers of the First and Seventh

Houses, stand in mutual square; the Moon in her fall and opposition with Saturn.'

'Which signifieth?'

'At this hour, all that for her I should most desire.'

'And of yourself what are they telling?' came from Martin, in faintly curious and amused inquiry.

'Mercury and Mars are in quartile, Mercury constituting the principal, with opposition of Saturn and Mars. The Moon comes to a direct opposition of Mars by direct direction, while she occupies the cusp of the Sixth House, representing – an adversary.'

'You talk in riddles, Jestyn. These prognostics –'

'Warn of secret and dissembling foes, from whom, not without danger, I may myself deliver,' was the reply, given with a respectful solemnity that yet betrayed the man's inward relish in mystifying his master.

'Ay, ay; one of my knaves playing some fool's trick on you, stealing or hiding some household bauble, for which, if he be reprehended or punished, you risk a broken head. Such, I have observed, is what these mighty significators amount to in the fulfilment. Well. But have a care, Jestyn. In the brooding on such figments, as in the wine-cup, one may leave one's wits; and haply find them harder to recover.'

It was lightly and friendlily spoken. Silently, furtively, as he had come, the man withdrew. Neither Martin nor Olwen turned, or saw the look he cast back at his master.

And only the Moon saw the sleeper stir and shift uneasily in his sleep; struggling with an impulse to cry out, the cry dying inarticulate as the dream swept him onward.

> 'I gave to its white wing to bear afar
> A message to her – my guiding star—'

sang Martin again, but broke off, saying: 'There, I have no skill. We must have Ivor here with his harp and musician's cunning that would charm the heaviest-hearted soul into some Paradise.'

Olwen did not respond, interposing quickly: 'Jestyn wants your hand over him, I think. He grows so wayward and fitful. At times I can do nothing with him.'

'Poor old soul! He has been with you since you had your first being; and you will always seem but a child in his eyes.'

'He talks so mysteriously, so wildly, of plots and persecutors. At moments he has put me in fear of him, even.'

Martin laughed aloud. 'Oh, you can see how it is with him. A quaint-tempered knave from his birth up, and mocked for that by his fellows. This has held him aloof, and now he needs must go cumber his wits with studies that serve for naught. He loves me not, I fear. But his devotion to you is the seal of his fidelity.'

'Father! *Father*!'

Again came the child's cry from the inner room. Martin rose and went straight to the couch of the little son, who was sitting up, dreaming with his blue eyes wide open. He clutched the soldierly hand and sank back, still clinging to it tightly as, soothed by the touch, he fell into a deep, untroubled sleep again. Martin did not stir. A sudden gust of wind closed the door of the bed-chamber.

Olwen, alone in the outer room, rose suddenly, moving uneasily, as if possessed by some overhanging presentiment.

Then, in the dead stillness, from far off, sounds caught her ear; faint, soft sounds that smote her like a stab.

Not the mirth of the revellers in the hill-barn. A voice singing in the night, a song known only to herself and the song-maker – harping as he sang, out there in the wild; dim, broken sounds, but to her, fatally intelligible.

Young Ivor, of Dinasmadoc, her boy neighbour during her maidenhood at her father's castle; the youngest of his house, musically gifted above his fellows, and so framed as to secure welcome and indulgence from all, wherever he showed his

face. One in whose company Martin took pleasure, treating
him as a younger brother, and interfering many a time to
preserve him from arrest or imprisonment from some daring
outburst of defiant patriotism.

Enamoured of her now, and to the point of valuing neither
his own life nor aught else in reckless persistent pursuit of
his purpose. Love's cunning had taught him to dissemble till,
not long since, he had suddenly let fall the mask; since when
she had lived in torment, faced by a woman's dilemma, more
heart-aching, more hopeless than any man's.

Not the common, old, daily recurring tale of the alienated or
double-minded wife meeting more than half way the promise,
false or true, of a love more alluring than the first in its outworn
zest. But Olwen's perfect heart-and-soul union with Martin
could not save her from what was pending now.

Call for fire from heaven, but not for an arbitrator between
those two men: Martin, the one in there – whom she loved with
a love too rare and intimate perhaps for man's understanding –
and the dare-devil young dreamer yonder, akin to her by race,
yet by virtue of it as remote from the Anglo-Norman Martin as
their two languages; one she had striven her utmost to reclaim
from the self-destruction on which he was blindly rushing.
She stood, as it were, high above them both; but that fury once
inflamed, her hand could not allay it. So much she knew.

Dismay, despair, was in her beautiful face. No dread had she
of Martin's anger or shadow of distrust for herself. But, once
they met, Ivor's wild and outspoken passion confessed, *she*
knew the look that would pass between them; the revengement
flame neither women nor gods can abate. To repent afterwards
of their murderous violence, it may be – but they will have had
their revenge. At best the smirch of blood would be over the
path of her life henceforth – Ivor's ghost cry to her in the night,
like the ghost of a child who, by some demon's maddening
trick, has drawn on itself the blow that made of it a ghost from
that hour.

Hatred, deadly combat between Martin and Ivor, and herself the cause! It would go to her heart to see Ivor perish. But the issue was at this moment beyond her control.

Never had she felt so mortally helpless. For one moment she buried her face in her hands, mazed, fate-entrapped, and held fast in that painful iron grip.

On there wall there hung an old mosaic, a thing brought long ago by her husband from the Far East, presenting a wondrous face of mystic, divine-seeming power and expression. The Face of One as pictured by Byzantine tradition and handed down for nigh on two thousand years.

Olwen stood gazing into the sorrowful eyes.

'Ivor, Ivor,' she whispered intently and low, 'may Christ save you! I cannot!'

SCENE 2

Away down in the marshland under the moonlight a witching picture arose.

No fancy figure or stage puppet, but a very human youth, whose garb, careful though simple, and whose aspect of fearless confidence bespoke his high condition, singing to the small harp he carried and handled as familiarly as an archer his bow, song-snatches in a language every son of Adam knows without learning.

It was Love speaking; Love the conqueror and omnipotent; Love enamoured of itself as desperately as of its object; Love that casts all else freely to the winds, owns no allegiance else, and infatuated to the pitch of the feeling the will confer the power to carry all before it and achieve the impossible, its quest.

Young Ivor ("young" he would always remain), Olwen's boy friend of old, Martin's protégé – endeared to them both by his charm and his gifts – dropping disguise, ignoring all that lies between him and his desire, all that may stay or weaken his purpose.

Yet in the beginning there had been no disguise, and his fellowship with those two and the song and verse-making for song's sake no mere pretence. How or when the change had come he could not tell and did not care. With the desire had been born the cunning to hide it and its growth. He had abandoned his mind to the thought and his heart to the dream, and welcomed their mastery. That it now rested with him to master the heart of Olwen was the very essence of the dream.

Wedded to an alien by her father, whose estates adjoined Martin's, such a mating was a matter of policy on the face of it. Say she loved her lord in dull, orderly fashion. That should be no enduring bar to his resolute siege, to a poet-lover's enticing snares. Had a voice calling from heaven warned him that Olwen's heart, gone out from the first to the Norman stranger chief, had by him been placed beyond recall by Ivor or another, that her love for him was woven inextricably into the web of her life, he would only have laughed. That, hand in hand with her husband, Olwen had entered a larger world of wider thought and more various action – the world their Cecil belonged to and would have to tread – was an idea Ivor could not entertain. He knew he was distanced, but not knowing why, thought he could overtake. Ah, but over and above the Norman's manliness and courtly grace, was there in his glowing eyes no spark of zeal or enthusiastic sympathy with the poet's fire? Ivor's creed – that these are chords only Welsh hands can strike – had perhaps once been Olwen's, though she no longer entertained it.

So, harp still in hand, but silent, the song ringing in his ears and bearing him onward as on wings, he was climbing the slope with the even, steady tread of the hillman that he was.

The face of the castle was dark, a solitary light gleaming from an upper chamber. There the adventurer pictured to himself Olwen listlessly awaiting the return tomorrow of her lord and master.

He approached by a private way that he knew, but could spy no sign of watch or ward. The guards might have gone forth to meet Sir Martin, leaving the steward with my lady, in charge, Jestyn, his, Ivor's, furtive ally, of whose connivance – whose secret aid – he was sure. Neither pact nor open word passed between them. They understood each other without.

Not many days since, meeting the astrologer, and accosting him as in jest concerning his fortune, he had by him been promised changes in life, journeys, love-making, the winning of friendship and favour of a lady of rank. The star-gazer, speaking on, made as though he were troubled about his home-coming master, mumbling of threatening losses, love converted into enmity; evil fixed stars in opposition, a train of malevolents. Fixed in Ivor's memory were his last words:

'One there is, not far from here, who, drawing near to the consummation of his desire, may yet be over-mindful of hidden perils and hazards lying between. He need not fear. He has his appointed defence. It is not he who by violence shall die. Good speed and success to you, Sir Ivor!'

And now, as he went he saw his visionary purpose, and every stop of the way thither, as vividly as though it were already accomplished. An immortal tale re-enacted; the tale of Nest, the Welsh Helen, borne off by the Welsh chieftain from Gerald, her Norman consort, faintly resisting it may be, but at heart nothing loth to surrender. Audacious though his flight with Olwen, it would be safe. All ways and paths were known to Ivor, and not a Welshman but would befriend, shelter, and protect them and lie skilfully to put pursuers off the track.

Placing his harp in a niche behind the postern gate he stood now under the shadow of the walls that held her; deserted looking, but for that light. He was used to find those doors open to him. None, Welsh or English, ever sought to repel Ivor, no more than if he were a little child.

But a child's hand can wreak havoc.

At the finding of the chosen entrance unlocked and unguarded

quite, his daring dream went farther. She had divined what
was coming, some revealing flash or veiled hint from the star-
gazer had told of a poet-lover speeding thither to snatch her
from the coming of her lord, dreadingly awaited, and delight
her with sweeter and more spiritual embraces and caresses.
His exalted mood accepted the idea of this sudden yielding to
his song-wooing unhesitatingly and without wonder.

Pausing a moment on the threshold, with the spontaneous
vigilance of those days and of that wild world when and where
every man carried his life in his hand, and stood upon his
guard, he had a fleeting impression as of the vanishing shadow
of a figure stealing up the stair; but not the faintest movement
was audible. Pooh! a moonlight flicker, or some ugly jest of
Satan's to daunt him.

Neither angel nor demon shall stop him now. In another
minute he will be in Olwen's presence, his arm round her; and
she – rapt, amazed, hesitating timidly, but not for long.

Forth, then. Sweet the compulsion, fond the captor taking
her from prison, the radiant moon lighting their path, Love the
leader, directing and protecting the steps of his devotees. In an
hour hence they will be out of reach of my lord's anger. Let him
threaten, let him pursue! He cannot overtake or prevail. Ivor
knew himself safe wherever the Welsh language is spoken;
and Olwen is safe in his arms.

SCENE III

His hand was on the chamber door when a shriek, a woman's
cry of nameless agony and terror, rent him through like a
sword. His dream-fabric fell to pieces at the shock, as a rose
whose petals are scattered by a sudden blast. In a moment it
had ceased to be. A moment more, and in the quenched light
of the room into which he stepped he felt he had burst into
the presence of deadly peril, if not death itself. Here were
the dim forms of two men locked in a mortal struggle, the

one unarmed and sorely wounded, and the other, with uplifted knife, was aiming a second deadly blow at his throat when Ivor's arm spontaneously interposed, arresting the thrust.

Beside him something white fluttered in the gloom. That whispered moan to him to save was Olwen's voice. In her defence Ivor felt the strength of five men come to him. But his assailant, though thin and slack of frame, showed the strength of ten. Fiercely he turned on the unseen intruder like a wild beast, and it would have been all over with Ivor had not the wounded man retained hold of the murderer's left arm.

There was a tense life-and-death conflict in the dark; before Olwen, having found and kindled a torch, brought light on the ghastly scene. Still Ivor knew no more of the combatants than that the Thing he was struggling with was possessed of the strength of seven devils.

Martin's countenance, unseen by Ivor these three years, and white with loss of blood, was but slowly recognisable; while in the adversary, his features distorted by maniacal hate and ferocity into a hideous, inhuman mask, well might he fail to know the harmless, self-absorbed, studious fool of a steward, Jestyn.

Neither could succeed in wrestling the knife from him. Foiled in the attack of Martin, with an incredible effort he shook them both off and turned savagely on the rescuer. The torch-bearer flashed the light full on Ivor's face. At that, the assailant, as at a jarring, painful shock, recoiled, staring wildly, trembled, tottered, and fell down in a fit, frothing at the lips.

Olwen, voiceless from the sudden horror sprung on them like a wolf out of the dark, was binding Martin's wound with sorely trembling tender fingers; Ivor, dumb and half-stunned, like the fairy-boy who, having touched Cold Iron, is flung violently and evermore out of the land of phantasy – the Kingdom of Love. Only Martin retained the mastery of his wits and sayings and doings.

'The fellow is mad,' he said. 'Like a ghostly enemy he stole in upon us, then fell upon me in a fury and had maimed me before I knew. What brought you to hand in such a pass, Sir Ivor? Go down, one of you. Ring the curfew bell that hangs in the forecourt, I pray, to recall the swaggering knaves in the hill-barn. Had one or two of the serving-men stayed at their posts this mischief had not been.'

At the bell boom, such of the men as were sober came running. Soon a dozen men were crowding in the doorway. Martin, dominating the physical effects of his wound, spoke with the balanced, forceful demeanour that rules men, whether they will or no:

'Our steward's mind is disordered. In a fit of frenzy he fell upon me and had made an end of me but for young Sir Ivor chancing by. Yet I never gave him just cause of hatred that I knew.' His eye searched the faces of the group. 'Morgan,' he said, instantly detecting a tell-tale movement on the part of one, 'know you aught of this? Speak, man! Have no fear!'

'Maelwas the Northman –' began the man, obeying at once, though unwillingly.

'That clever devil – yes. What of him?'

'Was here some while since. He told a woman whom he visited he had come for his revenge for his dismissal, and should get it through the hand of a madman, the evil in whose head and heart he had worked on, to convince him you were his persecutor, and would be his tormentor your life long. This I had from the woman, but thought it all the Northman's vain boast. Now he was often with Jestyn there, in secret places— '

'Ah. His moonstruck mind and the stars abetting, there has followed – this! Where is Maelwas now?'

'Gone back to his own place – to Merioneth. They say he has joined the Red Band of Robbers who hold the country there in thrall.'

'His own place… truly!' echoed Martin grimly.

'One who knows how to work in the dark. He saw his tool in our steward – in Jestyn there. The falling-sickness has now overtaken that poor wretch. When he comes to, he may do himself or others a mischief. So bind his hands – gently now – and bear him below to the hall. There lay him; and when he wakes, as he will presently, carry him down to the Priory Hospital in the plain, where the Brothers care for the sick. Tell them of his state; and, if there be a cure, the will find it.'

'And fetch hither one of them who is a surgeon,' added Olwen, 'to dress Sir Martin's wound.'

'Nay, 'tis too late to bring the old man this far long way tonight. Tomorrow will serve. You have done it already; none could do it better.'

As if by clockwork the men obeyed.

Martin turned to Ivor.

'He had let my life out with his ugly weapon in another moment had you not come. Christ sent you, I think!'

'I think not,' said Ivor quickly. Olwen alone marked the sardonic ring of his tone. Recovering his wits, he found himself precipitated to a new point of vision that dizzied him. In one unforgettable moment he had seen Olwen as she was; as eternally out of his reach as the star to which he had likened her.

'What then?' asked Martin simply.

His composure, his perfect self-control, were communicative, moving Ivor unconsciously to emulate them.

'I am bound for Brycheiniog,' he said curtly.

'A disturbed shire, at this hour.'

'The tell of a rising among the Welsh. I have kinsmen there and their business – and mine now – is to see that my countrymen get fair play. Some travels are better made by dark than by day. Between my home and that region lies your castle – whose doors have so often been open to me, and I halted before them, thinking – it might be for the last time. Then as I stood below fancy showed me, as it were, the devil's shadow stealing up the stair, and I followed to – I knew not what. I was ever a dreamer, my lord Martin, as you know.'

The crafty words, true to the letter, were convincingly spoken. There was no mistaking the attitude of farewell. What else might lie behind the haughty self-mockery and aloofness of his tone and bearing Olwen might surmise, though feeling in the depths of her heart it was better not to know.

To Martin they bore a simpler significance. He sighed and responded:

'I say nothing. You are bent on a dangerous errand. Well, if you find yourself flung into a wilful and heady enterprise, and a life is needed to preserve yours – send. You command mine. It is a debt that is due.'

And now he was gone, silently and mysteriously as he had come; and Olwen knew that she would never – God be thanked for that – see the look she dreaded pass between him and her heart's beloved, by whom she now knelt, her head on his breast, sobbing for joy unuttered – unutterable.

Ivor stood outside in the shadow of the postern-gate, motionless as a tree-stem or a pillar; a bitter cry in his heart. 'Love's Fool!' His paradise was worse than lost; it was destroyed.

Lights moving slowly down the slopes towards the plains marked the course of the convoy bearing the sick man to the Friary lazarhouse. Ivor lingered, his hand resting on his harp where he had left it standing in the niche, musing. He cast one look back at the castle, clearly and strongly outlined there in the moonlight. Than taking the little harp, he tore the strings across, broke the frame to pieces – as a soldier snaps his sword – and flung them away. 'Perish, together with my dream!' The action spoke for itself.

Turning on his heel he sped on his way to the open, murmuring low and defiantly the native rhyme of the rebel of olden time:

'See'st thou the wind? The rain dost thou see?
See'st though yon little bird on the lea?
See'st thou the men in leathern hose fling
Darts at the ship of the English king?'

Then, as he went farther, farther, he abruptly sang out in another strain, a variant just come to him, of an even more ancient foreign ditty:

'I have been Love's Bondsman this many a year.
Bondsman will I be no more:
On Song, on Love, I close the door.
All the days that I shall my sword wield,
Go I where stirs the strife;
Where Wales calls sons to the battlefield
There will I lead my life.'

But still, as he went, brooding on wars and fightings, he sang and sang.

At an early daylight hour a puzzled-looking cyclist, standing on the precise spot where Ivor had halted to look his last on the scene before him, was doing the same thing.

He, Alan Johns, had woken up, not as you wake from a natural slumber, but as a man who has been thrown into an artificially produced trance might rouse suddenly. Nothing real, nothing clear to his mind but the dream. Another moment and that would have gone out, eluded recall for ever. With a supreme mental effort he managed the instantaneous transfer of the fleeting impression, as it were, to the plate of his conscious memory, where it remains graven to this day.

So vivid had been the mental picture that he half expected to see the snake-like figure of the steward stealing up, as he descended the gatehouse stairs; found himself looking involuntarily for the returning convoy that had carried the sick man to the plains below; and in the opposite direction, for Ivor's vanishing figure.

Intruders had been here before him, farm-folk excavating and carrying off stones for repairing their pig-sties or barns; leaving shovel and pickaxe. Hereupon the journalist, still possessed by the visions of the night, found himself poking about the unearthed rubbish, seeking he knew not what, then laughed at himself, dropped the pick and desisted. Just as he turned to go his foot struck a small metal substance. He picked it up, pocketed it and carried it off, as a memento of the spot.

Looking at it afterwards more closely, it appeared to be a tiny T-shaped tool, of which he could make nothing. Only Alan Johns knows why one day after his return to London he chose to show it to the musical critic on his newspaper, asking if he knew what it was.

'A tuning-hammer,' answered the expert at once. 'But,' examining it curiously, 'I say, where did you get this?'

'Found it among some excavations down in South Wales.'

'I should call it the wrest of a harp,' he said, inspecting the shape of the aperture, 'were it not for the size. Too small for any modern instrument.'

'Didn't they use… weren't there small harps in former days,' ventured the other, 'that could be carried about and placed on the table when played indoors?'

'Like the lute or the zither. Yes. The wrest of an ancient table-harp. That is it, no doubt. If I were you I should keep it as a curiosity.'

Alan Johns is of the same opinion.

Zebedee;
or, A Latter-day Prophet

'I never met but one prophet in my life, and that was in South Wales.'

'Was he a true or a false prophet?' I asked him.

'False, let us hope. Time will show. But a prophet, out of doubt.'

And my friend, Jaques Robinson, a distinguished member of Oxford University, the Civil Service, and the Alpine Club, told me how it happened, as follows.

I

The Shepherd Guide

"Take a guide? For what? A short day's tramp over the humpy ridgway separating one Welsh dale from another. Guides for your grandmother! Am I not a member of the Alpine Club, one who has negotiated many and many a Swiss peak and perilous pass unescorted, piloted many a novice safely, unerringly, through long and difficult mountain excursions?"

So Jaques Robinson bethought himself, starting from Pont Berwyn leisurely and late, with no more doubt of reaching Llanwastad, his destination, by dinner-time than that his valise, already on its railway journey of forty minutes thither, would be there before him.

For a mere promenade the long drag upward by the old drovers' road proved incredibly toilsome. But how rewarding was the view sprung upon you all in a moment from the summit!

'Why don't you sing?' So an effusive American lady tourist had once cried out to him, when confronted on Toy's Hill, Sevenoaks, with a much milder spectacular surprise. The Alpiner was too out of breath for singing or shouting as he stopped to behold all the glories of West Wales, seemingly on parade for him below. 'Come and rest you on my mossy banks awhile and watch for trout,' said the little neighbouring mountain tarn to him prettily. The invitation was irresistible.

In less than a minute he found himself sunk waist high in a peaty bog, that gave absolutely no outward and visible hint of its underlying presence. His startled flounder sunk him deeper, well up to his armpits. With recovered presence of mind and a supreme and scientific effort he extricated himself and, bespattered all over with black mud, thankfully felt firm ground under his feet again.

He would be shot sooner than own it, but that had been a bad scare. All but "stogged," like a Dartmoor pony or bullock, or a "mysteriously disappeared" gentleman, come to an ignominious end in a perfidious morass. Fairly and might lie at the bottom of that bog, but Jaques Robinson preferred to stay in the wicked world that he knew. Surely the swamp had spread during his immersion! In wary avoidance of its borders he presently lost touch with his course and his bearings.

Now in the most formidable Alpine ascents the perils and dangers of the route, methodically studied and set down for you in the guide-books beforehand, may likewise be methodically met. Here you have to take things "according as they come." No kindly danger-signals or landmarks provided by luckless forerunners. No shelter-huts, nor so much as a cairn of stones nigh to aid, when presently the rain descended and the floods came and warred with his new Harris tweeds, destroying the bloom of their youth. He wondered if a suit of Welsh flannel would have met with more mercy from elements presumably patriotic. Before long the squall wearied of sustained effort and desisted of a sudden. But the sun seemed to be setting out of all due time. The mountain-tract was wild – inspiring; sky and clouds effects chimerically lovely; but he felt certain he had missed his way – a mere figure of speech this, since there was practically no way to miss – hence it was clearly lost labour to look for it.

Matchless, even in Jaques Robinson's experience, was the impression of lone lorn manhood and lifeless solitude. Mont Blanc, the Ortler, the Matterhorn, seemed places of public amusement by comparison. Dusk found the expert astray on rocky uplands where curlews nested and sheep ran, of the breed used to find bed and board among tussocks of coarse grass and rushes and clumps of fern and heather. He could have sworn that the map must be faulty or the lay of the land have altered since he set off. The M.A.C. had escaped being devoured alive by the Marsh King, only to get benighted, famished, possibly done to death by cold, bruises, and exposure, like many a poor traveller before him.

Ho! a light gleams yonder. Thank heaven, a house. But it danced up and down. The devil! a fen-fire. Then at his shout, 'Ahoy!' the fen-fire stood still. Jaques Robinson, making for it, plunged into a rocky stretch, a well-planned pitfall of break-leg holes, picturesquely disguised in fern and heather. But there – oh providence! – on the edge of those treacherous slopes stood a lantern-bearing man and a brother, regarding him and awaiting developments.

"Developments," in other words the Alpiner, after traversing what proved to be half a mile of very cross country, came up with one whose garb denoted a lowlier class; hence his plain duty to put himself then, there, and unreservedly at the holiday-maker's service, unmindful of his own business, to minister to the stranger Saxon's wants and whims.

To his surprise, Jaques Robinson learnt that he was in the right direction after all; but at the mileage named as yet lying between him and Llanwastad his bones cried out. The hill-man, tacitly and unasked, assumed his guide's office, and they tramped silently down a wild ravine, every sheep's footstep of which the Welshman seemed to know. He was strange-looking, but it was too dark for particular observation. He might be a criminal flying from justice, or an escaped lunatic, or a tramp of easy morality, with an incurable mania for theft, which the lantern-flashes on the Englishman's watch-chain might bring on at any moment.

Now Jaques Robinson, though he happened to be well conversant with the Welsh language, never fell into the vulgar error of accosting a native in his mother-tongue. Always presuppose his acquaintance with the language of the Empire.

'You belong to these parts?' he asked him by and by.

The man assented, adding, 'So do not you.'

'If I did, I should not be taking you out of your way to put me in mind, I hope,' answered Robinson with lordly civility.

'I am a herdsman,' the other told him presently. 'My way is on the mountains. It is the way of my flock.'

'Where are they now – your sheep?'

The shepherd waved his hand expressively. 'Up and down, in the folds of the hills yonder. Some I am finding here below in the valley. But tomorrow they will come all of them together to the fold. I am the principal of the flock.'

His voice was a pleasing voice. A passing jerk of his hand flashed the lantern light full on his face. A face of a well-known local type, as distinct from the tall, fair, languid Celtic tribe, as from the swarthy, long-headed vivacious Iberian. Dark-haired, with grey eyes; well-cast features, and a countenance of thoughtful, quiet intelligence.

'Your flocks don't seem to need much keeping,' remarked Robinson.

'Nay, but they wander on the mountains, and on every high hill. I have to search them out, and deliver them from the miry places and marshes,' (Robinson shuddered audibly at the terrible reminiscence), 'the cloud and dark places, where they have been scattered. I have to strengthen the sick, and bring again that which was lost, to feed them in good pasture – a fat pasture. So shall they dwell safely in the wilderness, and sleep in the woods.'

Jaques Robinson was silenced, mystified by these high-flown utterances, which fell as naturally, as inevitably, from his companion's lips, as slang from the low-born London loafer. He was sensible of a distinct, almost mesmeric-like attraction about the man at his side. Moreover, such poetic phraseology seemed perfectly in tune with the dimly seen magnificence of the mountain gorge they were descending, its sides clothed with clinging woodlands of birch and scrub-oak, the sounding river a cascading torrent below.

Some sort of a ferny, heathery path began to be under their feet at last, as they threaded their way downwards, alongside of a ravine becoming wilder and grander at every step. Could such precipitous rocks, boisterous mountain streams, such tremendous intersecting boulders exist, except in the romantic defiles of the Italian Alps? Of a sudden the strange thing, for which the tourist seemed to be waiting, happened.

A detonation first, overhead; but that was not it; a mere bolt from the blue would have been in the natural course of events.

Rounding a river-bend, they beheld a jet of water spout up some twenty feet, and on the opposite bank, torchlight flared on the darkling forms of four or five black-faced demons, brandishing torches and forks – engaged in what devil craft? – as they bent over the deep, stilly pool, gibbering and jabbering low to one another. Positively Robinson looked for the cloven foot and horns, then at his guide who, obviously nervous, was hurrying him past with suspicious apprehensiveness. But a wild yell from the group opposite let them know they had been seen. There was a savagery in its ring. Quick as an echo came from the shepherd guide a resonant, responsive shout – watchword or countersign – as he led on, but quickening his pace.

'I say!' began the member of the Alpine Club as, on rounding another bend, they lost sight of the lurid group. The next moment he suddenly understood and laughed aloud. 'Oh, Salmon, Miners, Poachers – eh?' The man nodded. 'Dynamite? What? Gaff and a net? What wickedness!' The sportsman in him righteously indignant. 'Don't your water-bailiffs look better after things than that?'

'Oh, they do look. There may have been one or two water-bailiffs among them just now,' came the grimly humorous reply. 'It concerns me not. I gave up poach— fishing, when I became what I now am – a fisher of men.'

The lower slopes they were approaching showed a fringe of civilisation. At the point where they emerged from the mountain gorge, the track became a rough road. On a grassy stretch alongside, the dark outlines of a small building of recent-looking erection but prehistoric simplicity were discernible.

'That,' said the shepherd, stretching out his arm, 'is Hermon. That is my sheepfold.'

Over the doorway, by some simple illuminating device, there shone out the inscription, 'The Lord is there!'

The fisher – or shepherd – of men had spoken in parables. 'You are a preacher, then,' said Robinson respectfully, 'and this is your chapel.' He assented, adding, 'There, tomorrow, what is given unto me will I speak.'

Here the spent candle-end in the lantern spluttered and went out.

'The night she is dark, as the fountain of all blackness,' the Welshman continued, 'and the road she is naughty. It is seven miles to Llanwastad, but one mile or so onward is an inn where I sleep this Saturday night. They do not take everybody; but since you come with me, they would lodge you if you so will. What we now wants is a candle. Follow you me.'

He opened a roadside gate that closed the approach to

a whitewashed homestead, ensconced there in dignified isolation, its back to the mountain side. He named it – a farm of ancient legendary local fame – so Robinson might name Temple Bar or the Monument, a landmark known to the world at large –and continued:

'A cousin, the daughter of the brother of my mother, is here on a visit to Mrs. Jones. She will give us a candle. A cousin from England – from London.'

And 'England' on his lips had a remote ring, as though it were Texas or Tasmania.

A damsel came to the door, ruddy-haired and comely, very.

'Oh, Cousin Zebedee,' she said, shaking her pretty head with womanly reprobation, 'why must you go wandering after dark on the hill-tops? One of these Saturday nights you'll fall and break your neck, and then – there will be no Hermon any more.'

At the familiar sound of her careless English accents, so remote from the bilingual variety, which was all of his native tongue that Robinson's ears had heard for some weeks, his heart went out to her on the spot. It was a curious revelation of the gulf that the difference of home language – the language in which you think – creates.

Coming forward he said, 'I think your cousin would have got down earlier but for me. It was I who went nearer to getting a neck broken. But for him I should have fared very badly.'

'You could have no better guide,' responded the girl, with a smile in her voice. 'There are some really dreadful places about here, but with Zebedee I feel always safe.'

She replenished the lantern and they tramped on, down a half-made road – crossing the river by the airiest quivering footbridge – to the tiny tavern where "they did not take everybody", which no doubt was why but small provision was forthcoming of any kind for anybody. But Zebedee's recommendation won the most charming civility for the new-comer, who accepted meekly the supper he was too tired to swallow and the bed he was too tired not to fall asleep on; his slumbers the weirdest jumble-dream of choking in a horrible quicksand, sheep without a shepherd, a shepherd without a flock, wayside temples, ape-faced demons thrusting nasty-looking weapons into uncanny pools, and the sweet smiling face, aureoled in beauteous hair, of a damsel who spoke English as he knew it – a damsel who could not be called anything but what she was: Rhoda.

II

A Sermon on a Mount

That on the morrow he should stay to walk up to Hermon and hear Zebedee's discourse was a proceeding on the part of Jaques Robinson that astonished no one but himself.

The inn-keeper's wife had meanwhile supplied him with a few particulars concerning the shepherd-guide of yesterday night.

Zebedee was not his name, but for some apparently forgotten reason he was commonly so called – perhaps because he had no children, all that we know of his namesake in the Gospels being that he had.

He was a widower, approaching forty, doing a poor trade at his little store in Llanwastad, but had been a notable member of a powerful chapel community there – up till a year ago, when dissension had led to a split, ending in his practical expulsion.

At the head of a suffering minority he had set up Hermon, refashioned out of a tumbledown mountain smithy, coming up there weekly to hold forth; and his reputation just now was very great and terrible. He could draw tears from a rock, Robinson was assured. Sunday evening last there was not a dry eye in the house.

'At the risk of being held up to derision as a godless and

obdurate Saxon I'll go and hear him,' this passer-by decided.

Bright was the Sabbath morn; pleasant the saunter by the light of day up the valley to the chapel. Bishop's son and man of mark though he was, he felt absurdly shy about going in, having never intruded on an unestablished place of worship in this country in his life. Discreetly he waited outside till the preliminaries, secular and other, of the meeting were over, slipping in without commotion just as the sermon was about to begin.

The tiny chapel was well filled. From up and down the valley the sheep had come. There was the pretty cousin Rhoda, whose attractive attire offered a dangerous rivalry to the coming address. Such neatness and fashion combined were a revelation alike to the admiring male and despairingly envious female section of the community assembled.

But from the moment Zebedee, pale, rapt, and magnetic-looking, stepped into the pulpit, the attention of the crowd – as one mind – was on him, held tight there as by the turn of a screw.

He straightened himself, and his face became as the face of a much younger man as he gave out his theme:

'*Surely the Lord God will do nothing but He revealeth it to His servants the prophets.*'

A voice of natural sonority and power, with a note in it that, like thunder, seemed to come from a distance.

He waited a few moments as if expectant, like his hearers, then proceeded slowly, in the same tone of gentle but emphatic confidence:

'*Be still, ye inhabitants of this isle, whom the merchants that pass over the sea have replenished. The harvest of the river is her revenue, and she is a mart of nations. Behold now your joyous city, whose might is of ancient days: the tumultuous city – full of stirs – whose merchants are princes and her traffickers the honourable ones of the earth.*'

The faint ring of distant mockery became nearer and louder

as he went on:

'*What aileth thee now, that ye have changed your glory for that which hath no profit? Surely a famine has come upon the land – not a famine of bread nor a thirst for water, but of righteousness and of judgement.*'

Letting drop the veil of obscurity he proclaimed, as it were, his prophet's message, clear, trenchant, every word made alive and of telling import.

'*Evil – mischief – shall come upon thee. Thou shalt not know whence it cometh nor be able to put it off. Desolation shall fall upon thee suddenly that thou shalt not know!*'

Jaques Robinson was stirred, in spite of himself. 'What's this? What is he talking about? For he knows!'

It was indeed with an emphasis inspired by something more penetrating than conviction that the shepherd-guide spoke on.

'*The leaders of the people do cause them to err. They err in vision and stumble in judgement. For they have made lies their refuge – under falsehood they have hid themselves. Among all the sons that the Isle has brought forth, there is not one able to guide.*

'*Her watchmen are all blind. They are ignorant and look every one to their own way, for gain, every one to his quarter. None careth for justice nor for truth. They trust in vanity and speak lies. So justice is turned away backward, for truth has fallen in the street, and equity cannot enter.*'

'Can this be mere Anglophobia and rhetoric?' wondered Jaques Robinson, listening on as he had never listened to a sermon in his life. This singular man might not be speaking his own words, no more than is an actor, or reciter of genius, who yet says what he has to say with a magic that imparts to it, however well known, the significance of a thing never heard before.

'*Lo, He that formeth the mountains and createth the winds, He that maketh the morning darkness and treadeth the high places of the earth, and declareth unto man what is His thought*

– He hath given his commandment against eh merchant city: "Why gaddest thou about so much to change thy way?" I said, "In quietness and confidence shall be thy strength, and ye would not." Ye have made children to be your princes and set babes to rule over you, causing you to err by their lightness and their lies.'

Passing for a moment from the stern severity of his tone of warning to one of appealing sadness:

'Yet I had planted thee a noble vine – a fine seed. How then art thou turned to the degenerate plant of a strange vine?'

Then the fire kindled, and the prophet broke out and delivered his indictment with a force and directness that electrified the stranger within his chapel gates.

'The diviners have seen a lie – and cause them to stumble out of the ancient way into paths not cast up. They are wise to do evil, but to do good they have no knowledge. They have altogether broken the yoke and burst the bonds. The youth behaveth himself proudly against the ancient and the base against the honourable. They have set servants to be their oppressors and let women rule over them. They hunt every man his brother with a net. Every one loveth gifts and followeth after rewards. They found as a nest the riches of the people, and as one gathereth eggs that are left they gathered, and there was none that moved the wing nor opened the mouth or peeped.'

A visionary – well, but if so, one after the grand manner – the manner of Ezekiel!

'Destruction cometh out of the North. They shall be delivered into the hands of the people of the North. Those who have conceived a purpose against them, saying, "Arise, get you up against the wealthy nation that dwelleth without care, that hath neither bolts nor bars – that dwelleth alone."'

The modulation from plain to fervent speech, becoming ecstatic – and thence to the singular vocal chant called "hwyl", in which it is customary for the latter part of a Welsh sermon to be delivered, was being effected so smoothly and spontaneously that the process was almost imperceptible. This intoning, a practice whose origin seems lost in antiquity, admits of a certain free, informal variety of cadence. On Zebedee's lips it became no mere musical device; the transition sounded natural, nay, inevitable. It seemed to focus, as it were, the interest of the oration, expressing some inherent message that might otherwise be missed. The effect was stirring as a war-drum or pibroch; the message was one of warning:

'Then I will make drunk her wise men. They shall sleep a perpetual sleep and not wake.

'But their prophets they say unto them, "Thou shalt not see this thing, and famine shall not be in this land, but we will give you assured peace."

'A false vision. For they speak a divination out of their own heart, and not the mouth of the Lord. They say to every one who walketh after the divinations of his own hear, "No evil shall befall you."

'They are vanity and the work of error. In the time of their visitation they shall perish. How say ye, "We are might and strong men for the war"? Oh madmen, the sword shall pursue you till ye be cut down. Then shall ye wander and cry, "We looked for a time of health, and behold trouble."'

The rise and fall of his voice was like a peal of bells, worked in masterly fashion by the ringers – mourning funeral bells. The mild and serious-faced Zebedee speaking there might have been the mouthpiece of the destroying angel, sounding, in rhythmic accents, the death song, the knell of a nation.

'Howl, ye ships, for your strength shall be laid waste and your harvest be made a heap in the day of grief and desperate sorrow.

'I will bring a nation upon you from afar – an ancient nation – a mighty nation, a nation whose language thou knowest not, neither understandest the purposes of their hearts.

'Out of the North an evil shall break forth on the inhabitants

of this isle and sweep it with the besom of destruction. Then shall be their perplexity. Then shall ye run to and fro and seek wisdom and shall not find it. Within three years shall the glory of the isle be contemned. There shall be a great forsaking and the remnant shall be very small and feeble. Their moorings are loosed, they could not well strengthen their mast; they could not spread sail. Then is the prey of a great spoil divided!'

Passing abruptly to the plain tones of simple speech, he concluded:

'The inhabitants of the world would not have believed that the enemy should have entered into her gates.'

Then the last word, as of the revealing presence, the warning sound, fading, flying away:

'Destruction cometh out of the North; a great commotion that shall make all thy cities desolate. Oh thou that dwellest by many waters, they end is come!'

III

The Hand of Rhoda

It was over. A gurgle of approval arose from the benches. 'Ah, well done! Good, very good! Better than you often hear at the Tabernacle, Llanffelix. Ah, he has the gift.' Zebedee had maintained his reputation; perfect complacency sat on the countenances of his faithful partisans. But it seemed to Jaques Robinson that the only genuinely impressed person present was himself.

Here in this little upstart of a meeting-hut of some nameless section of a sect he had been moved – carried away as by a voice from heaven. Had this dreamer-dweller in mountain fastnesses, closed to the world except in summer time, heard, like the augurs of old, in the rustling of the leaves of the oaks, the telling of pending doom and of evil to come?

For Zebedee's audience, gratified by the heights to which

their pastor had risen, the main thing was the personal element. The emotional excitement of mere sound had been wrought to a high pitch, the sense was relatively unimportant – thus the downfall-general fore-shadowed, which presumably must involve the Principality, had no power to depress them in the least. They broke into groups and fell to discussing matters audibly personal and secular. The preacher had left the pulpit, ruddy-haired Rhoda her seat, and passed through a door opposite to the main entrance. Thinking presently to make his exit that way, Jaques Robinson followed.

He stepped into a bare little ante-room, where the orator sat at a table leaning his head on his hand, in a state of such abject, helpless, nervous agitation as the Englishman had never witnessed but once.

That was in the artists' room of a London concert-hall. A performer of world-wide celebrity who had just been surpassing himself on the platform, succumbing to the vengeful reaction that follows – as the night the day – on any undue imaginative effort, unable to hide the pitiable depths to which he, a star of the first magnitude, was reduced.

Here in 'Hermon' was the exact scene repeated. There sat poor Zebedee, trembling and unstrung, speechless, helpless as a child, with the tears streaming down his cheeks, and a feminine comforter at his side administering suitable attentions, mopping his face, and talking continuously and low just to distract him and relieve the tension till the nervous crisis abated. The virtuoso's ministering angel was a countess, Zebedee's his cousin Rhoda.

Robinson walked straight through into the open. Before long the other two came out, Zebedee still pale but partly restored. He seemed not to see Robinson as he went off – Rhoda in the doorway watching his figure till it disappeared in the valley wood.

'Well,' Jaques Robinson broke out to her, 'an extraordinarily impressive speaker is your cousin Zebedee!'

'Yes, my cousin has an excellent voice, one that many of our teachers and school-professors might envy,' said Rhoda moderately.

'I little expected... Such a stirring address took me completely by surprise.'

'Oh, the words,' she rejoined indifferently, 'they all come out of the Bible, which he knows by heart, both in Welsh and English.'

'Yes, yes, I dare say. Still, the putting and weaving of them together, and the wonderful eloquence of his delivery gave to it the force of a composition – almost a creation,' returned Robinson, half amused to find himself expressing and apologising for his feelings to this girl. 'And surely he can never have spoken those words thus without some sense of their application, their present significance? It was to Britain, not to Judæa, he was speaking. We have heard the warning note before. Do you think it has reached him and inspired his discourse today?'

'Oh, he may have overheard people talking, or read something in a newspaper – he reads a lot,' said Rhoda, as unconcerned, obviously, with the substance of the discourse as the Hermonites. 'I know too,' she added, 'he thinks the country in danger through the people forgetting religion, and that vengeance will come. But I wish and am trying to make my cousin give up all this preaching. It is bad for his health, injuring his nerves, and ruining his business. By this secession he has made enemies of his best customers in and about Llanwastad. Such a pity!'

Here she raised her pretty head. Robinson, as he looked at her, "had an idea." It checked the vehement protest on his lips. The spiritually-gifted preacher cousin was likewise one of a distinctly well-favoured countenance. There was no more, he felt, to be said.

Before leaving Llanwastad on the morrow, after a comfortable night at the Castle Inn, Jaques Robinson went to look up the prophet, who when he was not prophesying sold tea and sugar at his store. A melancholy place this, with one mouldy melon in the window and a litter of unassorted comestibles on the counter and the floor, but no storekeeper. A stray infant customer with a penny to buy sweets was visibly deterred only by the stranger man's entry from helping himself.

A passage ran through into the back garden, a pleasant patch of colour where orange-lilies, rose-campion, stocks, and roses bloomed freely. There Robinson saw the prophet in a meditative attitude, watering-pot in hand, and went out to him, just to tender his thanks, he said, for ministrations received, including, he hinted, the remarkable harangue at Hermon. Zebedee received the compliments with becoming modesty, disclaiming credit, merit, or even full understanding of the word that was given him to speak. He was preoccupied just now with his bees – of which he had a few hives – the only things, together with the flowers for their nourishment, about the place that flourished.

'A mysterious lot, the Welsh, as certain also of their own commentators have said,' mused Robinson when he left.

But later in the day, driving past the store on his way to the station, the traveller saw another picture.

A country cart drawn up at the door, where the storekeeper stood handing up some packages to the purchaser on the driving-seat – Rhoda the ruddy-haired. She was bending down, her hand in her cousin's hand, her eyes on his.

The West can call you back as irresistibly as the East, and next Whitsuntide found Jaques Robinson revisiting Llanwastad and the Castle Inn.

Zebedee had married his cousin at the New Year, he was told, and soon after came to terms with his foes, abandoning Hermon, now a blacksmith's forge again. As a rebel that repenteth he had risen in favour; his store prospered, he had introduced Danish butter, advertised cleverly, adored his charming wife, now soon to become a mother. Preaching? Oh, he gave that up long ago. But he was a lucky man, averred the jolly innkeeper, with a twinkle in his eye. Such a wife as that was worth more than a fortune – would be the making of any husband.

But Jaques Robinson decided not to look him up, preferring to remember the seer of Hermon as he had parted from him, a lonely poet-figure, dreaming dreams in his garden, 'a populous solitude' of bees and flowers.

From *Camera Lucida;*
or, Passages from Common Life (1897)

Hand in Hand;
A Comedy of Yesterday

'The sea hath many thousand sands,
  The sunne hath motes as many,
The skie is full of starres – and love
  As full of woes as any.'

OLD SONG

I

Because people always spoke of the Miss Rodericks in the plural, like 'the snuffers' or 'the nutcrackers,' you might easily suppose they had not more individuality than the sides of a triangle. Reader, they were as dissimilar as the wick, the candle and the flame. All were delightful, but they were most delightful of all when you could get them together.

At church, in the singing-seats, they would take the shine out of an angel choir. Rosy complexioned Madge, with her black, glittering hair, and the mischief dormant in her dark innocent eyes; Charlotte, straight as a wand, thorough-bred, handsome, alert, a mysterious link between gipsy-faced Madge and Stella, a St Cecilia to look at – St Cecilia before she came out.

Children of a deceased landed gentleman in a small way in South Wales, they grew up on the weather-beaten hillsides of Cefn Cwm (pronounced Keffin Koom), near St Teilo, looked after the garden and their mother, who was delicate, and were happy, though with next to no society and no male society at all, except Gwyn, who didn't count because he was a real cousin and a pseudo-brother besides, having been about the premises all their young lives. But Penfynnon, Gwyn's paternal heritage, had to be sold when Gwyn was one and twenty, to pay the paternal debts, and now, after a year or so spent in helping to manage other people's property under Lord Knighton's agent at St Teilo, he was about to start for South Africa as a first step towards acquiring some of his own.

Madge Roderick was twenty-four, and the accredited guardian angel of the family in mind, body and estate, an estate of a dozen small farms. Madge understood Welsh, arbitrated between rent-collector and tenants, and imparted music and morals to the younger Celts, apter at the first than at the second study.

Charlotte, called Charlie at home, was the clever one. Charlie was wildly scientific. Not upon orthodox, certificated, specialising lines. Charlie wanted to know all things, and prove them too. She proved Madge's patience sorely by trying chemical experiments in the dairy, and putting jam into damp cupboards to study the different forms of mould as they grew. But the recent birthday present of a Kodak had diverted her awhile from the paths of serious research. Charlie who did nothing by halves, worked her camera so indefatigably that, according to Stella, her room-mate, she would get up in her sleep to 'take you' in yours.

The Rodericks had no 'advantages'. Every Board School child gets more so-called education than ever Madge got from the German governess to whom she so successfully imparted the English tongue. The 'Chits,' a nursery term for her juniors, that died hard, had spent two years at an expensive school, whence Charlie brought back all the dangers of a little knowledge and Stella fabulous tales of knavish tricks, and many excellent subjects for mimicry. For recreation the Rodericks, providentially, were self-supporting. Their only near neighbours were Mr. Ducane, the elderly valetudinarian who had bought Gwyn's little patrimony a year ago, and Louise, his relatively young wife. Yet Stella, just turned seventeen, was the only one of the sisters three ever heard to complain that they were wasting their youth in a desert.

When one November Madge went on a month's visit to some cousins, fashionable folk in Melbury Road, Kensington, that was an event, even in the lives of her sisters who remained behind. Then when she returned, having stayed nearly two months, that was another event.

Madge was radiant, her eyes like dancing stars, her face all smiles and dimples. 'Madge, you've been having a good time,' said Stella instantly, when they met her on the St Teilo station-platform. 'And now, Madge,' Charlie struck in, 'you'll have to let me "take you" before the bloom wears off and the ravages of care begin.'

That *enfant terrible*, Stella, all the way home, kept pursuing the returned native with a thought-reading gaze that Madge vainly tried to dodge, boxed up with the Chits in the hired vehicle that drove them from the station.

'It's another Madge,' said Stella privately to Charlie at home. 'There's a far-off look in her eyes, and she smiles at us from a distance, like an angel come down to visit the poor.'

Charlie stared in blank consternation. Can the pole-star wane or shift its position?

Later on, by firelight in the lancet-windowed schoolroom at Cefn Cwm, Madge, kneeling on the rug and studying the hearth while Charlie roasted chestnuts in the smokeless coal fire, was put by the Chits through a searching cross examination about one thing and another and one person and another, out of which she did not come well.

'Madge, you're keeping something back,' said Stella remorselessly. There was a fearful silence. Stella broke it with a little cry: 'Madge, you've been and gone and done it, I knew you had!' Madge blushed incarnadine, said, 'Oh me!' and covered her face with her hands.

Just their triumph, their reproaches! 'I couldn't help myself, dears or I would, indeed I would,' she pleaded, with naïve sincerity.

'Engaged, in so many words?' whispered Stella fiercely.

'It wasn't so very many!' Madge laughed softly, tearfully too.

'Ah, but, Madge,' – Charlie spoke more in sorrow than in anger – 'you'd no right – without so much as letting us see him first.'

'I've not been so bad as that, no really not,' protested the culprit, 'and if you only knew all—'

'Well?' came the other two in a breath.   And Madge imparted.

His name was Joscelin Carew.   He was an officer in the Royal Engineers and quartered at Chatham, namely, the Naval and Military Club, Piccadilly.   A frequent guest of Madge's hosts at Melbury Road, his name had recurred frequently in her letters home.

'I always thought,' said Madge meditatively, 'that an officer had only two ideas – horses and his moustache.'

'And you were his Third Idea, Madge,' groaned Charlie.   'I wish, oh! How I wish he hadn't had it!'

Madge told how she had heard him spoken of by everybody as such a dreadfully clever young man that she felt intimidated in advance.

What she saw was a tall, spare, light-haired, prepossessing and not too rigidly military looking guest addressing himself to the business of a ball with the zest of twenty-five, which he looked, and the discrimination of blank and thirty, his veritable age.

'Perhaps he saw I was the country cousin,' said Madge demurely, 'and didn't know many people.   For he asked me to dance with him three times.'

'Kind of him, wasn't it?' put in Stella with withering sarcasm.

'I told him I was raised in the backwoods, and that my cousins call me "Wild Wales".   He has heard before of this part of the country, from the Ducanes whom he meets in town, and who have often asked him to come down to them for the shooting.'

They met at dinners, dances, People's concerts, and smart musical and dramatic entertainments. Carew, a seriously accomplished amateur, made Mayfair and the slums akin by his admirable talents displayed, vocal and histrionic.

Then came a Cinderella dance at Melbury Road, on which Madge did not dwell, but after which it seemed a moral impossibility that Carew should not call in the course of the morrow. That impossibility occurred, and Madge knew despair. But of that she would not tell. The day after he presented himself; she and Despair were all alone in the drawing room, and Carew spoke words that made Madge as happy as she can never be over again.

But Madge was good, and her private bliss awoke her to a proper sense of the grave cares and responsibilities of the Home Office she filled so unostentatiously – Mrs Roderick's shaky health, finance that needed as minute attention. Only Madge and the agent knew all the tedious particulars, and he had one foot in the grave. It was flat desertion she was contemplating. How shift the burden on to the Chits, unused as the lillies of the field to taking thought?

'He agreed that the first thing – the Thing of Things – is for him to come here "on approval for admission to the family", he says. So if mother invites him for a fortnight from the 10th he will come. And, Stella, I haven't quite promised yet. You can't call me engaged. I'll not tell anybody so.'

'Not even Gwyn?' asked Stella.

'Gwyn will be gone before then.'

'Coming on the 10th,' exclaimed Charlie, 'and sings and acts beautifully? Madge, it will be the making of the Penny Reading at St Teilo on the 20th. You must get him to perform.'

'Charlie,' said Stella disgustedly, 'you were born to be an old maid.'

II

Dear Jos,
   *What is this that I hear concerning you and a certain
Miss Roderick? Is there any truth in it?   Yes or no?
– Yours,*

J. COURTNEY HERWIN

Challenged thus by his most intimate friend, Carew pleaded
guilty in four pages of self-excuse, called for by the special
case. Other sons of men might marry and be given in marriage
without more ado.   But when Joscelin Carew disposes of
himself by proposing, men, gods and goddesses will know the
reason why.

Nice-looking, nice-mannered, well-connected, Joscelin
Carew "went everywhere"; one of those gifted gentlemen who
take society seriously.   Society had repaid him with a really
notable circle of feminine admirers.   That those men who
called him a conceited ass were jealous was as self-evident
as that those gay coquettes who joked apart and unkindly
about the "flittings of a superannuated butterfly" had had their
addresses rejected.

But even on a man a dozen London seasons tell, bringing fits
of disaffection for the eternal round of fascinating frivolities;
when, believing the book of fresh sensations to be closed for
him, he is specially exposed to be carried away by a fresh
sensation, such as Madge created at the ball.

Like a Hamadryad who has stepped straight from her oaken
haunt into a supercivilised London crush, she brought the
breath of the Cefn Cwm woods along with her.   Gipsy-eyed,
with queer, mulberry-coloured scabious blossoms in her wavy
black hair and white frock, slight in figure but not insignificant,
brimful of spirit and playful intelligence, she came before
him like a new thing in girls, and took his experienced fancy
prisoner without the ghost of an intent.   'During our first

dance,' he wrote, 'I felt as if I had caught some delightful, undiscovered, wild creature – the wildest are not shy, Jack, you know. As unlike other people's country cousins as possible. A novice in London society, she holds her own there without trying, for nothing escapes her quick perception. She brings a fresh eye to bear on these matters and sees novel aspects that escape our blunted sense'… etcetera, etcetera. There was a wasted but distinctly literary knack in Joscelin Carew, and his pen was the pen of a ready writer.

Hers was a cheek to brave the dawn, the archest, merriest mouth ! the soul of inviolable honesty shone in her eyes. And should any immaculate reader in the sequel, come to think that hanging is too bad for Joscelin Carew, be it set down and remembered on his behalf that he did spontaneously mark, admire, seek out, and seriously woo Madge Roderick; proof in itself of some unperverted instincts.

At the Cinderella dance at Melbury Road he had gone as far as unattached man well can go and back out becomingly, and he knew it. Something said: "Pause and think it over somewhere else". So he fled to Chatham and thought.

Well, he wished he were not a third son, and that landed property in South Wales brought the widow and orphan more than 2½ per cent. But he had "influence", hence hopes of an appointment by-and-by; and… and… he felt he really could not stop, so he went on. It was left for Madge to point out the lions in their path.

'Seems she has a family dependent on her,' he wrote. 'Little sisters, bronchial mother, helpless housemaids and what not? Madge thinks if she goes the children will cry and the mother take to her bed, and there will be nobody to order the dinner or do the accounts, and Hodge will say he can't pay his rent. That's absurd of course. Still Madge is an angel to worry about these matters, for she's – well she's most unreasonably fond of your humble servant, Jack, though he tells you so who should not. However, as our affair has been "rushed" rather, we are going to begin it all over again from the very beginning for the benefit of her family. Next week I start for Carmarthenshire in the new character of suitor in form, but sworn to bring down the house. It is called Cefn Cwm. I will make love to my mother-in-law elect, play Badminton with the little girls; but I will not have Madge's happiness sacrificed to their selfish comfort. I don't promise you I shall be a bride-groom in three weeks, or even in three months. I'm cursedly hard-up, as usual in the decline of the year, and unless my governor at the War Office comes to my relief it's a problem to know how I'm to get married at all. But you know where there's a will there's a way – to the altar.'

Stella – who was naughty – having solemnly promised to keep Madge's confidence, went and dropped a broad babbling hint the very next day to Gwyn, who, as aforesaid, didn't count, and was going to South Africa immediately.

In consequence when Gwyn, on the eve of his departure, spent his farewell afternoon at Cefn Cwm, he worked for and secured half an hour's private talk with Madge. Then between long and weighty silences he expressed himself to the effect that, since it appeared he might not find her there if he came back, there was something of importance he must say to her before they parted now.

What it cost him to get that something out only Madge knows, who will never reveal. A confession of murder would have been easier in the articulation. Nothing less than the fact that he was taking his heart with him to the Dark Continent tomorrow would have forced it to his lips today. But when it got there Madge was not a little scared by the inadequate glimpse it afforded her of its powers of action and grave disturbance, then secretly tickled to learn that the provoking agent of all this moral and spiritual rout was – the Chit, Stella.

Stella and Gwyn had fought gaily with fists as children, with words as schoolboy and schoolgirl, Gwyn the tyrant, Stella the tease. Last year they met again, but with a difference; Stella a precocious-looking maiden on sixteen, Gwyn a ridiculously overgrown fellow of twenty. He had shot up suddenly like a beanstalk; there seemed much more of him than he knew what to do with, and his reserved and backward habits to protest against those six feet two inches of person that would not let him efface himself in any company. Since then Gwyn, whose life at St Teilo was lonely and his occupation prosaic, had harboured the divine folly of an infatuation springing up for an idealised, fair-haired cousin with large limpid eyes and a mutable countenance, now grave as befits a heroine of romance, now gay as the charming nonsense that broke from her lips. He could not see the childish side of Stella, whereas for Madge it was the leaven that leavened the lump.

It simply took her breath away to learn that Stella, who would sell her soul for a day's skating, who wept bitterly if scolded by her violin teacher, who spelt abominably, who made fun of everything in season and out of season, specially out, and who was probably employed the while Gwyn was telling his love in sowing mustard and cress in his hat, could have it in her irresponsible hands, if not to make or to mar his felicity for the term of his natural life (as he stated convincedly), at all events to tamper very powerfully with his present peace and content.

Gwyn had discovered that while bullying the provoking infant ten years back, and bantering the pretty schoolroom hoyden later on, he had been adoring her unbeknownst. Madge did not even smile. Instinct told Gwyn that recent events would make of her a soft-hearted confidante, thus emboldening him to confide in her and inquire, Could Madge, who knew everything, say how the land lay for him in that quarter? Would she advise – permit him to 'speak' to Stella before he sailed, as his impulse prompted?

People who would thrust upon you the responsibility of making up their minds for them in their love affairs would do very wrong were there the slightest chance of their abiding

by your verdict, if distasteful. There never is. This case was
quite exceptional. Yet Madge did not hesitate for a moment,
though she knew her word would be law.

'Gwyn, I cannot be certain, but I believe that Stella likes
you – more – better than she knows herself. Only she is so
used to regard you as a chum, Gwyn. I would not say anything
to her now. The change would be too abrupt.' "Comical",
Gwyn feared she meant, and winced inwardly. Madge went
judiciously on:

'Though Stella looks grown up, you cannot think what a child
she is still in some ways – too young for this, Gwyn. It would
just upset her mind and not bring you any satisfaction.'

Reminiscences of past cushion-fights might intrude and
provoke a thoughtless rebuff Gwyn would feel horribly. In
short, to tell his love now would spoil his chance, but Madge
would not say chance for his there was none.

Poor Gwyn's soul was burning to deliver itself of its errand,
and to take his suspense away with him into exile seemed the
one intolerable course. He paid a signal tribute to Madge's
reputed infallibility in that he chose it.

The last of a long line of sires who had lived and died welded
to the petty piece of land they had owned and farmed with,
of late, ever-vanishing profit, Gwyn's special faculties and
knowledge, though in themselves by no means despicable,
were of the sort that, in the new order to which the old has
given place, would not at the time of his majority help him to
the "living wage" of an agricultural labourer.

Very acceptable was the offer from a friend, once somewhat
similarly situated, who was now doing well in South Africa
in a farm up country, to come out and look around him,
undertaking to help him to a start.

But he was unusually out of spirits and heavy in hand that
last evening at Cefn Cwm. He always looked rather like a
camel, hulking about those undersized apartments, picking his
way among the doll's-house-like furniture. Depression sat on

everyone except Stella, who kept the room alive by her merry chatter. Wild and nonsensical, it made the wisdom of Madge's warning seem clear as the noon-day.

'You are to write by every mail, Gwyn, and give account of all your adventures, sporting and romantic. But the women of those parts are not very beautiful, are they?'

'I believe there are none where I am going to,' said Gwyn.

'Do you?' said Stella, her eyes twinkling. 'Gwyn, you're mistaken. There are two, believe me. I know all about the South African romance. Is it not written in ever so many novels? The story is getting stale.'

'What is it?' asked Gwyn.

'The scene is an ostrich farm,' began Stella. 'Enter two girls; one a commonplace blonde, the other a pale and impassioned brunette. Enter, to these, a young man, whose complexion I forget.'

'Stella, hush,' said her mother.

'He engages himself with precipitation to the fair girl, but the romance is between him and the soulful brunette. Hence the novel.'

'What's the end of it?' asked Gwyn.

'The soulful sister dies – an unnatural death, and the youth never smiles again. Oh, Gwyn, beware of that soulful sister!'

Gwyn observed that he was going out there to make – not love – but money, if only he found the thing could be done; then presently he gathered up his long limbs to depart. He was starting from St Teilo tomorrow at the break of day.

'Make haste and get settled, Gwyn,' was Stella's parting injunction, 'in an ostrich farm of your own. Then Charlie and I will come out to see you. Charlie, what fun! Gwyn shall take us up country in an ox-waggon, and show us round. Diamond mines, goldfields and big game. Charlie shall write a book about it when we come home which will clear our expenses. Do you think you'll be settled in a year, Gwyn?'

'If so I might have to come back for a bit to settle up here first,' said Gwyn, with an odd, tell-tale look at Madge. Stella shrieked with delight.

'Gwyn, swear you'll bring me back a mail cart with an ostrich to draw it. Charlie, wouldn't it be heavenly to go and call upon the Ducanes driving an ostrich?'

III

Dear Jack,

You are pleased to joke about what is a very serious matter. Observe the post-mark and beg my pardon. You see I date from the Principality.

Cefn Cwm is a pretty little shooting-box in a hilly country where the rain is constant and the cattle are black and all C's are K's. There is a river, a church at a safe distance, and a view of a ruined castle with an unpronounceable name. The shooting itself is deplorable. Ladies are Gallios about game, and Mrs Roderick's tenants have poached every flying fowl off the land. Madge is sorry now, and going to tell them they mustn't.

My reception was rather a damper. Madge is the dearest girl in the world, but her people are not civil.

The mother is a little Grey Lady you might easily mistake for a cipher in the household. Man, they would set themselves on fire to keep her hands warm, if filial piety gave the word. She greeted me as if I were a bailiff come to distrain for rent. However, Madge, who knows her weak point, pressed me to sing, the first evening. Now you know, old man, vanity is not my weak point. (Here Jack roared.) But you know also that I can sing 'The Message'. By the third verse the old lady was entirely – overcome. She gives me no further trouble.

Both sisters are grown up. In some ways Madge is the youngest-looking of the three. Number two,

Charlotte, is a fearfully and wonderfully well-informed girl – pulled me up in a misquotation from Madame de Stael. She dabbles in photography, and the way to her heart, as usual with those people, is to let her "take you" at will. A lout of a cousin, recently shipped of the Karoo, recurs in her album as an iterated warning: "Gwyn and dog"; "Gwyn and a haystack"; "Gwyn taking a wasps' nest", confirming me in my vow never, whatever the circumstances, to get mixed up with amateur portraiture. All three are uncommon girls and seem – how shall I put it? – to belong to each other. Now, my sisters were always badgering when they were not boring one another, and the thanksgiving was general when Nora married and got off to India.

The youngest, Stella, is a most diverting study. The first day she was mute, literally; the second rude, positively. The rudeness, methinks, is only sisterly affection gone wrong, for by taking pains you can make her forget her discourteous intentions, when she becomes delightful. She plays the violin, poorly enough, as I have told her, but has a fine voice and we are teaching her the duet, 'Friendship', to sing with me at an amateur concert coming on at St Teilo. Madge is the one I see least of. If a barn on the estate leaks, or a cow coughs, or a child has croup she is sent for. However, here I have been many days without feeling bored for a moment.

We are now off to call on the Ducanes, who are at their place hereabouts for the shooting. She was Louise Tierney, among whose following, the Lord knows how long ago, this child made himself pretty conspicuous, as you may remember, before she gave her hand to this Gold-headed old Walking-Stick of a husband. Tout lasse, tout passe, tout casse, except, I suppose, a substantial income. Ducane is a Malade

Imaginaire and *Louise* fosters the delusion so that he
may order himself to Nice or Monte Carlo.

Postscript, after the call:

*That girl Stella is a regular little demon. Louise and
I have met again and again since her marriage, and
I have never showed nor felt the least inclination to
dangle in her wake. That is a part for boys, or for
men who have failed in life. She has money (which is
what she cares for and cannot live without) and her
unimaginable bore of a husband, and I have – or
have had – my liberty. My engagement has not been
published abroad yet, but Louise probably suspects
something. She is chic incarnate as ever, and gets up
so well you could almost forget she is sur le retour.
Ducane has a terrible deal of conversation. No bore
like one with pretensions to intelligence! But the
matter-of-fact topics that came up this afternoon for
discussion were, if I rightly recollect, ensilage, the site
of a new railway station, and the contents of his orchid
house. As we were leaving he actually made Madge
turn back with him to look at some herbal monstrosity.
I sauntered on ahead with the girls, and we were hardly
out of hearing when Stella began:*

'Now, Mr. Carew, you can tell me something I am
burning to know.'

'Very happy to enlighten you to the best of my ability,
Miss Stella.'

'What is the secret of Mrs Ducane's attraction?'

'Of Mrs Ducane's – attraction?'

'Charlie and I call her "The Sorceress". Girls come,
have their day, and go off. But Louise Ducane's day
seems like the world, that being round can never come
to an end, you know. It's a charm, and I want to find
out all about it.'

'That is surely a question for Mr Ducane,' said I

discreetly.

'We in the country are still brought up to believe,' Stella ran on, 'that not only is it odious to rouge and dye and all that, but that nobody will respect you if you do and are found out. I think Louise Ducane began to dye her hair early, and adds to it little by little till there's no telling how much of it is silver gilt. But she paints quite straight-forwardly, and why aren't we allowed to if you – if men of taste like rouged cheeks best, and touched-up eyes, and hair that would come off if it came down?'

I pointed out that Mrs Ducane's perfections, natural or artificial, could not concern me in any way.

'Ah,' she let fall, 'you mean no longer – not now – because of Madge?'

Our glances met, and hers made me positively thankful that Louise had long ago forfeited any hold over me she may ever have possessed. Nothing less would have enabled me to disappoint the curiosity of so sharp a young lady. But her impertinence nettled me, and knowing that nothing makes her so angry as to be treated like the child that she – is not, I said:

'Wait until you are a little older, Miss Stella, then you will understand, without requiring to have it explained to you, how, although Mrs Ducane may never want for attentions, her most ardent admirer would hardly name her together with your sister Madge.' Who rejoined us at this moment, saving me a scratched face, I think. Stella was white with rage at my patronising tone.

But how on earth did she find out, what I am convinced Madge never remotely suspected, that Louise was an old flame of mine? I know how deadly sharp jealousy makes some women. But it is for Madge that Stella is jealous.

Looking over his letter, Carew cut out the latter end of it.

* * *

If moved thereto by satiety, that old society hand, Joscelin, had
succumbed irresistibly to the fresh beauty of "Wild Wales",
how much more was Madge, in her sensitive inexperience,
foredoomed to yield up her heart and mind to the ascendency
of this suitor, her first suitable suitor, as it chanced. Even
Carew, in whom vanity was no mere attribute but a vital organ
of his moral being, had no adequate notion of the impression
the descent of his brilliant self was calculated to produce upon
the place beneath; that quiet, far-away home that had hitherto
entertained nothing more romantic in the form of the adult
male than one Price Edwards, ex-Methodist parson (nicknamed 'Madge's proselyte' at Cefn Cwm, where ran the legend
that it was his humble, hopeless adoration of Miss Roderick,
shadowed in a poem he wrote on the sisters, comparing them
to a Garland, that had lured him into the alien bosom of the
Anglican Church, bringing his whole chapel flock along with
him); a drawing-room seldom filled with vocal strains more
emotional than those of some obsolete Hymnal, and whose
young occupants, with as complete a knowledge of social life
as can be obtained from the study of the best novels, had never
had the ghost of an objection in applying the same.

Enter, as into an empty space, Joscelin Carew like a comet.
Not unto every county magnate's son is it given to combine
with the natural advantages of good looks and good breeding
and the graces born of ease and leisure the stamp of the
spirited officer in one of the more intellectual branches of his
profession, the prestige of the man of the world and society
favourite, and the powers of the highly cultivated amateur:
the dazzle of it all agreeably tempered by every semblance of
a gentle nature, quick and delicate feeling, and a conspicuous
freedom from anything likely to jar on youthfully sensitive
tastes.

Madge's subdued but intense happiness was beautiful to see.

She was unconscious of any divorcement from the old life; this new and higher one was to include and develop it by-and-by. Her heart went out to her fellow-creatures, especially if in trouble. Less than ever could she deny herself to beggary in all its forms. A mother with a sick child, a returned prodigal, a drunkard's wife – she wanted to give them her last shilling. Then she thought of poor Gwyn, just landed at the Cape, and wondered if ever things would come right for him.

In a week, Carew was more at home in that house than ever Gwyn had become in all the years of his life. Comparisons were unavoidable and Gwyn, alas! was nowhere. Certainly Joscelin could not take the bees when they swarmed, prodding them with no more ado than if they were butterflies nor familiarly tackle a sullen bull stopping the way, nor turn a packing-case into a serviceable piece of furniture at short notice like the absent one, but he could tell them all about people and things and books and plays, and sang Schumann, and recited one or two monologues in a finished manner.

Charlie's attitude was one of respectful approbation. He was resolute in refusing to be photographed, which put cordiality on her part out of the question. And to lose Madge was unspeakably horrid – like losing hand or foot. Even now she was not their Madge, as aforetime. So the losers sadly felt in every waking moment. But Charlie thought Stella took it too hard.

The girl looked positively sombre some days, and once or twice left the room in a marked manner when Carew came in. Never had Joscelin been treated so. She was too young for her behaviour to alienate him, too handsome for him not to mind. He puzzled over it one day, felt huffed on the next, interested on the next, the day of the call. Two days later he betted to himself that he would break through her reserve. On the morrow he won his wager.

IV

The day after that Carew took up a pen to ease a mind
powerfully perturbed.

> *Jack, old man, you were right. Fate bosses the world,
> and mine, as you warned me, was never to jogtrot
> tamely to the Temple of Hymen along the Queen's
> highway.*
>
> *Yet, Jack, I swear I came down here with as straight
> intentions as ever an officer and a gentleman should
> – profess. And they have led me into more devious
> paths than ever. Man proposes, the devil disposes, and
> Heaven knows how it will end. It has not taken me into
> its confidence.*
>
> *She has the eyes of a young Christian martyr in
> the most ravishing combination with the mouth – the
> mouth of Lady Hamilton as "Sensibility": you know
> the picture by Romney. She puzzles, charms, checks
> and draws me on in equal measure. You have guessed
> it is not Madge of whom I speak. Madge is picturesque;
> this other one might be a beauty, did she know it.*
>
> *Jack, I'm not fickle, though it looks like it. My feeling
> towards Madge is absolutely unaltered, but contrast
> with another has shown me more plainly what it really
> is – and – and what it is not. I don't believe a man
> among us is safe from passing self-deception such as
> mine. A fatalist might say that my semi-engagement in
> London was all expressly ordained to bring me to my
> real destiny down here. Had I stopped on at Chatham,
> done as you and prudence would have advised, I should
> never have seen Stella. I should have been the poorer
> by the unique experience of the last few days.*
>
> *I think it began with the first instant and grew with
> every fresh one spent in each other's company, bad*

friends though we were, and never alone together.

Madge, to be sure, is always being wanted by agent, tenant or domestic, at whose beck and call she seems to live. Then the youngers are told off to take me for a walk on the fells, or in the "Owls' Dingle", as they call the little wood by the stream that waters their domain. Charlie soon strays aside after some bird, beast or fish, or stops to photograph. Then I improve my acquaintance with Stella, try to draw her out and get drawn in myself by the dangers and delights of the operation.

Jack, she has never touched her fiddle since the day when I told her she could not play one little bit! Her voice is a fine mezzo-soprano, but wants cultivation sadly.

This morning, in turning over some of Charlotte's photographs, I came upon a vignette of Stella, with her inspired look on, that I fancied and wanted to take for my own. Stella snatched it away. Here Charlotte happening to leave the room to look for a lost dictionary, I suppose I pled rather warmly.

'What do you want it for?' she asked.

'To put in my book – of Beauty.'

'So you collect beauties. I knew you did.'

'Portraits of my lady friends.'

'Beginning with Mrs Ducane and ending with Madge?'

Could you have seen her when she said that! She looked so delightfully perverse!

'I don't seem to see myself,' she added presently, 'among the charmers.'

Then I said what I ought not to have said, but could not keep back for the life of me.

'You would not, Stella. You would rob them, and kill them too.'

Enter Charlotte, having found the dictionary.

Never have I seen Stella look so handsome as today at lunch. I did not know if I were eating chicken or mutton. Stella, Stella, are you scared or angry with me for what I said? Or rather is that all? But dolls' houses like this were never built for underplots and secret understandings. You cannot so much as wash your hands at Cefn Cwm without apprising everybody on the landing. Just now I met Stella at the top of the narrow staircase intercepting her passage. She flashed me such a look of indignant defiance that – you could have knocked me down with your little finger.

'Say you forgive me, Stella, or – '

'Let me pass, let me pass,' she said hurriedly and low. I dared not persist, it was too risky. Her mother – the servants – might appear at our elbow; there were spies behind every door. It was not a little exciting. And she looked so damnably handsome! It was the fear of losing her altogether, not a sense of duty – duty to Madge, that – I ought to be shot for going on as I am doing, but—

Carew broke off, looked at his letter, which struck him as having been written in his sleep, tore it up, flung it into the fire and sat absently watching it consuming. He had delivered his mind and felt his head clearer for it.

Piano chords sounded from the schoolroom underneath. Madge was coaching Stella for the last time in the duet he and she were to sing at St Teilo that night:

'My true love hath my heart and I have his,
By just exchange one to the other given:
I hold his dear, and mine he cannot miss –
There never was a better bargain driven:
My true love hath my heart and I have his.'

So far the ditty, which drew Joscelin downstairs to join in the rehearsal. At length Madge pronounced them perfect in their parts. Carew's book of Schumann's songs stood open on the desk, and he ran through a string of them to Madge's accompaniment, Stella standing by. All three in a while became so mazed with music, Heine and private emotion as to lose touch with the sober side of life.

'If you please, Miss,' – Keziah the parlour-maid stood before them full of sly malicious enjoyment in her warrant to interrupt – 'Evan Jones he wants to see you most particularly, he says.'

'Oh Keziah,' moaned Madge distressfully, 'tell him, oh, tell Evan Jones his particular want can't take place. I can't come now and I won't, really.'

'He says, Miss, as you promised to write him a recommendation for his boy; and if you could let him have it tonight,' etcetera.

Exit Madge, with a sight and a departing glance at Joscelin. In the dusk she cannot discern the responding expression on his face.

Now the door is shut and Stella, seated at the piano, takes up the suspended strain, striking the first bars. Stella has the electric gift of touch. Carew lifts up his well-trained tenor voice and sings as eloquently as he knows how:

> 'When May, the wonder month, began,
> And buds broke into blossom,
> Befell within this heart of mine
> Love's wakening and uprising.'

> 'When May, the fairest month, began,
> And every bird was singing,
> 'Twas then that I my secret told,
> Told her my heart's desire.'

In the fast-fading light he must stoop down to decipher the words. Stella, seated gazing straight before her, like 'Harmony' in Dicksee's picture, turns suddenly to him with a flashing mirthful smile that affects Carew's head like a whiff of oxygen gas. His voice quavers slightly, then he sings on with subdued energy:

> 'The Rose and the Lily, the Dove and the Sun's Light,
> Was a time when I loved them with Love's mad
> > delight.
> I love them no more, but I love, I the lonely one,
> The Little one, Pretty one, Darling one, Only one,
> She herself is Love and its mad delight,
> Is my Rose and my Lily, my Dove and Sunlight.'

There was only the fire's glow to see by now, but they sing and play on as if possessed. Carew knelt down to bring his eyes on a level with the page. His head almost touched Stella's shoulder; his voice rang close to her ear, fervent, eager and low:

> 'If but mine eyes on thine I stay,
> Then pain and sorrow pass away;
> But if my lips to thine I press,
> Comes perfect ease and happiness.

> 'Leaning my head upon thy breast,
> I dream in paradise to rest.
> But when thou say'st, 'I love thee so,'
> Tears, bitter tears, arise and flow.'

Stella's fingers lost their way; she forgot; her hands sank down on the keys and the symphony died in discord. Rising abruptly she crossed the room unsteadily and sat on the sofa, white in the face, her hands tightly clasped as in pain unendurable. Carew was at her side in an instant.

'Why – *why* will you tease me so cruelly?' murmured the girl painfully, in a stifled voice.

Carew unclasped her hands in the gentlest manner, holding them in his own tenderly, like something that was meant to be kissed.

'Oh, how wicked, how wicked I am!' she sobbed under her breath; 'and you, you are wicked too.'

'It was worth it – it is worth it,' he said, slipping the halter of a sudden. 'Stella, my sweet, kiss me. I was to be your brother – '

Stella shrank away as from an evil spirit; was on her feet and at the door before he could interpose.

'That was yesterday, and it is over,' he affirmed eagerly. 'I – said it to try you. Ah, Stella, listen, look at me!'

At the genuine pain and entreaty in his tone Stella turned in her flight and wavered.

'Never mind, now,' said Joscelin agitatedly, 'what now can never be. I know it, I have known it, ever since I set foot here. Madge – is so kind, so unselfish, she may even forgive. But you, Stella; am I to understand that you hate me for loving you – dearest?'

'I think so.' She said it so simply that Carew, taken aback, dropped the hand he had taken.

'Tell me that again,' he said in cold displeasure, 'before I leave here, leave you for ever. You mean that your face, your voice, your self have spoken falsely to me?'

'Oh God!' Stella sobbed voicelessly, despairingly; 'Do not go. Or – take me with you. Can you not see? I have cast myself out by this. I have been false to them all, to myself, but not – but not – '

'Not to me.' He surrounded her with his arms; her eyes were full of tears as he kissed them with the passionate fondness sprung from that glad, fleeting, irretrievable moment of conquest. The next, she slid from his clasp and left the room.

* * *

Two hours later Stella, dressed for the concert, walked into Madge's room.

'I am not going to sing the duet, 'Friendship,' Madge. You must put in something else.'

'But why?' asked Madge unsuspiciously.

'I have not the nerve,' said Stella. 'I should break down.'

Madge regarded her and must concur. If the mere anticipation had made her so pale, so distractedly nervous, the chances were that she might begin to cry, just when she should take up the canon.

V

'Children, you had much better stay at home. It will rain in an hour.'

So preached Mrs Roderick wisely on the morrow to a party of four, starting on a long walk to the ruined Castle with the unpronounceable name, but preached to stopped ears.

Carew felt the pressure of the entanglement – to which his love of sentimental journeys of discovery yet lent a fatal attraction – less in the open air. Stella – come rain, hail, snow, or Jove's thunderbolts – the one impossibility for her was to sit at home and think. Something *must* happen to reconcile the two Stellas, one imparadised, the other self-loathing, at war within her.

Madge was struggling with a foolish-seeming fit of low spirits. For the friendly familiarity of Joscelin's manner, which affected her imagination today as distinctly tainted with indifference, *might* be held to signify mutual understanding too perfect, too sacred to have anything to gain by demonstrative sentiment in the presence of others. Charlie was the single cheerful excursionist. Her Kodak was her only care, and there was a ruined archway in an upper storey of the Castle that would make a lovely picture. At Carew's request, as they went, she narrated the history of the fortress, from Urien, Knight of the Round Table's time up. Then he put a question that betrayed that he had not heard one word.

'Engaged people are no good,' thought Charlie sadly. 'Heigho! The sooner he and Madge get their affair over the better now.'

The unseasonably mild air was heavy with moisture. When they reached the foot of the craggy hillside crowned by the Castle, low clouds were rolling up, filling the valley.

'That's fog on the way,' said Charlie. 'I must race it.'

No paths but straggling sheep-tracks led up to the declivity. The climbers attacked it in single file. Sure-footed Charlie was soon far ahead; Stella came next, walking as if for a wager, or to get away from herself. Madge, feeling tired already, lagged behind with Carew, but she could hardly keep up with his manly stride. The least exacting of engaged girls, she was keenly chagrined by the sudden inattention, the silence of the erst so punctilious, so winning-spoken Joscelin. Half-way up she halted to take a breath, and saw the absent-minded man go marching on, unaware that she was not beside him, nor so much as looking round to see. Madge could have sat down and cried.

The insensibly preparing atmospheric change took visible effect in a moment of time. An opaque white mist filled the air as by precipitation. Like a shroud it fell round Madge where she stood panting. She struggled on, but such a fog puts you on a level with the blind, and she went stumbling into a cairn of stones – a hint that she had lost her direction and must wait until the haze broke. At length a rift in it gave her a passing glimpse of the Castle turrets above, and Charlie's figure somewhere among the battlements.

Charlie had reached her vantage ground and photographed her archway the moment before the fog fell, blotting out the world beyond the parapet. She was searching in the rubble for a lost screw. Stella, some thirty feet below, stood still by the massive brickwork of the outer Castle wall. Two minutes later Carew, emerging from the fog, was at her side. And the white shroud encompassed the pair, shutting off the earth with its dumb and other witnesses: the sheep huddled on the grassy slopes, Madge astray on the declivity far below, and Charlie on her perch aloft. They two, a yard apart, could not have seen each other.

'Am I something so terrifying, such an evil spirit, Stella, that all this long day you have grudged me one word, one look?'

He got it now, the look Circe herself could not have improved upon for witchery. Then the other Stella spoke.

'Joscelin, I cannot bear for Madge to know. I could never look her in the eyes again.'

'Ah, but I do not see how that is to be arranged,' he said playfully, reckless just then of all beyond the strange revelations surprised from Stella's blue eyes by his own, and that concerned him more nearly.

'I'll tell you.' Stella spoke with low feverish insistence. 'Say you are called back suddenly to Chatham – obliged to start tomorrow.'

'So you wish me gone – is that it?'

'I will join you in town as soon as you write to tell me all is planned and ready,' said Stella desperately. 'Let it be soon, for *then* I can write Madge a letter and tell her all.'

For they would be married then, and hand in hand with Joscelin, not otherwise, she felt she could defy the recording angel himself.

It was the harum-scarum notion of a school-girl. Carew did not give it a thought.

'Tomorrow I was going to the Ducanes' shooting party, and had meant to send an excuse,' he said meditatively. 'How if I went there, and stayed the two nights as invited? I should be near – and it would give us time to think.'

'I cannot bear another tomorrow like today,' said Stella.

'You cannot tell what it is like for me.'

'Everything shall be as you wish, I promise,' he said caressingly. 'But, Stella, if you care as I care, for our love above all things, you will be silent one more day, for our love's sake.'

He drew her nearer to him and she raised her face which shone with the fervid, transporting life he had evoked. 'What you will,' she murmured confusedly. 'Nothing else matters now.'

How should they two remember to attend to the freaks of the treacherous fog? It was present still, but on the shift, breaking, closing, melting, re-forming here and there. For an instant the foreground was clear as though no fog had been, and there – there stood Madge, so close she could almost have touched them.

VI

'I told you so, girls. There is Madge looking like a ghost, quite knocked up. And Stella – what have you done with Stella?'

'Stella has a headache,' Charlie stated officially. 'She won't come down to dinner tonight.'

The soul of unsuspicion, Charlie was nevertheless the sharpest person in the house. She had heard nothing, seen nothing but the masked faces of the three as they trudged silently home through the rain. Charlie had guessed.

That was not a pleasant evening. The coward in Carew caught at the opportunity afforded by his semi-promise to the Ducanes, of shirking what would be worse, the inevitable domestic explosion on the morrow. Tonight all alike seemed smitten with a senseless impulse to dissemble, to spare Mrs Roderick.

But that lady had eyes in her head. They told her that Madge, whose function was to dry other people's tears, had been crying, which was rather like feeling the house rock.

Madge temporised till Carew was out of it, then she explained matters to her parent, her magnanimity so shielding the culprits in the telling that she talked, nay, half felt, as though they, not she, were the victims and the wronged – Madge who was staggering and bleeding under a blow from a triple-edged blade. Her love was lost, Joscelin was false with the Chit, – with Stella. Present, past, future, were stained ineffaceably.

Mrs Roderick had never been so angry in her life. Angry with Stella, yes, as you are with your troublesome little darling who, playing with matches, fires the curtains. It was simply inconceivable to her that the child could have been grievously to blame in the affair. But Carew, who must have acted knowingly, deliberately, stood branded past redemption in her sight as unworthy to touch the hand of a daughter of hers. That verdict was given in Stella's presence with an irrevocable conviction from which there seemed no appeal, the unsparing condemnation passed, for once, by a kindly, but clear and upright judgement. With a blanched and hardened countenance Stella left the room.

The terrible, miserable day dragged on. Charlie, tossed about with sympathy for Madge, indignation with her betrothed, and growing compassion for Stella's utter misery, wondered grimly how many birds had fallen to Joscelin Carew's gun that afternoon.

At night Madge watched wearily over the fire in her room, bowed down by a dull pain at her heart. No sense of heroic self-sacrifice to solace her secretly. Small generosity in giving back his word to a sinner who has unrepentantly jilted you for your sister! It was a ghastly mystery Madge was far too stunned, too mazed by the stroke, to try and unravel.

Charlie entered on tip-toe. 'Madge, you must come. Stella frightens me to death. She will worry herself into a brain fever before tomorrow to a certainty, if she hasn't done it already. I daren't leave her alone for many minutes. She seems quite off her head.'

'Does mother know?' asked Madge mechanically.

'Madge! You know she would only give her a dose of nitre, – and that would be the last straw. Madge, I've tried my best, but I can't. I don't know what to do.' And Charlie's voice quavered oddly.

Marge came and sat on Stella's bed. The occupant was a sufficiently disturbed and disturbing spectacle. She might have been ill for a month; her cheeks looked sunken and pale, with hectic spots; her eyes hollow ringed, dry, distraught; and her skin was burning. Sleepless excitement and trouble had wrought up her nerves to that pitch when it is an everlasting, terrible puzzle how far the human animal is responsible for his misdoings. Stella had cause. She felt she had sold her soul for something nice, and was going after all to be cheated of the fee.

'Oh, go. Can't you let me alone? You – you'll kill me between you,' she complained, as Madge approached. 'Killing's no murder, I know, when it is done by inches; but leave me – oh, do!'

Madge moved away to the window and stood silent and perplexed. Stella lay still with closed eyes, then of a sudden she sat up, saying with a crazy little laugh: 'Charlie, for goodness' sake take that hideous little monster away. I can't have it there, mocking and grinning at me.'

Charlie removed the Japanese enormity referred to, hitherto accounted sportive, or decorative, even. Stella looked round like some caught wild animal under vivisection. Oh those four walls and her sisters' eyes! Flinging herself back she smothered her face in the pillows, exclaiming: 'Why, *why* can't one die when one wants to?'

There was silence, silence that might be felt. Clearer, louder rose the sound of the running river below in the wood.

And this was Stella, the Merry Maid of Cefn Cwm, who only the other day was playing practical jokes on her cousin Gwyn!

Then spoke a voice not in the least like Stella's, and Madge, who was watching furtively, felt a queer chill down her back:

'That such a little river should talk so loud! To say – to say – "I am deep enough to drown in" – as that servant girl of the Ducanes found who tried it.'

'Oh Stella, don't,' said Charlie, wretched and dismayed. Stella did not hear. She was talking to herself in broken snatches.

All the ghastly things Madge had ever read of in the papers now came back on her to molest her imagination. Young people, reckoned of sound mind and amiable temperament, timid, inoffensive and well-behaved, suddenly cutting their throats or their neighbour's, or otherwise insanely misdemeaning themselves, and mysteriously disappearing thenceforward from the rolls of recognised human life.

Stella's passion of despair was beyond the control of her will; her violent distress, envenomed by remorse, seemed to be tearing her defenceless soul to pieces as she lay. Madge, to whom the task had been set of mastering the lessons of a lifetime in half a day, put her hand to the rescue, quickened by Charlie's imploring gaze.

'Listen, Stella; you must! Mother was bound to be very angry – to feel as she felt. Be reasonable one moment, child. She could not do less than she did – at first' Madge choked for a moment, then went valiantly on. 'But she is much too fond of you to resist for very long your real and earnest wish. Have patience only, and you will see.'

Stella sat bolt upright, her eyes like saucers. 'What do you mean?' she said eagerly, then distrustfully, 'No shamming, Madge, for pity's sake!'

'She will come round,' said a voice, presumedly Madge's voice.

'Too late!' moaned Stella. 'Not till she has said and done more than enough to estrange and separate us. But if he is not fit to stay here, neither am I! Let her send me away. I would go of my own accord— '

'I will talk to her,' said Madge.

'You?' Stella's eyes dilated; they were now like the Round Tower at Copenhagen, but her voice had a ring as of dear life coming forth.

'You?' she repeated and laughed nervously. 'You can do everything, but you will not do that. I see. You are humouring me, like a mad person till you can get the strait-waistcoat on me, I suppose.'

'I think I can make her – understand things differently – as I understand them, and so alter her mind. Do you understand me now?'

'You promise me?'

'Yes.'

'Oh, Madge!' Stella broke into a flood of uncontrollable weeping, distressing to behold. But the tears relieved her brain somewhat, while exhausting her further, and at length she slept from sheer prostration. Charlie passed a watchful, wakeful night, with a sense of the advantages of fancy-freedom, for a mournful consolation; Madge in schooling herself so to advocate the cause of her sister and supplanter as to secure for Carew such a reception on the morrow as should not mortally wound his pride and send him away in exasperation and disgrace, forbidden to communicate with Stella, and leaving her heartbroken.

He returned before he was expected. The Penfynnon party had been broken up by the sudden indisposition, real or imaginary, of the master of the house. 'He thought he was a little hoarse,' said Carew, 'and where I or another man would have taken a voice lozenge he ordered himself to Nice by the next *train de luxe*.' The Sorceress had behaved admirably, neither betraying her annoyance nor feigning unnecessary fears. Carew, who felt he had not improved his position among Stella's people by running away from it, and who had further disgraced himself by bad shooting, reappeared to receive his deserts in so extra-sensitive a mood that to mete them out to

him would, as Stella had surmised, have been the way to
bring about an irreparable breach.

What Madge had said to her mother is no matter; but in
the interview with the latter that Joscelin had to go through,
Mrs Roderick expressed herself on the subject of his conduct
with a dignity and moderation that, for the first time, made
him feel thoroughly ashamed of it and eager to rehabilitate
himself in her estimation. He confessed his fault, in that,
mistaking his regard and admiration for Madge for a different
feeling, he had deceived her, and himself also. But as to
trifling basely, heartlessly with Stella – perish the thought
of an iniquity of which he was utterly incapable! Stella he
loved; and Stella he desired to marry as soon as her mother
gave leave. He was as serious and sincere as ever he was in
his life, and Mrs Roderick's prejudice was a little shaken. He
was very melancholy at the prospect of the curtailment of
his leave. His company was moving to Shorncliffe and his
colonel wanted him. Mrs Roderick said it was for the best.
He and Stella might correspond. She would not forbid that.

So after all he had won. Even in the matter of reproof he
had been let off easily, and things made as little unpleasant
for him as possible. Madge, with Red Indian-like fortitude,
refrained from so much as a look which might seem to
reproach them with their happiness, and kept her desolation
to herself.

Stella, who knew without being told that the tide was
setting in her favour, was triumphant, buoyant, defiant. She
looked uncannily handsome. Her boundless youthful vivacity,
restrained, not subdued, flashed through her eyes, and when
these and Joscelin's met he vehemently regretted that the
period of probation insisted on was not long enough to afford
decent excuse for an elopement, and railed inwardly against
the sense of propriety, domestic ties, and to her paltering
considerations which, now that his conquest was tacitly
sanctioned, deferred his possession of the prize.

Charlie, the outsider, was the only one he could not look in the face.

VII

In the interminable-seeming home calm that now followed, and that was more trying than storm and tempest, Madge was reminded of poor Gwyn and his story, and felt bound at once to acquaint him, in the far Karoo, with these facts: that her engagement was not; and that Stella, his Stella, was irretrievably engaged to Joscelin Carew.

Gwyn, who was peculiar, and further sunk in Stella-worship than was conceivable to the liveliest sisterly imagination, wrote back from the cave of the Giant Despair, too wretched, poor fellow to be keenly alive to any one's feelings but his own. The best of men, those whom no amount of prosperity could corrupt, may turn selfish and cruel in adversity, so morally improving to the egoist; and for the same reason: for grief wrests a disposition from its natural self, whilst happiness gives nature freer play.

What maddened Gwyn was the fatal conviction that had got hold of him, one past disproving from henceforth, that by blindly taking orders form Madge he had given away his only chance, annihilated now. Had he spoken to Stella, who can tell what might have been? Say that in the depths of her young heart she, divining his preference, returned it in some wise. His leaving England thus for years or for ever without a hint to her of what it cost him to go, or that she was more to him than others, must hurt and piqued her to the quick. And even Gwyn knew that if five out of every ten matches were not made more or less out of pique, those who pretend marriage is a failure would have no case at all. Mortified by this apparent indifference and neglect where she had perhaps looked for their opposites, she would be in a mood to fall the readier victim to such a skilful practitioner as Joscelin Carew.

Such was Gwyn's ingenious but absurd theory, expounded with such eloquent conviction that Madge was staggered. Was it possible, she asked herself, that he, not she had been right? Right or wrong she was bitterly to rue to counsel so glibly given.

Gwyn – this was the next news – had grown restless, and quarrelled in advance with the monotony of farming life and 'chucked it' for the present. There were disturbances threatening on a newly acquired frontier, and he had enrolled himself as a volunteer in a special constabulary force. He was starting up country at once, to help to keep the peace in a half-known district, still too unsettled to tempt the colonist

Thus Madge might know, for her comfort, that while Gwyn in his present sinister humour to 'chuck' his life in some foolhardy exploit, or succumb to the sickness that destroyeth the more easily those who have no particular mind to exist, she would, however remotely, have his blood on her head. That he was exposed to both issues she knew from his letter.

Torments she could confide to none. Meanwhile she must overlook the rentals, pronounce for or against the eviction of a drunken or dishonest tenant, and the felling of timber, and superintend the Sunday school, just as if nothing were.

At least Stella was happy in a fashion, love's own fashion. She spent the best part of four months in writing letters and reading Carew's answers, an increasingly absorbing correspondence which took up her whole mind. Mrs Roderick, who had counted on her finishing her studies, was in despair.

Only Charlie retained a natural healthy interest in the weather, the garden and such local events as occurred, as, for example, the installation of a learned professor of many sciences at the brand new college at Llandyfrig, some fifteen miles off, whose interesting lectures on popular scientific subjects, coming on at St Teilo, she proposed to attend.

Then there would soon be new faces at Penfynnon. Old Mr Ducane, fleeing from the mild damp of South Wales, had been killed off by the fierce winds of South France shortly after he got there. By dying her cad cleared himself, in the only effectual way, of the charge of being a pseudo-invalid. The unexpected conduct of his widow, again, had put all her detractors, notably the Miss Rodericks, to the blush. They had never concealed their assurance that she had married him for his money, with one eye, Stella used to insinuate, to preserving at least a comparatively juvenile appearance set off by his decrepitude. And a thousand merciless jests had been passed on poor Louise as a 'verdant antique,' a mercenary, third-rate coquette. Judge not, young people. Here the *malade imaginaire* proved to have had a heart complaint all along, and the slandered Louise, though he had left her a clear £3000 a year, was inconsolable; her life endangered by mourning, and sunk in woe and crape she was going to renounce the world and retire into a sisterhood, bestowing all her goods upon the poor, on Mr Ducane's relations. And this was the Sorceress, whom Stella had regarded with a retrospective jealousy, which even now peeped out in her half-contrite: 'Poor old thing!'

Everybody was sorry and would have liked to recall hard things said; and Madge wrote a nice letter and felt she had no right to quarrel with the markedly cool reply, not even in Louise's handwriting. Mrs Ducane was too ill to hold a pen. Her health was broken by the shock she had sustained; the stir and gaiety of Nice had become hateful to her, and she was leaving it to seek in some suitable seclusion the perfect quiet insisted on by the doctors, in whose hands she must be for some time to come.

One day a South African telegram in the morning paper threw all such trivial matters into oblivion. The latest news from the debatable frontier: the pioneers had been surprised in a narrow mountain pass by a hostile force. Killed – Smith; wounded slightly – Robinson; dangerously – Brown and Roderick. But the enemy had made no serious resistance

and the skirmish was of less than no account in the annals of
colonial progress.

Gwyn was many thousand miles away; Gwyn was not
a hero of romance, but he was a solid fact in his cousins'
existence, and that it should be wiped out for ever and ever by
the hand of the savage was a suggestion of domestic calamity
serious enough to throw the whole house into mourning.

Except Stella, who had just had such a pretty letter from
Carew and who, in her private paradise, vehemently resented
anything that presumed to reproach her with being perfectly
happy. She proved to them all that they were torturing
themselves quite unwarrantably. The report was imperfect,
the very name of the spot garbled in transmission, the
rumours might be exaggerated or even wholly false. And
though mail after mail came in, bringing no news which is
not good, and Madge looked worse every day and was forced
to confide her fearful secret to Charlie, who vainly racked
her brain for a hopeful comforting word, Stella stopped her
ears and would hear no ominous knell. The next mail, or the
next or the next would bring a letter accounting somehow for
his long silence. Whereas if Carew was silent no conjectural
explanation satisfied her hungry soul, absorbed in those
letters, now given, now received, whose giving and taking
was more to her than all the world outside. If some chance
delayed his token, as once when he was suddenly called to
London on business, it was distressing to see her ravenous
anxiety. Indeed, the second time it befell that she had to wait
rather longer than she expected she worried herself into such
a state of nervous agitation that Mrs Roderick, looking on,
came sorrowfully to the conclusion that the protraction of this
intermediate state could serve no useful end.

There was a sense of relief felt all through the house when
the morning's post brought the desired missive to Stella's
address in the well-known, clear, distinguished-looking
handwriting. Stella devoured the outside with her eyes, then

vanished to her room to read, mark, learn and inwardly digest the contents of her letter.

Mrs Roderick told Madge she had made up her mind to write that day to Carew to intimate that he might consider his probation ended, and come down to Cefn Cwm as soon as he could get leave, with a view to making arrangements for introducing Stella to his family and fixing the date of their marriage.

VIII

Stella raised the seal to her lips, then breaking it, she read as follows:-

> *Do you not know that the least service you allow me to render you is to me the most precious of pleasures? I spent two hours this morning with the men of law and have thus spared you, I trust, some trying discussion and the fatigue of a journey to London. Expect me at nine this evening with the papers I have induced Messrs Furlonger to entrust to me as your delegate.*
>
> *This unhoped-for renewal of our old friendship has lent a brightness to my existence I little thought it could ever regain, and that I am soon going to forfeit again for ever, by my own deed. Why am I not free? Not, – need I say it? – that anyone has ever come between us so as to eclipse the memory of the past, but that forbidden to meet you on the old terms, or any terms but those of ordinary acquaintanceship, I became careless what befell.*
>
> *My word was given under a complication of events that bind me in honour not to ask for it back. You know partly how it all came about – how I was drawn into it, how circumstances are our masters sometimes and force us – you said it once, of yourself – to do what yet*

> *we never should, if it were to do again. Certainly I was*
> *reckless when I bound myself, I who whatever betide*
> *can but sign myself, – Yours always, Louise, bound or*
> *free,*
>
> *JOSCELIN CAREW*

Yesterday evening at nine sharp Carew, not for the first time, had presented himself at the door of a furnished house recently taken at Folkestone for Mrs Ducane, who had removed thence from the country, which her doctors pronounced too relaxing. Her old-standing acquaintance with Joscelin, quartered at this time close by, warranted him in proffering and her in accepting his assistance in some legal business that had arisen in connection with the disposal of her late husband's property; to the details of which she felt unequal to attending, and in which he served her both with zeal and discretion.

Louise was awaiting him in the mournfully luxurious, dimly and religiously lit apartment in which Carew already felt so remarkably at home. She had never been more seducing than in her artfully art-concealing garb of widowhood. Her interesting and unaccustomed pallor and gracefully negligent coiffure served somehow to heighten the singular enticement, akin to that of forbidden fruit, in her eyes, and the subtle play of lines round her mouth. Louise was not a beauty or even a particularly clever woman, but her energies had never been divided, and she knew how to please.

As he marched in, confident of his own welcome, she confronted him with an extraordinary expression, and her greeting was to hand to him his own note received a few hours ago.

'Now I want to know,' she said to the astonished man, 'what you mean by sending me this?' Carew glanced at the paper, and his countenance had a great, a terrible fall.

This is what he saw:

DEAREST STELLA

Are you not a little over-exacting at this time? You send me four pages of reproaches I hardly seem to myself to have deserved. You know I have been overdone of late with duties that may not be shirked. The world does contain other matters, Stella, outside ourselves, that will now and then claim our attention. The worst remains to be told. It is that I have lost all prospect of getting leave from headquarters to absent myself immediately, and it seems probable I may be forcibly detained here for longer than I had reason to expect. Forgive me for writing, as I must, in haste, but at least my love will not have to complain of my absolute silence. And I will speedily follow up and make amends to her for all that is wanting in these few hurried lines.

Louise leaned back on the couch where she was resting and covertly enjoyed Carew's passionate discomfiture. He was storming round the room in a fever and a fury, denouncing his unlucky star and his near sight so pathetically that her mischievous relish was presently merged in soft compassion.

'How could such a thing happen to Joscelin Carew of all men?' she asked him, laughing faintly.

'Two envelopes – yours to go by hand, Stella's by post *I stamped the wrong one*, yours, inadvertently. That misled me, and I addressed and posted it to Stella.' And he called himself names, and cursed destiny.

'Now hush, you excitable man,' said Louise. 'Have some regard for my poor shattered nerves. Sit down and try to compose yourself a little. One thing I must know, though, before I tell you what I think of you.'

'Eh?' He looked up at her ruefully. The disconsolate, defenceless Joscelin had never been more attractive to her than at that moment.

'WHAT have you despatched to that girl – to Stella?'

Carew could blush, for he did now. 'The truth,' he answered truthfully. 'You have nothing whatever to forgive me, Louise; it is she – Stella, who has got the affront, and she won't. Merciful heaven! what a fracas there will be! Hanging will be too bad for me in that quarter.'

Louise closed her eyes, and a faint smile played round her lips as she said with wistful irony:

'There, go and make your peace with the little Welsh girl. You are clever enough to manage that. Only don't pretend that it is I who "forcibly detain" you. How can I ever wish to see such a bungler again? A pretty adviser I have chosen for my affairs! My poor Joscelin, don't let them trouble you further. I had better take them back into my own hands, weak as they are.'

Carew looked dreamily down at the delectable, well-tended, jewelled hand, gleaming white against the jet-black folds of her dress. In a moment he was on his knees, metaphorically, imploring her to pity him. For she must know that she it was who did forcibly detain him. Since it had been borne in upon him that he might lay himself and his fifteen-year-old devotion at her feet, he was torn in two between his Lover, which was hers, and his Troth, which was another's. That Stella should find this out – well. But to have betrayed himself in this blundering fashion!

'You graceless boy!' murmured Louise (Carew loved to be called a boy, and boy he will continue to be now and then called at fifty). 'And you thankless boy! For Fortune, who favours the undeserving, has played your featherhead a good turn. I hope, for decorum's sake and my own, that you have written nothing too terribly foolish for any eyes but mine to see. But had you deeply conspired to escape from the bond you want me to believe irks you so, you could hardly have done better for yourself than by this error. There need be no breach of promises on your part now. She will release you without your asking, by return of post'

Louise sat upright and said suddenly, rather sharply, 'By the way, Joscelin Carew, I suppose those envelopes *did* get mixed up by accident and not – and not – '

'Oh no, no.' He impetuously repudiated the suggestion. Louise regarded him dubiously for one moment, but preferred to believe him. She would rather have him lucky than cunning – so cunning as that.

But even she could not make a perfectly happy man of him in this hour, as he sat silent and crestfallen. For he cared for his reputation, did Joscelin Carew.

'You couldn't make up your mind to jilt openly,' Louise told him, 'yet you don't like the idea of being dismissed. Was ever a man so hard to please?'

No, Carew did not like it. He covered his face with his hands and was troubled. Louise soothed and consoled him expertly, dropping well-inspired words of flattery into his ear. He, throw himself away on a raw schoolgirl, without money or *chic* or *savoir faire*! She would have dragged him down into the crowd of middle-class husbands, stupidly restricted his pleasurable activity, and dimmed the brilliancy of his existence. It was gospel truth, and comforted him not a little, as insinuated by those lips. The contrasting picture he might draw for himself. The thorn of wounded self-respect still rankled, but for Louise and £3000 a year something assuredly might be endured, and he left her sure of a future there awaiting him more alluring by far in certain respects than any he could have anticipated with Stella; prospective considerations which must enable him to endure the ordeal of the next few days.

'The girl is young,' mused Mr Ducane's widow, 'and will most indignantly send him about his business. Well, I put no hand to the manner of the breach, but in the matter of it I feel no compunction whatever. Joscelin Carew, I have saved you from a thoroughly inadvisable match, and your Stella from a most undeserving bridegroom.'

IX

The "Garland" was broken; the sundered flowers drooped apart.

No one ever knew exactly what Stella had said to Carew in a certain letter, her latest to his address. He wrote repeatedly in self-exculpation, protesting against harsh and unfair condemnation, hastily passed, but acquiescing tacitly in his summary release.

Stella, who was born to astonish her family, exhibited an amount of self-control quite incompatible-seeming with her previous unresisting yielding to impulse. Brain-fever, hysteria, or the turning of her despairing soul inside out for the torment of her own people would have been more in the natural order, and thus to her sisters less disquieting than this portentous, unaccustomed reserve.

Only Mrs Roderick, who had not lived fifty years in this world for nothing, understood. To Madge and Charlie she said: 'Leave her alone. You cannot get near her or help her. However she comes through it, well or ill, it must be alone, in her own way.'

The deadly bitterness of it all was nowise lessened to her by the secret dim knowledge that, bad though the thing that had happened, the worse thing was that which had not. Married to Madge, Joscelin might have been shamed into decently upright behaviour. Married to Joscelin, Stella would have sunk to his moral level.

All this was between herself and her pillow. But her mere surface reflections must be of the sorest. Jilted, jilted! and Poetical Justice, summing up, said: "Serve her right". The maidenly freshness of heart and countenance was gone. She was a girl with a story, and the wisdom it had taught her was not wisdom from above. Fortunate Charlie could still snatch a recreant distraction in Professor Anstey's lectures. Men were deceivers and hearts like pie crust and lovers crazy, but the Transformations of Tadpoles could be relied on to exhibit the same phenomena faithfully, and the steady interest of observations, microscopic, telescopic and other, never changed or waned. Assisting at his able expositions and experiments that never disappointed the votary, Charlie could be beguiled into temporary oblivion of the cloud on Cefn Cwm awaiting her on her return. Then she hated herself and disloyal, she who could enjoy herself, even for an hour, with so much tribulation at home. Carew was faithless, and Stella eating her heart out, and Madge looking daily more worn and ill, and Gwyn was dead.

Although as Stella pointed out they need not, and she for her part would not, believe the worst. Of that no proof had reached them. For the best and worst of reasons. Heavy floods had supervened in the outlandish district under annexation, and for months cut off the exploring party from communication with more civilised stations, and, alas! intercepted the supplies of food and medicine sent for their relief.

Then Mrs Roderick fell ill with bronchitis and was shut up in her room for two months. Still no news of Gwyn, and the arrival of the mail that might bring it was now treated merely, as, till it came, Stella's conjecture that he was alive and well, only for some reason had neglected to acquaint them with the fact, might be hung up for a counterfeit hope to cling to.

* * *

A changed, dejected group of three were gathered in the evening dusk round the schoolroom fire one winter evening. Madge had left her mother asleep and had come down for a rest pending the doctor's expected visit. Poor Madge, worn to a shadow, with half a murder on her conscience, was looking so wretchedly ill that Charlie said gravely:

'When Dr. Rice comes, Madge, I shall call his attention to you.'

'Oh, don't,' said Madge with a pitiful attempt at levity. 'He's no good, and if it was you, Charlie, you'd be the first to say so. You are like those men – Agnostics they call themselves – who make their wives go to church regularly.'

Silence fell, like a pall. Charlie, aged twenty, was looking back wistfully like a grandmother, on the 'old days' when they went gipsying in the Owls' Dingle by the river, and sat telling ghost stories till the moon was high and the "Goody Hoos" (owls in the vernacular) sang out, and Stella, in a panic, led that laughing, madcap uphill scamper home.

Or went boating with Gwyn, in a coracle of his own construction, on the river or the pool in the cavern whence the stream flows forth, after a mysterious underground course of ten miles, which Gwyn once started to explore with a packet of candles; his cousins bidding him an eternal farewell. Or stayed improving their minds in this room, with long intervals for relaxation, when Madge played bewitching bits of Chopin on the piano, and Charlie roasted chestnuts in the smokeless coal fire, and Stella lay on the sofa and read *Far from the Madding Crowd*.

Charlie, in a well-meant but futile effort to be jolly, had brought in a handful of chestnuts today, but had let them char to ashes in the embers, forgotten. With Stella in one of her brooding fits, looking like a Tragedy Muse, and Madge apparently on the verge of a bad illness, better let crumbs of comfort lie, though Charlie. Sackcloth and ashes and a dirge were more cheerful than the crackling of thorns under the pot. And again she thought of the day, not a twelvemonth ago, when the light-haired, light-hearted Joscelin, light-coming and light-going, first trod the threshold and was hailed as a messenger of grace. Results: Madge was ill, and Stella embittered, and Gwyn was dead.

'Oh, but this won't do,' thought Charlie, with a manful effort to keep off the pessimist fiend by striking up a conversation about Mr Anstey's 'Electricity at Home' lecture that afternoon.

'Such glorious fun! Pity you missed it, Stella. There stands the professor, like a conjurer behind his table of tricks; bits of lamps, batteries, clocks, gongs and bells and cleaning machines, with an air that says: "Here there is no deception. You shall see how perfectly easy it all is." And he makes them work. Then he explains to you how it is done.'

'And you're none the wiser,' rejoined Stella trenchantly.

'No, but your opinion of the conjurer and his art goes up. Oh the many inventions they have sought out, and that he showed us! A miner's lamp burning under water, and an electrophone, letting your ears know what's going on at any distance. And he *thinks* we shall next come to seeing by electricity, what's out of sight, you know. Then people sitting here in South Wales may take a look at some other country and see – and see – '

'What their relations are doing in South Africa, for instance,' supplied Stella gloomily.

Charlie gave it up. No subject was safe. The ground was volcanic wherever you trod.

Upon the dreary hush that reigned within, rose the drearier sound of the wind roaring round the house, shaking the sheltering trees. Then a deeper vibration stirred as of wheels coming down the drive and staying at the front door.

'The ghost-carriage,' Stella let fall involuntarily. Cefn Cwm was one of the many lonely country houses subject traditionally to the visitations of a phantom coach, the sound of whose wheels on the drive was invariably the first intimation of the death of a member of the family. The Miss Rodericks were nothing less than superstitious, but all felt that if the next post brought news confirming their fears for Gwyn, they would become so. An uncomfortable moment passed, then a matter-of-fact tinkle broke the spell.

'The ghost-bell is a novelty,' said Charlie, sensibly relieved. 'Idiots that we are! It's just Rice, the medicine-man.'

Madge started up from the sofa and began wearily

readjusting her disarranged hair. 'You needn't hustle,' said Charlie. 'Keziah will show him into the drawing room and come and tell us.'

Madge was ready before the handmaid's footsteps were heard outside. She opened the door and murmured something as explanatory as the name of a railway-station officially announced, fogging their minds.

At the sight of the figure behind her, Madge's brain in the twinkling of an eye went through some remarkable psychic experiences. First it told her the phantom coach had brought a phantom passenger, next that Dr Rice had sent a stranger deputy. She did not know the black-bearded, upright, muscular intruder.

'So you didn't expect me so soon,' said a voice she had always known.

'*Expect you*?' gasped Charlie, staring and losing her head. 'Why, Gwyn, we thought you were ill – we thought – '

'Thought I was dead, perhaps,' he suggested, as in jest. They were speechless. Then Stella came to the rescue.

'Not I. Not so foolish as that, Gwyn. But mother and Madge would let their funereal imaginations run away with them. I tried to hold them in, but they were too much for me sometimes. It was all your fault for not writing. What possessed you to leave us in the dark so long?' She stopped for another look, then added with a little laugh, 'And they weren't so far wrong after all. For, Gwyn, you really have departed this life and come back – somebody else. But oh, how glad, how, how glad – mother will be! So it's really you?'

'To the best of my belief it is,' said Gwyn, who seemed not a little fogged himself by the sensation his advent had created.

'And how are you? You don't look so bad, Gwyn!'

'Well, I'm just all right,' said Gwyn, seating himself, waiting silently for the flutter to abate. His tone, his movement, his address had undergone a change the girls could make nothing of at first. They were not even sure that they liked it.

'But weren't you even wounded?' asked three voices with an audible ring of disappointment.

'Nothing to signify. My comrade Robinson, came off badly, and I hear our names got mixed in the report. But we had fever afterwards both of us, and the doctor, when at last we got him, ordered me home as soon as I could go. The voyage set me right as he little expected. I never was better in my life. I'm quite fit to start again tomorrow, and shan't put it off long any way. But I felt I must see you all first.'

Floods at first, then fever, had for some months prevented his sending news of himself. A letter subsequently written, saying he was coming to England when convalescent, had miscarried on it precarious way to the nearest post-station. Finally his latest, despatched just before sailing, would arrive tomorrow morning, his own vessel having made an unprecedentedly quick passage, outstripping the mail by some hours. Gwyn was prepared to come upon the household by surprise, but not to this extent. Three pairs of cousinly eyes were fastened upon him with more curiosity than he had ever in his life excited before, or in all likelihood will excite again. Was it possible to change in so short a time? It was taking a liberty, almost. He should have asked their leave first.

'There's mother's bell,' said Madge; then with a quick, reviewing glance at the situation, 'Stella, do come with me,' she implored, 'and break the good news to her. I should make a boggle of it, I know.'

Having closed the door upon them, Gwyn stood up in front of the remaining sister, saying:

'Look here, Charlie, Madge wrote that Stella – that Stella, you know, was to be—'

Taking the *Morning Post* from the table, Charlie pointed out to him the following announcement:

> *On the 20th inst., at St George's, Hanover Square, Joscelin Carew, Captain, R.E., to*

Louise, widow of Edward Ducane, Esquire, late
of Penfynnon, Carmarthenshire.

Gwyn read, all agape. 'Good Lord!' he ejaculated, 'but what sort of a flipperty-gibbert is this gentleman?'

'I never liked him from the first,' Charlie stated, with pardonable pride. 'I never could see what Stella – what Madge – could find there to admire or care about. But oh, Gwyn, it has been so horrid. First one mortal blow, then another! Many mornings lately I've looked tremblingly in the glass to see if my hair hadn't turned grey in the night.'

'Did you ever really think I was dead?'

'I had no doubt of it whatever,' confessed Charlie candidly. 'Misfortune seemed to have taken such a fancy to us that the worst was a foregone conclusion. I see now we were morbid, but it wasn't our fault. What are you doing with my photograph book?'

'Looking to see if you've taken me out of it. No. Then you hadn't buried me outright.'

'That was Stella. She was the only sensible one of us where you were concerned. She scouted the notion. Gwyn, how well you do look I didn't know you the first moment.'

Poor Gwyn always came in for these left-handed compliments.

Madge rushed in to say that Gwyn must come up to his aunt, or his aunt, at peril of pleurisy, would come down to him.

That was the first cheerful evening at Cefn Cwm for *years*, if the girls' feelings could be trusted. The warmth of his reception was to Gwyn most embarrassing. That he should be a welcome guest was natural, proper and expected. But it staggered him to find himself hailed as the godsend that he really was, walking in just at that moment. His mere re-appearance meant, to Madge a morbid nightmare removed, to Charlie restored faith in the benevolent government of the world; to Stella the healthy distraction that would help her to recover her balance; while Mrs Roderick was old-fashioned enough to find unspeakable comfort in the reflection that here was a thoroughly reliable make relation at hand, a help and protection for her fatherless girls if she did not get over her bronchitis, which, however, began to mend from that hour.

X

We need follow no further the fortunes of Mr Ducane's widow and Joscelin Carew. If their wedded life had a story it can never affect the Miss Rodericks, with whom mainly we are concerned.

Gwyn's return safe and sound was the immediate, though indirect, cause of the breaking up of the "Garland" for all time. For Charlie, relieved of her apprehension for Madge, who now picked up magically, and Stella – ah, Stella was so young she might, she must, live down what was past, – well, Charlie, set free to think a little of her own private affairs, became engaged within the month to Professor Anstey, an eligible, honest-hearted young suitor, over head and ears in love with his intelligent pupil.

'He came to call on Saturday,' Stella told Gwyn, 'with his microscope. They were going to dissect the heart of a crayfish in the school room. I never thought it would take so long. Then when at last I looked in, I found they hadn't touched it but sat there looking so foolish, so foolish, as only the wise and learned can look.'

The wedding was fixed to come off very shortly at St Teilo. Gwyn needed no pressing to say for that; but the mother-country would not hold him much longer. Although he had come back from South Africa no richer in pocket than when he started, he had made himself a footing out there he was anxious to improve. He, with his country-training, active disposition, small capital, and a knack of managing people under him, had been recognised in more than one quarter as the stuff that

was wanted at the particular stage then reached. He had been
through a good deal and come out of it with credit. A mining-
claim had been assigned him out of which the profit might
one day accrue; his friend in agriculture was pressing him to
come back and help him. He was returning with prospects
of the choice of more than one good position. All pointed to
his lengthened residence if not permanent settlement in the
colony.

Now it was counted among the many virtues of Charlie's
professor that his appointment was at Llandyfrig College,
which would allow Mrs Anstey, *nèe* Roderick, to live with
one foot, so to speak still in her old home.

But a special leave of three months had been accorded him,
for the purpose of spending them, as he and his bride planned,
in a wedding trip to the Cape. The bridegroom had a scientific
errand to fulfil which would take him to Kimberley. It was
arranged for Stella to accompany them. What more natural
than that Gwyn should take his passage out on the same boat?
Why did Madge shake her head as the trippers' starting-time
drew nigh?

Gwyn – travelled, hardened, developed, with extended
ideas and new-awakened interests – ought by rights to have
been cured of his boyish infatuation of the Chit, Stella. But
in the course of the preparing and making ready for Charlie's
wedding, in which he, as their nearest male relative, did
sometimes participate, Madge saw and heard passages between
the twain that made her her open her eyes very wide.

She sounded Stella and ascertained that, whether ignorant
or not in the past, she was perfectly well aware at the present
hour of Gwyn's tender sentiments towards her, as also of their
old standing. Her own were past Madge's finding out, perhaps
inscrutable to herself. To expostulatory hints she only replied,
with an incorrigibly naughty twinkle in her eye, 'How do you
know I haven't been his good angel, Madge? If it was with
him as you say, the thought of me may have saved him from

declining on a barmaid at Kimberly. So many of them do. I know, for he told me so.'

This was unanswerable. Then Madge tried Gwyn, who remarked to her profoundly that Stella was 'quite different now to him from what she used to be.'

As if, to the end of time, a heart sorely wounded as hers had been would be in a condition steadfastly to refuse such balm in Gilead as Gwyn's unshaken predilection and silent homage were offering her today! 'Oh Gwyn,' thought Madge, 'you who thought it quite natural she should accept the flattery of another's addresses out of pique at your imagined indifference – how much, do you suppose, does pique count for in her softened attitude towards you now?' It was not easy to put forward the delicate suggestion, but Madge managed it.

'Well,' this was Gwyn's parting promise, 'I give you my word I'll hold my tongue for three months – till their return tickets are up. If at the end of that time Stella doesn't know her own mind I don't think she ever will.'

So, Madge, at any rate, can wash her hands and say: 'I am innocent of the fate of these young people.' With this and the certainty that Gwyn will keep his word and not precipitate the issue, she must rest content.

My Friend Kitty

That my friend Kitty was a very clever girl was a fact about which there could not be two opinions. It was her misfortune but not her own fault. Kitty was fond of praise – being born of woman – but of longings to shine among ladies intellectual, she was more than destitute, she was incapable. I tried hard to kindle that flame in her. It would not burn. Fond of her fine eyes she might be, though fine eyes are as common as field daises; but her mental commodities – perception, memory, judgment, logic, fancy and insight enough to set up half a dozen average mortals of either sex – she valued no more than her good appetite.

Kitty's cleverness was an old household jest. When a child in short frocks she wrote her Harrow brother's holiday task for him: an essay on 'Spanish Influence in England in the Middle Ages'. The crowning joke was that it got the prize. Her own schooldays ended with a shower of medals and certificates, promptly forgotten by the medallist at the sight of her first ball-dress awaiting her at home on the bed.

Born in a scholastic medium Kitty might have gone on to Girton and glory – or brain-fever and collapse. Hers was the common, natural feminine lot.

Her father was a half-pay General with a military appointment at Archminster. Her mother's health was breaking up. There were three big brothers and one rickety little scamp of eight. All wanted Kitty in sundry places and divers manners, and generally at once. Her papa wanted an ornament for his home, a charm and relaxation in his hours of ease; her mamma tactful care and nursing; the elder brothers sympathetic and refining influences; and Tim, the veriest little demon ever faked up as a cherub, a fair godmother to keep him clear of the police courts. Kitty at home found no difficulty in killing time, nor had she been a Napoleon in petticoats would scope for her universal genius have been wanting, if she proposed to be perfect in all her parts: social treasure, medical companion, mentor to six servants older than herself, special providence to a curly-headed imp, who from his cradle went into convulsions whenever he was crossed, and mistress of all the knowledge – chemical, mechanical, sanitary, aesthetic and economic – whose practice we disrespectfully lump together as 'good housekeeping'. Kitty never pined for a 'higher life'. She was what is called 'a true woman', by which I do not mean that she had no sense of humour and was incapable of thought, but that the natural affections came first with her and their all-embracing demands swallowed her all up. She read at odd times, just as her brothers smoked, but no more dreamt of writing for the press for instance than they of manufacturing tobacco.

One evening Kitty sat composing – a love of a cap for her mother – while her father and brothers were abusing the Mayor and Corporation. These being commercial gentlemen could never do anything right in the eyes of professional gentlemen. Kitty, cap engrossed, heard nothing till Reggie, her curate-brother, wound up a long lament sighing, 'Yes, the Roodgate is doomed!'

'*What?*' cried Kitty, aghast.

It was the last left standing of the old city gates, a massive semi-circular archway of the time of Edward II, turret-flanked, with carved shields on the face of it and stone figures of men at arms on the battlements. A treat to the eye, and full of story.

But the Roodgate was to go. Why? Well, it wanted repairing, and the suggestion to spare this trifling outlay by spending some thousands on its demolition had prevailed with the authorities. A job, a flagrant job, the Rev Reggie insisted. A contractor who would profit, an alderman whose adjacent premises would be bettered. But the reasons assigned were that it served no purpose of public utility, and a sack-laden waggon could not pass under it. Enough. The citizen-representatives had spoken and the represented were too busy to take heed.

Next morning at breakfast Tim lifted up a shrill voice:

'Kitty, what were you doing last night? I got up at five to pinch nurse's nose. The door was open, and I saw the light under yours.'

Kitty blushed, and laughed, as if at herself.

'Oh, something kept running in my head – I – I was trying to get rid of it by putting it down,' she said. 'Only a joke.'

'Give us the benefit of it,' said the Rev Reggie. Kitty promised. But the housemaid was leaving. Kitty was busy interviewing candidates all the morning; there was a lawn-tennis party in the afternoon, a choir-practice in the evening. The morning after she came with the butcher's book in one hand, in the other a few sheets in her own neat writing, to Reggie, who read, and roared.

'Oh, good, Kitty,' he exclaimed. 'Good!' Then with an illuminative flash, 'Kitty, I'll take this to Dulford,' a local Conservative editor, 'and get him to print it in tomorrow's *Gazette*.'

'Not really?' said Kitty incredulously.

'Without your name, of course,' he added. 'It'll make them squirm, at any rate.'

In that paper's next issue appeared a lively plea for the thorough regeneration of Archminister on the principle of improving away everything that was not palpably useful or that stood in anybody's way. The flowers in the public gardens were to go that the dear little children might walk on the beds, the ancient, stained-glass cathedral windows to be plain-glazed, that short-sighted folk might see the preacher and congregation. A famous cromlech in a certain field was to be broken up for conversion into a new drinking fountain, and the rookery elms in the precincts to be cut down that the canons might see the time of day by the church clock. More sweeping proposals followed. The fun of the fooling lay in pertinent local allusions; the point in the neat sly hits at the motive of personal profit that prompts public waste, as exampled in the affair of the Roodgate. Only a joke. But people heard of it, read it, and for the first time in its career the *Gazette* went into a second edition.

Quite suddenly the citizen-readers perceived that the Corporations' project on foot was monstrous and intolerable. That body, dismayed at the wasp's nest they had brought round their ears, put the plan aside for mature consideration. It has been six years maturing. Many Town Councils have come and gone. Nobody now recollects that the Gate was ever in danger, much less the skit that saved it, which was ascribed to different gentlemen residents. But Kitty's secret was kept.

Kitty's second literary sally led to our acquaintance. 'Read "Teddy", in the *Cornhill*,' so Hartley Beddome, a distinguished young friend of ours who reviewed the magazines for a leading weekly, kept telling me till I did.

Who has not known a "Teddy"? The Benjamin of irresistibly lovable passive qualities and actively perverse instincts, making it a lottery whether he stands or falls, pulling down his homestead around his ears. Kitty's was a social tragedy of two generations ago.

"Teddy", the cathedral organist's son, is at once a domestic joy and a cupboard skeleton, ordinary methods not sufficing to implant in him the moral sense. Patronage procures for him paid employment in the Post Office at fourteen, where he is accounted steadied and secure. Too soon. On sudden, light temptation he tampers with a letter, is detected, convicted of what was then a capital offence, withal an offence against the State, hence no allowance made for youth and its distemper.

Struck thought I was with "Teddy", the greater surprise was the sight of the bright, pleasing, flower-like, happy-looking

girl who had put forth this gruesome invention; a tale so
spontaneous, so direct in the telling as to reveal afresh the
inevitableness with which dreadful things may come to pass
without any one being dreadfully to blame. The only comfort
was that this particular dreadful thing couldn't happen now.

'What put it into your head?' I asked her. It was in the
Archminster Deanery drawing-room, where we first met and
made friends quickly.

'Everybody asks me that,' said Kitty, 'and I remember now.
It was in church. Old Archdeacon Wordie had been preaching
half an hour when he said, 'The other remarks which I wish to
make before I come to the substance of my discourse…' and
a little groan ran through the pews. I was trying not to smile
when "Teddy" shot suddenly into my head, like something
thrown in at a window. Weeks before at a dinner-party they
were talking of a postman here who had got three months for
stealing the contents of a letter, and the Archdeacon said: 'I
remember when a lad of fourteen could be hanged for that'.
Everybody said it was impossible, but it seemed it was a fact.
I had never though of it since; then it was blown back, or the
seed sprang up suddenly like the Bean Stalk.'

'And you came home and wrote your story?'

'Oh no. That was Sunday. Sunday afternoons the boys and
I always go for a long walk by the river; then we have late
supper at home. Monday there was a Royal inspection at the
depot; and some of the suite were stopping in the house. But
Tuesday the gentlemen were dining at the Mess; mother went
to bed at nine. A pen seized me,' said Kitty, ' and I had written
the first lines when the cook burst into the room and sobbed
out that the kitchenmaid was dying. It was only hysterics, but
we thought she had had a stroke. I got frightened and forgot
all about "Teddy". Next day was Mrs Bland's dance; and my
dress – it was beaded tulle and white poppies,' said Kitty
musingly, 'came home all wrong, and my spare time went in
altering it. Then when you've danced till four you're not fit for

much the next morning.'

And so on; but at length "Teddy" got written, and was sent to the *Cornhill*, because they took it in at home, and was printed at once, and the editor wrote polite letters soliciting further contributions and sent twelve guineas which fell on Kitty like a golden shower from heaven. Her family prated of her as a kind of prodigy; same kind as the pony that knows his alphabet and the poodle that dances the polka, but urging her seriously to go on and get more gold and more glory. 'Do write something else, Kitty. And now you're flush of money you'll lend me that sovereign you said you couldn't.' Kitty readily lent the sovereign, but did not follow up her little success. How many of our disconsolate sex are perishing with aspirations they are incompetent to fulfil! Here was Kitty, who certainly could have done something had she chosen, too unconcerned to try.

So when, before leaving Archminster, I was invited to spend a few days under her father's roof, I went sworn inwardly to rouse Kitty to a proper sense of her duties to the public.

Then the first morning Tim was missed after breakfast and disappeared for the day. Kitty was on tenterhooks, making vain inquiry. Late at night the little scamp turned up from the races, which he had managed to attend, and there got rid of all his pocket-money, and, I suspect, some of Kitty's to which he had helped himself, but with such a bad bronchial cold as to shield him from rebuke.

Between nursing him, and writing invitations to a large garden party, and interviewing beggars from her brother's parish, the next days' hours melted away, for Kitty, like small change. Now it was a flood in the kitchen, due to a servant's carelessness; today a round of duty calls, tomorrow of hospital visits, or family shopping that would not wait. And she had her college brother, Cecil, very much on her mind just now, since the discovery that he had been courting a pretty barmaid furiously. At the filial alternative offered him of a clandestine misalliance or a Breach of Promise action the General's wrath knew no bounds. Providentially the barmaid, a woman of sense, saved everything by making up her mind to marry the publican, who was courting her too. But Cecil was melancholy, talked of shooting himself, which was nonsense; but he wanted much judicious petting, humouring, cheering and consoling, to help him to his feet.

Kitty would never do anything, i.e., write anything, I saw, and saw why. Her life was brim full, and she was bound to it by her affections. Only she remained subject to fits – penseizures, we called them. Things that struck her in a certain way would call up a picture or a drama in her mind, which must out with the product, unless circumstances made it a material impossibility. Almost invariably they did so, but the impetus itself was as involuntary and as irresistible as a sneeze.

I think it only befell her twice in the next four years, but once too often, as will appear.

One summer she and her people spent at Felixstowe. The weather was atrocious, but her brothers brought down all the last new novels, each outdaring its forerunner in startling originality of plot. Anne Radcliffe's notoriously wild conceptions are tame beside the miracles of inconceivable improbability dealt in by the authors and accepted by the readers of an age that is nothing if not realistic and sceptical.

Some such impression in Kitty found vent in her *Fairy Tales for Adults*, a very pretty little joke at the expense of these purveyors of the marvellous, and a joke that ran through three editions. Kitty's bishop who lived two lives, that of a reverend divine by day and of a crack comic music-hall singer by night – detected only by accident; her Cabinet Minister before whom monarchs and Parliaments crouched, and who after all was a woman; her High-School girl-detective, whose prowess was the wonder of Scotland Yard, and who ran down the most accomplished criminals in her holidays; these and other skittish fancies, sketched in a light and sprightly vein, excited much amusement in many quarters, but perhaps not a little wrath in some.

There was a deeper vein in Kitty, but her way of life was irreconcilable with its working. "Teddy" was an accident, unlikely to recur.

It is an article of faith among men that women have no sense of humour. The evidence to prove it is overwhelming. But so is the supreme artfulness of the sex. Perhaps they have it and squash it, knowing what an unsafe thing it is for them to carry about. What self-respecting man would tolerate it in them if he chanced to call it into activity? And there might be no accounting for the event.

Several family changes, long pending, now befell Kitty in rapid succession. The flickering taper of her mother's life went out rather suddenly. The General was quite broken down, and leaned heavily on Kitty. They went to Dinan, and he came back much improved. His appointment had expired; and they settled at Chiswick. The brothers were scattering, one had taken to himself a wife, another a degree and a tutorship. Tim's health and morals had so far been coaxed into existence that he could be sent to school without the certain consequence of physical breakdown or condign expulsion.

Now the General was a nice old man; not too old to be courted energetically by three maiden ladies and two widows. His surrender to one of the widows everybody but Kitty saw was only a question of time. I feared the shock for the poor girl. The only mitigation – one all her friends must desire – would be for her first to get married herself.

Kitty was still fancy free. Once she had been courted by young Reckitt of the Blues, but her brothers were positive he was a gambler and a sot, and she never let it come to an offer, being too good-natured to wish to inflict on him the slight of a refusal. Next came Weaklin, the unsuccessful artist, whom she defended against her brothers' merciless ridicule. But it was more on his side than hers, and he died prematurely. Dr Septimus Scott, a widower, with three bouncing children, had proposed to her not once but twice, and Kitty had said 'No,' gently, for she was sorry for Dr Scott, who was a good man though a heavy one and a bore – like a thoroughly good pair of boots – boots that creak.

Matchmaking is heaven's business, I know. Still if I saw Kitty and Hartley Beddome upon their first introduction remain mutually engrossed for the rest of the evening, and saw him afterwards go repeatedly out of his way to meet her, well, if I went out of mine once or twice to promote their acquaintance I merely in doing so, followed heaven's lead.

Both were hit, equally but differently. To Kitty the experience was new, thus it moved her the most. Yet it seemed the other way. He was constantly coming to see me now, all to talk about Kitty. Might he call at Chiswick, did I think? Would I bring her to his evening at Toynbee Hall or his lecture on Dante at the Artisans' College? He was the warmest admirer of her literary feats, and always urging her to add to their number.

Hartley Beddome was a clever, many-sided man of mark. But Kitty regarded him and his intellect with a respect I thought simply preposterous. The notion that he could condescend to care for her more than for others was, to her, an inconceivable impossibility.

But he did, for he told me so, or what amounted to it. He regarded her as a discovery; such a blend of fine intelligence with the 'eternal feminine' charm realised an ideal that had always eluded him. He said Kitty was the one bright spot in his life; called regularly whenever I had the bright spot under my roof, escorted us to the opera, the Royal Institution and a People's Party at the East End, where I had to do duty for the three, so busy was he making himself seriously attentive to Kitty.

Now though these attentions gave her extraordinary pleasure Kitty, deluded by her absurd modesty or exaggerated idea of his superiority, did not take them seriously. She was perfectly unembarrassed and perfectly charming. How well they looked together! Rather tall was Kitty; her thinness was of the sort that makes for grace alone; her pretty countenance one of that that elude you if you try to recall them, though the singular impression of charm remains clear. Her eyes took on a strange new light when Hartley Beddome was with her. Oh, very soon she would understand, and the surprise would be sweet. Well for Mr. Beddome, whose heart had known storm and stress, to drift into this fair haven! Well for Kitty to enter with unbuttered heart on the wifely vocation she was so admirably gifted for, with one who was her secret heart's choice and her mental equal or superior. So I prospected: together I saw them stand before the altar at Chiswick Church, the Rev Reggie officiating. It seemed hardly too soon to begin casting about for a suitable wedding present.

Now Hartley Beddome, though a literary figure, and almost a great man in our estimate, had, like many greater than he, what the crowd are pleased to call a 'crank'. Sometimes the crank proves right in the end; then the crowd call him discoverer or benefactor. More often he is wrong, and goes down as fool or monomaniac on the point. Cranks are very various in this age. There are Vegetarianism, Sanitation, Symbolism, Astrology, faith in unlucky days, numbers and colour; the Original Mystery of Freemasonry, the occult meaning of the Book of Daniel, or the Great Pyramid. Hartley Beddome's crank was Soul Transference, perhaps the oldest extant, but highly elaborated and brought up to date. The uncomfortable part of it was that you who held it could not so much as call your soul your own. It might have been possessed in the past by some person, or even some animal – Mazeppa's horse, or the whale that swallowed Jonah – whose destiny, whose doings and misdoings, had power to tamper with yours; an incongruous influence from which you were never quite safe. For myself, I refuse to believe in such wanton complication of the difficulties of life for us. It was said of Hartley Beddome that he was persuaded he had met with the soul of Queen Anne reincarnated in his washerwoman; and that the real explanation of the murder of President Carnot was that the souls of Cain and Abel, safely reincarnated, it was thought, in two peasants of different countries, had come into collision with all but inevitable result we know.

To Kitty, as to me, it seemed so much nonsense, but it did not affect her estimate of our friend, who moreover never forced the belief on any one's notice. It was a hobby, which she regarded as he might the mole on her cheek: a trifling personal defect, unimportant to the whole.

One evening Kitty and I went to a soiree given by the Independent Discussion Society. Hartley Beddome, who had invited us, was kept away by influenza. But two dull disciples of the Soul Transference theory discoursed upon it at length to the assemblage. Their arguments were promptly forgotten in the music and recitations that came later on. Kitty and I drove home together, talking fast, when in the midst of an animated dispute about the merits of Mascagni's operas the girl was taken with a sudden fit of inextinguishable laughter. I asked what amused her so.

She made no answer; her eyes wandered; all the rest of the way her replies showed her mind absent, till I dropped her at her own door.

Soon after, seeing Kitty's name in a prominent magazine, I sent for the number. Her effusion was entitled 'My Wife's Soul'.

I read. I daresay it was very humorous; everybody said so. The happiest *reducto ad absurdum* of the Soul Transference creed. But my sense of humour was unequal to the occasion, my taste of fun quite spoiled by an apprehension of the hole it might make in my project for making two people very happy. At the finish I hid my face in my hands and cried out: 'O Kitty, Kitty, what have you done?'

Who just then should walk in but Hartley Beddome? It was too late to whip the magazine out of sight. He began talking at once about 'My Wife's Soul'. Not so weak or so vain as to bear her a grudge for her *jeu d'esprit*. Kitty's was very pretty fooling indeed. She did not understand his point of view, but he did not expect that. He praised the style and seemed perfectly frank and friendly in his comments. Yet when he left I could have cried with vexation. I knew that my cherished scheme for those two was checkmated. Could a clever woman be so stupid as to commit such a blunder? Or can a clever woman not sacrifice her vanity and ambition to what even she must value much more? Throw away Hartley Beddoe for a magazine article? Good heavens! That was what Kitty had done.

These affairs are so delicate. At least critical stages come when lesser things than Kitty's lively, ill-timed sortie nip the thing in the bud. Matters were just at that point when, if anything came of it, people would say it had been love at first sight; if nothing came, that there never had been anything between them. There would now be nothing more.

Any lingering hope vanished next time I saw them in company together. The footing was altered and final. It was all over. Only I know that he ever contemplated marrying Kitty. Possibly he now would disclaim it. Kitty never believed it. They are the best of friends whenever they meet, but their lots have trended apart.

Poor Kitty's home position was becoming untenable. The General's widow-bride-elect might be an archangel in the house; my sympathies were with the superseded angel there – the grown-up daughter. A day came when Kitty confided to me that Dr Scott, the importunate widower, had written again, imploring her to think if she could, if she would, and so forth. And she had thought, and he was kindness, goodness itself, and had sworn to be Tim's special providence, now and always, and seemed so unhappy without her that – well, she had made up her mind to consent. What did I think? I would not say. Besides, I hardly knew. But I had done with meddling. Perhaps Kitty was right.

Then we fell to idle talking of Life and Love and Duty and Woman's Questions and the report in a society paper that Hartley Beddome was engaged to Dolly Simpleton, the handsome and the rich. The mention of it brought the faintest flush to Kitty's cheek, and a glance passed, like a look back on the incomparable memory of your life. I forgot myself and cried out:

'Kitty, Kitty, why did you write "My Wife's Soul"?'

She looked up intelligently, but oddly. 'Did he mind, do you think?'

'Well, did you think he – or any man – would enjoy having his pet belief shown up as a mental infirmity? Do you know I once thought you cared, or might care for each other? I must have been mistaken so far as you were concerned.'

Kitty's face changed again and her eyes let me know she had cared as she never could again. Quite out of patience now I said: 'Then, my dear Kitty, why didn't you let Soul Transference alone?'

Perplexedly she tried to think, to recall the incident, then described to me how the fancy was sprung upon her in the cab as we drove from the conversazione, and almost the next thing she clearly remembered was the housemaid coming in to call her, and finding her writing at her desk, never dreaming it could be morning yet. What she had written she had written, and it passed out of her hands the same day.

'Having eased your mind by writing it, you might have put it into the fire,' I said crossly.

Kitty shook her head. 'Not then,' she declared, 'not while the fit was on. If you have something you must say, it is of no use saying it to yourself in a whisper. But you don't understand. What I did I simply couldn't help – not then, you know.'

Kitty's blunder, so far as I could make out, was committed with her eyes wide open but in a state of irresponsibility – of spontaneous trance. Repent it she could not, for repentance implies choice, and against this mental visitation she was helpless. I could not understand quite, but must believe her.

'Would you do it again, knowing the consequences?' I asked curiously.

'I should do it,' said Kitty, ' but not because I would. If giddiness seizes you on a height you jump down; to know you will hurt yourself cannot stop you.'

I try to think all has happened for the best. But except for Dr Scott I see it has not. Kitty's highest qualities are thrown away in her marriage and Hartley Beddome's is rapidly making him common-place. Then I wish Kitty had been just a shade less clever. But then she would not have been Kitty, inimitable in her charm. It is one more of life's innumerable little riddles, one for which I can find no satisfactory solution.

From *Fraser's Magazine* (1874)

Latest Intelligence from the Planet Venus

It may not be reckoned among those things not generally known that within a short time direct telescopic communication, by means of signals, has been established between the earth and the planet Venus, and that at certain stations regular interchange of intelligence is now carried on. The results have hitherto been kept secret, partly, it is said, owing to the disappointment of the astronomers at finding in the new country but a mirror of our own, with an hereditary constitutional monarchy, two Houses, a civilisation in about the same stage of advancement as ours, and political and social institutions remarkably similar. The single remarkable difference presented to their notice is one they are loth to reveal, for fear, we believe, of the family discords it might possibly excite at home, and we are the first to acquaint our readers with the curious fact that in the planet Venus, though the present sovereign happens to be a king, all political business, electoral and parliamentary, is allotted to the women. Women only have the right to vote or to sit in the House of Commons, and the Upper House is formed of the eldest daughters of deceased Peers. Politics, therefore, are included among the usual branches of ladies' education, but except in this respect their social condition presents no unusual features.

This monopoly by women of political power is as old as their system of government, and until a few years ago no one dreamt of complaining or of questioning its wisdom. But a pamphlet advocating the enfranchisement of males has lately been published by a clever female agitator, and caused a considerable stir. It is not pretended that a majority of the sex ask or even desire the privilege. The plea put forward is abstract justice backed by possible expediency, and, the cry once sounded, arguments are not wanting, petitions flow in, idle men have taken the matter up and find supporters among the younger women, and last night a member of the Government redeemed the pledge made to her constituents last election, to bring forward a bill for removing the electoral disabilities of men. She has no lack of supporters, some sincere, some interested. Her greatest difficulty was in persuading the House to treat the measure seriously. The notion of admitting young cornets, cricketers and fops of the Dunready pattern to a share in the legislation, the prospect of Parliamentary benches recruited from the racecourse, the hunting field, and the billiard-room was a picture that proved too much for the gravity of the Commons. A division however, was insisted upon by the original proposer. At this juncture the leader of the Opposition, a lady as distinguished by her personal attractions as by her intelligence, moderation, common sense, and experience, arose, and made the following forcible speech, which we transcribe for the benefit of all such as it may, directly or indirectly, concern:

'Madam, – Before proceeding to state my opinions on this question, or my reasons for holding them, I wish to impress on you a sense of the importance of the measure just brought forward, that it may at least obtain from you the attention it deserves. I must urge you not to allow party or personal motives to blind you to its nature and bearings. The supporters of Male Suffrage are seeking not only to introduce a startling innovation into a system of government that has hitherto worked remarkably well, but in so doing they would tamper with the foundations of society, and in a blind cry for equality and suppositious justice ignore the elementary laws of nature. The question is not a political, it is a scientific and physiological one. About the equality of the sexes we may go on disputing for ever, but with regard to their identity there can be no manner of doubt. No one has ever ventured to assert it. Each sex has its special sphere – mission – call it what you will, originally assigned to it by nature, appropriated by custom. What now are the special and distinguishing natural characteristics of the male sex? Assuredly muscular strength and development. With less quickness of instinct, flexibility and patience than women, men are decidedly our superiors in physical power. Look at individuals, men of all classes – mark their capability for, nay their enjoyment of, exertion and exposure. If these do not naturally fall to their lot they find artificial employment for their faculties in violent games and athletic exercises; some indeed go so far as to seek it in the distant hunting grounds and prairies of uncivilised continents. This quality of theirs has its proper outlet in the active professions. To man, therefore, war and navigation, engineering and commerce, agriculture and trade, their perils and their toils, their laurels and gains; to man, in short, all those callings in which his peculiar endowment of greater physical force and endurance of physical hardships is a main and necessary element. Those with superior mental gifts will turn to such scientific pursuits as specially demand courage, exposure, and rough labour. It is most essential that their energies should not be diverted from these channels. We should then have bad soldiers, bad ships, bad machines, bad artisans. Government, on the other hand, is no game to be played at by amateurs. The least of its functions claims much honest thought and watchfulness. Either, then, the manly professions will suffer, or else – and this is the worse danger of the two – the suffrage will be carelessly exercised, and the mass of new voters, without leisure to think and judge for themselves, will be swayed by a few wire-pullers, unprincipled adventurers, who, seeking only to feather their own nests, will not hesitate to turn to account the ignorance and preoccupation of the electors.

'Now turn to the woman. Her organisation no less clearly defines her sphere. With finer natural perceptions than man, less ungovernable in her emotions, quicker and clearer in intellect, physically better fitted for sedentary life, more inclined to study and thought, everything seems to qualify her specially for legislation. For the judicious application of general rules to particular cases, peculiar delicacy of instinct is required, and in no capacity have any but women been known to approach the ideal of government – that perfect rule – all-efficient, yet unfelt.

'Take the family as a rough type of the nation. To whom, at home, is naturally allotted the government of young children? To the mother. To whom that of the domestic household? To the mistress. Widowers and bachelors are proverbially the slaves and victims of spoilt children and ill-trained servants. In all such home matters the husband defers to his wife, and would as soon expect to have to instruct her in them as she to teach him fortification, boxing, or mechanics. Little time or thought, indeed, has the professional man to spare for household superintendence; how much less for matters requiring such careful study as the government of a nation. The clergyman, wearied with his day's visiting of the sick, teaching or preaching; the doctor after his rounds; the merchant or tradesman overwhelmed with business; what they require when their daily toil is over is rest, relaxation, not to be set down to work out complex social and political problems, to study the arguments for and against the several measures to which members offer to pledge themselves, and to form a judgement on the merits of respective candidates. What time or opportunity have they for qualifying themselves to do so? But the wives of these men, on the other hand, have lives comparatively unoccupied, and of physical and intellectual leisure enough and to spare. Here, then, is a commodity; there a demand and a field for it, and this surplus, so to speak, of time, strength, and attention with us has been always supplied to the science of government, nor do I see how a happier or more judicious arrangement could have been made.

'I will proceed now to enumerate a few of the dangers to which the enfranchisement of men would inevitably expose us. Male voters will view each political question in a narrow professional light, irrespective of its justice or general expediency. Large proprietors will stand up for the game laws, eldest sons for primogeniture. Publicans, brewers, and railway directors will exercise a baneful, blind, one-sided influence on our counsels. An impartial debate or decision will soon become a thing of the past, fairness sink in to the shade, and a majority of direct pecuniary interest turn the scale in all cases.

'Again, the bulk of the national property being in the hands of the men, the openings and temptations to bribery would be enormously increased. Few women have the power, had they the will, to offer bribes sufficient to suborn a constituency, but when millionaires are admitted to the suffrage we may expect to see parliamentary elections bought and sold, and going, like other wares, to the highest bidder.

'But there is a more alarming danger still. The muscular force of the community being male, an opportunity would be afforded for an amount of intimidation it would shock us now even to contemplate. Right has never been might in our land. Shall we reverse our motto? Shall we, who have ever taken pride in the fact that our counsels are swayed by reason and judgement alone – a fact from which men have benefited at least as much as women – invite the fatal indefensible element of force to enter in and meddle with our elections, and let the hustings become the scene of such struggles and riots as in certain countries where, by a singular distortion of judgement, the management of political affairs is thrust entirely on the men? Supposing that the suffrage were irrespective of sex, and supposing it to happen that the men in a wrong cause were arrayed against and outvoted by the women in a right, would they not, as they could, use force to compel the women to submit? And here we are threatened with a relapse into barbarism from which the present constitution of our State affords so admirable a guarantee. And that something of the sort would ensue I have little doubt. Probably the next step would be to oust women altogether from the legislature – the standard of female education would then decline, and woman would sink lower and lower both in fact and in the estimation of men. Being physically weak, she must always, among the rough and uneducated classes, be especially exposed to ill-treatment. Of this in our country, I am happy to say, there are but rare instances, nevertheless. But there are lands where men monopolise the suffrage, and where a state of things exists among the lower classes – let us hope the upper and civilised orders do not realise it, for their apathy would otherwise be monstrous – which if widely and thoroughly known would be recognised as the darkest page of modern history, something to which a parallel must be sought in the worst days of legalised slavery. Penal laws have utterly failed as a remedy, and it is obvious that they must always do so. What has been our guard against this particular evil? Is it not that point in our social system which raises women's position, both actually and in the eyes of the men of her class, by entrusting to her functions of general importance, which she is at least as well qualified by nature to fill as man, and which we take care that her education shall fit her for, as a man's, necessarily unequal, semi-professional, and engrossing, can never do? Thus men have an irksome, thankless, exacting, life-long labour taken off their hands, which are left free to work out their fame and fortune; educated women their faculties turned to the best account; while among the lower orders, the artificial superiority conferred on the female sex by its privilege of the suffrage, raising the woman's status in fact and in the eyes of her husband, acts as an effectual check on domestic tyranny of the worst sort, and the nation has the advantage of being governed by that section of the community whose organisation, habits, and condition best enable them to study political science.

'That any wrong is done to men by the existing arrangement, I entirely deny. Most of them are married, and it is so seldom that a wife's political opinions differ materially from her husband's, that the vote of the former may fairly be said to represent both. The effect on the sex itself would be most undesirable. It is a fatal mistake to try and turn men into women, to shut them up indoors, and set them to study blue-books, and reports in their intervals of business, to enforce on them an amount of thought, seclusion and inaction so manifestly uncongenial to their physical constitution, which points so plainly to the field, the deck, the workshop, as the proper theatre for their activity. The best men are those who are most earnest, and do not trouble themselves with politics. Already they have sufficient subjects to study – special studies imperatively necessary for their respective occupations. Do not let us put another weight on the shoulders of those who, from the cradle to the grave, have so much less leisure than ourselves for reflection and acquiring political knowledge, or else, let us look no more for calm and judicious elections, but to see candidates supported from the lowest motives, and members returned by a majority of intimidation, bribery, private interest, or at best by chance, all through the ill-advised enfranchisement of an enormous body of muscular indeed, but necessarily prejudiced, ignorant, preoccupied members of society.'

The honourable member here resumed her seat amid loud cheers. On a division being taken, the motion was rejected by an overwhelming majority, and the question of Male Suffrage may be considered shelved for the present on the planet Venus.

A View Across the Valley: Short Stories by Women from Wales c. 1850 – 1950
Edited by Jane Aaron

Stories reflecting the realities, dreams and personal images of Wales – from the industrial communities of the south to the hinterlands of the rural west. This rich and diverse collection discovers a lost tradition of English-language short story writing.

978 1870206 358   £7.95

Queen of the Rushes: A Tale of the Welsh Revival
by Allen Raine

First published in 1906 and set at the time of the 1904 Revival, this is an enthralling tale of complex lives and loves that will capture the heart of any modern reader.

978 1870206 297   £7.95

Other titles in theHonno Classics series

The Wooden Doctor
By Margiad Evans
Introduction by Dr Sue
Asbee
ISBN 978 1870206 686
£8.99

The Small Mine
By Menna Gallie
Introduction by Jane Aaron
ISBN 978 1870206 389
£8.99

Strike for a Kingdom
By Menna Gallie
Introduction by Professor
Angela John
ISBN 978 1870206 587
£5.99

Eunice Fleet
By Lily Tobias
Introduction by Dr Jasmine
Donahaye
ISBN 978 1870206 655
£8.99

The Rebecca Rioter
By Amy Dillwyn
Introduction by Dr Katie
Gramich
ISBN 978 1870206 433
£8.99

**Welsh Women's Poetry
1460 - 2001: An Anthology**
Eds Dr Katie Gramich and
Catherine Brennan
ISBN 978 1870206 549
£12.99

**A Woman's Work is
Never Done**
By Elizabeth Andrews
Ed Ursula Masson
ISBN 978 1870206 785
£8.99

Iron and Gold
By Hilda Vaughan
Introduction by Jane Aaron
ISBN 978 1870206 501
£8.99

**Betsy Cadwaladyr: A
Balaclava Nurse**
*An Autobiography of
Elizabeth Davis*
Ed Jane Williams
Introduction by Professor
Deirdre Beddoe
ISBN 978 1870206 914
£8.99

About Honno

Honno Welsh Women's Press was set up in 1986 by a group of women who felt strongly that women in Wales needed wider opportunities to see their writing in print and to become involved in the publishing process. Our aim is to develop the writing talents of women in Wales, give them new and exciting opportunities to see their work published and often to give them their first 'break' as a writer.

Honno is registered as a community co-operative. Any profit that Honno makes goes towards the cost of future publications. To buy shares or to receive further information about forthcoming publications, please write to Honno at the address below, or visit our website: **www.honno.co.uk**.

Honno
'Ailsa Craig'
Heol y Cawl
Dinas Powys
Bro Morgannwg
CF64 4AH